ROBERT LUDLUM'S

THE
TREADSTONE
TRANSGRESSION

THE TREADSTONE SERIES

Robert Ludlum's The Treadstone Exile (by Joshua Hood)
Robert Ludlum's The Treadstone Resurrection (by Joshua Hood)

THE BOURNE SERIES

Robert Ludlum's The Bourne Treachery (by Brian Freeman)
Robert Ludlum's The Bourne Evolution (by Brian Freeman)
Robert Ludlum's The Bourne Initiative (by Eric Van Lustbader)
Robert Ludlum's The Bourne Enigma (by Eric Van Lustbader)
Robert Ludlum's The Bourne Ascendancy (by Eric Van Lustbader)
Robert Ludlum's The Bourne Retribution (by Eric Van Lustbader)
Robert Ludlum's The Bourne Imperative (by Eric Van Lustbader)
Robert Ludlum's The Bourne Dominion (by Eric Van Lustbader)
Robert Ludlum's The Bourne Objective (by Eric Van Lustbader)
Robert Ludlum's The Bourne Deception (by Eric Van Lustbader)
Robert Ludlum's The Bourne Sanction (by Eric Van Lustbader)
Robert Ludlum's The Bourne Betrayal (by Eric Van Lustbader)
Robert Ludlum's The Bourne Legacy (by Eric Van Lustbader)
The Bourne Ultimatum
The Bourne Supremacy
The Bourne Identity

THE COVERT-ONE SERIES

Robert Ludlum's The Patriot Attack (by Kyle Mills)
Robert Ludlum's The Geneva Strategy (by Jamie Freveletti)
Robert Ludlum's The Utopia Experiment (by Kyle Mills)
Robert Ludlum's The Janus Reprisal (by Jamie Freveletti)
Robert Ludlum's The Ares Decision (by Kyle Mills)
Robert Ludlum's The Arctic Event (by James H. Cobb)
Robert Ludlum's The Moscow Vector (with Patrick Larkin)
Robert Ludlum's The Lazarus Vendetta (with Patrick Larkin)
Robert Ludlum's The Altman Code (with Gayle Lynds)
Robert Ludlum's The Paris Option (with Gayle Lynds)
Robert Ludlum's The Cassandra Compact (with Philip Shelby)
Robert Ludlum's The Hades Factor (with Gayle Lynds)

THE JANSON SERIES

Robert Ludlum's The Janson Equation (by Douglas Corleone)
Robert Ludlum's The Janson Option (by Paul Garrison)
Robert Ludlum's The Janson Command (by Paul Garrison)
The Janson Directive

ALSO BY ROBERT LUDLUM

The Bancroft Strategy
The Ambler Warning
The Tristan Betrayal
The Sigma Protocol
The Prometheus Deception
The Matarese Countdown
The Apocalypse Watch
The Scorpio Illusion
The Road to Omaha
The Icarus Agenda
The Aquitaine Progression
The Parsifal Mosaic
The Matarese Circle
The Holcroft Covenant
The Chancellor Manuscript
The Gemini Contenders
The Road to Gandolfo
The Rhinemann Exchange
The Cry of the Halidon
Trevayne
The Matlock Paper
The Osterman Weekend
The Scarlatti Inheritance

ROBERT LUDLUM'S

THE
TREADSTONE TRANSGRESSION

★ ★ ★

JOSHUA HOOD

G. P. PUTNAM'S SONS
New York

PUTNAM
— EST. 1838 —

G. P. Putnam's Sons
Publishers Since 1838
An imprint of Penguin Random House LLC
penguinrandomhouse.com

Hardcover ISBN: 9780593419793
Ebook ISBN: 9780593419809

Printed in the United States of America
1   3   5   7   9   10   8   6   4   2

ROBERT LUDLUM'S

THE
TREADSTONE
TRANSGRESSION

PROLOGUE

Dallys Carver sat in the passenger seat of the dented sedan, the light breeze blowing in off the ocean doing little to temper the sultry suck of the Haitian night. Even with the windows open, it was stifling inside the car. The sweat ran down her face, dripping onto the screen of the Iridium sat phone in her hand.

C'mon, ring, dammit, she implored it, but the Iridium remained obstinately silent, forcing Carver to just sit there and listen to her partner bitch.

"How in the hell did I let you talk me into this shit?" Chico Long asked from behind the wheel.

Carver was about to reply when the Bluetooth in her ear chirped.

Here we go.

She answered, the call connecting with a rush of static and the double beep of the encryption packet coming online. Then the connection cleared, and she heard the words she'd been waiting for all night.

"Echo One, this is Control . . . Execute."

"Echo One copies," she said.

Carver was out of the car before the line went dead, shoving the sat phone into her pocket and darting across the street. She ducked into the alley, the oppressive stench of stale piss and rotting garbage sending her stomach rushing into her throat. She gagged but kept moving, right hand snaking the SIG P226 from the holster on her hip.

She angled for the rusted metal door to her left and bumped the SureFire X300 WeaponLight mounted to the bottom of the pistol with her thumb, the momentary flash of the high-output LED sparkling off the pristine Master Lock snapped through the slate-gray hasp.

The sight of the shiny lock sent a stream of questions rapid-firing through her mind. *Is the mission blown? Do the Haitians know we're coming? Did Toussaint talk?*

Carver stopped short of the door, suddenly cautious. The current of fear that came with the momentary hesitation spread like a contagion through her body.

"What is it?" her partner hissed.

"The lock," she said, "it's brand new."

"You want to abort?" he asked.

It was the right call—the decision they'd trained to make at the Defense Intelligence Agency's training facility at Harvey Point, North Carolina. That was where she and the rest of her class had been schooled in the dark arts that would become their stock-in-trade as intelligence officers.

Shit. What do I do?

Like everyone else, Dallys Carver was hoping for a European posting, somewhere glamorous like Paris, Berlin, or Budapest. A place where she could get into the action, make her name, and rise through the ranks.

Instead, she got Haiti. A backwater posting, the kind of place the DIA sent their burnouts and fuckups—*not* a hard charger like Carver.

"You think *anyone* wants to be here?" her boss at the US embassy in Port-au-Prince asked when she arrived. "Do you think *I* want to be here?"

"I have no—"

"Hell, no, I don't want to be here," he said, slamming his fist on the desk. "Yet here *we* are."

"So what can I do?"

"Ride it out. Get a tan. Work on your French." He shrugged.

"I didn't join the DIA to sit on my ass."

"I don't really care *why* you joined up," he said. "But let's get one thing clear: I'm running the show here and I will *not* tolerate any cowboy shit. You got me?"

"Yeah," she lied, "I got you."

She tried to keep a low profile, but in the end, it just wasn't in her nature, and despite her boss's warning, Carver was soon immersed in research and intel through trolling bars, nightclubs, coffeehouses, and bistros—wherever diplomats, officers, entrepreneurs, teachers, and even regular working folk hung out—searching for any diamond in the rough, the source who would get her information that would get her noticed by the big shots back in DC. But by the time a month had passed, she was happy to find even a cubic zirconia in the rough—anyone or anything she could add to her network of informants.

Unfortunately, it didn't take long for Carver to realize that when it came to national, or even regional, intelligence, the Caribbean didn't have much to offer.

But just when she was ready to throw in the towel, a friend of a contact's uncle heard about a disgruntled manager from the Banque de Port-au-Prince, and everything changed.

"Breach it," she said.

"You sure?"

"Open the fucking door," she hissed, jerking her thumb at the assault pack strapped to her shoulders.

"Okay, okay, fine with me," he said, unzipping the pocket and tugging out the Bladetricks tactical pry bar they carried for this occasion.

While she watched the street, Long wedged the pick into the shackle and then, with a deep breath, snapped the lock free.

Ten seconds later they were inside, Carver hooking left, digging her hard corner, the SIG up and ready to fire. Finding it clear, she rejoined her partner, who was holding on an open doorway.

"Whatcha got?" she whispered, tucking in behind him.

"Stairs."

They moved silently up the steps, then through the rust-pitted door they found on the landing. They wound up on the roof.

Carver hustled to the north corner and dropped to a knee, the fresh air a welcome relief after the fetid stench of the alley. She laid the assault pack flat on the tarpaper roof and unzipped the main compartment, revealing the suppressed Barrett REC10 stowed inside.

With the ease born of a thousand repetitions, she pulled the rifle free and got it into action, slapping the magazine home and racking a Hammer 166-gram monolithic bullet into the chamber before laying the weapon across the ledge.

"I'm up," she said, the emerald halo of the PVS-14 night-vision monocular mounted behind the scope pooling over her eye as she scanned the street.

On a normal night the Rue Champ de Mars was a hive of activity, the shouts from the vendors hawking their wares and the diesel roar of the brightly painted tap tap buses rattling down the street so loudly that it was hard to think. But with the start of Carnival just around the corner and most of the city busy making last-minute alterations to their costumes, the street lay silent and still. Which was the only reason her superiors back at DC had given her the green light for the mission.

"You do this by the book. No mistakes, no fingerprints, and *no* fucking bodies. Do you understand?"

She'd been irritated at being spoken to like a child, but it was a good mission, one she could potentially make her name with, and Toussaint had assured her that the building would be deserted.

"They'll never know we were there," he'd promised.

At first glance the disgruntled banker wasn't much to look at. He was short and doughy with the hunched shoulders and poor eyesight of a man who spent most of his time chained to a computer.

But Carver didn't give a shit about how Toussaint looked; all she wanted was actionable intelligence. Proof to back up what she already suspected—that Felix Pasquette, the director of the feared Haitian intelligence service, the ANI, was using the Banque de Port-au-Prince to help three international scumbags skirt international sanctions.

According to Toussaint, everything she needed to pull off "the intelligence coup of the century" was sitting on an encrypted flash drive not one hundred feet from her current position—so close that Carver could see it when she swung the rifle back to the alabaster building on the far side of the square.

Nothing's going to stop me now, she thought, depressing the push-to-talk button on the PRC-163 dual band radio attached to her low pro plate carrier.

"Little Bird, this is Echo One. We are in position," she said into the radio.

Nothing.

"Little Bird, this is Echo One—do you copy?"

Silence.

"Twenty bucks that tubby fuck got cold feet," Long whispered.

"He's got too much riding on this not to show," Carver said, hoping that she sounded more confident than she felt.

"Maybe . . . or *maybe* he figured out a free trip to the

States wasn't worth getting his head cut off by that machete-wielding psycho who's running the ANI."

"Trust me, he'll be here."

C'mon, Toussaint, she begged.

Then she heard it: a hiss of static followed by the heavily accented voice of her source. "I—I am here," he said. "O-on the east side of the building."

"Let's do this," she responded.

Toussaint stepped into view and Carver tracked him to the front of the building, watched him swipe the card over the reader and step inside.

"We've got eight minutes until the security guard makes his rounds. Start the clock," she said to Long, moving the reticle up the side of the building, counting the windows until she reached the bank director's sixth-floor office.

While she fine-tuned the focus, working the scope's magnification ring until she could see through the glass and into the office, her partner kept her abreast of Toussaint's progress. "He's out of the elevator and moving down the hall," he said. "You should have him in five, four, three, two . . ."

Right on time, the door of the office swung open and Toussaint stepped inside. Leaving the door ajar, he moved to the computer sitting on the desk in the center of the room and got to work.

"I've got him," she said. "What's the time?"

"Seven minutes left."

So far everything was running smooth, and while Carver wasn't expecting any problems, she wasn't taking any chances. "Go ahead and bring the pickup team into the area. Have them hold at the end of the block."

"A little early, don't you think?" Long asked.

"I want all the eyes we have on the street."

"On it," he said, keying up on the team's internal net.

By the time the rest of the team was in position, waiting in the white panel van at the end of the street, Carver was sweating, the heat from her face fogging the scope's ocular lens, the rivulet of sweat running down her nose, stinging her eyes.

She lifted her cheek from the buttstock of the rifle and, wiping her sleeve across her forehead, wished she'd thought to bring some water.

"Three minutes left," Long said.

Three minutes . . . we're going to make it.

But the thought had no sooner crossed her mind than everything went to shit.

"We've got movement . . ."

"What? Where?" she demanded.

"At the elevator—someone is getting off on six," Long replied.

Carver's first impulse was to swing the rifle off target and confirm what he was telling her, but she fought it, knowing that right now she was the only protection Toussaint had.

"Get him out of there," she said.

Long hit the transmit button, but instead of the usual hiss of static of an open frequency Carver heard the high-pitched warble of a broken transmission.

"The signal is jammed," Long said. "What the hell do we do?"

Before Carver could answer, the hallway lights flashed to life, the fluorescent blaze seeping through the cracked door of the office, flaring her night vision. With the lights on, the

PVS-14 was now useless, so she hit the throw lever, rotating them away from the scope.

When her vision cleared, Toussaint was nowhere to be seen.

Shit! Where did he go?

The answer came a second later when Toussaint's harried voice came rushing through her earpiece.

"S-someone is coming . . . I can hear them running down the hall," he panted.

"No shit," Carver said.

"Get the pickup team rolling," she ordered Long before keying up on the radio. "Where are you?"

Before Toussaint could respond, the door to the office burst inward, the shadow of a man spilling into the darkened room like a wraith.

"We're burned," Long advised.

"Shut the hell up!" Carver snapped, settling the reticle over the shadow's chest.

At first all she saw was a caricature of a man—a wide torso, a thick neck with a haze for a face. But as she worked the focus knob, the distortion disappeared and she found herself looking at Emerie Barbot—the ANI's second-in-command.

"We're not burned, we're *fucked*," Long moaned.

Through her earpiece she could hear Barbot speaking in French. "I know you are in here. Come out now and I won't kill you."

She knew it was a lie and, from Toussaint's ragged breathing in her ear, assumed he knew the same.

Barbot started toward the desk, Carver tracking him through the scope, the light flashing off the silver automatic in his right hand bright as a flash-bang. At the sight of the pistol, her training took over and her thumb moved unbidden to the rifle's selector. The metallic *snap* of the weapon being flicked from *safe* to *fire* was impossibly loud.

"What the hell are you doing?" Long demanded. "We don't have authorization . . ."

But Carver was in another world, her mind laser-focused on Barbot and the realization that he was seconds away from killing her source—destroying her one chance of getting the hell out of Haiti.

Not this time.

Then she fired.

GRANT COUNTY, NEW MEXICO

Adam Hayes opened his eyes, instantly awake and ready. He lay there assessing the darkened bedroom, left hand snaking across the sheets, seeking the reassuring warmth of his sleeping wife, his right searching for the cold steel of the Archon Type B under his pillow.

Finding both where they were supposed to be, Hayes turned his attention to the digital clock by the television.

It was four a.m.

Might as well get up, he thought.

Careful not to disturb his wife, Hayes secured the pistol in the Vaultek safe mounted to the nightstand before easing out of bed. He got to his feet and crossed to the chair by the window, the puckered scar tissue from the bullets he'd taken in Luanda tight across his thigh.

Hayes dressed in the dark—pulling on the black running shorts, gray T-shirt, and a worn pair of Salomon trail runners he'd laid out the night before—snagged a faded beanie from the dresser, and slipped out of the room. Hayes tugged the hat over his shaggy blond hair and started down the hall. He paused to look in on his son, Jack. Seeing the boy had kicked free of his blankets during the night, he stepped in to cover him.

But he wasn't halfway across the room when Týr, the black Malinois he'd bought to protect his family, was growling at him from his spot on the bed.

"*Stil,*" he said. *Quiet.*

The dog went silent but remained on guard, its eyes tracking Hayes all the way to the bed like a pair of aiming lasers. "*Braaf,*" he whispered, giving the dog an affectionate scratch behind the ears before turning his attention to his son. *Well done.*

Being back with his family was the dream that had kept Hayes going during his government-imposed exile to Africa, and discovering that Jack no longer slept in a crib was one of many surprises he'd found waiting for him upon his return. When he'd left, Jack was just learning to walk; now he was on the verge of turning four. Covering the boy, Hayes couldn't help but reflect on how much he'd missed.

How much time they'd stolen from him.

"I promise I'm going to make it up to you," he whispered, kissing Jack lightly on the forehead before stepping out of the room.

The kitchen, like the rest of the house, was dark and still, the only light the pale white glow from the security panel that illuminated the weighted vest and headlamp sitting by the door. Hayes picked up the vest and strapped it to his torso, his mind already compiling a list of reasons why this was a bad idea.

It is too early and way too cold out there for this crap. Stay inside, forget about this nonsense.

Hayes silenced the chatter and typed his code into the security panel, disengaging the interior alarm and the motion detectors he'd emplaced around the house before throwing the lock on the Level 3 GSS security door.

He stepped outside and closed the door behind him, the *chunk* of its multipoint locking cylinders sliding into place muted by the howl of the early morning wind. With the door secure, Hayes tugged the headlamp on and stepped off the porch, cursing the cold and forcing himself into a stiff-legged jog.

Located two and a half hours south of Albuquerque, New Mexico, the Lazy A was as isolated as it was beautiful, a three-hundred-acre paradise of desert grassland, pine-studded foothills, and mesquite-tangled canyons nestled in the shadows of the Black Range.

It was an untamed land, a remnant of the once great wildernesses that covered the southwest. The kind of place where a man could leave his past behind and start a new life, which was exactly what he'd been looking for since returning home, and the reason he'd bought the ranch from his brother-in-law nine months prior.

Unfortunately for Hayes, it wasn't the ranch's natural beauty but the ache in his knees that had his attention.

He'd never liked running, and even as a younger man he'd seen it as an annoyance, an unnecessary suffering that was to be ended as fast as humanly possible. But with the big 4-0 just around the corner and with Hayes feeling every ding and broken bone that he'd collected during his tenure with Treadstone, that annoyance had blossomed into a full-on hatred.

So why not make it worse, right, macho man? the voice chided him.

Hayes knew the voice wasn't real, knew that it was a synthetic by-product of the behavior mods the Treadstone docs had used to turn him into a genetically modified assassin. He'd tried to get rid of it, to purge it from his brain. But despite his best efforts to remove it, the voice remained, buried like a splinter in the recesses of his mind.

So instead he tried to ignore it and focus on his breathing as well as the rhythmic bob of the headlamp off the gravel beneath his feet. He maintained the slow jog for a quarter mile, letting his legs loosen up before starting the timer on his watch.

Hayes cut east across the pasture, the downward slope of the terrain and natural cushion of the buffalo grass beneath his feet a welcome reprieve from the unforgiving hardpack of the gravel drive. Taking advantage of the conditions, he snugged the weighted vest tighter across his shoulders and raced down the slope, hitting the first mile thirty seconds ahead of time.

He continued to push his pace and by the end of the third mile, Hayes had gained a full minute. He was flying, but more important than that, he was in position to conquer the course that had been beating his ass for the past month and a half.

Might want to keep something in the tank, the voice warned.

The advice was solid, but Hayes was in the zone and with his body running like a machine, he wasn't interested in holding anything back.

It's payback time.

Hayes was on his last mile and still pushing hard when the undulating terrain and the steady bounce of the forty-pound vest against his diaphragm began to take their toll. The cramp started small, a stabbing pain beneath his right rib cage that forced him to loosen the vest.

Maybe you might stop trying to prove how tough you are.

"The hell with that," he said, eyes locked on the graphite shadow to his north that marked the final leg of the run.

By the time he made it, the horizon had begun to purple in preparation for the dawn, the muted light filtering through the shadow revealing the arroyo that would lead him up to the finish line.

The sight of the wash rising up before him like a giant ramp sent a rush of endorphins coursing through his bloodstream.

This is it, he told himself.

Sure it is, the voice replied. *It's half a mile to the top.*

Ignoring the voice and the spreading pain in his side, Hayes pushed himself into a sprint, the alluvium that lined the bottom of the wash threatening to suck the shoes from his feet as he raced toward the summit.

The first two hundred meters were gentle, almost easy,

and Hayes was still confident he could make it, but then he hit the wall. In an instant he was out of gas, his throat and lungs raw from the cold morning air, legs burning hot as fire from the lactic acid rolling through his thighs and calves.

He tried to power through it, to keep pushing, but he'd pushed too hard and now he was paying the price.

So, the same old, same old, the voice chided. *How's that working out for ya?*

By the time he made the apex, Hayes was gassed, his legs shaking like someone had hit his muscles with a cattle prod. He slowed to a walk and checked his watch to see that he'd run the course in forty minutes.

It was a good time for a Navy SEAL, but too slow to get him back on Treadstone operational status.

He turned his attention east, cursing his lack of judgment and his deep-seated need to prove that he could still hack it. The napalm glow of the rising sun reminded him of Angola and the gunfight in Luanda that had damn near killed him.

Going to Africa hadn't been his choice. He'd been given an ultimatum—get the hell out of the States or spend the rest of his life rotting away in some government-run black site.

It was a shit hand, but that was nothing new, and Hayes was determined to make the best of the situation. Atone for the many hell points he'd acquired during his time in Operation Treadstone and come back the kind of man Annabelle and little Jack could be proud of.

With that thought at the forefront of his mind, Hayes went to work for an aid group flying food, water, and much-needed medicines to the beleaguered refugee camps in Burkina Faso.

It was a shit job and, thanks to the gauntlet of extremist gun positions encircling the camps, dangerous as hell. But people were dying and, after all, helping people was the reason he'd become a Green Beret in the first place.

Unfortunately, no amount of altruism was going to change the fact that Hayes was a shit magnet, and it wasn't long before he found himself sucked into a conspiracy that had almost cost him his life.

"That's enough," he told himself. Time to focus on the here and now, not the past.

Good idea, said the voice. *And what exactly is the here and now?*

Hayes took a deep breath, closed his eyes, and turned his head back to the sunrise. By then it had shifted from napalm fireworks to the glow of a fireplace. In the wafting rays he could see the glint in his son's eyes and the warmth of his wife's smile.

Yeah, said the voice. *Maybe it's time to concentrate less on your bad ass, and more on what's really important . . .*

The thought galvanized him. After knocking out a hundred burpees, Hayes ran back the way he'd come. By the time he hit the gravel drive his legs felt like they were full of air. All he was thinking about was getting to the front door and laying eyes on who was waiting inside.

Even so, he made the last hundred yards on willpower alone. When he reached the stairs he was done, mouth dry as a bone, the sweat-soaked vest feeling like it weighed a thousand pounds. He unstrapped the thing and let it fall, the resounding thump of it hitting the ground followed an instant later by a sultry voice from the front door.

"Where you been, cowboy?"

Hayes looked up, the bone-crushing fatigue instantly forgotten as his wife, Annabelle, padded lithely across the porch—effortlessly beautiful despite just rolling out of bed, or maybe because of it.

"I . . . uh . . . couldn't sleep," he finally managed. "What are *you* doing up so early?"

"I'm just enjoying the view," she said, a mischievous glint in her green eyes.

"Is that a fact?" Hayes grinned, starting up the steps. "And where is our son?"

"Still asleep," she said.

"Oh, really?"

"But don't you get any ideas until after you take—" she began.

Before she could finish, Hayes was on the porch, right hand snaking out to grab her around the waist.

"Too late," he said, pulling her close and kissing her hard on the lips.

For an instant the world fell away, the pain and uncertainty that had been his constant companion since coming back to the States receding like a bad dream.

But it wasn't to last. Seconds into the embrace, Hayes felt eyes on him. He looked up to see his son standing at the screen door.

"Ewww, gross," the boy said, his tiny voice popping the moment like a bubble.

"So much for that," he said.

"Don't worry, cowboy," Annabelle said before pulling

away, "now that you're home, we've got all the time in the world."

Then she was gone, and Hayes was alone on the porch, wishing he shared her optimism, but knowing it was only a matter of time before Treadstone showed up to pull him back into the fight.

PORT-AU-PRINCE, HAITI

It was seven thirty a.m. in Port-au-Prince when the convoy turned onto the Route de Delmas, the flash of the blue lights and the wail of sirens from the lead Land Rover barely noticeable over the lively beat from the revelers gathered in the street a hundred yards ahead.

At the edge of the crowd, Junior Noel stood with the scrum of musicians, a patinaed trumpet pressed to his lips. The instrument was old and, thanks to the dry-rotted cork valves, sounded stuffy compared to the other horns, but Junior didn't care. His father had given him the instrument shortly before he died, and Junior played it with pride.

Junior paused to wipe the sweat from his brow, the band

ready to launch into another song when one of the drummers saw the convoy.

"Now what do these sons of bitches want?" the man wondered.

"Who cares?" another man said. "Let them go around."

Junior nodded and licked his lips, ready to get back to the music when he saw the blacked-out Mercedes G-Class SUV coming up fast behind the Land Rover.

Shit.

He opened his mouth, ready to yell a warning, but before he could, a woman in a feathered headdress and sequined bikini beat him to it.

"Dyab la ap vini!" The devil is coming.

"Run!" a second voice shouted.

In an instant the crowd was moving, musicians and revelers stampeding for the sidewalk. Junior turned to follow, crashing into one of the broad-shouldered musicians, the wooden *tanbou* drum swinging from his shoulder, clipping Junior in the side of the head.

The blow sent him spinning, ankle twisting beneath him, and then he was falling.

Junior hit hard, the impact knocking the air from his lungs, but the pain was overshadowed by the clatter of his trumpet into the street.

"No!" he shouted.

He scrambled to his feet and lurched forward, ready to jump out and save the instrument, when through the car's front windshield he saw the figure in the rear of the Mercedes. The sight of the man's malignant eyes and the garish

21

scar that crisscrossed his face froze Junior in place, leaving him helpless to do anything but watch the tire flatten his prized possession.

On most days, Felix Pasquette would have savored the moment. Ordered his driver to slow the car so he could feast on the fear written across the faces of the men and women jammed together on the curb. Their abject terror coursed through his blood like a shot of morphine. Reminding him that while the president and his ministers were busy convincing themselves that *they* were the ones running the country, the people knew the truth. Knew that Pasquette and his dreaded Agence Nationale d'Intelligence, or ANI, were the island's *real* power.

But today he sat silent in the back of the Mercedes, his fingers tapping impatiently against the silver-plated hilt of the machete in his lap. His thoughts were on the phone call that had woken him at dawn.

Felix had been out late, drinking and whoring at Casino El Rancho, and he'd gotten home around one and promptly passed out. Three hours later, the woman he'd brought home was kicking him awake, her voice husky from sleep.

"Felix . . . your phone."

His eyes had fluttered open and he'd tried to make sense of her words, but with his mind still hazy from the booze all he could think about was going back to sleep. Then he'd heard it, the rattle of his burner phone vibrating across the nightstand, and the name displayed on the screen cut through the fog like a snort of amyl nitrite.

Captain Bernard? Shit.

In an instant Pasquette had been out of bed and moving to his dresser, the phone pressed to his ear, knowing that there was only one reason his source within the Haitian National Police would be calling him at this hour.

"What is it, Captain?" he'd asked.

"There is a problem at the bank."

"What kind of problem?"

"Barbot is dead. Killed trying to stop a break-in last night."

The news had hit like a blow to the face and suddenly the room was spinning. Feeling like he was about to pass out, Pasquette had braced himself against the wall, the voice on the other end of the line receding to a dull buzz.

This can't be happening. Not now.

"Sir, are you there?" Bernard had asked, his voice cutting through the spell.

Pasquette had gathered himself by sheer force of will and stood upright, knowing that he had to get control of the situation before it was too late.

"You said this happened last night. Why am I just now hearing about it?"

"Inspector Dorval has personally taken control of the scene, so I was not alerted until this morning when I came on shift."

Of course, Pasquette had thought.

Like all federal agencies, there was no love lost between the ANI and the Police Nationale d'Haïti, or PNH, and with both departments constantly seeking to expand their power, a bitter rivalry had developed. However, despite the animosity and the willingness on both sides to do whatever they could to undermine the other, it was agreed that all skirmishes would be conducted behind closed doors.

But that had changed when Inspector Dorval took command of the PNH nine months prior. Since then, the once-contained conflict had blossomed into open war.

"Where are you now?" Pasquette had wanted to know.

"I am at the bank, awaiting your instructions."

"And your men?"

"They are waiting for you at the bank," Bernard had replied.

"Good. I am on my way."

The instant he was off the phone, Pasquette had had his men rolling, and by the time he was dressed and downstairs the convoy had pulled up at his house. As a rule, he was a realist, a man who usually dealt with the facts as he found them, but as he'd climbed into the Mercedes, Pasquette found himself praying that this was some kind of elaborate misunderstanding.

Even now, as the convoy turned onto the Rue Champ de Mars, he was still clinging to a sliver of hope. But then he saw the bank and his hope vanished at the sight of the yellow caution tape and the cluster of PNH vehicles parked haphazardly around the building.

"I will kill them," he snarled, fingers tightening around the machete's handle.

As the convoy closed in on their destination, Captain Bernard came bounding into view, a scarred nightstick in his right hand. "Stand at attention, you fools!" he yelled at the officers lounging around the white and orange sawhorse pulled across the drive. "And you, move that damn barricade."

The men leapt into action and the convoy pulled into the parking lot, Pasquette's men bailing out of the Land Rovers before the trucks had even come to a halt. In an instant half had formed a loose perimeter around the Mercedes while the rest started up the stairs—barking orders and shoving the police officers out of the way.

"I apologize for my men," the young captain said when Pasquette climbed out of the car. "They are lazy shits, but they are loyal."

"Where is he?" Pasquette demanded.

"On the sixth floor," Bernard said. "I will take you to him."

Despite its stature as *the* preeminent banking establishment in Haiti, everything about the Banque de Port-au-Prince was woefully out of date. The lobby that had once been considered an architectural masterpiece was now a sad caricature of its former self. The gleaming marble floor had faded to a dull gray and the gilded mirrors that hung behind the massive reception desk bore a hazy fog.

But it was the rumble from the basement that came when his guide pushed the call button for the elevator, the reverberations shaking the floor, that gave Pasquette pause. The tortured scream of stressed metal and overworked gears grew to a crescendo seconds before the car bumped to a halt and the patinaed bronze doors slid open.

"After you, sir," Bernard said.

Growing up, tight spaces had never bothered Pasquette, but that all changed with the earthquake of 2010. He'd been in the kitchen helping his son with his homework, his wife humming contentedly at the stove when the quake hit. One second, he was checking his son's addition by the sallow glow of the bare bulb, and the next instant he was alone, buried beneath the rubble that had once been their four-story apartment building.

He'd spent the next eighteen hours trapped under the mass of shattered concrete and twisted rebar. When the rescue service finally pulled him out, Pasquette was more animal than man, his mind twisted by the hours spent listening to the screams of the living and the hushed prayers of the dying.

All that was left was the rage.

By the time the car came to a grinding halt on the top floor, Pasquette was sweating, his guts twisting against the caustic stench of hot metal and lithium. The door slid open and all he could think about was running from the car and getting to a window for a breath of fresh air, but he refused to give in and held himself in place with an inward snarl.

Get ahold of yourself.

Grabbing the fear by the throat, he shoved it back into its box and calmly stepped out of the car. He followed Bernard down the long hall, ignoring the salutes of the officers who snapped to attention.

He could hear Dorval now, the inspector's booming laugh rolling out of the last office on the left, the sound sending the blood boiling in Pasquette's veins.

The moment he stepped into the office, the idle chatter he'd heard from the hall fell away, all eyes swinging to the fat man standing in the center of the room.

"Ah, Director Pasquette," Dorval said, "so kind of you to join us."

Pasquette ignored him and moved to the window, his dark eyes taking in the jagged star the bullet had punched through the glass.

"I took the liberty of having the body removed," Dorval said. "It was starting to smell."

Still silent, Pasquette turned, following the trajectory of the bullet to the back wall where the clotted blood and pinkish clumps of Barbot's brain matter was sprayed across the white paint.

"Clear the room," Pasquette said.

"You forget yourself, Director," Dorval challenged. "*This* is a police matter—which means you and your thugs have exactly *zero* authority."

"One of my men is dead," Pasquette said, stepping forward. "Which makes *this* a matter of national security."

"Over my dead body," the fat inspector sneered.

"Well, if *you* insist," Pasquette shrugged, yanking the machete from its scabbard, the early morning sunlight glinting off the blade as he slashed at the inspector's throat.

Dorval stepped back, his fingers rushing to his neck. He touched the wound, the fear in his eyes receding when he saw only a dab of blood on his fingertips.

He smiled scornfully at Pasquette and opened his mouth to speak, but with the bob of his Adam's apple the flesh ruptured, the rush of air through the gaping maw that had once been his throat followed by a torrent of blood.

Dorval dropped to his knees, both hands wrapped around

his mangled throat, trying to stanch the gush of blood through his fingers.

"Anyone else wish to question my authority?" Pasquette asked, wiping the blade across the dying inspector's shoulder before returning the machete to its sheath.

"No, *sir*!" the men in the room said as one.

"Excellent," Pasquette said, turning his attention to Captain Bernard. "Close the airport and the harbor. No one comes in or out until we find out who is responsible for this. Do you understand me, *Inspector* Bernard?"

"Yes, sir," the man said, already heading to the door.

"And Bernard," Pasquette said, "I want them *alive*."

GRANT COUNTY, NEW MEXICO

While Annabelle got to work on breakfast, Hayes hob-
bled over to the chest freezer and threw it open. He
frowned down at the three bags of ice he found lying
at the bottom.

"I swear I just filled this damn thing up," he grumbled.

"You did," Annabelle said. "Takes a lot of ice to keep
those old bones working."

"Old bones, my ass," he muttered, leaning over the edge
and retrieving the bags. He stood up, about to tell her that he
was in his prime, when the dry pop of his right knee cut him off.

"What was that?" she asked.

"I . . . uh . . . guess I need to get more ice when I go
to town."

"Maybe next time you'll think ahead," she said with a smile.

Oh, yeah, that old refrain.

"Speaking of town," she continued, her voice dropping to a whisper, "Ed called and the decorations I ordered for Jack's birthday came in. Would you mind picking them up?"

"Did he say anything about the fireworks?" Hayes asked hopefully.

"Please tell me you didn't order *more* fireworks."

"The boy said he wanted to shoot fireworks at his party."

"You've already got two boxes out in the barn," she said, her hands finding her hips. "How many fireworks could a four-year-old possibly need?"

"Better to have too many than not enough," Hayes grinned.

"I swear, Adam, sometimes it feels like I'm raising *two* children around here," she sighed. "And don't you dare mess up my bathroom."

"Yes ma'am," he said, closing the freezer lid.

He stepped out of the kitchen and kicked off his filthy shoes and socks in the laundry room before hobbling down the hall, the terra cotta tiles cold against his bare feet. Closing the bathroom door behind him, Hayes dumped the ice into the cast iron tub, turned on the water, and stripped out of his clothes.

While he waited for the bath to fill, he turned to the mirror and studied the scars that crisscrossed his muscled torso like lines on a topographic map. To an untrained eye there was nothing to differentiate the patchwork of knotted tissue— they were scars and nothing more. But to Hayes they were a living history, a tapestry that reminded him of friends lost, mistakes made, and hard lessons that had been paid in blood.

His eyes dropped to angry red welts marking his lower abdomen and upper thighs left by the bullets he'd taken in Luanda. He remembered the surgeries and the pain, his burning desire to get the hell out of the hospital and be with his family.

"When can I leave?" he'd asked.

"Mr. Hayes, the fact that you are even *alive* after what you've been through is a miracle," the chief of surgery had said. "But now that you are on the mend, you *must* give your body time to heal."

"How long, doc?"

"Optimistically?" the man had asked.

"Yeah."

"Another two . . . maybe three months."

By this time Hayes had already been away from his family for more than a year and there was no way in hell he was staying in a hospital for another three months.

"That's not going to work," he'd replied.

Eager to get home and make up for lost time, Hayes had checked himself out of the hospital, returned to the US, and three weeks later they'd sold their house in Tennessee and were heading west.

His brother-in-law had warned him that the ranch was a fixer-upper, but nothing prepared him for what he found waiting in New Mexico. To say the ranch house was dilapidated was an insult to the word. The place was wrecked with gaping holes in the roof, a dangerously sagging porch, and a bathroom that made a crack house look nice.

Physically, Hayes hadn't been much better. He'd been gaunt and weak, his skin an ashen gray from the months spent in the hospital. Annabelle suggested they hire someone to make the necessary repairs.

"That's not happening," he'd said.

"But you can barely swing a hammer without getting winded."

"Then I'd better get stronger," he'd grinned.

Hayes had known it was going to be hard work, but he hadn't cared. They were a family again and that was all that mattered.

Not that it didn't suck.

The first few weeks toiling beneath the blowtorch heat of the New Mexico sun had damn near killed him, but he knew that he was getting stronger by the day. He'd kept at it, pushing himself harder than any foreman, and by the end of the first month he'd regained most of the muscle mass he'd lost.

But now, standing there in the bathroom, still hurting from the run, Hayes knew he was a long way from being dangerous.

Might as well get this over with, he thought, turning away from the mirror.

He cut off the water, stepped into the tub, and slowly lowered himself through the ice floating on the surface. Once he was sitting down, he took a deep breath and, before his body could talk him out of it, sank beneath the water.

While Hayes knew that he was in no danger of freezing to death, his brain didn't get the memo. Sensing the sudden drop in body temperature, the primal part of his brain went into full-on fight-or-flight mode.

Officially known as the cold shock response, the sudden dilation of the blood vessels, erratic skipping of his heart, and the sudden involuntary inhalation were designed to save his life, but to Hayes it felt like a revolt.

Not wanting to suck in a lungful of cold water, he surfaced in time to take a gasping breath. While his brain screamed at him to get out, Hayes held fast. He closed his eyes and turned his attention inward, forcing himself to focus on his son's upcoming party.

To Jack there was nothing special about turning four, but after all the birthdays Hayes had missed, it was the most important event of the year. And he wanted everything to be perfect.

He was still freezing when he got out of the water, but the pain and disappointment that had come with the run were gone and his mind was clear. Hayes got dressed, this time in a pair of faded Kühls and a long-sleeve thermal top under a fleece button-down. He stuffed his feet into a pair of worn Tony Lamas, and grabbed the pistol from the safe and tucked it into his holster before following the smell of bacon and eggs to the kitchen.

He was starving and wolfed down his breakfast while Annabelle wrote out a list of everything he needed to pick up while he was in town.

"Am I forgetting anything?" she asked.

"Can't think of anything," he said, stuffing the list into his pocket before stepping into the den where Jack sat locked on the television.

"I'm out of here, buddy," he said. "Anything you need from the store?"

Silence.

"Earth to Jack," he said, snapping his fingers.

"Huh?" The boy blinked and looked away from the television long enough to flash a smile and a small wave. "Oh, hey, Dad."

Curious to see what had the boy's undivided attention, Hayes stepped closer to the screen and saw a young boy playing with the exact toys Jack had scattered around the den.

"What's this?" he asked.

"*Ryan's World* . . . it's a YouTube channel."

"And you like this show?"

"Yeah, Ryan is *awesome*," Jack grinned.

"So . . . instead of playing with *your* toys, you are watching this Ryan kid play with *his* toys?"

"Yep."

"Well, have fun . . . I guess," Hayes said, kissing his son on the top of the head. "I love you, buddy."

"Love you, Dad," Jack smiled.

"He's watching some kid play with toys," he said, passing Annabelle on his way out the door. "You believe that?"

"That kid is worth eleven million dollars," she said, following him outside.

"You're shitting me."

"Nope."

"Damn . . . you think Ed has any video cameras?" he wondered.

"How about we hold off on exploiting our son," she frowned as he started to the sun-faded 1979 Ford F-250 parked in front of the house.

"Good call," he said, climbing behind the wheel.

The pickup was old to the point of being obsolete, its tired engine and rust-pitted frame long past its prime. But Hayes had a soft spot for old things, and there was something about the old Ford that appealed to him.

Annabelle, on the other hand, harbored no such sentiment.

"Be careful," she said.

"I'm going to town, not Beirut," he said, sliding the key into the ignition. "What's the worst that could happen?"

"With you driving that old bucket of bolts there is no telling," Annabelle sighed.

"You're talking about a classic." He closed the door and turned the key, ignoring the flash of service lights that danced across the dash as he pumped the gas.

The starter whined, the truck making a halfhearted attempt at turning over before going silent. "Give her a second," he said, adjusting the manual choke he'd installed in the cab. "She's just cold."

"Whatever you say, babe."

Smartass, he thought.

On the third try, the engine roared to life, the jet-black smoke that poured from the exhaust pipe sending Annabelle rushing into the house. Hayes hooted in triumph and slapped the wheel. "That's the girl," he said, knowing the Ford would likely stall the second he took his foot off the gas.

Keeping his foot firmly on the accelerator, Hayes yanked the truck into gear, the acrid choke of the exhaust burning the back of his throat. He pulled off and started down the gravel drive, the old Ford bucking and sputtering like a stubborn mule beneath him.

He used the remote to open the gate at the end of the

driveway and pulled though, making sure the gate closed behind him before following the service road east for a mile and a half.

By the time he hit the end of the drive, the Ford was running smoothly. He cracked the window, the rush of clean mountain air venting the exhaust from the cab. Living out in the middle of nowhere had its advantages. The air was clean and the crime low, plus with his closest neighbor being five miles to the east, Hayes didn't have to worry about uninvited guests. On the flip side of that coin was the long commute to just about anywhere with nothing but the stunted chollas to break the endless gray wash of the desert.

To deal with the monotony of the drives, Hayes had ordered a satellite radio to replace the Ford's antiquated radio, but, until it came in, he was stuck with the handful of cassettes he kept in the center console. He selected the Allman Brothers's *At Fillmore East* album and shoved it into the tape deck before turning onto state route 27.

With the hypnotic opening riff of "Whipping Post" playing through the speakers, Hayes settled back in his seat, fingers drumming on the wheel as he drove south. For a moment everything was right with the world. But then he saw it—a dark green speck in the sky racing toward him.

What the hell?

Hayes pulled off the side of the road. By the time he threw the truck into park, the object was gone, hidden behind a pair of low hills fifty yards to his front. He killed the music and hopped out of the truck to scan the sky—but there was nothing.

For most men, the lack of a discernible threat would have

signaled the end of the matter, but Hayes had spent enough time as both the hunter *and* prey to know that just because he did not see the threat didn't mean it wasn't there.

Knowing that he needed to get to higher ground, Hayes clambered into the bed and was stepping up on the toolbox when the helicopter came rocketing over the crest of the hill. The sight of the helo froze him in place and before he could snap free, it was thundering overhead—the superheated blast of its rotor wash shoving him backward.

Then it was gone, Hayes standing vapor-locked in the back of the truck, helpless to do anything but watch it streak west across the desert like an arrow shot from a bow.

The ranch, the voice said. *They're heading for your family.*

The sudden realization of the helicopter's destination hit like a cattle prod. In the next instant, Hayes was moving, leaping from the back of the truck. His only thought: beating the helo back to the ranch.

DOÑA ANA COUNTY, NEW MEXICO

The UH-72 Lakota lifted off from Las Cruces airport and raced west across the desert. In the back, Director Levi Shaw tugged his harness tight and closed his eyes, the exhaustion of the previous eighteen hours crashing over him like a tidal wave.

When he first joined the CIA, Shaw had prided himself on his ability to function on as little as four hours of sleep a night. But thirty years later there was no denying that he'd lost a step, and he cursed himself for not taking a nap during the flight from Andrews Air Force Base.

He tried to clear his mind, but even with the white-noise hum of the engines it refused to settle. Instead, it skipped back to the call he'd received eighteen hours prior.

He'd been on his way home from the Defense Intelligence Analysis Center, or DIAC, at Joint Base Anacostia–Bolling, his only thought the lowball of Bushmills waiting for him at his newly rented condo in Alexandria, when the phone rang.

He tugged the encrypted phone from his jacket and frowned at the number he found displayed on the screen. "You've got to be shitting me," he said.

"Sir?" his driver asked, eyes darting to the rearview mirror.

"It's the office."

"Roger that," the man replied, already merging to the exit.

While his driver got them turned around, Shaw answered the call and pressed the phone to his ear. There was a moment of silence followed by the double click of the end-to-end encryption suite coming online and finally the voice of the watch officer at the DIAC.

"Sorry to bother you, sir, but there's a situation in Haiti . . ."

"Haiti?" Shaw asked, momentarily confused.

"Yes, sir, Port-au-Prince, to be exact."

As the director of Operation Treadstone, Shaw was responsible for running operations all over the world. He knew for a fact that none of his agents were anywhere near Haiti.

"What's that got to do with me?" he finally asked.

"No idea, sir," the man said. "All I can tell you is that the general wants to see you ASAP."

"Okay, I'm on my way," Shaw said, the low throbbing at the base of his skull signaling the start of another migraine.

The migraines, like his position at the Department of Defense, were new, by-products of the CIA-sanctioned ambush meant to end his tenure as the director of Operation Treadstone nine months earlier. The plan was to hit him on his way home—run him off the road and make it look like he had been the victim of a hit and run.

The operation was well planned, every detail meticulously scripted to ensure his assassins had the upper hand, but not only had Shaw survived, before he put his would-be killers in the dirt he'd learned that the kill order had come from Mike Carpenter—the CIA's deputy director of operations.

Knowing that it was only a matter of time before Carpenter found out that he was still alive, Shaw needed more than just an escape plan, he needed a protector. Someone with enough firepower, money, and influence to shield him from the agency—and Shaw had known exactly where to look.

The meeting with General Joseph Mitchell, the chairman of the Joints Chiefs of Staff, had cost him every favor that he'd collected during his thirty years with the government and even then, all the man would give him was five minutes.

Not that it mattered, considering what Shaw was bringing to the table.

Just as he'd suspected, the general jumped at the chance to bring the world's sharpest scalpel to the DoD's toolbox. But what Shaw *hadn't* expected was how quickly his newfound protectors would seek to broaden the terms of their agreement by attempting to use his highly skilled Treadstone operatives for just about everything *but* their primary function.

What bullshit are they going to try to pull this time? he

wondered as they drove through the security gate and turned off MacDill Boulevard heading north toward the six-story glass and concrete building that housed the Analysis Center.

His driver guided the Suburban around the back and down into the garage where his Department of Defense liaison, Major Gunner Poe, was waiting for them at the bank of elevators.

Like most officers who'd served with the US Army's elite Delta Force, Major Poe was a seasoned warfighter, calm and collected thanks to the ten years he'd spent conducting combat operations in some of the most inhospitable environments known to man. Which is why the sight of the young major pacing back and forth in front of the elevators, like a junkyard dog on a leash, put Shaw instantly on guard.

Before his driver stopped at the curb, Poe was tracking the Suburban like a wire-guided missile, his muscles straining beneath the navy-blue polo.

"What do we have?" Shaw asked, climbing out of the truck and starting to the elevators.

"Officially, there isn't anything going on in Port-au-Prince," Poe said, falling in beside him.

"And unofficially?" Shaw asked, swiping his ID card over the reader and stepping inside the elevator.

"None of this is confirmed, but word is that a human intelligence team was compromised during an operation at the Banque de Port-au-Prince," Poe said. "General Cantrell is playing this one very close to his chest, but from what I gathered he is looking to send in a team to get them out."

"You've got to be shitting me," Shaw said, pressing the button for the top floor.

"Like I said, nothing's confirmed."

Dammit, Shaw thought.

"What do you want me to do, sir?" Poe asked, as the elevator car settled to a halt beneath them.

As an intelligence officer, the only thing he hated more than rumors was going into a situation with more questions than answers, but with the door sliding open, Shaw was running out of time to get ahead of the situation.

"I need you to find Adam Hayes," Shaw said, stepping out of the elevator. "And Poe, I need you to keep it quiet."

"Roger that, sir."

Shaw waited for the doors to close and then started toward the glass-fronted room at the end of the hall. He flashed his badge to one of the armed guards flanking the door and then stepped to the retina scanner mounted to the wall on the right side of the door. He pressed his forehead against the rubber plate and there was a flash of light followed by the metallic click of the magnetic lock disengaging.

While the hallway and elevator had both been well lit, the interior of the operations center was downright gloomy, the recessed lighting in the ceiling designed to reduce the eye strain of the analysts who spent their days staring at either the monitors on their workstations or one of the many LCD screens mounted on the far wall.

It took a moment for Shaw's vision to adjust to the wan lighting, but when it did his gaze settled on the scrum of intelligence officers watching a live feed from a General Atomics MQ-9 Reaper.

His professional curiosity piqued, Shaw started over, curious about what they were watching, but he hadn't made it halfway before a young lieutenant was angling to inter-cept him.

"Director Shaw," the man said, "if you will follow me, I will take you to the general."

Casting a final glance at the screen, Shaw stepped in be-hind the man, who led him along the back wall to a breakout room with frosted glass. Motioning for him to stand fast, the man moved to the speaker mounted on the wall and pushed the call button.

"General, I have Director Shaw for you," the man said.

"Send him in," an authoritative voice answered.

From the outside the breakout room didn't appear much bigger than a broom closet. However, like everything in the intelligence world, looks could be deceiving. When Shaw stepped inside he found himself in a full-scale situation room complete with an oak conference table, a bank of LCD mon-itors, and a square of leather chairs in the far corner.

Yet despite its size, the room was empty save for the stocky gray-haired general sitting at the head of the table.

"Thanks for coming in, Levi," said General Cantrell, the ribbons on his uniform gleaming in the light as he got to his feet and came around to greet him.

"Didn't know I had a choice."

The smile fell from the general's face and he stopped short, his dark eyes suddenly hard as a pair of rock drills. "What was that?"

"A joke, sir . . ." Shaw said, inwardly cursing himself for the failed attempt at humor. "I was just . . . kidding."

"That's funny," the general said with a humorless smile. "Now sit the hell down."

"Yes, sir," Shaw said, pulling out a chair.

"We are already behind the eight ball on this, so I'm going to get right to the point," the general began. "Two months ago, I was advised that a human intelligence officer had recruited a high-level source from the Banque de Port-au-Prince," Cantrell said, sliding a crimson briefing folder across the table. "The source's name is Hugo Toussaint. In exchange for a new life in the States, Mr. Toussaint agreed to provide proof that the ANI was working with a foreign conglomerate to skirt international sanctions. Yesterday Toussaint was compromised by a member of the ANI while trying to retrieve the intelligence."

"What happened?"

"Dallys Carver, the team leader, went off script and terminated the compromise with extreme prejudice."

"How extreme?" Shaw asked.

"She put a one-hundred-and-sixty-six-grain bullet through his cranial vault."

"And the intel?" Shaw asked.

"Recovered."

"So what's the problem?" Shaw questioned.

"The man she killed was Colonel Barbot," Cantrell said.

That information gave Shaw pause. "That *is* a problem," he finally said. "Pasquette definitely won't be happy."

"I agree, but the boss wants that intel. He wants you to send in a team—"

"Send in a team?" Shaw asked in disbelief. "With all due respect, sir, Treadstone's not in the rescue business."

To an outsider it was a heartless thing to say, but not for Shaw. He'd spent his time in the mud—he'd lost more blood and friends in more third world shitholes than he could count. He knew what it felt like to be left out in the cold, on the run, praying that somewhere, *someone* was doing everything they could to get him the hell out.

So, if General Cantrell or any of the brass at the DoD wanted *him* to send one of his boys into harm's way—they better have a damn good reason.

"This isn't negotiable, Levi," Cantrell said. "You either make it happen, *or . . .*"

"Yeah, I got it," he said.

The pilot's ten-minute warning brought Shaw back to the now and he opened his eyes to find Major Poe staring at him from the other seat. Shaw had ordered him to come along to pick up the sure-to-be-reluctant Adam Hayes.

"Something on your mind?" Shaw asked.

"I tried to look up Hayes's file," Poe began, "but there's nothing in the database. Hell, if he hadn't applied for a New Mexico driver's license, I doubt I'd have even found him."

"That's because they scrubbed it from the system when he left," Shaw said.

"I heard you recruited him personally."

"That's right," Shaw said.

"Anything I should know about him?" Poe asked.

"Yeah. Try not to piss him off," Shaw grinned.

GRANT COUNTY, NEW MEXICO

ayes didn't bother to close the door; he simply yanked the Ford into reverse and stomped down on the gas. The truck shot backward in a spray of gravel, and he let it pick up speed before cranking the wheel to the left.

At almost five thousand pounds, the big pickup wasn't designed to handle this kind of high-speed maneuver. It was too heavy, and the ancient shocks and struts gave it the handling of a barge with a stuck rudder, but Hayes didn't care.

As he let off the gas, the truck's momentum swung it around, and Hayes shifted into drive the instant the hood was pointing north. The transmission thumped into gear and he drove the gas pedal down to the floor, fully expecting the truck to die on him.

For once the old truck complied with a surge of power and took off, the big V8 roaring beneath the hood. Steering with his left hand, Hayes ripped open the center console with his right and dug through the mound of receipts that filled the interior, desperately searching for the phone Annabelle had bought him.

Like many men in his line of work, Hayes had a natural distrust of anything that could be remotely controlled, accessed, or exploited. While on operations, he'd seen how the government could hack into phones, computers, and cameras to get him the targeting info he'd required to complete a mission, and he wanted nothing to do with it.

But despite his protests, Annabelle had finally forced him to join the digital age when she gave him a phone for his birthday.

"You know how hard it is to find a flip phone without internet access these days?"

"Nope."

"Well, it's hard, so you better use it."

At the time all Hayes could manage was a begrudging "thank you," but as he dialed his house line and pressed the phone to his ear, he said it again for her foresight. Instead of the line connecting, though, all he got was the "no signal" beep.

"You piece of shit!" he yelled, about to throw the phone out the window, when he saw the rise in the road a mile ahead.

You need to get to higher ground, the voice advised.

"Yeah, no shit," Hayes said.

But even with the accelerator pinned to the floor, the

speedometer had yet to creep past sixty miles an hour. With his family's safety on the line, the slow charge up the hill felt like an eternity.

Finally, a service bar appeared, and then another, and he let out a triumphant shout, kissing the phone before hitting the redial button. This time the phone connected and with the first ring Hayes let out the breath he hadn't realized he was holding.

His relief was immediate but short-lived. No sooner had the phone begun to ring than a bright red Porsche Carrera GT came zipping over the hill, the gray-haired man behind the wheel too busy staring at his own phone to realize he'd drifted out of his lane.

Hayes let off the gas and punched the horn, but the Porsche was flying and in the few seconds it took for the driver to look up and see the massive truck barreling down on him, the two vehicles had closed to within twenty yards.

During Hayes's time at Treadstone he'd been sent to countless performance driving schools, where he'd learned how to push a car to its absolute limit. During the thousands of hours on the track he'd learned that the typical human reaction time was 250 milliseconds—or a quarter of a second. Which gave the driver of the Porsche plenty of time to realize that his fancy German sports car was seconds away from becoming a hood ornament. It was an easy fix, and Hayes was expecting the man to swiftly move back into his lane. But instead of taking the easy way out, the driver seemingly panicked— stomping on the brakes and jerking the wheel to his right.

If the man had picked one or the other, they would have been fine, but stomping on the brakes *and* yanking the wheel sent the Porsche instantly out of control—sliding down the middle of the roadway at eighty miles an hour.

With the Porsche screeching down the centerline, Hayes had to pick a side and, with the large dropoff on the right shoulder, the only viable option was to go left. Clutching the phone to his ear with his shoulder, Hayes cranked the wheel hard over, steering for the relative safety of the open desert.

The truck clattered off the roadway, the bang of the front tires off the mounded dirt shoulder bouncing the Ford sky-ward. With all four tires in the air, Hayes sat behind the wheel, staring up at the pale blue sky and marveling at how fast this day had gone to shit.

Then gravity took over and the nose dropped, the impact whiplashing him into the steering wheel and blasting the phone from the crook of his shoulder. Dazed by the blow and blinded by the pall of ochre dust that filled the cab, Hayes grabbed the wheel and hit the brakes, but instead of slowing down, the Ford continued to accelerate.

"What in the hell?"

The brakes were working—he could feel them engage, hear the grind of the pads against the rotors—but even with his foot off the accelerator, the truck kept gaining speed. A quick glance at the floorboards and he saw the reason.

The accelerator was stuck.

He pulled at it with his toe, tried to pry it free, but the arm was twisted, pedal wedged firmly against the firewall. A crunch of metal from the front of the truck followed by the sharp crack of a hard object hitting off the windshield ripped him from his work, the cracks spiderwebbing across the glass drawing his attention back to the terrain.

Just drive, dammit, the voice commanded.

From his current position, the shortest distance to the ranch was due west but it was also the most rugged, a fact that sent Hayes reaching for the seat belt. He snapped in and adjusted his heading, centering the hood on the series of low hills that guarded the east side of the property.

At first glance the sand-blown wasteland appeared flat, almost level, and the large boulders that littered the terrain easily avoidable. But Hayes had spent enough time exploring the area to know about the unseen hazards: the tire-swallowing sinkholes, the axle-breaking fissures cut into the ground by centuries of erosion and the hood-crumpling boulders.

He tried to pick the path of least resistance, but no matter which line he picked or how many times he swerved to avoid one rock it was only to slam into another. The Ford was built like a tank, engineered to take a beating and keep on running, but he could tell by the play in the steering and the unnatural lean of the vehicle from the broken springs that there was only so much abuse it could take.

Skidding around a sinkhole, he inadvertently slammed into a shelf of rocks that sent the front end bouncing into the air. Hayes fought to keep the truck under control, but whatever had snapped caused the truck to pull hard to the right, toward the arroyo that ran down into the low ground.

He was fighting to keep the truck straight when the helo came flashing across the front of the truck, the sight sending a spark of rage coursing through him.

Jump, the voice commanded.

With his body finally on the mend, Hayes had no interest in jumping out of a moving vehicle.

Break a bone or lose your family? the voice asked.

Realizing that jumping out of the vehicle was the only way he was going to beat the helo, Hayes stopped fighting the truck and let it pull back toward the arroyo. With the accelerator pinned in place and the steering already tracking to his destination, Hayes unbuckled his seat belt and, using the glass slider, crawled into the bed.

Holding on to the roof, he stood up, eyes locked on the sandy ridge at the lip of the arroyo. Calculating the distance, he knew he needed to time it just right or break his neck.

This is going to hurt, he thought.

Then he threw himself from the truck.

LANGLEY, VIRGINIA

It was one p.m. at Langley and Mike Carpenter stood in the anteroom of the CIA director, the Tom Ford suit he'd bought for the occasion fitting like he'd been poured into it. As the deputy director of operations, Carpenter was the second most powerful man in the Agency, and this was the day he'd been waiting for. It had been rumored for weeks that the director was ready to step aside, and that could only mean that he would be asked to step up.

The culmination of all the hard work he'd put in during his twenty-plus years in the CIA, Carpenter was nervous despite his outward calm, and it took every ounce of willpower not to keep checking his watch.

Feeling the director's administrative assistant watching

him from his desk, Carpenter moved to one of the leather chairs on the far side of the room and took a seat.

Just breathe, he told himself.

Finally, the phone on the man's desk beeped and he lifted the handset. "Yes, ma'am," he said, and then returned the phone to the cradle. "The director is ready for you."

Carpenter got to his feet and checked his reflection in the glass of the framed American flag hanging on the wall. Smoothing a hand over his slicked-back hair, he moved to the door and opened it.

Here we go, he thought.

Unlike the ultra-modern all-glass-and-chromium offices favored by Hollywood producers, stepping into the director of the CIA's office was like going back in time. The wood-paneled walls, matching oak desk, and battered filing cabinet took him back to the early eighties.

This wasn't Carpenter's first time in the director's office. However, if his suspicions about the meeting were correct, then it would be the last time he came as a visitor.

"Good afternoon, Michael," Director Bratton said, coming around the desk.

"Lisa," he replied. "How are the kids?"

"They're good. Thank you for asking," she said. "And your wife?"

"Eden is doing well," he lied.

"Excellent. Shall we take a seat?" she asked, motioning to the pair of chairs by the window.

"After you," Carpenter nodded and unbuttoned his jacket, studying his boss as she took her seat.

With her tidy shoulder-length hair, stone gray pantsuit,

and owlish eyes, Director Lisa Bratton looked more like an overworked professor than America's chief spy, but Carpenter knew better. There was steel beneath those brown eyes, a toughness that he'd seen firsthand during their training at the Farm.

Back then there was no such thing as political correctness, and the tough-talking Cold Warriors who'd been their instructors made no attempt to hide their opinions that women had no place in the CIA.

"I'll be damned if I let a *skirt* make it through," they'd promised.

For Carpenter, those early days had been the hardest of his life—the daily runs and nightly exercises through the mosquito-infested swamps damn near broke him. But at least they *wanted* him there. The same could not be said for Bratton. While many in her shoes would have tucked tail and run in the face of the constant harassment and off-color jokes, the fact that Bratton not only survived but excelled in a culture of toxic masculinity was a testament to both her grit and determination.

"What are you smiling at?" she asked.

"Just thinking back to those days at the Farm," he said. "Trying to remember the name of that instructor who used to torme—"

"Jeremy Astin," she said with a tight smile. "But we aren't here to talk about the past, we are here to talk about your future. So, if you could take a seat."

He did as he was told, the ice in her eyes putting him instantly on guard.

"Legal has just sent down their Treadstone findings," she said, nodding to the stack of papers sitting on the small table to her right.

The realization that they were not here to talk about his promotion hit Carpenter like a Mack truck and sent a range of emotions rapid-firing through his mind. There was anger, outrage, and dismay—but in the end it was fear that stood out.

Shit. What does she know? he thought, eyes drifting to the stack of documents. *Focus, dammit.*

Carpenter felt her eyes on him, knew that she was watching, searching his expression for any admission of guilt. But Bratton wasn't the only one with steel in her soul.

As the director of operations, Carpenter had been responsible for planning and executing some of the most secretive operations in intelligence history. These so-called special projects were black bag ops: assassinations, extraordinary renditions . . . hell, he'd even overthrown governments. If there was one skill he'd perfected, it was how to cover his ass.

"Interesting," he said, "but I'm not sure what this has to do with me."

"Michael, how long have we known each other?" she asked, getting to her feet.

"Long enough to know if there was anything in there about me or any of my people, we'd be having this conversation in a cell," Carpenter replied.

"It's because of our history that I am giving you this chance to come clean. If you tell me what you know about Director Shaw and Adam Hayes, I've been authorized to give you full immunity."

There was a long silence where no one said or did any-thing, both faces seemingly frozen. Then, finally, Carpenter spoke.

"I can't tell you what I don't know, Lisa."

"Very well," she said, somewhat sadly. "But until we get this sorted out, I'm transferring you out of Operations."

"You're demoting me?" Carpenter asked, jaw muscles flaring with anger.

Bratton didn't blink. "Moving you to a less conspicuous posting," she corrected.

Carpenter leaned forward, his face clouding. "After everything I've done for this country!"

"You might wrap yourself in a flag, but you're no patriot," Bratton said, her voice cold as ice. "I still believe you had something do with the plot to kill Levi Shaw."

"Prove it," Carpenter said, getting to his feet.

"I intend to," she said. "But until then, you can get the details of your new assignment from my assistant."

"This is bullshit!" Carpenter spat, heading for the door. She didn't let him reach it.

"Oh," she said, freezing him in his tracks. "And one more thing."

"What's that?" he asked without turning around.

"I've instructed security to revoke your access to the building when you badge out tonight," she explained. "So, do make sure you take any personal items home with you."

"Is that it?"

"Yes," she said placidly before returning her attention to the files. "Now get the hell out of my sight."

Carpenter stomped out of her office, pausing only to

snatch the envelope from her assistant, and then he was out the door. Marching fast down the hall, he ignored his open-mouthed assistant and went into his office, slamming the door behind him.

Rushing to his desk, he yanked open the bottom drawer and tore out the bottle of Blanton's. In one practiced motion he ripped the cork free and put the bottle to his lips. He took a long pull, the heat of the whiskey at the back of his throat no match for the rage building in his guts.

Finally, he came up for air and dropped into his chair, wondering what in the hell else could go wrong when his cell phone started buzzing across the desk.

"Pasquette, this is *not* a good time," he began, about to tell the man that he needed to call him back, when the Haitian cut him off.

"There was a break-in at the bank," the man snapped. "Barbot is dead, and we are fucked."

"Slow down," Carpenter said, his meeting with the director instantly forgotten. "Catch your breath and tell me *exactly* what happened."

"It happened last night," Pasquette began.

"Last night? Are you fucking kidding me?" Carpenter snarled, his fingers curling around the phone hard enough to crack the plastic.

"I just found out three hours ago," Pasquette stammered. "Y-you were the first person I called."

Carpenter reached for the alcohol, wanting another hit to steady his nerves, but, knowing that he needed a clear mind, left it sitting on the desk. "What's done is done," he growled. "Now tell me what you're doing to fix it."

"We've identified the thief," Pasquette said. "A bank employee named Hugo Toussaint. But despite our best efforts, it seems the man has disappeared."

"How hard can it be to find a banker?" Carpenter asked.

There was a long pause on the other end of the line.

"What *aren't* you telling me?" he demanded.

"We can't find Toussaint, and I'm sure your government is the one that's helping him," Pasquette said.

"Say that again," Carpenter demanded, his knees suddenly weak.

GRANT COUNTY, NEW MEXICO

ayes's senses came online like a computer after a hard reset. The pain that accompanied each breath and the copper taste of blood in his mouth welcomed him back to the land of the living. His eyelids fluttered open, and he blinked the world back into focus, wanting nothing more than to just lie there and catch his breath.

But the buzz-saw roar of the helo from near the ranch house told him that wasn't an option.

Hayes grunted to his feet, the tangle of chaparral that had broken his fall tearing into his flesh like wooden talons. He spit the mouthful of blood into the dust and ripped himself free, the pain breathing new life into the ashes of his rage as he turned toward the ranch.

He lurched into a limping run, his eyes hot as coals beneath the mask of dust that covered his face. After the morning run his legs were all but useless—each step agonizingly painful. But his time at Treadstone had taught him more than just how to kill.

It had taught him how to suffer.

A year ago, he would have been quick to smother the rising fury, tamp it down before it could consume him. But now he let the rage build, the searing heat flowing through his blood driving him forward like a machine.

Someone is going to wish they'd never been born.

By the time he reached the low ground, his shirt was soaked with sweat and he was thoroughly pissed off. His first thought was to attack, hit the helicopter before it had a chance to land, but having lost his pistol in the fall, the only weapons at his disposal were the handful of rocks scattered near his feet.

Yeah, that's not going to cut it, the voice said.

Knowing there was nothing to be gained by running out into the open, Hayes took a knee, forcing himself to stay still and let the situation develop. Focusing on his breathing, he worked to clear his mind, and come up with a plan that would give him the advantage.

The most obvious course of action was to try for the shop he'd built in the back of the barn. There were weapons there as well as the remote security panel that would allow him to lock down the house and activate the host of anti-intrusion devices he'd emplaced around the property.

But with his legs feeling like they were full of lead, Hayes knew he'd never make it. The closer and more accessible option was the weather-beaten toolshed twenty yards to his left.

Only problem was, thanks to his overzealous bush-hogging, there wasn't so much as a shrub or blade of grass to conceal him from the helicopter.

So how do I get there?

The answer came from the helicopter and the scattering of dirt and dust already being kicked up by its rotors. Allowing the pilot to land so Hayes could use the brownout to mask his movement was a smart play. Hell, it was his *only* play, but once again the idea that he was actually going to let the helo land was a hard pill to swallow.

Take your sweet fucking time, he thought.

Finally, the pilot found a suitable spot and began his descent, Hayes waiting until the Lakota was enveloped in the pall of dust before grunting to his feet. Staying low, he half-limped, half-jogged the twenty yards to the toolshed, pushed the door open, and stepped inside.

Leaving the door cracked behind him, he went to the back of the shed and studied the tools hanging from the pegboard. After first crashing his truck, then being forced on another run, Hayes was in a medieval mood—eager to do bodily harm to whoever came out of the helicopter. But as much as he wanted to inflict the maximum amount of damage on the intruders, he bypassed the freshly sharpened wood axe, as well as the eight-pound sledgehammer, and settled on a seven-inch sickle.

He lifted the mini-scythe off the peg and slipped back to the doorway, a quick look outside revealing two figures already emerging from the cloud of dust. There was something familiar about the man in the lead, but Hayes couldn't make out his face.

Not that he tried.

The men were threats and nothing more. Whoever they were ceased to matter when they showed up at the ranch.

That there were two of them didn't bother Hayes. He'd been trained to work as a single operator, and being outnumbered and outgunned was part and parcel of the job. However, the reason he was still alive, while so many of his Treadstone classmates were feeding worms in some third world shithole, was because he'd made it a point to avoid anything that resembled a fair fight.

As an assassin, his job was to attack from the shadows, find a weak point in his target's defense, then hit them at the time and place of *his* choosing. Unfortunately, with the men closing in fast on the front of the house, waiting wasn't an option.

The second man was big and built like a fireplug, but more than his size, it was the way he carried himself that made him a priority. Hayes's plan was to come in hard and fast, take the big man down and then deal with the other one.

The only problem was that his target saw him coming.

The man was fast—Hayes had to give him that. Before Hayes could close the gap, his target was shoving the other man to the ground and his right hand was flashing to the SIG holstered at his waist, tugging the pistol free.

Before he could bring it up on target, Hayes was on him, the sickle hissing through the air. He was aiming for the wrist, but the man parried the blow with the pistol, the impact snapping the blade from the handle.

With his weapon all but useless, Hayes threw the broken handle at the man's face and then stepped in with a tight left hook to his gut. The man grunted, but instead of folding over as Hayes had hoped, the man brushed it off and tried to backhand him with the pistol.

Off-balance, all Hayes could do was duck his head and throw up an arm. He blocked the blow, but the crash of the SIG against bone left his arm instantly numb. His opponent was quick to take advantage and stepped in, swinging the pistol like a club.

But Hayes was ready and, using his good arm, grabbed the man by the wrist. He twisted hard, pulling the man off-balance, then kicked his legs out from under him. The man dropped like a stone, and before the dust settled Hayes twisted the SIG from his hand, planted a boot in his chest, and shoved the barrel in his face.

"You even think about getting up and I will empty your skull," he snarled, pressing the barrel into the man's forehead.

"Enough," a familiar voice shouted.

Hayes froze. Then, with a shake of his head, he took his finger off the trigger and stepped back. "I should have known."

"You're a hard man to find," Levi Shaw said as he finished pulling himself up from the dusty earth.

"Not hard enough."

Hayes had known the day would come. It was only a matter of time before the Treadstone director reached out and told him it was time to go back to work. But the fact that Shaw had shown up in person and unannounced told him everything he needed to know.

Somewhere, something had gone horribly wrong.

GRANT COUNTY, NEW MEXICO

"What are you doing here, Levi?" Hayes asked.

"I could ask you the same thing," Shaw said, a bemused look on his face. "Last time we talked, you were living the family life in Tennessee. Next thing you're gone. No phone call. No, 'Hey, Levi, I'm going to play cowboy in New Mexico'—just gone. Had me worried, son."

"So you decide to fly down here and bring a fucking spook to my house?" he asked, his voice icy.

"If it makes you feel any better, I told him to wait in the helo," Shaw shrugged.

"My family is here," Hayes stressed, his voice getting tighter.

"Look, I . . ." the director started, taking a step forward, when the distinctive *cha-chunk* of a shotgun being racked came echoing across the yard. All three men turned to the porch where Annabelle stood, the SPAS-12 Hayes kept in the hall closet rock steady in her hands.

"Everything okay out here, babe?" she asked.

"All good," he lied.

"Good afternoon, Mrs. Hayes," Shaw said with an appreciative smile.

"Something wrong with your phone, Levi?" she asked, her eyes hot as cannon fuses.

"No ma'am . . . I . . . uh . . ."

"Hmph," she grunted, lowering the shotgun a fraction of an inch. "Well, since you're here, you might as well eat."

"I appreciate the offer, ma'am," Shaw said, "but, unfortunately, this isn't a social call."

With a nod from Hayes, she expertly racked the shell from the shotgun and stepped back inside, leaving the men alone in the yard.

"Cooler in the barn," he said, stepping out of the sun.

"She know how to use that thing?" the other man asked.

Hayes looked at the house with a hint of a smile. "She's a good student."

The other man began falling in behind Hayes and Shaw. "She wouldn't have . . ."

"Shot you?" Hayes asked.

"Yeah."

"For you I'd say it's fifty-fifty," Hayes said. "Now, Levi on the other hand—she's been itching to shoot him for years."

As the trio walked, Levi motioned at the spook.

"Adam Hayes, Gunner Poe." He motioned in the other direction. "Gunner Poe, Adam Hayes."

Neither man said "nice to meet you" or anything similar. Instead, Poe was silent for a moment, taking in the information, then changed the subject. "Nice spot you picked out," he finally said.

"Yeah, we like it," Hayes replied as his eyes drifted east to the pair of mule deer grazing on the sagebrush.

"Ten more months and I'll have my twenty," Poe said. "Hope to get a place like this when I get out."

"Ten months, huh?" Hayes grinned, reaching for the door. "I must have hit you harder than I thought."

Rather than smile, Poe decided to take offense. "What the hell does that mean?" he demanded.

Hayes remained unfazed. "It means that once Levi gets his claws into you," he explained, "there's no such thing as getting out. Remember that, kid."

Before Poe could take offense at the "kid" moniker, Shaw interrupted. "Enough talking," he sighed, turning to Hayes. "Are you ready to get back to work?"

Hayes was smart enough not to get coy. "What's the job?" he asked as he stepped inside the barn and turned on the light.

"A DIA human intelligence officer named Dallys Carver was approached by a high-level source from the Banque de Port-au-Prince," Shaw immediately replied, taking a briefing folder from his attaché case and handing it over. "In exchange for immunity in the States, the source agreed to provide us with a flash drive that has proof that certain parties, with the backing of the ANI, were using the bank to skirt international sanctions."

"Interesting," Hayes said cautiously, taking the folder and spreading the contents on the table.

During his time at Treadstone, Hayes had flipped through more mission folders than he cared to remember and, despite his time away, this one was laid out exactly like the others. At the front was the intelligence brief and the operations plan—two critical pieces of information meant to inform the reader about the situation on the ground and the reason for the mission.

"Looks good on paper, but I'm pretty sure you aren't here to tell me that everything went according to plan."

"No. The asset was compromised inside the building by a member of the Haitian Intelligence Service and instead of breaking contact and getting out of the area, Carver went off script."

"Off script?"

"She smoked a colonel in ANI—head shot from a hundred feet away."

"Jesus," Hayes grimaced. "Bet that pissed someone off."

"You have no idea," Shaw said.

"Oh, I bet I do," Hayes disagreed. He studied the report a moment more. "This Carver seems a tad green to be running ops by herself, don't ya think?" he said to Shaw.

The director all but ignored the comment. "The DoD wants that intel, which means someone has to go down there and get her out."

Hayes's eyebrows raised. "So we're doing that now, too? Why me? You need somebody to lead the pickup team?"

"No," Shaw said. "Your part of the pie is purely logistical. Fly in, set up in the safe house, and wait for Carver to make contact."

"Then what?"

"You babysit the assets until the extraction team arrives," Shaw said.

"Sounds easy. How long do you need me on the ground?" Hayes asked.

"Forty-eight hours. Have you back home in time for Jack's birthday."

That comment caused Hayes to look directly at the director. "Oh, you know about that, do you? You didn't stop by the town store and pick up the fireworks, by any chance?"

Shaw was unfazed. "Figured we were already bringing enough fireworks," he replied. "So, what do you think? About the mission, I mean."

Hayes didn't mince words. "Kinda thin."

"You've done it before," Shaw countered.

"I've done a lot of stupid stuff before," Hayes said. "Doesn't mean I want to do it again."

Shaw sighed. "Let's cut the crap, Adam. You know as well as I do that this is a time-sensitive operation, and we're already behind the curve," Shaw said. "So, unless there is something you're not telling me, I need you in Haiti."

Hayes almost laughed. "Me, not telling *you*? What are *you* not telling *me*?"

Shaw's placid expression would have done a high-stakes poker player proud. "Well, son," he nearly drawled, "you took a hell of a beating in Angola and, let's face it, you're not exactly a spring chicken."

Brilliant, said Hayes's inner voice. *But do* not *fall for this reverse psychology!*

It was too late. "Don't worry about me, old man," Hayes said, rallying to his defense. "When the chips are down, I can still run and gun with the best of them."

"No need to get testy," Shaw said, raising his hands in mock surrender. "I had to ask."

Oh, your damn macho ego, the voice said. *You know there is more to this than what he's saying. Tell him to fuck off. Better yet, kill them both and bury them in the desert.*

"What are you smiling at?" Shaw asked.

"Nothing," Hayes answered. "Look, if I do this, we're square, right? We're done."

"Yeah, sure," Shaw said. "You pull this off and we are good."

But Hayes wasn't buying it. "I want your word."

"You don't trust me?" Shaw asked.

"Oh, my God, you're playing the 'trust' card?" Hayes laughed. "Levi, what have you ever done to earn my trust?"

Shaw barked a laugh right back at him. "Oh, I don't know," he replied with more sarcasm than Hayes had ever heard from the stone-cold spymaster. "I suppose you got out of Africa all by yourself, didn't you?"

It suddenly got very cold and very quiet in the barn. Hayes didn't have to answer and both men knew why. If it hadn't been for Shaw saving Hayes's ass, this conversation never could have happened.

Even so, Shaw seemed to pretend that cross, sarcastic words had not been spoken. "You bring that drive back," he concluded, "and we're good."

Great, the voice warned. *His word and a dime will get you ten cents.*

Hayes knew the voice was right, but he also knew that Shaw even being here, and bringing a helo and a spook to boot, meant that his home's security was truly compromised. It was all well and good that the director enacted this charade of asking for Hayes's assistance, but they both knew it wasn't a request. As he had told Poe earlier, there was no such thing as getting out of Treadstone. And that went double for Adam Hayes.

"Fine," he said. "I'll do it."

"Good. Let's go," Shaw said, extending a hand.

Hayes ignored the gesture and nodded toward the house. "I have to grab a few things."

"Okay, but believe me, it might not feel like it right now," Shaw said, dropping his hand, "but this is the best decision for you and your family."

Hayes stared at Shaw, seemingly trying to decide whether to laugh or spit. "Yeah," he finally said drily. "Right."

By the time Hayes stepped inside the house, he was in full-on mission mode, his mind so focused on the task at hand that he barely noticed Annabelle watching him from the couch with an expression that mixed sympathy and concern. She waited for a few seconds to see if Hayes would notice, then slowly stood and spoke to their son.

"Jack, please go to your room," she said.

"But Mom, I want to talk about the man in the heli—"

"We'll talk about that later, dear," she said, seemingly

softly, but Jack knew that tone well. Without another word, the boy headed to his room.

Annabelle and Adam waited until the door to Jack's room closed quietly, then the woman stood on no ceremony.

"Well?" she asked, letting him decide how to break the news to her.

"I've got to go away for a few days," Hayes said simply.

Annabelle's face nearly crumbled with care and dread, but she managed to collect herself. He knew she was ready to talk again when she unclenched her fists. But what she then said reminded him how well she knew him, as well as the import of Shaw's personal appearance out of the sky and onto their land.

"Was there any way to say no?"

He exhaled, then shook his head.

"Can you tell me where you're going, then?" she asked. "Can you tell me how long you'll be gone?"

"Baby, you know I can't . . ."

His attempt at being considerate had the opposite effect. "No," she interrupted. "Don't say that. You know you can. You know you can because wherever you're going, whatever you're doing, it will have an effect on this family. No matter how hard you try not to affect us, it will. It does. After all you've already put us through, you're letting half-truths, even outright lies, take you away from us again—just days from your son's birthday—the first birthday you would've had with him . . ."

Before Hayes could respond, movement at the top of the stairs caught his attention and he looked up to see Jack staring down at them. "This might not be the best time to talk about this," he said evenly.

Annabelle followed his gaze to the landing, then looked back at him, her face a mask of tragedy and foreboding. "Or it might be the absolute best time to talk about this," she said sadly. "Don't you think your son wants to know why his father might not be here for his birthday?"

"Daddy, is that true?"

Hayes was no stranger to pain, and during his career he'd been shot, stabbed, blown up, and beat down more times than he could remember. But all those injuries combined couldn't hold a candle to the agony that came with his son's question.

"No way, buddy," he said, moving to the stairs. "I swear that I'll be there."

"Adam," Annabelle warned, "don't make *another* promise that you can't keep."

"You have my word," he said, eyes shifting from his son back to his wife. "There is nothing on this earth that will keep me from being here for Jack's birthday."

"Please," she said, stepping in close, her voice thick with emotion, "because as much as I love you, and want to believe you, you know we have no choice but to prepare ourselves in case you're not here . . ."

PORT-AU-PRINCE, HAITI

It was nearing three p.m. in Port-au-Prince, fifteen hours after the hit on the bank, when the white panel van pulled off the Avenue Maïse Gaté into the Chatelain Cargo Services lot. "All the way to the back," Dallys Carver said, pointing to the rusted gate that separated the weed-infested freight yard from the flight line.

They should have been off the street hours ago, but with Carnival picking up steam and the roadways flooded with a sea of flesh, progress was measured in feet, not miles.

As per the plan, they had released the rest of the team. Now only Long and she were left to watch Toussaint.

What a shitshow, she thought, as Long negotiated the

trailers and rusted loaders haphazardly parked around the diesel-stained asphalt.

"This is good," she said, grabbing the bolt cutters off the floorboards.

When Long brought the van to a halt, she hopped out and hustled to the rusted gate, the Haitian sun beating down on her like a bully with a magnifying glass. With the rush of adrenaline that came from pulling the trigger long gone, Carver was running on fumes. Her head was pounding from the onset of dehydration, her nerves shot from the stress of the mission.

But she'd been here before. Despite her discomfort, she still had a job to do.

Get your head in the game, she told herself.

Shifting the bolt cutters to her left hand, Carver raised the pair of Vortex binoculars hanging around her neck to her eyes and scanned the row of cargo aircraft arrayed around the line of weary hangars, their paint long ago sandblasted clean by the salt-laden air.

She took her time, searching for any sign that their primary escape route had been compromised, waiting until she was sure that it was clear before cutting the chain.

By the time she climbed back into the van, she was soaked with sweat, her shirt clinging to her back and her mouth bone dry. "Third hangar on the left."

"Whatever you say," Long said, guiding the van across the tarmac.

Carver ignored him, dug the half-empty tube of Dexedrine from her shirt pocket, and shook one of the triangular pills into her hand.

"Might want to go easy on those . . . killer," he suggested.

"You got something you want to say to me?" she asked, dry-swallowing the pill.

"Yeah, you fucked up back there," he said. "Put the mission in danger with your cowboy shit."

"But I got it done," she said, nodding to the back of the van where Toussaint sat, "and if *you* can keep your shit together for another five minutes, we *might* just get the hell out of here alive."

"You sure about that?" Long asked, looping around the backside of the hangar. "Because from here, it doesn't look like anyone is home."

You've got to be shitting me.

"It's fine," she said, for her benefit as well as theirs, "just stop here and I'll take a look."

"By yourself?"

"I'll be right *there*," she said pointing to the seam between the pair of roller doors. "Keep your radio on and I'll be back before you know it."

"Wait . . ." Long said.

Carver ignored him and slipped out of the van, easing the door shut behind her before trotting across the tarmac. From the van she estimated it was twenty yards to the doors, a short jog, but halfway there Carver realized it was more like fifty.

It wasn't until she was standing beside the doors that she understood the cause of her error, realizing that the doors weren't just big, they were massive and what had looked like a tiny seam was wide enough for her to fit through.

She worked to catch her breath and peered into the

hangar. The relief that came with seeing the Antonov An-24 she'd chartered to get them off the island sitting in the center of the stained concrete pad settled on her like a warm blanket.

"Plane's still here," she said over the radio.

"What about the pilots?" Long asked.

"Hold on," she said, inching into the hangar.

"No, no, no," he warned. "Going in there is a terrible idea."

It was the right call, and with fifty yards separating her from the van, Carver knew this was neither the time nor the place to break line of sight with the team. But before she could turn around, two figures stepped out of the shadows.

Shit, she thought.

Carver took an involuntary step back and was thinking of making a run for it when the men stepped into the light. One of them yelled at her to stop and moved to unsling the ancient M16 from his shoulder. It wasn't the sight of the rifle but the man's uniform that froze her in place, however.

The PNH? How?

Going into the operation, she'd known that Pasquette wasn't just going to sit on his ass and let her smuggle Toussaint out of the country. So, before seeking the green light from Washington, her team had spent weeks surveilling the ANI. Trailing their agents around the city, studying their routes, capturing their radio frequencies, and hacking their computers—searching for a weakness she could exploit.

By the end of the allotted time, they had compiled a list of shortcomings: outdated equipment, poor training, and the general complacency that came with being the bully of the block. But in the end, it was the open hostility between the ANI and the National Police that sat at the top of the list.

Carver had been so confident that this mutual hatred would prevent them from mounting any kind of coordinated effort that she'd submitted the operations order for approval. It was only now, standing in the hangar with the pair of PNH officers closing the distance, that Carver realized she'd misread the situation.

Any other time, the sight of the two armed men would have been more than enough to gain her compliance. But as the man swung his rifle to bear, it wasn't the fear of being shot but the realization of what Pasquette would do to her if she lived that sent her heart hammering in her chest.

"I said stop!" the man repeated, his voice booming loud as a shotgun inside the hangar.

"That's *not* going to happen," Carver said, reaching for her pistol.

Before the man had a chance to bring the M16 into action, the SIG was out, Carver squeezing the slack out of the trigger as she brought it up into a two-handed grip. She settled her front sight on the center of the man's forehead and pulled the trigger.

Her aim was true and the 115-gram hollow point punched through the man's skull and into his cranial vault at eleven hundred feet per second. He dropped like a marionette with cut strings. Before his body hit the ground, Carver was transitioning to his comrade.

She dropped him with a neat double tap to the chest and

then, not sure if the PNH issued body armor to their officers, stepped forward and put a single round through his right eye. Holstering the pistol, Carver reached down and ripped the man's radio from his belt. Then she was running out of the hangar, screaming at Long to bring the van.

CARIBBEAN SEA

It was the flaps that woke him up, the whine of the hydraulic actuators followed by the sinking feeling in the pit of Hayes's gut as the Gulfstream G650 began its descent. He opened his eyes, instantly awake, the back of his throat scratchy from the recycled air circulating through the cabin.

He lifted the bottle of water the steward had given him from the cupholder and unscrewed the cap. Taking a long pull, his mind circled back to his last exchange with Annabelle.

That she was upset about him leaving was to be expected, especially considering Hayes still hadn't fully recovered from the wounds he'd sustained in Angola. However, it wasn't the fear in her eyes, but the sad certainty of her parting words that had caught him off guard.

If you break that boy's heart, we won't be here when you get back.

Annabelle hadn't said that, but that was what Hayes heard.

Well, then, you might want to get your head in the game, the voice suggested.

With that thought at the forefront of his mind, Hayes turned his attention to the task at hand.

Shaw had designated Poe as Hayes's handler for this mission, and according to Poe, the situation in Port-au-Prince was "fluid," which Hayes knew was a polite way of saying the bosses back in DC had no idea what in the hell was going on.

"So, what's the plan?" he had asked on his way to the airfield.

"You'll fly to Naval Air Station Key West, meet up with the extraction team, and try to get on the same page."

"How long do I have on the ground?"

"Carver is scheduled to check in at seven p.m."

"*Three* whole hours," he'd scoffed.

"Better than going in blind."

The man had a point.

With its pair of Rolls-Royce BR725s running full-out, the flight time from New Mexico to Naval Air Station Key West was scheduled for a little over two hours. But looking at his watch now, Hayes saw that it was almost four thirty p.m. and they still weren't on the ground.

What the hell? he thought.

Leaning forward, he took another drink of water and accessed the touch screen on the forward bulkhead, swiping through the menu until he came to the navigation screen.

There was a pixelated blink and then a map popped up. Hayes almost spit the mouthful of water across the cabin when he saw the digital icon of the Gulfstream cruising southwest across Haiti.

"I'm going to kill him," Hayes said, digging the Iridium phone from his pack and dialing Poe's number.

Pick up the phone, you son of a bitch.

The line connected with a rush of static followed by the double click of the encryption package coming online, and finally Poe's voice in his ear. "I was wondering when you were going to call."

"Mind filling me in on what the hell is going on?"

"There's been a change in plans," Poe said. "This situation in Haiti is *rapidly* deteriorating."

"What's the problem?"

"ANI is responding faster than anticipated," Poe replied, his voice sounding tired through the line. "Word from my guy at the State Department is that they've got Port-au-Prince on lockdown and were in the process of closing the airport when someone blasted a pair of PNH officers. I'm taking bets that it was Carver."

"Then why the hell am I looking at a map that tells me I'm about fifteen miles from that damn airport?"

"Because," Poe said, "I need you on the ground *now*."

"If they closed the airport, how do you expect me to land?"

"About ten minutes ago your pilots advised the tower they had an engine failure and requested permission for an emergency landing."

"This is because I punched you—isn't it?" Hayes asked.

"Don't flatter yourself, tough guy," Poe said. "I've had harder knocks rolling out of bed."

"I'll remember that next time I see you," Hayes said.

"Listen, smartass," Poe said. "There are two ways the situation is going to play out. Option A has a bunch of angry Haitian cops coming out to the flight line and finding a Gulfstream registered to a company that doesn't exist, a crew carrying diplomatic visas, and one unarmed redneck with a bad attitude."

"And option B?" Hayes asked.

"You take your bite of this shit sandwich, think on the fly, do what you signed on to do, and get home to your family. It's your choice."

"What about my gear?" Hayes asked.

"You mean all those shiny toys you requested?"

"Yeah," Hayes said.

"There's a truck waiting for you in the parking lot," Poe replied. "Everything you asked for is in the back."

"And how exactly do you propose that I make it to the truck without getting shot or arrested?" he asked.

"You're Adam Hayes," Poe said. "I'm sure you'll figure something out."

And then the line went dead.

"Asshole," Hayes said.

Asshole with your life in his hands, said the voice.

Good point, Hayes thought. This whole op was rapidly starting to stink as a suicide mission set-up. Well, then, it might be a good idea to stop sitting back, waiting for info they're withholding, and start taking control.

Shoving the phone into his pocket, Hayes shouldered his

assault pack and started to the flight deck. The steward saw him coming and got to his feet. "Sir, we are on final approach. You need to stay seated." But Hayes ignored him and pushed his way into the cockpit.

"You guys couldn't have given me a heads-up?"

"Sorry, sir, it wasn't my call," the copilot said, nodding to his superior in the left seat.

"Is that true?" Hayes asked the pilot.

"Just following orders," the man said.

"Back in the army we had a name for guys like you," Hayes said.

"And what was that?" the pilot asked.

"Blue Falcon," Hayes said.

"Blue Falcon?"

"Stands for buddy fucker," the copilot said, a smile forming at the corner of his lips. "But to be fair, it's not *totally* his fault."

"Oh, yeah?" Hayes asked. "And why is that?"

"He was in the Marines," the man said. "They don't know any better."

"What about you?" Hayes asked.

"I was in the Air Force," the copilot grinned, "and I never was very good at following orders."

"Well, unless something has changed while we've been in the air, *I'm* still in command of this aircraft," the pilot snapped.

"Consider yourself relieved," Hayes said.

"On whose authority?" the pilot demanded.

"Mine," Hayes answered, his voice cold as steel. "You got a problem with that?"

The pilot took one look at his eyes and swallowed hard, the defiance rushing out of his posture like air from a busted tire. "N-no . . . sir," he said.

"Good choice," he said, turning his attention to the windscreen.

At first glance, Port-au-Prince International looked abandoned, its single ten-thousand-foot runway and the apron in front of the squat concrete terminal void of life. But Hayes wasn't fooled and, considering what Poe had told him about the two dead PNH officers, he knew that somewhere down there were men with guns.

But where?

He found what he was looking for a thousand yards to the east of the terminal: four white pickups and a scrum of men in body armor milling around one of the hangars that lined the cargo ramp.

"Anything in particular you're looking for?" the copilot asked.

"Yeah, something soft," he answered, "and far away from the cargo ramp."

"Not much of that around here," the man replied.

"What about that strip of grass on the west side of the taxiway?" the pilot muttered.

"You mean the one *right* in front of the tower?" Hayes asked.

"You got a better idea?"

He didn't, and, with the Gulfstream less than a mile from the runway, Hayes knew he didn't have the time to figure it out.

"Just get me close," he said.

Leaving the pilots to handle the landing, Hayes stepped out of the flight deck and turned his attention to the next problem on his list. Mainly, how the hell was he going to get off the aircraft without attracting the attention of the PNH officers around the hangar. Luckily, the Gulfstream came with six separate emergency exits: the main cabin door, two removable windows over each wing, and a smaller door in the aft cargo hold.

With the aircraft in motion, Hayes wasn't crazy about trying his hand at wing-walking and would have preferred to use one of the doors. Only problem was both the main cabin door and the cargo hatch were located on the left side of the aircraft—the same side as the hangar full of the PNH officers he was trying to avoid.

Might as well get this over with, he thought, cinching the pack straps tight against his shoulder.

Hayes headed back to the port side emergency window and pulled down on the red locking tab. The top of the frame popped free of the bulkhead and he pried the window free, the noxious rush of burnt AV gas that came rushing through the hole slapping him hard in the face.

Blinking away the tears, Hayes set the window on the floor and was about to climb out onto the wing when the steward began waving his arms in the air and pointing at the opposite window.

He turned and followed the man's outstretched finger to the window, in time to see the first PNH pickup come racing out from behind the hangar, red and blue lights strobing off the tarmac.

PORT-AU-PRINCE, HAITI

The Gulfstream wasn't even halfway down the runway when the PNH pickup came racing across the tarmac, its lights strobing, rapid fire, off the terminal. As a pilot himself, Hayes knew it was common practice for an airport to send rescue crews to assist any aircraft landing under emergency conditions. He also knew that typically they dispatched fire trucks and ambulances, *not* pickups loaded down with heavily armed men.

Don't think they're here to help, the voice opined.

"Yeah, you think?" Hayes said, tracking the truck across the tarmac.

Initially it appeared the driver intended to meet the Gulfstream at the end of the runway and escort the aircraft back to the terminal. But halfway there, the driver changed his mind and cranked the wheel hard to the left, centering the hood on the strip of grass Hayes had picked out from the air.

Realizing that the driver meant to cut them off before they made it to the taxiway, Hayes was searching for another option of extricating himself from the plane when the pilot shoved the throttles forward. The sudden surge of power bowled him off his feet.

"What the hell are you doing?" he shouted over the freight train roar of the engines.

"Getting out of here!" the pilot screamed back.

With the truck full of armed goons barreling down on them, *not* sticking around was the right call. One any rationally minded person would have made in that situation. The only problem was that Hayes had a mission, and thanks to his debt to Shaw he was unable to cut and run when he knew that Carver was counting on him to bring her home.

Determined to hold up his end of the bargain, and not wanting to spend the foreseeable future locked in a Haitian cell, Hayes yanked the fire extinguisher from its mount and started to the emergency window.

"Might want to buckle in," he told the steward before ducking through the opening.

He twisted his upper body until he was facing an engine, left hand holding the frame, right curled tight around the fire extinguisher. Pressing his thigh against the bulkhead, Hayes steadied his body and, ignoring the shake of the aircraft beneath him and roar of the wind past his ears, sent the fire extinguisher spinning toward the engine.

Watching the bottle rising through the air, he was sure

that he'd missed. But just as it appeared to be sailing over the cowling, it vanished, the big turbo fan gulping it in like a bass swallowing a lure.

Before he could get back into the cabin, the engine exploded. With the port side engine still running full bore, the Gulfstream was shoved hard to starboard. Hayes was unable to do anything but hang on tight as the sixty-five-million-dollar aircraft went skittering off the runway and headed toward the culvert that ran the length of the infield.

In the cockpit the pilots cut the remaining engine and fought to keep the stricken bird out of the ditch, but before they could steer clear, the right landing gear slammed into the culvert and snapped free. With the gear gone, the Gulfstream was off-balance and that, combined with the downward grade of the infield, sent it toppling onto its side, the wing cutting a deep furrow in the blood-red clay.

Taking advantage of the situation, Hayes released his grip on the bulkhead and let gravity do the rest. He slid down the wing, tucked his head, and rolled clear. Then he was on his feet running through the knee-high grass on the far side of the culvert, heading south toward the line of baggage carts parked in front of the terminal.

He kept his head down and weaved across the tarmac, back muscles tense in expectation of the scalding burn of a bullet that never came. After the arid climes of New Mexico, the muggy suck of the Haitian afternoon was a shock to the system. By the time Hayes made it to the terminal his shirt was soaked with sweat, his heart jackhammering in his chest. He dropped to a knee behind one of the baggage carts and tried to catch his breath, but the moisture in the air made it feel as if he were inhaling through a straw.

Keep moving, the voice suggested.

After a quick scan of his surroundings, Hayes forced himself to his feet and trotted to the iron fence that separated the terminal from the parking lot. He reached up, grabbed the tines at the top, and hoisted himself over, dropping to the bushes on the other side.

Crouching in the shadows, he fished the Bluetooth earpiece Poe had given him from his pocket and pressed it into his ear, waiting until he'd caught his breath before hitting the redial button on the sat phone.

"What kind of truck?" Hayes asked when the line connected.

"Excuse me?" Poe responded.

"The truck you said was waiting for me in the parking lot," Hayes sighed. "Can you give me a make or model . . . maybe a license plate or something?"

"Wait . . . you're on the ground?" Poe stammered. "You mean you actually made it?"

"Are you fucking with me right now?" Hayes asked.

"No . . . hold on, I've got it right here," Poe said, the sound of rustling paper coming through the line. "It's a dark gray Pathfinder, keys are on the back left tire."

Hayes scanned the vehicles parked around the lot in front of him until he found the Pathfinder in the second row from the back.

"Got it," he said, getting to his feet and strolling casually across the lot.

"Is there anything else you need?" Poe asked, suddenly the picture of helpfulness.

"Actually, there is one more thing," he said.

"What's that?"

"That Gulfstream of yours," Hayes said, bending to retrieve the keys from the tire. "It's insured, right?"

"Yeah . . . why?" Poe asked, a touch of concern creeping into his voice. "Did something happen to it?"

"I'm sure everything's fine," Hayes said, opening the door and tossing his bag on the passenger seat. "There's probably nothing to worry about."

Before Poe could respond, Hayes ended the call and started the engine, immediately cranking the a/c to the max and cracking the rear windows to vent the mix of hot air and the sickly-sweet stench of the air freshener someone had used to mask the fact that the previous occupant had been a smoker.

With that done, he reached beneath the seat, fingers probing in the darkness for the pistol that routinely would have been left there.

As a rule, Hayes didn't go to the bathroom without a pistol, and he was not happy about finding himself alone in a hostile country with nothing but the Spyderco Para Military folding knife in his pocket with which to defend himself.

Where the hell is it?

Finally, his fingers brushed the edge of the nylon bag. He ripped it free and unzipped the flap to find the FN Tactical, four-inch Thompson Machine suppressor, and an Odin outside-the-waistband holster he'd requested before leaving New Mexico.

That's what I'm talking about.

Hayes lifted the pistol, making sure that it was clear, before checking the sight picture through the Trijicon RMR mounted to the slide. Satisfied everything was in working order, he slapped the magazine into the magwell, racked a nine-millimeter hollow point into the chamber, and returned the pistol into its holster.

Properly armed, Hayes typed his destination into the Pathfinder's GPS and pulled out of the parking spot, following the signage past the unmanned security shack and then merging onto the Boulevard Toussaint Louverture.

He was unaware of the CIA MQ-9 Reaper stalking him from twenty thousand feet.

LANGLEY, VIRGINIA

Mike Carpenter stood in the corner of the basement, steam coiling from the cup of coffee in his right hand. He scanned the room, taking in the analysts at their stations, their faces backlit by the blue glow of their monitors. They kept their heads down and, besides the occasional furtive look to the back of the room, stuck to their work. But he knew that they were all thinking the same thing: Why in the hell was the deputy director of operations watching a drone feed down in the basement and not up in the operations center?

Not that Carpenter really gave a shit what they thought. All he cared about was that they did their jobs and found the information he needed.

"How much longer is this going to take?" he asked, shaking out a stale cigarette from the pack of Marlboro Reds he'd found at the back of his desk.

"Sir . . . you can't smoke in here," one of the analysts said, pointing to the sign on the wall.

"You've got to be shitting me."

"Uh . . . no, sir, it's bad for the equipment."

Fuck.

"Fine, I'll be out in the hall. Let me know when the feed is up," Carpenter said, moving to the door.

He stepped out and was about to light up when he noticed the smoke detector mounted to the wall above him. "Give me a fucking break." But knowing the last thing he needed was for the fire department to be dispatched, Carpenter dutifully shuffled to the stairwell.

He stepped inside and, leaving the door cracked so he could hear the analyst when he called, touched his lighter to the tip of the cigarette and took a deep drag.

It had been hours since the showdown with Director Bratton and as much as he wished that he was sitting in some bar, boozing away his sorrows, leaving the building wasn't an option.

Especially after the bombshell Pasquette had dropped on him.

"We can't find Toussaint, and I'm sure your government is the one that's helping him."

The words had hit like a bolt of lightning and for a moment Carpenter had been struck dumb, unable to think or to speak, unable to do *anything* but stumble to his chair before his legs gave out on him.

Then his mind came back and with it the realization that *if* that flash drive contained the information he thought it did, Director Bratton would have everything she needed to bury him. The fear that followed would have crushed a lesser man, sent him back to the bottle, or worse, the barrel of a pistol.

But Carpenter wasn't in the "possibility" business and, until he had proof that corroborated the Haitian's accusations, it was all a bunch of hot air.

If Pasquette had called earlier in the week, or, hell, even earlier in the day, verifying the man's story would have been as easy as picking up the phone. But while word of his demotion had yet to leak from the director's office, Carpenter knew conducting an off-the-books investigation from his office into another country was probably not the best idea.

The smart play would have been for him to leave the building entirely, drive to one of the agency's annexes, and use their systems to get the answers he needed. But getting out required Carpenter going through the security checkpoint in the lobby and he knew the instant he swiped his badge over the reader he would be locked out and cut off from the tracking software, databases, and computer monitoring systems he'd need if Toussaint's story checked out.

No, he was going to have to stay.

Despite the loss of his office, Carpenter had been busy and, after finding a computer terminal in one of the empty conference rooms on the second floor, he accessed the ADS-B Exchange and ran a search of every aircraft that had flown in or out of Port-au-Prince in the last three months. Downloading the data into Excel, he dismissed all the commercial aircraft, compiled a list of all remaining tail numbers, and fed that data into the FAA's Aircraft Registration database.

Thirty minutes later he got a hit: a Gulfstream G650, tail number 651RT that, according to the FAA, belonged to Evergreen Aviation out of Olympia, Washington. A company Carpenter knew also happened to be a sole source contractor for the Defense Intelligence Agency.

"Levi Fucking Shaw," he snarled, "I can read you like a book."

But it wasn't a DIA-contracted Gulfstream that had flown to Port-au-Prince in the past few months that had him smoking in the stairwell. No, it was the fact that, according to a recently amended flight plan, tail number 651RT was on its way to Port-au-Prince right now.

He was still thinking about his options when the tech's voice came bouncing down the hallway.

"Sir, I've got one," the man said.

Carpenter dropped the cigarette on the ground and gave it a quick crush with the toe of his wingtip before stepping out of the stairwell and power-walking down the hall.

"What is it?" he asked, falling in behind the tech.

"It's a Reaper, sir," the man replied, striding back to his station. "One of the older models we loaned out to the Coast Guard for their counter-narcotics operations."

"How much play time do we have?" Carpenter asked as the man took his seat.

"Not long," he answered, pulling on the headphones that would allow him to talk to the pilots operating the drone from their base in Nevada.

Carpenter nodded and leaned in, his eyes laser focused on the screen.

For the uninitiated, getting their bearings among the pastel sea of buildings and gray-washed roofs scrolling across the screen would have been impossible, but Carpenter had spent enough time watching Kill TV—the nickname the CIA had given to UAV feeds during the beginning stages of the war in Afghanistan—that it was almost second nature. After comparing the latitude and longitude coordinates displayed on the green heads-up display in the center of the screen, with the map of Port-au-Prince already spread out on the table, he knew that the Reaper was on the west side of the city, a few miles short of the airport.

Seconds later the view shifted to the east as the pilots made some adjustments. The feed was leaning to the left as they brought the Reaper into a lazy orbit over the target.

"Pilots say we've got five minutes until they have to return to base," the man said.

But Carpenter wasn't listening; his eyes were locked on the runway and the Gulfstream lying crumpled on its side.

"I need them to zoom in on the tail number," he said.

The tech relayed his instructions to the pilots and the camera zoomed in, until the 651RT painted in block letters on the tail was crystal clear.

Fucking Shaw, he thought.

Carpenter stepped back, the rush of rage through his veins like battery acid, and his mind already shifting to his next move, when a flicker of motion near the right edge of the feed grabbed his attention.

What in the hell is that?

At first, he thought it was a piece of trash being blown by the wind, or maybe one of the thousands of dogs that roamed the city of Port-au-Prince had made it onto the runway. But when he leaned in closer, Carpenter instantly recognized the shape for what it was.

"We've got a runner," he said just as the figure ran out of the camera's field of view. "Tell them to zoom out and rotate ten degrees to the right."

It took a few seconds for the tech's instructions to make it from DC to Las Vegas, and a few more for the Reaper to receive and comply with the pilot's corrections. And while Carpenter guessed it hadn't even been ten seconds before the UAV was moving, it felt like an eternity.

"He's gone," the tech said.

"Not gone," Carpenter said, scanning the tarmac. "Just . . . hiding."

"Right there, running for the fence," the tech said, already relaying the information to the pilots. "Target is going for the parking lot."

With the pilots locked on to the quarry, the lag vanished and they followed the man in real time, maneuvering the UAV over the parking lot, the camera tracking him as they reestablished their orbit.

"I need to see his face," Carpenter said.

"Roger that, sir," the tech said. "Be advised the pilots are reporting they have three minutes until they are out of fuel."

"I don't care if it runs out of gas and crashes in the middle of fucking Port-au-Prince. You tell them to get me a positive ID or it's their ass," Carpenter snapped.

"Y-yes, sir," the tech stuttered.

While the Reaper started its second rotation, the MTS, or Multi-Spectral Targeting System ball on the bottom of the UAV, was in constant motion, continuously rotating back and forth to keep the reticle in the center of the heads-up display locked on target. Thus, when the figure stepped out of the bushes and started across the parking lot, the camera was in perfect position to capture the man's face.

A face Carpenter instantly recognized as that of Adam Hayes.

PORT-AU-PRINCE, HAITI

A dam Hayes pulled away from the airport, any hopes of slipping into Port-au-Prince without alerting the ANI vanishing with the column of smoke rising from the mangled Gulfstream. Merging south onto Route Nationale 1 and knowing that it wouldn't take Pasquette long to realize that someone had fled the crashed plane, Hayes was eager to get to the safe house and contact Carver.

He pushed the Pathfinder hard, ignoring the groan of its engine as he guided it up one of the many hills that surrounded the city. But when he reached the summit, it wasn't the postcard-perfect sunset over the Caribbean that held his gaze, but the smashed foundations and piles of shattered concrete that served as tombstones for the neighborhood that had once occupied the plain to the east.

At first Hayes wasn't sure what he was looking at, then he remembered—*the earthquake.*

Like most westerners, what he knew of the 2010 earthquake that hit Port-au-Prince with the force of a seven-kiloton nuclear warhead came from the news, and even now he vividly remembered the apocalyptic scenes that had been beamed into his living room.

But more shocking than the destruction he'd witnessed from the apex were the gaunt-faced children he saw picking through the trash piles outside the cardboard city of a refugee camp he found at the bottom of the hill. Hayes spent the next five miles trying to understand how the level of suffering he'd just witnessed was possible after eleven years and the billions of dollars that had been sent to Haiti to aid in the rebuilding. But before he had an answer, Hayes was pulling into Pétion-Ville, the luxury shops, nightclubs, and walled compounds that lined the streets of the wealthy commune, leaving him feeling like he'd been transported to another planet.

He followed the GPS up the hill, past the Cuban embassy and what looked like a casino before finally ending up in a quiet cul-de-sac, complete with manicured lawns and a smiling couple out walking their dog.

Using the clicker he'd found in the center console, Hayes pointed it at the ornate metal gate and pressed the button. The gate hinged open, and he pulled through, following the cobblestone drive until he came to a Mediterranean villa painted a garish burnt orange, the house in striking contrast to the dumps that had been available during his time at Treadstone.

Hayes backed the truck into the garage and killed the engine, the steady beep from the alarm panel echoing loudly off the concrete walls.

"All right, all right, I'm coming," he said, grabbing his assault pack from the front seat.

Climbing out of the truck, he moved to the security panel and used the code Poe had given him to kill the alarm and then pressed the remote to close the garage door. Then he stepped inside, the heavy Class III door thumping closed behind him.

The luxuries of the exterior notwithstanding, the inside of the safe house was spartan, with the only non-mission equipment being the stainless-steel appliances in the kitchen and the TV in the den. Everything else was fully functional: fire-resistant curtains, ballistic windows and doors, and the medical suite with its surgical table, stocked pharmacy, and array of monitors there to keep the occupants alive.

While the lack of any visible creature comforts might have bothered someone else, Hayes wasn't planning on being there long enough for it to matter. By the time he stepped into the control room and sat down behind the desk, he found himself already planning the trip home.

First things first, the voice cautioned. *You still have a job to do.*

"Yeah, yeah," he said, firing up the computer.

He brought up the security system, ran a diagnostic test on the perimeter motion sensors, and when he was confident they were functioning properly, turned his attention to the cameras. He studied the feeds and was wondering why no one had thought to put a camera at the front gate when his sat phone rang.

It was Poe and, as usual, the handler got right to the point.

"That was a sixty-five-million-dollar plane you destroyed," Poe chided.

"You say that like you gave me a choice," Hayes replied.

That stopped Poe's scolding, but only for a second. "Well, General Cantrell certainly isn't pleased."

"Look, if you guys are going to get this bent out of shape every time I break something, this is going to be a *long* forty-eight hours," he said.

Poe didn't find the comment amusing. "You do realize that this is supposed to be a low-visibility operation?"

"Well, then, maybe next time you won't wait till the last second to inform me about any decision that seriously compromises the operation." When Poe had no complaint about that truism, Hayes took the advantage. "So, is there a point to all this or do you have a ball-busting quota to maintain?"

Thankfully, Gunner Poe decided to lower the temperature of the conversation and get down to business. "I got the NSA to tap into the Digicel Haiti network. Thirty minutes ago they intercepted a call from one of Pasquette's lieutenants to an individual named Jimmy 'Barbeque' Chérizier."

"I'm guessing his nickname doesn't come from his way with smoked meat," Hayes said.

"Not of the cow or pig kind, at any rate," Poe replied. "Looking at the packet State sent over, this guy's a real piece of work."

"Give me the highlights," Hayes said.

"Seems that Jimmy started out in the army, worked with one of those anti-narco paramilitary teams the CIA set up back in the early nineties. After Congress cut the funding for those programs, Jimmy took his skills to the PNH, where he quickly developed a reputation for excessive violence and stealing cocaine."

"Did they fire him for that?"

"Actually, no," Poe said. "They fired him because he started using Molotov cocktails on the locals."

"Hence the nickname," Hayes sighed. "What was the call about?"

"Pasquette has put a bounty on Toussaint," Poe replied. "Ten thousand American bucks if he is brought in alive. Seeing how most of the city is in G9 territory, I thought you could use the heads-up."

"Okay, sounds like we've got to speed things up. I'm not waiting around for Carver to check in. Give me her number and I'll contact her myself."

For once Poe agreed without any argument and passed along the contact information.

"Anything else?" Hayes asked.

"Yeah, the National Weather Service is tracking a couple of tropical storms in the area."

"Wow, this just keeps getting better. Thanks for telling me before they were outside the window."

"Keep your shirt on," Poe said. "By the time they make landfall you'll be long gone."

"You just make sure that extraction team is ready to go wheels up when I make the call," Hayes said. "I don't want to be stuck in this place one second longer than I have to."

"Then I suggest you hurry up and call her," he said, ending the call.

SAINT-GERARD, HAITI

Dallys Carver stood on the balcony outside their room at the Hôtel Oloffson and scanned the street. In the west, the sun hung low on the horizon, its dying light spilling across the slate gray sea like liquid gold.

It would be dark soon, and already she could hear the relentless beat of the *tanbou* drums and the twinkling laughter of the revelers rising over the cityscape. Soon the streets would be filled with revelers in papier-mâché masquerades, along with bare-chested musicians and dancers in feathered headdresses. A truly rousing sight if it hadn't been for her sense that the ANI was closing in on them like an invisible noose.

With a sigh, Carver shook a cigarette from the pack of Camel Lights, pressed it between her lips, and lit it off a patinaed Zippo. She took a deep drag, the warm soothing rush of nicotine going to her head.

Oh, God, that's good, she thought.

But the relief was short-lived. Before Carver had even exhaled the smoke from her lungs, Long was there to ruin the moment.

"You're out of control," he said. "You're going to get us all killed."

"I understand you're upset," Carver said, "but we got to deal with it."

"Deal with it? Are you serious? Do you have any idea how screwed we are?"

"Keep your voice down," she hissed, stepping past him to look in on Toussaint, who lay sleeping on the couch.

"Why? You worried I'm going to wake up your precious source?"

"No," Carver said, closing the patio door and turning to face her partner. "What I'm worried about is one of the guests calling the cops to complain about the crazy American on the second floor who's losing it."

"So, now *I'm* the crazy one?" he asked.

This wasn't the first time Long had lost his shit during an operation. In fact, in the past twelve months Carver had been so concerned about his poor judgment and increased volatility that she'd put him in for a psych eval.

According to Long, the shrink said he was simply exhausted, worn thin by the pressure cooker of adrenaline and fear that came with the DIA's high op tempo, and sent him back to work with a bottle of Ambien and a clear bill of health.

But Carver wasn't buying it. She knew there was something

wrong with Long, but it wasn't until that moment on the patio that she finally figured it out.

He's lost his nerve.

"I think we should split up," Long declared.

"Now?" Carver exclaimed. "You're joking, right?"

"You got a better idea?" Long asked.

"Yeah, we follow orders," she said. "You know, just sit tight, wait for the cavalry to arrive."

"Listen to me," Long said, leaning in intently. "I don't know who the hell they're sending, but unless he's John Fucking Rambo, it isn't going to matter, because if Pasquette closes the border, it's game over."

"It's only game over if you panic," she said.

"He's not going to stop," Long said. "Not after how many of his people you've killed. No, now he'll use that machete of his to peel off our skin."

Carver blinked. He wouldn't listen to reason, so she had to change her tack. "So, what's your plan?"

"I know a guy in Pedernales," Long said. "If we can make it to the border, he'll help us across, then we drive to Cabo Rojo, rent a plane . . ."

Carver tried hard not to roll her eyes. "The risks on that trip are far greater than if you just follow orders and wait for pickup."

"Follow orders," Long laughed, throwing open the door and stepping back into the room. "That's rich, coming from you."

"Let me call Washington," she said, trying to defuse the situation. "I'll get a sitrep and *then* we can decide the best course of action."

"*You* can do what you want," he said, crossing to the door, "but I'm done with this shit."

Then he was gone, stepping out into the hall, the door slamming hard in her face.

"W-what's going on?" Toussaint asked from the couch.

"Nothing," she said, about to follow Long out into the hall when the sat phone began vibrating across the table. She snatched it up.

"Who are you and why are you calling me?" she snapped. "The plan was for me to call you."

"Listen, killer," a man's voice said, tinged with irritation. "I know it's been a rough time, but I'm going to need you to take a deep breath. Can you do that for me?"

"Y-yeah . . ." she said. "Sorry. Dealing with insubordination on top of everything else."

"I'm not surprised," the man said. "Just stow the attitude and tell me where you are."

"Hôtel Oloffson," she said, stepping back out onto the patio. "Room 211."

"A hotel?" he marveled. "How'd you manage that during Carnival?"

"The owner owed me a favor," she said, looking around the area musingly. "A lot of people around here owe me favors. I saw to that . . ." Carver's attention snapped back before she spoke again. "And before you say anything, yes, I trust him."

There was silence on the other end of the line and, for a moment, Carver thought the satellite had dropped the call, but then the man spoke.

"I'll be there in twenty minutes," he said. "We are only

going to get one shot at this, so I need you ready to roll when I hit the gate."

"I understand."

"Good. Now, do you have anything for me?" he asked. "Any questions, gripes, or complaints?"

Carver moved to the railing and looked down to see Long fast-walking down the stone path that led to the bar, his hands balled into angry fists. She debated telling the man that her partner had become a liability, but just as quickly as the thought crossed her mind, she pushed it away. She was in enough trouble with the brass back in Washington as it was, and knowing that whatever she told the man would undoubtedly end up in the nightly situation report he was required to send back to his handler, she decided to keep her mouth shut. Besides, with Long's gear stacked neatly at the foot of his bed and the keys to the van safely in her pocket, it wasn't like he was going anywhere.

"You there?" he asked.

"I'm here."

"Any questions?"

"There is one thing," she said.

"What's that?"

"You never told me your name."

"It's Hayes. Adam Hayes." And then the man hung up.

Well, I hope you're more charming than you sound, Mr. Hayes, she thought, flicking the cigarette over the edge and turning back to the room.

15

SAINT-GERARD, HAITI

Five miles to the north, in the commune of Delmas, Jimmy
Chérizier sat at his desk with a phone pressed to his ear.

"They are not at Pacot Breeze," the voice said.

"You're sure?"

"Yes, boss."

"Keep looking," Chérizier said, sweat beginning to glisten
on his broad forehead.

He ended the call, threw the phone onto the desk with the
others, got to his feet, and stomped angrily to the map tacked
on the far wall. Digging the red felt-tipped pen from his
pocket, he scratched an *X* over the Pacot Breeze Hôtel, his left
hand slipping to the *gris-gris* hanging around his neck.

He rubbed the talisman between his thumb and forefinger,

the steady *tick-tick* of the Simplex clock on the wall taking him back to the call from Haitian intelligence.

For most men in his position, getting a call from the ANI was a logical prelude to a painful death, especially considering the active arrest warrants and sanctions the United States had imposed on Chérizier following his orchestration of the 2018 massacre in the La Saline slum. But he wasn't worried.

Mainly because it was Pasquette who'd contracted him and his G9 gang to kill the twenty-four government protesters in the first place. But as much as Chérizier had personally benefited from his close relationship with the Haitian intelligence service, he'd been in the game long enough to know that the second he stepped out of line the ANI wouldn't hesitate to put him down.

So, when he first heard about the incident at the bank, Chérizier knew that it was only a matter of time before one of Pasquette's intermediaries reached out for help.

"I've been waiting for you to call," Chérizier had said when he had answered the phone.

"Good, then I can cut to the point," the man had said. "Can you find them?"

"For the right price, *anything* is possible."

"Ten thousand dollars," the man had said, "but the boss wants them alive."

Jimmy had whistled.

"That's a lot of money," he'd said. "How much did this Toussaint steal?"

"That's not your concern," the man had said. "Can you find them, yes or no?"

"Yes," he'd said.

"Good, you have until the end of the night."

Then the line had gone dead.

The time limit had caught him off guard, but he'd been quick to recover and soon had his army of informants out on the streets. Honestly, he'd thought they'd be easy to find. After all, there were only so many places in Port-au-Prince for a foreign team to hide, but studying the ragged X's that dotted the map, Chérizier realized he was running out of places to look.

"Where the fuck could they be?"

He didn't know, but with darkness falling outside the building and still no word of his quarry, Chérizier could feel the walls starting to close in.

Then the phone rang, the weight of the world falling off his shoulders when he answered and heard the woman's voice on the other line.

"I found them."

"Where?"

"The Hôtel Oloffson," she said.

"You're sure?"

"Yes, one of them is drinking at the bar right now."

"Do *not* let them leave," Chérizier said.

SAINT-GERARD, HAITI

Ten minutes after getting off the phone, Hayes was speeding west on the Avenue Lamartiniere, the roadway coiling across the Morne l' Hôpital foothills like a jet-black snake. It was obvious from his drive that the Pathfinder was the wrong vehicle for the trip, but with Carnival in full swing and, no doubt, every lowlife in the city searching for Carver and Long, all Hayes could think about was making the pickup, getting back to the safe house, and calling in the helo that would get them the hell out of Port-au-Prince. He pushed it hard, ignoring the squeal of the tires as they navigated the switchbacks.

By the time he reached the neighborhood of Bois Verna, the brakes were hot and the *check engine* light burned bright orange on the dash. He let off the gas and turned south on the Avenue Christophe, praying the SUV would start when he needed it.

In the distance he saw the Hôtel Oloffson nestled among the trees, the light of the moon off the bleached white wood and dark black windows of the Victorian gingerbread mansion giving it the look of a sinister dollhouse.

That's creepy as hell, he thought, dialing Carver's number.

For someone who'd been on his share of blown ops, Hayes was fully expecting Carver to be holding on to her phone for dear life, but to his surprise there was no answer to his call.

"You've *got* to be shitting me," he said, pounding the wheel with the flat of his hand.

Pushing down the irritation he felt simmering in his guts, Hayes circled the block and angrily dialed the number again only to have it go straight to voicemail.

He felt the blood rush to his face as he gripped the steering wheel tightly. Then as suddenly as it had come, the heat of his anger was gone, replaced by the icy finger of dread, and the realization that there was a reason Carver wasn't answering her phone.

Because she can't, he thought.

Knowing there was only one way to find out, Hayes killed the lights and pulled the Pathfinder into an alley on the west side of the hotel. He cut the engine, and rolled down the windows, senses straining in the darkness for any sign of life.

From the front seat, he had a clear view of the hotel but even then, he almost missed the dented pair of pickups snugged up near the front door.

Could be anyone, the voice unconvincingly said.

Hayes pulled a tan hard case from his assault pack and opened the lid to reveal a palm-size drone, a controller, and a ruggedized tablet. He'd never been a big tech guy and, while most of the operators he worked with at Treadstone loved getting to field-test the latest gear and gizmos the engineers developed, Hayes usually ended up breaking them.

But thankfully, the tiny UAV was Hayes-proof and, after lifting it out of its protective foam and hitting the power switch, all he had to do was follow the prompts on the tablet. A few seconds later the drone was whizzing across the street, its four tiny propellers all but silent in the night air.

I've got to get one of these for Jack, he thought as he guided the UAV through the open gate and up the drive.

Afraid to fly too close to the hotel, Hayes worked the drone clockwise around the perimeter, the clarity of its tiny night vision camera beginning to suffer as it moved away from the ambient light of the street and into the shadows of the mango trees that grew thick over the property.

By the time he made it around the back of the hotel, the picture was so bad that everything looked like one dark green shadow. Hayes was about to recall the drone when he saw the muzzle flashes from the second floor.

A second later the sound came bouncing across the street, the precise *tack-tack . . . tack-tack* of a pistol delivering controlled pairs followed by the staccato chatter of an AK-47 firing on full auto.

"I hate it when I'm right," he muttered.

Practically grabbing the drone out of the air, Hayes pulled the Spyderco Para Military from his pocket and used the tip of the blade to pry the plastic housing from the dome light.

He removed the bulb, tossing it and the plastic cover into the backseat before opening the door.

Stepping out, he moved to the rear of the truck and opened the cargo hatch, his fingers sliding beneath the upholstery until he found the metal detent near the left firewall. He pushed down on the tab, felt the locking bar disengage, and then pulled up. The entire bottom hinged open to reveal a black Pelican case and an olive drab kit bag. He hadn't had time to examine the contents before, but there was no putting it off now.

Hayes opened the kit bag, pulled out the Ferro Concepts low-vis ballistic vest and the pair of PIG FDT Alpha gloves he'd requested. He strapped the vest tight to his chest, pulled on the gloves, and then turned his attention to the Pelican case.

He unsnapped the ruggedized clasps and opened the lid to find the tools of his trade nestled safely in their foam cutouts. Selecting an HK MP7 from the weapons arrayed inside the case, he pulled it free of its foam insert, activated the Aimpoint Micro, and after adjusting the brightness of the red dot, slammed a forty-round magazine into the grip and racked a 4.6x30mm armor-piercing round into the chamber.

Slinging the German-made submachine gun over his shoulder, Hayes stuffed three Dutch V40 mini-frags and an extra magazine into his pouches, grabbed the Ops-Core ballistic helmet with a pair of PVS-23 night vision goggles, and was about to close the hatch when the olive drab bandolier in the far corner of the case caught his eye.

Now we're talking, he thought, lifting the bandolier free.

Hayes closed the hatch and pulled the M18 claymore mine

from the bag before dropping to a knee. Turning the mine around so that the FRONT TOWARD ENEMY embossed on the plastic case was pointing directly at him, Hayes used a pair of plastic flex cuffs hanging from his vest to secure the three-and-a-half-pound mine to the back bumper.

He pulled them tight and, when he was sure the claymore wasn't going anywhere, screwed the remote-activated blasting cap into the fuze well, shoved the detonator into his pocket, and climbed behind the wheel.

It was less than a hundred yards from the alley to the front of the hotel, and Hayes stomped the accelerator to the floor. The Pathfinder leapt forward, its tires kicking up a spray of gravel, and shot from the alley. Hayes guided it down the incline and across the street, the RPMs redlining as the speedometer shot past thirty miles per hour.

There was a dip at the bottom of the alley—a shallow depression where the dirt met the road that Hayes hadn't seen on the way in. And while he couldn't tell exactly how deep it was, the voice in his head could.

Slow down! it bellowed.

But Hayes ignored it and kept the accelerator pinned to the floor.

He hit the depression with a full head of steam, the slam of the frame against the concrete as loud as a howitzer. *So much for the element of surprise,* he thought.

The force of the impact bounced the Pathfinder skyward, the tires spinning aimlessly as it sailed across the street. Hayes had no idea how long they were airborne, but with the rush of adrenaline coursing through his blood, it felt like forever.

Finally, the weight of the engine sent the Pathfinder nosing back to earth. The SUV came down like a meteorite, the front bumper crashing into the hotel's drive with a spray of sparks. Alerted to the threat, the men he'd seen in the drone feed came racing out of the shadows, and they converged on the limping SUV like ants at a picnic. But Hayes ignored them and kept his attention on the front of the hotel.

"Nothing's going to stop me now!" he barked.

But the words were no sooner off his lips than a broad-chested man stepped around the corner, lifted an RPG to his shoulder, and fired.

SAINT-GERARD, HAITI

Hayes should've known better. In every war movie he'd ever seen, someone saying "nothing's going to stop us" was the cue for disaster.

So now, the RPG came screaming across the lawn at nine hundred feet per second, the exhaust from its rocket motor coiling behind it like a snake. Even before Hayes had a chance to react, it came slicing across the hood, so close that he could see the guiding fins and smell the propellant through the open window.

Then it slammed into one of the palm trees that lined the drive and detonated, the overpressure from the blast back-handing the passenger side of the Pathfinder. The windows exploded, showering Hayes with glass. The heat singed his skin, but he bit down on the pain and kept the hood centered on the front of the hotel.

Here we go, he thought.

Hayes was aiming for the door, but after the collision at the bottom of the alley the damaged Pathfinder was almost uncontrollable. Realizing that he was about to go through the wall instead of the window, all that was left to do was brace for impact.

A split second after the grille made contact with the wall, the airbag came ballooning out of the steering wheel—the white-fisted punch of the nylon bag leaving Hayes feeling like he'd been kicked by a mule wearing boxing gloves on its hooves.

Shaking off the stars, he yanked up on the emergency brake and disconnected his seat belt. He clawed at the door handle, got it open, and threw himself from the SUV, the stock of the MP7 smashing him in the side of the face as he went skidding across the tile floor.

The Pathfinder blasted through the counter before burying itself into the back wall. Hayes's world went white as a geyser of masonry dust and shattered plaster kicked up by the collision inundated the room.

Coughing against the smokescreen, Hayes limped to cover behind a decorative planter and threw himself to the ground. Then the gunfire started. First, it was a few tentative shots from the top of the stairs, then the men he'd seen spread out on the lawn came rushing up the steps, the AK-47s in their hands chattering on full auto as they sent a wall of lead blasting through the gaping hole the Pathfinder had torn in the front of the building.

Hiding unseen behind the planter, Hayes watched the men form into a haphazard skirmish line and advance on the crippled vehicle. The orgy of gunfire rose to a crescendo as he casually pulled the detonator from his pocket and waited patiently for the men to blow their wad.

The shooters burned through their magazines. The rate of fire slowed, and then stopped, but even then Hayes waited until the last shooter had fired his last round before flicking the safety wire free.

Fire in the hole, he thought, squeezing the detonator twice.

The claymore exploded with a resounding boom, the blast sending seven hundred steel ball bearings packed over the pound and a half of C4 buzz-sawing through the line of gunmen. Hayes leapt to his feet and raced through the smoke, angling for the stairs. One of the shooters stumbled into his path so Hayes thumbed the selector of his weapon to full auto and sent a short burst stitching across his chest.

Before the man hit the ground there were two more to take his place.

"There he is!" the closest man shouted, the Uzi submachine gun in his hand spitting flame as tracked his target across the open ground.

Hayes threw himself out of the line of fire and scrambled behind an oversized couch, the burst of the nine-millimeter bullets snapping past his head like a swarm of angry hornets. Not to be outdone by his partner, the other attacker flipped his CAR-15 to full auto, locked it tight against his hip and proceeded to work the cut-down assault rifle across the room like a fire hose.

You don't have time for this, the voice said.

"You think?" Hayes asked. He tugged one of the mini-frags from his plate carrier, pulled the pin, and flipped it down the hall.

BOOM!

The scream of pain that followed the detonation was Hayes's signal to get back on the offensive, so he hurdled the two dead men sprawled out on the ground and bounded up the stairs.

With most of the shooters dead or dying, the gunfire had stopped, and the only sound was the voice of an angry man echoing down the hall to his right.

"This is your last chance, *blanca*!" the man shouted. "Hand him over."

"Go to hell!" a female voice replied, her tone defiant.

"Then I'll burn you out!" the man shouted.

Hayes ran toward the voice, and when he stepped into the hall, saw three men standing at the far end, one of them lifting a lighter to a Molotov cocktail in his partner's hand. He stopped and was bringing the HK up to fire when a wide-shouldered man came rushing from the open door to his left, a rusty machete in his hands.

Knowing there was no time for a precision shot, Hayes thumbed the selector to full auto and sprayed a long burst down the hall. There was nothing pretty about the shot, but with the MP7 capable of a firing 950 rounds a minute, there didn't have to be. Hayes held the trigger down and hammered through the magazine until he saw his target lurch backward, the unlit Molotov cocktail flying from his hands.

The man went down, the bolt of the now-empty HK locking to the rear, and he turned to face the man with the machete. With no time to reload or transition to the pistol at his hip, Hayes grabbed the buttstock with his right hand and the suppressor with his left, the heat from the aluminum tube melting his glove. He ignored the pain, turned the MP7 sideways and lifted it up, parrying the machete chopping down at his head.

The rusted blade sparked off the receiver and Hayes went to kick the brawny Haitian in the chest, but the man was fast, and before his foot left the ground the man hit him hard in the face. Dazed and off-balance, Hayes stepped back, the Haitian swiping at him with the machete, the blade slicing through the sling of the MP7.

He let it fall and circled to the right, the rush of adrenaline pumping through his veins slowing time to a crawl. In an instant Hayes was aware of every detail: the hiss of the machete through the air as his attacker slashed the blade at his chest, and the frantic voices of the men behind him as they scrambled for the Molotov cocktail.

I've had about enough of this shit, he thought.

Then the world snapped back into real time and Hayes stepped forward, grabbed the man by the front of the shirt and snapped his helmet into his face. The bridge of the man's nose exploded in a spray of blood and snot. He dropped the machete, hands rushing up to his face. But before he had a chance, Hayes kicked his legs out from under him and drove him to the floor.

The impact knocked the breath from the machete man's lungs and his mouth opened wide in a silent scream, but before he could catch his breath, Hayes jerked the suppressed FN from its holster. He shot the man between the eyes, but by the time he whirled back toward the other two men, they'd recovered their prize.

"It's too late," the taller man said, the orange glow from the flaming wick highlighting his twisted smile as he cocked his arm back.

But before he could throw it, Hayes had the RMR locked on the bottle.

"For *you*, maybe," he said, pulling the trigger.

This time his aim was dead-on, and the bottle exploded, the thwack of the suppressor inside the hall followed instantaneously by the *whump* of the flame igniting the vaporized fuel. Hayes threw himself into the open room, the fireball that came rolling down the hall singing his pants leg.

Then there was blessed silence.

LANGLEY, VIRGINIA

Mike Carpenter fast-walked down the hall, the uncontrolled panic that came with seeing Adam Hayes in the drone footage kicking his fight-or-flight response into high gear. He burst into the bathroom and, desperately holding back the nausea, managed to throw the lock before stumbling into the stall and dropping to his knees.

Carpenter vomited until there was nothing left but bile, and then sagged against the wall, the weight of the moment crashing over him. Even before his meeting with Director Bratton, his life had been circling the drain. His wife, Eden, tiring of the long hours he'd been forced to spend at the office and the frantic schedule that kept them from enjoying normal holidays, had demanded things change or she'd leave.

Being married to an intelligence officer was no easy task, but Carpenter had begged her to hold on, and promised that he'd be able to take a step back when he took the director's position.

But then came the failed hit on Shaw and everything changed.

He'd known that there would be blowback when he learned that his assassins had missed their man. He knew that, eventually, Shaw would have his dog Hayes try to finish him off and swore that when that time came, *he* would be ready.

Planning for the inevitable showdown became an obsession, one that slowly took up every waking hour, and it wasn't long before Eden pulled the pin on their marriage. By the time her lawyers were done she had it all: the house, most of the money, and all his pride.

And now with Adam Hayes on the ground in Port-au-Prince, Carpenter realized he was on the verge of losing the five million things he'd thought no one could take away from him: the dollars he'd painstakingly siphoned from the different black projects he'd commanded over the last ten years.

Letting the last of the vomit dribble from his lower lip, Carpenter got his wits about him. *That's not fucking happening*, he thought.

Carpenter got to his feet and moved to the sink. A splash of cold water over his fevered brow snapped him back to reality. Looking at himself in the mirror, he knew his only chance to get ahead of the situation before it blew up in his face was to contact his partners.

So far, Carpenter had managed to stay under the director's

radar by confining his movements to the old headquarters building where, thanks to budget cuts and the tight-fisted government comptrollers, security was still stuck in the early nineties.

But to contact his partners with any degree of deniability, Carpenter couldn't afford to use his phone. He needed a computer that would offer him some anonymity. There were plenty of those back in the main building, but it would mean taking one of the tunnels back to the new headquarters. Worse than that, actually logging on to one of the mainframes required the user to slide their ID card into the reader, and the moment Carpenter did that, the director would know he was still in the building.

In the old days it wasn't uncommon for someone running to the bathroom to leave their ID plugged into the readers, but with the recent crackdown on cybersecurity, Carpenter knew he had a snowball's chance in hell of finding an unlocked computer terminal.

No, if Carpenter was going to contact his partners, he had to do it the right way, and that meant sneaking back up to his office and grabbing the air-gapped Alienware m15 laptop he kept in his safe.

But how am I going to get up to my office without being seen?

If he'd been able to leave the building, he could have gone to the garage and used the express elevator to take him up to the seventh floor, but with that option off the table, the only other way was to take the stairs up six flights.

Awesome, he thought, stepping out of the bathroom.

By the time he made it up the final flight of stairs, Carpenter's legs were burning and his lungs were tight. Cursing the cigarettes, he eased the door open and looked out into the hall. Finding it clear, he stepped out, gently closed the door behind him, and slipped past the empty secretary's alcove and into his office.

Leaving the lights off, Carpenter moved to the silver safe on the far wall, stuck his key into the lock and spun the combination into the dial. The tumblers fell and he swung the door open. He had just retrieved the laptop bag when he heard voices outside his door.

Carpenter closed the safe behind him and tugged his key from the lock, his right hand dropping to his back pocket and the ten-ounce Ulster sap that he'd carried since his days in the field. Tugging it free, he moved to the hinge side of the door and squeezed in next to the coatrack, pressing his back to the wall.

A second later, the door swung open and the baby powder smell of his secretary's Chanel No. 5 came wafting in the office.

Dammit, Carol.

He inched his body to the left and looked out, seeing the back of his secretary's head as she stepped into his line of sight, a manila folder in her right hand. For an instant it looked like she was going to place the folder on his desk and walk back out, but then Carpenter heard the hiss of fabric off one of the chairs followed by Carol muttering. "That man can't even hang up his own raincoat," she sighed.

Realizing what was about to happen, Carpenter waited until he saw her wrinkled hand reaching for the knob and then, in one smooth motion, he bumped the door shut with his hip and stepped out.

As expected, his sudden appearance froze her dead in her

tracks, her mouth opening to exclaim. But before she had a chance, Carpenter had her by the throat, his fingers tightening around her larynx, choking off the sound.

"You always were a bothersome bitch," he hissed before slapping the blackjack down hard across the side of her skull.

It was a killing blow. Her knees buckled. Carpenter dragged her corpse to the closet, only then lowering her to the floor and checking her pulse just to make sure.

He shoved her inside and after a cursory check for any blood, grabbed the laptop case and stepped out of the office.

Ten minutes later he was back in the old building, the laptop open on the empty desk. He plugged it into the wall socket and moved the Alpha wireless antenna closer to the window ledge to ensure the best signal.

When the laptop booted up, he pulled an external hard drive from the bag, installed the VPN software that would protect his connection from any prying eyes and the modified internet browser that would allow him access to the hidden collective of internet sites known as the darknet.

Once the software was loaded, he typed the address into the search bar and a moment later, Carpenter was directed to a nondescript webchat log-in screen, the box in the center requesting his meeting ID and password. He typed in the information, a sudden wave of anxiety rushing through him as his index finger hovered over the enter key.

The people in the chat room were not to be trifled with. They were men and women with the connections, money, and firepower to bring anybody down. With Adam Hayes running amok in Port-au-Prince, Carpenter knew that, without their help, he was a dead man walking.

No use delaying the inevitable, he thought, hitting the enter key.

Colonel Quan Park, the hatchet-faced vice minister of Chinese counterintelligence, was the first to appear on screen, and the tightness of his jaw made it obvious that the man was not in a good mood. But then again, Carpenter had never seen him in a good mood.

"Do you have any idea what time it is?" the man demanded in accentless English.

"Four a.m. your time," Carpenter said, glancing at the row of clocks on the far wall. "Don't tell me that you were still asleep."

Before he could reply, a dark-haired woman appeared in the pane adjacent to the Chinese spy.

"Of course he wasn't asleep," Sofia Belov, the Russian black market and dark web master, laughed, her piecing green eyes flashing. "The MSS is much too busy trying to overthrow the West to allow him any rest. Isn't that right, comrade?"

Park bristled at the comment, but remained silent, choosing to wait for Paulo Morales, the Brazilian arms dealer, to appear before speaking.

"Now that we are all here," he said, leaning forward in his chair, "perhaps you'd be kind enough to tell us what is so damned important."

Carpenter quickly brought them up to speed on the situation in Port-au-Prince, including everything that he'd learned since his call with Pasquette that afternoon. When he got to the part about the unauthorized landing at the airport, he paused to upload the screenshot he'd taken of the drone feed.

"And this is the operative they sent to recover the data?" Park asked.

"Yes, his name is Adam Hayes," Carpenter answered. "He's one of the most dangerous men my government has ever put in the field."

"Doesn't look like much," Morales sniffed.

"Take my word for it—with him on the ground, everything changes," Carpenter said.

"How much is currently in the account?" Park asked.

"A little over twenty-nine million," Belov answered.

"And how much time would we need to move it?" Park asked.

"To move that much money without anyone noticing would take a few months," she said. "It could be done faster, but we would lose a substantial amount of capital."

"But what about the deal on the table?" Morales demanded.

"It would be wise to delay," Park said.

"That is unacceptable," Morales said. "The guns are already on their way, with the buyer set to arrive in forty-eight hours. My reputation—*our* reputation—will be ruined."

"Indeed," Park said, steepling his fingers.

"What does Mr. Pasquette think about all of this?" Belov asked.

"Who cares what he thinks?" Morales roared.

"I do!" She yelled back. "The only reason I agreed to put my money in that shitty little bank was because he assured us it was safe."

Carpenter let them bicker for a few moments and then finally stepped in. "I believe there is an alternative," he said.

"One that allows us to maintain both our positions and our reputations."

"Oh?" Park asked. "And what is that?"

"Hayes is good," Carpenter began, "but the fact that he came in alone leads me to believe that the DIA is going to send in an extraction team *after* he's secured the package."

"Go on," Morales said.

"Right now, Pasquette has his men tearing up the city looking for the missing flash drive," Carpenter said, "and while I might be able to offer logistical support, when it comes to direct action, my hands are tied."

"What are you saying?" Morales asked, then answered his own question. "Are you saying that you want us to fly a kill team down to Port-au-Prince and take out Hayes and whoever else shows up?"

"That is *exactly* what I'm saying," Carpenter said.

SAINT-GERARD, HAITI

Hayes got to his feet to find the hall ablaze. He took a deep breath, the dense black smoke from the burning carpet scalding his eyes and throat, then stepped out, snagging the MP7 from the ground on his way to the fire extinguisher on the far wall.

He shoved a fresh magazine into the magwell and dropped the bolt, slinging the submachine before ripping the extinguisher from its mount. As he advanced on the flames, the sweat on his skin evaporated in the face of the intense heat. Ripping the pin free, he mashed down on the handle, the flames retreating before the jet of white foam. He backed them down the hall and was almost to Carver's room when he tripped over the leg of the dead Haitian. As he went down, the extinguisher slipped from his hands.

With nothing to keep the fire at bay, the flames came surging back down the hall like a pack of ravenous wolves. Hayes was on the verge of being devoured by the blaze, when the ancient sprinkler system finally kicked on, soaking the hall in a shower of rust-red water.

With the fire dampened, Hayes rose to his feet and, hacking against the residual smoke, marched the rest of the way to Carver's room. He ignored the mangled door and the innumerable bullet holes in the sheet rock when he stepped into the room and activated the SureFire WeaponLight. He panned it over the splintered furniture and charred mattresses as the thick acrid smoke in the room threatened to strangle him. He grabbed a charred wooden desk chair and flung it through the nearest window, taking a greedy gulp of the fresh air that rushed in.

"C-Carver," he managed to croak.

Nothing.

"Carver," he repeated again. "It's Hayes, can you hear me?"

Shit, he thought, *they're all dead.*

Then he heard a weak cough from the door to his right. He pushed it open, his light reflecting off the spiderwebbed mirror.

"I'm coming in, don't shoot me," he said.

There was groan from the corner as he stepped in, light panning toward the large cast iron tub, revealing a young woman with soot-stained reddish-blond hair beneath a large beach towel, as well as a man with thick black glasses.

"Carver?" He asked, the relief in his voice evident.

"W-what took you so long?" she asked.

"Funny," he said, helping them out of the tub.

With the hotel room smoldering around him and no idea how many more shooters were in the area, time was not on his side. After a cursory medical check, he herded them out of the bathroom.

"We need to go," he said. "Where's the rest of your team?"

"There's just one other, and he's gone," she said.

"Who?"

"Chico Long . . . my partner," she replied.

"He's dead?"

Carver nodded.

"You saw his body?" Hayes asked.

"He went downstairs right before the shooting started," she said. "I . . . I tried to help, b-but . . ."

Before she could finish, headlights came sweeping up from the road and Hayes looked out the balcony window to see three PNH vehicles pulling up the drive.

"We have to go now," he said quietly but with dead certainty. "Where's your vehicle?"

"Down the back stairs," Carver said, getting to her feet and heading for the door.

Out in the hall, she turned left, Hayes bringing up the rear as Toussaint followed her around the corner and down a flight of metal stairs that led to the back of the building. Then they were outside, moving fast to a white panel van parked at the edge of the property.

Running up to the vehicle, Hayes was trying to figure out how they were going to get away with the PNH cramming the main drive. But moving around to the passenger side, and seeing the gravel access road to the front of the van, it was obvious that whoever had chosen the spot knew what they were doing.

Hayes opened the sliding door, helped Toussaint into the back, and waited for Carver to climb in behind the wheel.

"Put it in neutral," he said, "and keep the lights off until we're down the hill."

Carver muttered something about this not being her first rodeo, but did as she was told as he braced his shoulder against the frame. Old bullet wounds in his thighs burned as he rocked the van forward.

"C'mon, you big bastard," he grunted.

By the time Hayes got the wheels rolling and climbed inside, he was covered in sweat, his legs shaking from the effort. He collapsed into the seat next to Toussaint, his chest tight from the smoke he'd inhaled.

Carver guided the van down the hill and let its momentum carry them around the corner, waiting until they were out of sight before tapping the brakes.

"Which way?" she asked after starting the engine.

Hayes was too busy coughing up a lungful of black soot to offer anything but a ragged "east," until Toussaint pulled a bottle of water from the black duffel bag on the floor and handed it over.

"Take it easy with that water," Carver snapped. "We may need some later."

Hayes ignored her and took the bottle with a nod of thanks, cracked the top, and took a swig. He swished it around, trying and failing to get the taste of burnt carpet and gunpowder out of his mouth before spitting it out the open door.

"She always like this?" he asked the man.

"She's . . . complicated," Toussaint said with a smile.

Complicated, Hayes thought, draining the rest of the bottle in one long pull. *Just what I need.*

"Are you going to tell me where we're going?" Carver asked a few minutes later.

Hayes forced himself upright in his seat and checked the backtrail. When he didn't see any headlights, he pulled the sliding door closed.

"Pétion-Ville," he said, settling back into his seat and typing out a quick text to Poe.

By the time they made it back to the safe house, Hayes's body had begun to stiffen from the gunfight at the hotel, and while he should have been thinking about the cold beer in the fridge and the painkillers waiting for him in the infirmary, his handler had yet to reply.

Fucking Poe, he thought as he stepped into the kitchen.

Hayes dropped the MP7 and his sweat-soaked plate carrier onto the table and moved to the refrigerator. He opened the door and pulled out a six-pack of Prestige.

"Want a beer?" he asked, lifting one of frosted bottles free after he set the rest on the counter.

"No," Carver said. "I want to know when we're getting out of here."

"You're not the only one," he said, twisting the cap free and taking a long gulp.

"Wait, what does that mean?" she asked.

"Uhhh . . . it means that I'd also like to know when we are getting out of here."

"You don't know?"

"I'm just a mushroom," Hayes said.

"A mushroom?" Toussaint asked, reaching for one of the bottles.

"It's an expression," he shrugged.

"An odd expression," Toussaint said, struggling to get the cap off the bottle. "What does it mean?"

Before he had a chance to answer, Carver stepped in, snatched the beer from Toussaint's hands. "It means he doesn't know shit," she said, twisting the cap free. "That about cover it?"

"Pretty much," he said.

"Great, now that we've got that covered," Carver said, handing the beer back to her source, "how about you show us to our rooms?"

Hayes shrugged and took them upstairs, showed them their rooms and made sure they had everything they needed.

"Looks good," Carver said, shutting her door.

Got a real charmer on our hands, he thought, knees popping as he started down the stairs.

Hayes went back to the kitchen, grabbing his kit and another beer before limping down the hall. He stopped by the security room to drop off his gear and was on his way to the infirmary when Poe finally responded.

His text read: *I need a full after-action brief in ten minutes.*

"Sure, you do, asshole," Hayes said.

He stepped into the infirmary and moved to the glass-fronted shelves on the left wall. The neat row of pill bottles he found inside took him back to when he first joined Treadstone. He'd been twenty-nine. Just young and dumb enough to think that getting old was something that happened to other people.

They'd programmed him to ignore the pain, to push himself harder, faster, and further than anyone else, but he was quick to learn there was only so much damage the body could take.

By the time Hayes turned thirty-five, the bruises, broken bones, and bullet wounds he'd collected along the way had finally caught up to him. He was slowing down and often unable to sleep because of constant pain.

To keep him and the rest of their operators in the field, Treadstone had an army of support personnel: doctors, surgeons, and therapists who came equipped with a rainbow of painkillers—sky blue Vicodin, lemon yellow hydrocodone, and lipstick pink tramadol.

"Take your pills and get back into the fight" became the motto, and just like everyone else, Hayes took what they gave him—never seeing the hook embedded in the handful of pills he'd down after each mission.

They'd taught him how to stalk his prey and how to kill without leaving a trace, but when it came to addiction, they hadn't told him shit. No, Hayes had to learn that lesson on his own and it had almost cost him everything he'd ever cared about.

He'd been clean ever since, but standing there in the infirmary looking at those same multicolored pills in their translucent orange bottles, Hayes could feel their pull. Knew that any one of them would take his pain away for the rest of the mission.

You might even get some sleep, the voice suggested.

"Not happening," he said, grabbing a bottle of 800 milligram ibuprofen and then heading back the way he'd come.

Hayes stepped into the security room and shook three of the fat white pills into the palm of his hand and popped them into his mouth. He chased them with a swig of beer, dropped into his chair, and picked up the phone.

"What took you so long?" Poe asked.

Hayes filled the man in, telling him everything that had transpired since he'd left the battlefield.

"You burned down the Hôtel Oloffson?" Poe responded. "What's the matter with you? That place is on the historical registry."

"Hey, Jimmy Barbeque was the one who brought the Molotov cocktail to the party," he replied. "I was just trying to have a good time."

"Is that it?" Poe demanded.

"No," he said, getting to his feet and closing the door. "Carver's partner was KIA."

"Dammit, Hayes," the man said, "what the fuck are you doing down there?"

"Excuse me?" he asked.

"You've been on the ground for, what, three hours, and you've already crashed a plane, burned down a building, and lost a ma—"

"Let me stop you *right* there," Hayes snapped, his blood rushing to his face. "If I wanted an opinion from one of

Shaw's puppets, I'd shove my hand up your ass and move your mouth."

"What was that?" Poe demanded.

"You heard me," Hayes said. "A puppet, by the way, who's keeping his cards so close to his chest that he's endangering me, and everyone else I was supposedly sent down here to protect."

"Hey, I don't appreciate—"

"I don't give a fuck what you appreciate," Hayes snarled. "All I care about is getting home. Is that, in any way, unclear?"

"No," the man said tightly.

"Good, now if the next thing out of your mouth *isn't* the ETA of my extraction team, I am going to take a personal interest in seeing you suffer."

"We'll be wheels-up from Guantánamo Bay in five minutes," Poe said, his voice shaking with anger. "We can talk about your insubordination when I get there."

"Can't wait," Hayes said.

20

CARACAS, VENEZUELA

E leven hundred miles to the south, the Antonov AN-12
lifted off from Generalissimo Francisco de Miranda Air
Base, its four Ivchenko AI-20 turboprops spewing a
cloud of gray smoke over the Venezuelan capital. The Russian
Air Force pilots banked the transport north over the Caribbean Sea and by the time they leveled off at twenty thousand feet, all but one of the Wagner Group contractors they'd
picked up in Caracas had their sleeping bags spread across the
cargo hold floor and were fast asleep.

Maxim Popov sat on the nylon bench, the red-lensed headlamp strapped to his forehead illuminating the photo of the
blue-eyed man that had come with the dossier he'd been given
prior to takeoff.

Like the rest of his team, he was exhausted, his face sunburned and his skin raw from the leeches and various insects that had preyed on them while hunting government rebels through the jungles.

And just like the rest of his team, when word came over the TacSat that headquarters was sending a helo to pull them out, Popov had been sure they were finally going to get some of the R&R they'd been promised since coming to Venezuela six months prior.

"We're going home," Pavel Simonov, his second-in-command, grinned as they clambered aboard the Mi-17. "I'm going to drink myself into a coma."

After twenty-one days of near total silence, the clatter of the helo and the raucous laughter of his men was jarring at first, but by the time the helicopter began its descent into Caracas, Popov had begun to loosen up.

"What are you going to do with yourself, boss?" Ivan Baben, the team's sniper, asked.

He was about to answer when he saw Lieutenant Colonel Dmitry Yutkin waiting for them at the edge of the landing pad. "Don't think we're going home, boys," he said, pointing the man out.

At the sight of their iron-haired XO, the teams's booze-laden daydreams popped like a bubble, and the only sound was the metallic clicks of the men checking over their weapons and magazines.

"I guess I'll take the boys and go find some more ammo," Pavel said as they climbed off the helo.

"Take a shower while you're at it," he grinned. "You smell like a goat's asshole."

"Better not keep the old man waiting."

"Yeah," he said, slinging his AK-12 across the front of his grime-soaked plate carrier.

As the former commander of Group Vympel, Lieutenant Colonel Dmitry Yutkin was a legend in Russian Special Operations and the man who'd handpicked Popov to join the Wagner Group, a quasi-private military company the colonel had helped stand up in 2016.

According to Yutkin, the men who joined Wagner were no longer officially in the military, but they would still be connected to the Ministry of Defense through a series of cutouts and a patchwork of shell companies.

"Phantom soldiers," the man had said, "untraceable assets the government can use to conduct operations where we have no official presence."

But even though Popov was technically no longer in the military, when he stopped in front of his boss, he found himself snapping automatically to attention.

"For fuck's sake, Ghost," Yutkin said, using the call sign he'd carried over from his days in the GRU, "how many times am I going to have to tell you to knock that crap off?"

"At least once more, boss," Popov said.

"And where is that shitbird sergeant of yours going?" he asked, nodding to Pavel's wide back.

"We shot up most of our ammo, sir," he said. "Out of frags, too."

"Ammo?" Yutkin demanded. "What makes you think I didn't bring you out of the bush to send you home?"

"Hard to get home in that piece of shit," he said, nodding

toward the sterile Russian transport being fueled on the far side of the tarmac.

"You always were a clever son of a bitch," the colonel said.

"Am I wrong, sir?"

"No, you're perceptive as usual," Yutkin said, pulling a manila folder from the small of his back. "The tasking came in an hour ago. It's a priority target."

"Another one?" Popov frowned. "What? The boys back at the home office don't think we're busy enough?"

"This came directly from Moscow," the colonel said.

"From Moscow?" Popov asked, suddenly intrigued. "And the target?"

"See for yourself," the colonel said, handing him the dossier.

Popov opened the folder, looked at three photographs paper-clipped to the front, and then turned his attention to the single-spaced operations order. It was a kill order; that much he knew by reading the opening lines, but it was the second section, the one that identified the targets, that caught him off guard.

A Haitian and two Americans? he read. *No, that can't be right.*

He read it twice just to make sure he wasn't mistaken and then looked up, eyes wide in astonishment. "The targets are Americans?"

"It gets better," the colonel said. "Turn to the second page. See where the intelligence came from."

Since joining Wagner, Popov had traveled the globe conducting sanctioned killings at the behest of his government. He'd seen it all, or thought he had, until he flipped the page and saw the letterhead stamped in the center of the document.

"The CIA is authorizing us to kill two of its own?"

"Not only are they authorizing us to kill them," the colonel smiled, "but they've authorized a fifty-thousand-dollar bonus *if* you complete the operation by midnight."

"Who are they?" he asked, turning back to the photo at the front of the folder.

"Rogue agents, traitors . . . it is hard to know with the Americans," the colonel said. "In the end they are all simply targets."

"Of course," he said, closing the folder. "Consider it done."

Sitting in the back of the Antonov, Popov reread the operations order to make sure he wasn't missing anything. On the surface, the mission seemed simple enough. All he and his team had to do was hit a safe house in the city, kill everyone inside, and retrieve a drive from the Haitian in the photo.

But despite the colonel's assurance that the Americans were simply targets, there was something about the blue-eyed man in the photograph that sent the hairs on the back of his neck standing on end.

But what?

Popov didn't know, but looking at the pallet strapped to the cargo floor he was confident they'd brought enough explosives and ammo to offset any threats they might encounter at the target location.

PÉTION-VILLE, HAITI

Hayes stripped out of his filthy assault clothes, shoved them into a trash bag he'd found in the kitchen, and stepped into the shower. He turned on the knob, and the blast of ice-cold water against his skin took his mind off the headache that had been growing since he got off the phone with Poe.

That his handler seemed unwilling to grasp the complexity of the situation here in Port-au-Prince or understand that his poor decisions had made Hayes's job harder than it needed to be was beginning to wear thin.

But what really pissed him off was Poe needing to micro-manage the situation by coming with the team instead of staying in the States where he could respond to any problems that might arise during the extraction.

The hell with it, he thought as he turned off the water. *In a few hours all of this will be someone else's problem.*

Hayes got out of the shower and, after drying off, pulled on an extra pair of olive drab Crye Precision pants and an assault shirt he'd brought with him from the ranch. He stuffed his feet into the same smoky pair of Salomon Speed Assault boots he'd worn at the hotel and, once dressed, headed back to the security room.

The wind had picked up while he was in the shower, and he could hear it moaning across the eaves, see the camera feeds shaking on the monitor. He frowned and, knowing that the wind and the debris could trip the motion sensors, sat down at the desk to recalibrate the sensitivity.

When he was satisfied, Hayes went to the National Weather Service to check on the forecast. Sitting at the desk, he suddenly realized how tired he was, but with Carver and her source tucked away in their rooms and the extraction team still an hour away, sleep would have to wait.

The solution to all your problems is just a pill away, the voice said.

While Hayes had no interest in the narcotics he'd seen in the infirmary, the same couldn't be said about the Dexedrine—the government-issued speed—he'd seen. But before he could make a decision, the web page loaded. The warning above the storm track advising that the tropical storm was intensifying got his full attention.

"Ninety mile per hour winds. Possible landfall in the next few hours," he read. "Well, that's just great."

Leaving the browser open in the corner of the screen, Hayes got to his feet and went to the weapons mounted on the far wall, grabbed a cleaning kit from the top shelf, and carried it back to the workstation.

Spreading the contents out on the workbench, he broke down the MP7 and the pistol with a deft precision born of thousands of repetitions. When they were both disassembled, Hayes opened the bottle of Hoppe's No. 9, the pungent ammonia tang of the bore cleaner quickly filling the room.

He dipped a cleaning patch into the bottle and pushed it through the barrel to remove the carbon. The familiar smell of the solvent put his mind at ease. Weapon cleaning was mindless work, so his thoughts played over the day's events, critiquing the decisions he'd made at both the airport and the hotel.

Before joining Treadstone, Hayes had never considered himself a violent man. He was a soldier, a protector, but even so, taking another man's life had never come easy. That had changed with the behavior mods and neural reprogramming the doctors used to turn him into an unstoppable assassin.

After that, killing became automatic, a reflex like scratching an itch, and with his newfound abilities to kill without remorse or hesitation, Hayes became Treadstone's ultimate weapon. But in their rush to get him out into the field, the doctors failed to notice the glaring flaw in their design. They'd forgotten to give him an off switch.

Hayes was thinking about the damage the oversight had cost him and his family as he began to reassemble the MP7, and by the time he had it back together he was determined that this was his last mission.

No way in hell I'm putting them through this again, he thought.

After everybody you've already burned, replied his inner voice, *all you have to do is figure out how you're gonna pull that little trick off.*

Hayes did his best to ignore the words, so he repeated the process with the FN. He was wiping the gun oil off the pistol when there was a light knock on the door.

"Adam . . . you in there?"

Hayes got to his feet and opened the door to find Carver standing in the hall, her SIG in her right hand, her standard shirt and pants reinforced with a gray body armor vest, complete with small arms protective inserts.

"Everything okay?" he asked, looking down from the vest to the pistol.

"Too wired to sleep," she said. "Then I saw the light and smelled the Hoppe's. Since I'm up I figured I might as well clean this thing."

"Knock yourself out," Hayes said, stepping aside and motioning to the table like a maître d'.

She moved inside, dropped the magazine from the pistol, and ejected the round from the chamber.

"Where'd you get the vest?" Hayes asked as she set to work on her gun in a brisk, professional manner.

"Hanging in the bedroom closet," she explained. "Everyone has them. I even had Toussaint put one on."

Hayes shrugged. "Better safe than sorry, I guess."

Carver took the opportunity to glance over at Hayes. "I was a little ragged earlier," she said. "I want to apologize for that and thank you for saving our asses."

"I've been there," he said, passing her the bottle of

Hoppe's. "No apologies needed. Good news is that the team is on their way."

"Yeah?" she replied, her tone mixing relief and skepticism. She looked up from the pistol. "What happens now?"

"They get here, I get bitched out by my boss and then you, me, and Toussaint get the hell out of Port-au-Prince."

There was a pause while she cleaned her gun, but he could tell something was on her mind.

"You think it's gonna be that easy, huh?" she finally said softly.

"The hard part's over," he maintained.

The young woman cocked her head. "I wish I was as sure as you seem to be." She glanced at him. "Know the phrase 'maybe a little too easy'?"

Hayes got to his feet as if she had somehow just corroborated a concern he had been ignoring. And even though he wasn't planning on doing any more fighting, he carried his empty magazines over to the arms locker and began to fill them from the ammo he found inside.

"Well," he grunted, "I wouldn't say that what we've already been through was 'too easy,' would you?"

"No," she agreed, returning her attention to her gun cleaning, "but I can't shake the feeling that there's something we're missing."

Hayes felt his tiredness draining away, as if her words were cleaning his one-track mind. Suddenly Shaw and Poe's behavior started taking on extra shadows.

"What do you mean?" he asked quietly.

She put her gun down on the desk and shifted in the chair to look directly at him. "The reason I was sent down here was to get rid of me," she explained. She shook her head at his concerned expression. "Not kill me, but bury me someplace I couldn't bother them with my suggestions to do better. Do better? Hell, just do their jobs at all. You know what they called me?"

"Ball buster," Hayes guessed with a grim grin.

"I wish," she replied. "Cock Carver."

"To your face?" Hayes asked.

The woman grimaced slightly. "Not at first. But, eventually, yeah. They just wanted to play their ego and power games the way they always had without someone calling them on their shit. Their huge, stinking, growing piles of shit. Suddenly, overnight, I'm here, standing out like a sore thumb.

"So, I figured that if they aren't going to play by the rules, neither am I. The only way for someone like me to get ahead is to forget about the book, and do what needs to be done."

Hayes sympathized with her, but still couldn't focus on what was now bothering him about the setup, too. "How does being here change anything?" he asked.

Carver leaned in, her elbows on her knees. It was as if she had been waiting for months to tell somebody her suspicions. "I'm down here for just months, and I've already made more contacts, and done more, than the entire office has done for years. The poor people here have been waiting for somebody, anybody, to . . . to . . ."

"Help them?" Hayes suggested.

"Not even help them," she replied. "Just to take them seriously, for God's sake. So now I, alone, have uncovered an international scandal, and everybody around us seems to be . . ."

Before she could finish, Hayes got a text.

"Hold that thought," he told her, reading the message. When he looked back up at her his face bore a thin smile.

"Is that the extraction team?" she asked.

"Yeah, they're five minutes out," he said, slamming a magazine into the butt of the pistol and racking a round into the chamber.

The spell broken, Carver got back to business. "I'd better go wake up Toussaint," she said.

"Do me a favor," Hayes replied, the news dissipating his concerns. He returned the pistol to its holster, looking forward to the end of this little adventure. "I've got a feeling my handler is going to be a little tuned up."

"Because of what happened at the hotel?" she asked.

"No," Hayes said. "It's a personal thing, between me and him, but if you could stay upstairs with Toussaint until I come and get you it would really help out."

"No problem," she said, grabbing the SIG and heading for the stairs.

With Carver gone, Hayes turned his attention to the monitor and when he saw the lead Suburban pull up at the gate, he disabled the motion sensors. When both vehicles had pulled through, he rearmed the sensors, double-checked the magnetic lock on the front gate, and then, with nothing left to do, stepped out of the security room and headed down the hall.

Hayes could hear the extraction team out in the garage, loud as a band of Vikings, joking and trading insults. But the instant they stepped into the kitchen and saw him standing there they went silent, their hands moving reflexively to the grips of the assault rifles hanging around their necks.

The first few minutes of their arrival were filled with the usual posturing and butt-sniffing that came with the job, the men spreading out around the kitchen, feeling Hayes out to see if he was truly a member of the tribe.

It was a ritual as old as war itself, and he dutifully played his part, answering their questions and waiting for Poe to finish up whatever he was doing out in the garage.

"Can't remember seeing you around the office," said a broad-shouldered bearded man who'd introduced himself as Tex. "You work for the DIA, bro?"

"I'm a consultant," Hayes answered. "They brought me in for this one job."

"According to Poe, you worked with Director Shaw at Treadstone," a shorter, but equally muscular man said. "That true?"

The fact that Poe had talked about Treadstone caught him off guard, but he was quick to recover. "I guess that depends on your security clearance," he grinned.

Before the man could reply, Poe stepped into the kitchen and the room went quiet.

"I've got to tell you, Hayes," he said, shoving his phone into his back pocket, "until we pulled up to the gate, I wasn't sure if this place would still be standing when we got here."

"Funny," he said. "You about ready to get this show on the road?"

"Why, you got someplace you need to be?" Poe said with a humorless grin.

"Yeah," Hayes said, "actually, I do."

"Well, unfortunately," his handler said, "until this weather clears, we aren't going anywhere."

"You afraid of a little wind, Poe?" he asked.

"Nope, just don't see the need in taking the risk when we can just stay here," the man smiled.

"You want to stay, then stay," Hayes said. "Just let me get my stuff and I'll be out of your hair."

"Where the hell do you think you're going?" Poe demanded as Hayes turned to leave the kitchen.

"I did my job," Hayes said without bothering to turn around. "Now I'm going home."

SAINT-GERARD, HAITI

F elix Pasquette was the last to arrive at Hôtel Oloffson. He stepped out of the BMW and started up the stairs, his dark eyes dancing with anger. He'd known when he reached out to Chérizier what he was getting. The man was a blunt instrument. A rabid dog that most of his subordinates felt should have been put down years ago.

But Pasquette allowed him to run free because with the PNH unable to keep the peace, Chérizier brought a semblance of order to the otherwise unlawful streets. He also knew how to follow directions, which was the reason Pasquette had decided to use him to hunt down Toussaint and the Americans, but striding up the steps of the hotel, it was obvious that he'd made a mistake.

He ducked through the hole smashed through the front of the building and stepped into the entryway, where he found the newly promoted Inspector Bernard standing over the arc of the dead men scattered across the black and white tile.

"That fucking idiot Barbeque did all of *this*?" Pasquette asked, taking in the blood-splattered walls and the splayed bodies.

"No, sir," Inspector Bernard said.

"Then who?" he demanded.

Instead of answering, Bernard stepped out of the way and pointed to the mangled SUV embedded in the far wall.

"What about it?" he asked.

"You don't recognize it, sir?"

Pasquette frowned, annoyed at himself for not seeing the connection, and stepped over. He took his time studying the vehicle, taking in scorch marks on the back bumper and the shattered back glass before moving around to the driver's side.

He did not understand what the man was talking about until he looked through the window and saw the olive drab backpack sitting in the passenger's seat. Then it clicked, and he reached into his pocket to pull out the picture Carpenter had emailed him.

He unfolded the sheet of paper and quickly compared the SUV and backpack the man was wearing in the photo to what was in front of him. Then he looked up at Bernard.

"One man did all of this?" he asked incredulously.

"Yes, sir."

"That's impossible," he said.

"We have it on tape," Bernard said, pointing to the camera mounted in the corner of the ceiling.

Pasquette was about tell the man to show it to him when his driver stepped in. "Excuse me, sir."

"What is it?" He demanded.

"The American," his driver said, handing him the phone.

He nodded and took the phone. "Yes?"

"Where the hell have you been?" Carpenter demanded. "I've been trying to call you for the last hour."

"There was a situation that required my attention."

"You tried to go after him, didn't you? Even after I sent you the file and told you how dangerous he was."

"I can promise you that it was not intentional," Pasquette said.

"Forget it. I reached out to our partners, and they are sending help."

"Help?" Pasquette asked. "What kind of help?"

"Professionals—the first team will be there by midnight."

"You decided to send more foreigners without consulting me?" he asked. "I told you that I could handle—"

"Do you think I would have put my neck out and called them if I had even the *slightest* confidence in you or anyone else on that rat-fuck island of yours?" Carpenter demanded.

The condescension and raw arrogance in the American's words hit like a punch to his gut, and Pasquette recoiled from the phone, a rush of anger and loathing toward the man on the other end of the line crashing over him like a breaker.

That the United States considered Pasquette's country just another "third world shithole" was nothing new. Ever since the first American invasion in 1915, through sending covert CIA teams in 1986, and the second invasion in 1994, Washington's belief that Haiti was incapable of handling its own affairs had been well documented.

You fucking Americans, he thought. *So arrogant. So condescending. So determined to pull our strings.*

"Pasquette, are you listening to me?" Carpenter yelled.

"I am here," he said when he trusted himself to speak again.

"Good," Carpenter said. "The first team is thirty minutes out—"

"But my men are still searching for the safe house."

"I've got that covered," Carpenter said.

"How?" the Haitian asked.

"I figured you were going to screw up, so I bought some insurance," he said. "Cost me fifty grand, but I managed to get a man on the inside."

"A mole?" Pasquette asked.

"Something like that," Carpenter said. "Now, if you're done playing twenty questions, I need you and your men at the airport."

Twenty minutes later, the Antonov AN-12 touched down in Port-au-Prince. While the pilots taxied to the hangar, Maxim Popov tore the Velcro-backed Russian flag from the sleeve of his fatigues and dropped it, and his ID card, into the airsickness bag the loadmaster had given him.

He checked the rest of his pockets to make sure he wasn't carrying anything that could identify him, and then leaned over to his second-in-command. "Make sure you check them this time, Pavel!" he yelled over the roar of the engines. "We don't need a repeat of Syria."

The bulky NCO flashed him a smile, dropped his own flag and ID card into the bag, and got to his feet. "All right, you sons of bitches," he bellowed, "you know the drill!"

When the men were sterile, the bag was given to the load-master and the men filed past the weapons pallet, grabbing the extra guns and munitions they'd brought for the task at hand. Popov was the last one off the aircraft and, after a quick check to make sure nothing had been left behind, grabbed a GM-94 pump-action grenade launcher and a bandolier of thermobaric grenades from the pallet.

He followed his men down the ramp and across the tarmac where a squad of Haitians in jungle fatigues waited next to a pair of LT-79 TAG armored cars. "Who is in charge?" he asked in French.

A man in a black suit stepped out from the shadows, the orange glow of the Cohiba Lancero between his lips illuminating the scar that crisscrossed his face. "I am."

"Do you have the target information?"

"A full workup, as promised," he said, handing over a stack of satellite imagery.

"Then let's go kill some Americans," Popov said.

PÉTION-VILLE, HAITI

Hayes had no idea how he was going to get home, and honestly, he didn't care. All he knew for sure was that if he didn't get out of the safe house soon, there was a very real chance that he was going to put Poe's head through a wall.

Cursing his handler under his breath, Hayes was almost to the security room when Carver came down the hall. "So that's it, you're just going to leave?"

"I thought you were going to wait upstairs," he said.

"And I thought *you* were going to make sure we got home."

"Listen, I—"

But Carver wasn't having it.

"No, *you* listen!" she snapped. "I'm sick of this shit. Sick of men running for the door every time someone steps on their fragile egos."

There was a snort from the kitchen, and he turned to find Poe grinning at him from the doorway. "Looks like you got a real wildcat on your hands," he said.

"And who the hell asked you?" Carver asked.

The question elicited a howl of laughter from the rest of the extraction team and this time it was Poe's face that went red. "Fuck you. I'm not gonna take any lip off you, Little Miss Fuck-up," he said, starting toward her.

"What the hell did you call me?" she asked, hands curling into claws.

"You heard me," Poe said.

"Get out of my way, Hayes," she said.

If Carver's career hadn't already been in the shitter, he might have refused, or at least tried to talk her out of it, but considering all that had transpired since he'd been on the ground, Hayes was confident that her future with the DIA was pretty much nonexistent. With his decision made, Hayes shrugged and stepped to the side.

"You better think about this," Poe said.

"Oh, I am," Carver replied.

The blow shot out like a python directly from her shoulder, taking all her considerable pent-up energy with it. Poe's head snapped back as she split the handler's lips with the heel of her right hand. The others let out surprised and impressed noises.

"I was going to go for your balls," she said reasonably, "but, what with this audience, I knew the only thing you macho men understand is a punch to the mouth."

Poe looked at the blood on his hand, his eyes flashed, and his angry gaze snapped onto Carver's face like a laser sight. But rather than be intimidated, she took a step toward Poe, before Hayes grabbed her in a bear hug from behind.

"All right, champ," he said, lifting her off her kicking feet. "I think you made your point."

To his surprise, Carver then relaxed, turning her head until her lips were close to his ear.

"Something's wrong," she warned softly as he carried her back to the security room and dumped her on the couch.

Hayes was trying to kick the door closed behind them but Poe came barging in, while Tex and a second man did their best to hold him back.

"You're fucking finished!" he yelled, blood spraying from his busted lip. "Both of you are fucking done!"

"Tex, get this asshole out of here," Hayes said.

"Dude, I'm trying."

The hell with this, he thought, moving to shove the man out into the hall when a new hell descended.

24

PÉTION-VILLE, HAITI

The lead APC had raced south on the Route de Delmas, the road clear all the way to the target building thanks to the PNC units who'd been sent ahead to block traffic. In the back of the armored vehicle, Maxim Popov and the rest of the team had studied the satellite imagery of the target area and went over the plan.

The men had assaulted and cleared enough buildings in Syria that they could do it in their sleep, and they all knew that the success or failure of the assault relied on their ability to strike fast, strike hard, and kill everyone in their path. However, they were used to having a second fire team backing them up, and, at the moment, their only backup was the contingent of ANI paramilitary officers riding in the other vehicle.

His men had made no attempt to hide the fact that they were not happy to be working with the tactically inferior Haitians.

"What happens if those bastards get amped up and start slinging lead our way?" one of the men had asked.

As far as operation went, Popov had done his best to keep it as simple as possible and had already instructed them that there wasn't anything overly complicated about what was about to happen.

"We're going to keep this easy," he said pointing to the imagery. "The driver breaches the gate and stops. We come in behind. The initial rally point is this tree."

"Where are you putting those Haitian bastards?" Pavel had asked.

"They are going to be on our right flank with Baben and the PKM."

"It's a risk," Pavel had spat. "Those bastards know not to shoot anyone wearing green, right, boss?"

"With any luck, yes, but be prepared." While Popov wished he'd brought another squad with him, he knew that he was going to have to work with what he had. "You know your jobs."

"Two vehicles just pulled up," the ANI watcher advised over the radio.

"We will give them a moment to get settled," Popov said, "then I will stand behind the tree with the assault team while the breachers move to their objective and press their charges to the wall."

The breachers had worked in silence, and, in a matter of seconds, had completed their assignment—inserting the blasting caps—and headed back to the assault team. To Popov's eyes, it had been fast and sexy, but watching the roof-mounted camera swinging toward their position, he knew that it hadn't gone unnoticed.

Any second now, he thought.

The charges blew with a wink of orange flame and then the roar of the explosives came bouncing down the hill, setting off every car alarm within a quarter mile. Before the echo died away, the assault team was moving back to the breach.

Pavel yanked the pin off a concussion grenade and flung it through the cleanly cut hole that had been blasted through the wall.

While the number one and two men prepared to enter the structure, Ivan came over the radio and advised that he had movement at the front door.

That the men would actually come out of the safe house and try to fight them in the open was idiotic. In fact, it was so stupid that the team hadn't even briefed the possibility. Turning to his right, Popov saw three figures burst from the doorway.

This is going to be easier than I'd ever imagined, Popov thought, then centered his aiming laser on the chest of his closest target. He let the man take another step and then fired, three quick shots to the chest that sent the man stumbling backward.

"Man down!" a voice yelled in English, the rifle on his shoulder spitting lead while the second man tried to drag their fallen comrade to safety.

But they hadn't made it more than a couple of yards when Baben opened up with the PKM, the controlled-burst 7.62x54 millimeter putting all three of the men down for the count.

"Clear," he said.

"Nice shooting," Popov said. "Stay on plan. We'll be back home before morning."

PÉTION-VILLE, HAITI

Moments before, inside the no-longer-safe safe house, the monitor had flashed to life and the perimeter intrusion alarm began blaring from the speakers.

"What the hell is that?" Tex asked.

"We've got a breach," Hayes said, grabbing the joystick on the desk. With it, he panned the Axis P54 dome cameras across the front lawn. With their internal infrared illuminators, the cameras were capable of working during the day and at night, but with the wind blowing the rain directly across their clear plastic protective domes, the usually clear feed looked like something from a Picasso painting.

"Can't see shit," Poe said. "Going to have to go outside."

"Hold on, we've got thermal on the roof," Hayes said, transitioning to the Axis Q8752 bispectral camera.

But by the time the feed came up and Hayes saw the two APCs in the yard, as well as the breachers slapping wall charges to the north side of the building, it was too late. The men were already at the door, and all he had time to do was tell Carver to get down, step out into the hall, and shout a warning.

The wall exploded, a rush of hot gas and shattered concrete catching Hayes full in the chest. That blew him back into the room, bounced him off the doorframe, and dropped him to his knees.

Then everything went black.

It was the pain that brought him back, the tightness in his chest, and the metallic drip of blood down the back of his throat. Hayes sat up, a lightning bolt of pain in his side hinting of a cracked rib.

What the hell?

Then it came rushing back, the two men on the camera, the explosion. *Shit.*

Pushing the pain away, he grunted to his feet. The effort sent the world spinning before his eyes. He braced himself against the doorframe to keep from falling, his ears ringing from the roar of the explosion, and his lungs burning from the caustic choke of the plastic explosives.

Where the hell is Carver?

He stepped out into the hall and opened his mouth to call her, but then a figure in dusty green body armor stepped through the breach, his red aiming laser cutting through the smoke.

At the sight of the figure the pain vanished, and Hayes was

moving, pushing off the wall, throwing himself through the open door a split second before the man opened up.

The shooter fired on full auto, the bullets slapping into the wall, spraying Hayes with bits of masonry dust as he rolled out of the line of fire. He came up in a crouch, the FN in his right hand, the red dot centered on the man's chest.

He fired, two quick shots center mass, the bullets slamming into the man's body armor, staggering him backward, earning Hayes enough time for the kill shot.

The 124-gram hollow point hit the man in the center of the forehead and snapped his head back. He dropped, but not before the bullets sent the contents of his skull spattering across the face of the man following him through the breach. The assaulter staggered inside, left hand swiping at his face, trying to clear the gore from his night vision, when Hayes put a bullet through the side of his skull.

"Carver!" he yelled.

"Here!"

Hayes rushed back into the security room and found her under the workbench, shell-shocked and covered in grit, but otherwise unharmed. "Can you walk?"

"Yeah."

He helped her to her feet, picked up an MP7 lying on the floor, and slapped it into her hands.

"What's the play?" she asked.

With the roaring in his ears beginning to recede he could discern the firefight taking place outside. They could both hear the suppressed *thwacks* of the extraction team's M4s, and the louder, more distinctive counterfire of the assaulters' heavier AKs.

For most people there was no discernible order to the gunfire. For them, there was no way to tell where one shot began and the other ended. But to Hayes it was as clear as any conversation, and he knew from the volume of incoming fire that they were fighting a losing battle.

"Get Toussaint," he ordered.

"What about you?"

"I'm right behind you," he said, grabbing his plate carrier from the floor and strapping it over his chest.

She ducked out of the room, and he grabbed a green duffel bag from the shelf by the wall, dumped the contents onto the floor, and went to the weapons locker. He opened the door and snatched an HK416 from the shelf, turned on the EOTech holographic sight mounted to the rail, and slammed a magazine home.

As Hayes chambered a round and studied the weapons inside the locker, a plan began to form in his mind. That they were outgunned was obvious, but he hoped that the extraction team would be able to hold off their attackers long enough for him to get Carver and Toussaint away.

But with the defenders' fire steadily tapering off, he knew it wasn't going to happen. Which meant the only way any of them were getting out of there alive was if he created a distraction.

Grabbing a green duffel bag from the top shelf, Hayes shoved in a shotgun, a second HK, and one of the pairs of night vision goggles he found inside. Those would be for Carver, which left one pair of night vision, the HK he had around his neck, and the M320 standalone forty-millimeter grenade launcher for him to play with.

It wasn't much, but Hayes had worked with less, and after throwing a few cases of ammo and grenades into the duffel, he dragged it all out into the hall.

"Help me with this," he said as Toussaint and Carver came bounding down the stairs.

Together they dragged the duffel into the garage and flung it into the back of one of the up-armored Suburbans.

"Please say you've got a plan," she grunted.

"I do, but you're not going to like it," he answered as he pushed her toward the driver side door.

"Try me."

"The only way we are getting through that," he said pointing toward the gunfire outside, "is if I can draw their fire."

"You're nuts."

"Yup," he shrugged, "but unless you want to do it, I think we're all out of options."

"I've already had to leave someone here," she said. "I won't do it again."

"Well, that's good to know, because I sure as hell don't plan on dying here," Hayes said. "Just keep your radio on and I'll tell you where to pick me up, okay?"

Then he was gone, moving back into the house.

Hayes donned the pair of PVS-23s and eased out the back door, the HK up and ready to fire. He scanned the area and when he was sure it was clear, slipped around the south side of the safe house.

"Radio check," he whispered into the throat mike.

"Loud and clear."

"Go ahead and start the engine, but do not leave until I give you the signal."

"Roger that," Carver said.

By the time Hayes made it around the side of the safe house, the firefight was all but over. When he peered out, he could see a squad of what looked like Haitian soldiers high-fiving each other.

But he wasn't concerned about the Haitians as much as he was the men in the green body armor. He could see three of them left, two near the tree in the center and one on the flank with what looked like a PKM machine gun.

Up until that moment, Hayes wasn't exactly sure how he was going to pull off his so-called plan, but as he studied the scene and the post-firefight catharsis of the Haitians, it reminded him of the few times in Afghanistan his Special Forces A-team had partnered up with locals.

For the most part these joint operations consisted of Hayes and his men doing the fighting, while the Afghans hung back and smoked dope. During these missions they were hard-pressed to get their allies to fire a single round even if their targets were standing in the open.

But when those same Afghans found themselves on the wrong side of a Taliban ambush, they'd flip their AKs to full auto and spray down anything that even looked like a target. It was "pray and spray" at its finest, and Hayes knew if he could get the Haitians to start slinging lead, he might just be able to pull this off.

Knowing that he needed to get the heavy machine gun out of the fight first, Hayes loaded one of the forty-millimeter high-explosive grenades into the breech of the launcher and studied the scene. He guessed it was thirty yards to the target, and while that was an easy shot with a rifle, to get a grenade onto target required Hayes to point the stubby barrel up toward the trees.

He studied the limbs through the sight, not sure if he should take the shot, when the men in the green armor got to their feet and slipped toward the house.

You only live once, the voice said.

Hayes ignored it and keyed up on the radio. "Here comes your signal."

Then he pulled the trigger.

The forty-millimeter grenade left the barrel with a barely audible *thoop,* and while the sound was significantly quieter than the suppressed rifles the extraction team had been using, it was distinctive enough to send the men diving to the ground.

The Haitians, on the other hand, were too busy playing grab ass to notice. For them, the first hint of danger was the dull smack of the grenade ricocheting off a tree limb— followed a split second later by the explosion of razor-sharp shrapnel.

The blast killed two of the Haitians instantly, and before their bodies hit the ground, Hayes had a second grenade arcing after the first. This time his aim was dead-on and when the forty-millimeter grenade exploded, it took out both the PKM and the gunner.

At first the Haitians just stood there, frozen by the suddenness of the destruction, but then the Suburban came blasting out of the garage, its steel bumper peeling back the reinforced door like a tin can.

One of the men in green body armor leapt to his feet and leveled his rifle at the retreating SUV, managing to get off a few shots before Hayes had the HK on target. He fired three shots into the man's back, the 5.56 hollow points hitting like a sledgehammer, shoving the man forward.

He fired another burst at the man still on the ground, and then he was running. Sprinting across the lawn, a smile spread across his face when he heard the banshee scream of an RPG from one of the armored cars.

Hayes cut hard to the left, trying to get out of the line of fire, already knowing it was too late. One second, he was on his feet, and in the next instant he was skipping across the grass like a stone.

He tumbled to a halt next to the lead APC and rolled behind the wheel—away from the bullets the remaining assaulter was sending his way.

"Okay," he panted. "That . . . one . . . hurt."

He rolled onto his back, sweat stinging his eyes as he adjusted the night vision. He could see the hole in the fence the APC had made and the street beyond was not even ten yards away, but with the clanging of the bullets from whoever was shooting at him from the other APC against the rear armor, and the rounds of the remaining assaulter slapping against the side, it might as well have been a mile.

I'm not dying here.

Hayes reached to the front of his kit, found the last grenade, and tugged it free. He held it in front of his face and eyed the letters stenciled on the front of the canister. It instantly elicited a memory Hayes would never forget.

"This is a Number 80 MK 1 grenade," the instructor had told him, his southern accent thick as molasses. "It contains eleven ounces of white phosphorus—or Willie Pete. Now Ol'

Willie is what you call a pyrophoric agent, which means as long as he stays inside this here can, you've got nothin' to worry about. But give him a little oxygen"—the instructor had pulled the pin and hurled it inside a car—"and he'll go from zero to five thousand degrees in less than sixty seconds."

Hayes had watched the white phosphorus burn the Ford down to the wheels and swore never to be close to an MK 1 when it exploded.

But that was then and this was *right now,* so Hayes knew the only way he was getting out of here alive was if he used the smoke from the white phosphorus to cover his withdrawal.

"You only live once," he agreed with himself before ripping the pin free.

Hayes lobbed the grenade toward the second APC, heard the screams and felt the heat when it detonated, but stayed down until he saw the billowing white smoke come cresting over his own vehicle.

"I'm coming through the breach in thirty seconds," he said over the radio.

But as he got to his feet and took off toward the hole in the fence, the wind shifted, and the smoke came coiling around him. The effect was immediate: The scalding pain in his lungs and blinding burn in his eyes threatened to overwhelm him. But Hayes knew it was either keep moving or die.

He wiped his face on his shirt, picked himself up, and ran. Ignoring the pain in his body and the crack of the bullets over his head, he kept moving. The only thing that mattered was getting to the street.

He stumbled off the curb and dropped to a knee, not sure

if he could go any farther, when the Suburban screeched to a halt. Carver didn't even manage to get the words "get in" out of her mouth before he had all but vaulted into the passenger's seat.

Four things happened at once. Carver spun the steering wheel with one hand, stomped on the accelerator with her right foot, Hayes slammed the door shut, and a man in green body armor appeared from the white smoke clouds like an avenging demon—aiming his PKM right between Hayes's eyes.

Carver let out a screech as Hayes jerked the wheel in the man's direction and let all six thousand pounds of the Suburban lurch at the green armor. The man in the green armor managed to get one shot off as he tried diving out of the way, but the bullet screeched off the vehicle's ceiling as its left bumper caught the green armor's side. The resulting thump was gratifying, as was the roar of tires when Carver wrenched back control of the steering wheel, and aimed the Suburban back toward the street.

But just as Carver was ready to cheer or let out a sigh of relief, Hayes slammed his left foot between hers, mashing the brake to the floorboards as he also ratcheted up the emergency brake. The Suburban let out an agonized howl as it came to an unwilling, sliding halt. Both Carver and Toussaint grunted as they jerked forward, but the woman didn't leave it at that.

"Hayes," she howled, "what the f—"

He cut her off. "Be right back," he snapped, already halfway out the passenger door.

"F-f-fuck!" Carver shouted after him.

But he was already running back to the twisted heap of the green-armored man writhing on the ground.

Seeing him coming, the man tried to reach for his rifle, but the grotesque twist of his arm left it useless.

"That's a nasty compound fracture," Hayes commented quickly, bending over the man while unsnapping his radio pouch on the front of his vest. "I sure hope they've got orthopedic surgeons wherever the hell you're from."

"*Poshel . . . na . . . k-khuy,*" the man gasped in Russian. *Fuck you.*

Hayes paused in surprise as he pulled the radio free and stood up, but with more figures bounding from the open garage and starting across the lawn, there was no time for any additional niceties or interrogations.

"Sorry, comrade," he said, tugging the FN from his holster. "Nothing personal."

The man opened his mouth to speak, but before he had a chance, Hayes put a bullet through his forehead and ran back to the Suburban.

Shoving the radio he'd taken off the dead man into the cupholder, he wasn't even entirely in his seat before Carver stomped on the gas, sending him deep into the cushioning, slamming the passenger door closed via acceleration, and leaving the safe house flickering like a tiki torch in the acrid, smoky night.

PÉTION-VILLE, HAITI

Hayes's stolen radio bore fruit within seconds.

"They are coming down the hill," a voice said from the cupholder. "Cut them off."

The words were bad enough, but the fact that they were in English rather than Russian or Haitian Creole was even more disquieting.

Carver took the first corner, managing to keep all four wheels on the road.

"Head east to Route Nationale 8," Hayes instructed.

"What the hell for?" Carver all but snarled.

"That's the road to Pedernales where the bird is waiting to get us the hell out of here!" he barked back.

"What?" she exclaimed, turning the corner. "After all this, you still think . . . ?"

But at that moment any directions were rendered moot when they saw a pair of armored cars pulled across the road some fifty yards ahead—their searchlights beaming through the windshield impossibly bright.

"Shit," Carver spat. "Can this thing get through?"

"They've got a damn DShK mounted to the top of one of the vehicles . . ." Hayes started to explain, but before he could finish, one of the armored cars opened fire, spitting a line of fifty-caliber armor-piercing rounds at the Suburban.

"Heads down!" Hayes barked, as Carver spun the SUV back the way they had come.

A moment later the second gunner opened up with his DShK, its bullets slamming into the back of the SUV. The rear windshield exploded, sending a shower of safety glass cascading over Toussaint.

The man yelped and Carver hunkered down in her seat when the bullets came snapping through the cab like a swarm of angry hornets.

"I thought these things had bulletproof glass!" Carver seethed as she tried to push the accelerator through the floor-board.

"They do!" Hayes told her as he yanked up his FN, but before he could swing it around and get it aimed—for all the good that would do against armored cars, even ancient Haitian ones—he felt himself being jerked against his door as Carver took a speeding, extremely hard left. This time it was possible two of the tires did leave the ground.

"What are you doing?" Hayes barked. "Trying to get us killed?"

"No!" Carver barked back, her head down, her dark green eyes shining. "I'm trying to keep us alive! What, you think I'm gonna play chicken with armored—"

She never got to finish the statement since the Suburban's extreme contact ultra-high-performance all-season tires hit the curb, sending the SUV plowing into the upscale neighborhood's shrubbery that lined the road.

Hayes thought she'd start crashing through homes any second, but quickly realized she knew this neighborhood far better than he did. He was also relieved that the sounds of the fifty-caliber bullets were no longer echoing in his ears. But that didn't mean they wouldn't start up again any second.

"Lost them!" came a voice from the Russian radio Hayes had taken.

"Secure the commune entrances and exits!" another voice started, before a third, Russian-accented voice intervened.

"Close this channel," it snapped. "Use the PNH channel . . ."

The radio Hayes had killed a maimed man for immediately became a paperweight.

"Was that a Russian voice?" Carver exclaimed. "Why would the Russians invest in a Haitian bank?"

"The Russians'll use any bank that'll launder their shit," Hayes answered, keeping a sharp eye out as the back of hotels, cafes, stores, markets, and houses sped by while Carver navigated a glorified alley parallel to the road they had just left. "Where are we going?" he asked.

"Away from them," she answered as she expertly navigated the big SUV through spaces that should've been scraping the paint from its sides. "Until I can figure out how to get us out of here."

Hayes scanned the area. Outside of the safe house at the top of the hill, Pétion-Ville was crammed with plain rectangular houses painted in bright shades of yellow, pink, blue, and red—as if trying to disguise the fact that they were rudimentary constructions that made retirement villages in Florida look good.

He had a momentary vision of plunging down the hill, smashing through house after house until they exploded out of the gated community. But quickly following was another vision of the armored cars waiting for them, and an image of the Suburban skewered onto any one of the many barbed-wire-wrapped iron spike fences that turned each building in the area into a personal prison.

Hayes took a second from his lookout to stare at Carver's intense profile. "We've got to find a way to Pedernales," he insisted.

"Jesus!" she exclaimed without taking her eyes off the veritable path that now served as their street. "Don't you get it? The fix is in. What makes you think that Pedernales bird is any safer than your so-called safe house?"

Hayes was already achy and angry, but couldn't deny her logic. "But what reason . . ."

"There are probably a million reasons they want me and Hugo dead," Carver interrupted, "and within thirty seconds of meeting your 'friends' back at the safe house, I figured they wanted us dead, too. Why is Poe giving you such a hard time?"

Hayes wanted to say that was always the case with ego-driven warriors, but, thinking back on that very first bait and switch from Key West to Haiti, it sounded hollow even to him.

"Yeah," he finally agreed, then went right back into warrior mode. "Given how this commune is set up, the one place those armored cars are sure to be waiting for us is at the Pétion-Ville gate. Do we have any other options?" he asked. Her answer surprised him.

"Listen for music," she said. "During Carnival, Pétion-Ville has street parades . . ."

"So?" Hayes blurted. "I don't exactly feel like dancing."

"*Estipid,*" Carver cursed, eliciting a high-pitched, nearly hysterical giggle from Toussaint all the way in the back. The woman had used the Haitian Creole word for *stupid.*

By the sound of it, Hayes could guess that, too, but at least Toussaint's laughter was proof that he had survived the hail of high-caliber bees.

"How long do you think two Americans are going to stay unreported in this neighborhood?" she continued. "In any Haitian neighborhood?"

Toussaint's head appeared above the second-row seats, a wan smile on his exhausted face. "Where there are street parades there are costumes and . . ."

The end of his sentence was cut off when Carver suddenly whiplashed the vehicle beside a surprisingly clean mini-dumpster between the back of a small market and the back of a tiny beauty salon. By the time the engine stopped, they could all hear the music of guitars, horns, keyboards, and Haitian Creole singing.

"*Méringue,*" Toussaint breathed in relief.

"*Merengue* is the English word," Carver informed Hayes as she pointed through the buildings. "Right on the other side there."

"So why are we stopping here?"

Carver readjusted her pointing. Hayes followed her finger to see costumes hanging in the closed market's back window, consisting of long white robes with different colored hems, as well as thin, pliant, rubberized plastic, head-covering masks.

"Those are the cheap ones," Carver said, "but that's better to not draw attention."

After disembarking, Carver and Toussaint stood by the back of the market, staring at the barred grate screwed around the window.

"Anybody see a wrench, screwdriver, or crowbar?" Carver wondered. "Maybe we could use some tire-changing tool . . ."

She stopped talking when Hayes stepped up and grabbed the bars with both hands, like a jailbird waiting for lunch. "Get ready for an alarm," he suggested.

Toussaint sniffed. "No one has answered an alarm in Haiti for years," he said sadly. He hadn't even finished the comment when Hayes tore the bars off the window as if snapping strands of salt-water taffy, the four foundational screws tearing from the brick wall as if it were made of chalk.

Within minutes, the three stood at the mouth of a path facing Pétion-Ville's main thoroughfare, the Route de Kenscoff. Every kind of construction, from cheap to standard, lined the streets and hills, but almost every walk and road was filled with a riot of brightly costumed people of every age. The streets were so crowded, in fact, that there was no room for any vehicles, be they bikes, trucks, or armored cars.

Within seconds of appearing there, Hayes was in complete agreement with the woman. They were lost in a sea of colors and crowds. Hayes's kit was under his robe while his blond hair and all-too-noticeable face was hidden under a lion mask. Carver had on a tiger mask, Toussaint a horse.

"One bullet-riddled SUV in exchange for three costumes?" Carver had commented. "Not a bad trade."

"What now?" Hayes wondered, keeping an eye out for any uniforms or green armor, under a costume or not. They stayed close together, and not just for security, but to hear each other over the pulse-pounding, jubilant music.

"Follow me," Carver said, and began leading them southwest.

They hadn't gone two blocks when Hayes spoke again. "Do you know where you're going?"

"Yeah. I started making calls as soon as I got to the safe house," Carver explained.

"On your cell?"

"Of course not," she replied. "That's why I waited until you got us to the safe house. There were bulletproof vests in every closet and encrypted phone lines in every bedroom."

"Who did you call?"

"Contacts," she answered simply. "*Trusted* contacts."

"Like the owner of the hotel?" he asked.

Even through the robes he could see her shrug and could imagine her sardonic expression. "If each favor I call in results in that kind of destruction, I figure I better use them quick."

Hayes couldn't argue the logic of that, so he followed where the woman led as he kept his eyes out for any glints of green armor and anyone who could possibly be ANI or PNH. Thankfully, the costumed crowds remained plentiful, and the music remained loud. Even with the rapidly gathering clouds, the jubilation remained constant.

"When the storm moves in," Hayes said, "are we going to be the only ones left on the street?"

The horse answered. "I have seen Carnival party on in a cyclone. Thankfully, at the moment, that should be the least of our worries."

The trio mingled in with the revelers, swaying to the music as they made it past the wide-open Pétion-Ville gates. Sure enough, the armored cars were there, flanking the road, but at least some of the Haitian occupants were outside the vehicles, smiling, and one even swaying to the music, as the crowds surged by.

The change in the environment and constructions was immediate. As they passed the Haiti El Rancho hostelry and neared the Rue Jose de San Martin, the already poor quality of the buildings began to deteriorate further, as did the quality of the costumes around them. After all, why would any better-costumed Pétion-Ville resident leave the safety of their gated community?

Thankfully the number of revelers stayed large, making it tough, and hopefully impossible, for any Russian or Haitian hunter to pick them out. Just to be on the safe side, Hayes made sure to hunch so he would look to any observer to be the same height as the others. But just as they didn't see him, he wasn't able to make out any sign of them.

"How far now?" Hayes asked. He was all for staying safe, but he was also acutely aware of his personal timetable. *There is nothing on earth that will keep me from Jack's birthday* echoed in the back of his head on a seemingly endless loop.

The tiger mask jerked up toward what looked to Hayes like a pile of billowing debris tucked in a crevasse twenty feet from the side of the dirt road. To his eyes it appeared that a cut-rate hotel had been dumping its torn, stained, unwashed laundry there for years. For a moment he was concerned it might be a dead end, but Carver anticipated his concern.

"That is not a garbage dump," she said. "That's a standard Haitian shantytown."

Carver cautiously pulled back the billowing dirty cloth that served as a door. Standing inside was a little man who looked like he was ready to hack them to death with the jagged strip of metal he gripped in his hand.

She lifted her mask just long enough to let him see her face.

"Jevet?" The instant the man used the Haitian Creole phrase for "green eyes," the tension in the room evaporated.

Jesula Fidelus was short, wearing a ragged T-shirt and shorts matted with dirt and sweat. His features were strong, wide, and so sunken down his face that, to Hayes's eyes, he looked as if he were starting to melt. That's what years of poverty and oppression did to people. But there was no mistaking the strength in his wet, bloodshot eyes.

They all remained masked and hunched in his hovel under a low, rusting, corrugated metal roof, the dirt walls barely held back by obviously scavenged boards—some burnt, all damaged. The stench of nearby waste of every imaginable kind was strong.

As Jesula and Hugo spoke quietly in their native tongue,

Carver leaned toward Hayes. "Can you handle it?" she asked, not without sympathy and understanding.

"I've been in shitholes all over the world," he told her quietly. "But this one probably deserves a special mention."

Carver shook her still-masked head. Even if she felt good about not being seen by the police, assassins, informants, or any Haitian who would equate the sight of white people with distrust, resentment, and anger, the thin mask also lessened the smell a bit.

"This is nothing compared to Cité Soleil, just a few kilometers up the road," she informed him. "That's one of the biggest slums in the world."

Hayes nodded. He already knew three-quarters of the houses in the country didn't have running water, and around ninety percent of the children were diseased, but they were not here for a civics lesson. As he watched the hushed, intense conference between Toussaint and Fidelus, he was grateful for having a few minutes to recuperate, think, and thank heaven that his son didn't live here.

"Jesu is one of the most remarkable people I've met," Carver whispered as she watched the Haitians confer. "Before the earthquake he was a respected mechanic. Apparently, he could fix or rebuild anything. After, he had to collect garbage to survive."

Just as she finished, Toussaint looked in their direction and the squat, wide Haitian man approached them. Close up, Fidelus's body looked like it was made of one solid, coiled muscle.

"Jevet has done my family service," he rumbled in quiet, halting English, "for which we are grateful. The men who are . . ." He stopped, turned to Toussaint, and asked something.

Toussaint said, "Pursuing."

Jesula turned back to Hayes. ". . . pursuing you have also . . ."

Another turn, another question. This time Toussaint said "persecuted."

". . . persecuted my family. So I am at your service. What is it that you need?"

By the time they reached the southeast city area, the storm clouds overhead looked like thick descending curtains. The horse noticed the lion's eyes looking upward, so he sought to pass on the information he had gleaned from fellow pedestrians.

"The storm has been downgraded to a tropical depression," Toussaint told his companions. "If it's not as bad as Hurricane Matthew in 2016, Carnival will continue."

Well, how's that for good news? Hayes's inner voice asked.

Fidelus crouched beside Carver's tigress, wearing a blue, green, and orange jaguar mask above his T-shirt and shorts. They were all crammed into a brightly colored pickup truck along with as many Carnival revelers as could fit in the glorified taxis they called tap taps. If Hayes had wanted to know why the vehicles were called that, he didn't need to once Fidelus tapped the side to let the driver know they wanted off.

Hayes saw many other similarly crowded pickups rolling slowly past the Carnival crowds as he, the tigress, and the horse moved slowly onto a small, dark, crowded plaza consisting of an unfinished building facing a closed hospital, a squat office, and what looked like a municipal building.

Hayes assumed the unfinished construction was Port-au-Prince's idea of a skyscraper. Four stories of the thing were roughly outlined with floors and ceilings, but what seemed to be two extra floors looked like a steel skeletons of girders, poles, and even an innocuous circular stairway.

Hayes turned his attention to the municipal building Fidelus was slowly making his way toward through the milling, masked, and costumed crowd. He could see the French influences of the construction, the white stucco and arched brick reminding him of the faded Polaroids his father had brought back from Saigon. The only lights that were on inside any of the buildings surrounding the plaza came from the municipal one.

Hayes continued to follow Fidelus toward the side of the structure, hunching as low as he could to match the heights of the horse and tigress beside him. He thought Fidelus would check in with a guard or watchman, but all the man did was retrieve a stained, soiled plastic garbage can on wheels from a small, nearly hidden alcove, and roll it toward the building's main entrance.

"The chaos of the city precludes any extra security,"

Carver told him quietly. "The conflict between the ANI and PNH is bad enough, but add that to the growing gang presence and all bets are off. Besides, Carnival is everyone's excuse to play hooky."

She followed the jaguar and horse closely as they entered the building, while Hayes did a quick final check of the costumed figures on the streets for any shape, size, shoes, or green armor that looked familiar.

Since Carver had prepared him, Hayes was both grateful and careful about the empty lobby they stood in. There was one old wooden desk in the center of the white stuccoed back wall, with two standing lamps flanking it, though only one worked, feebly bathing the area in light no stronger than a small campfire. He froze when he heard a voice from upstairs calling out in Haitian Creole. He relaxed when Fidelus responded calmly while moving toward a once grand staircase on the far left that had certainly seen better days.

"'Yes, it's me,'" Toussaint translated. "'The usual tonight?'"

"Wonder what 'the usual' is," Hayes muttered, gripping his pack tightly beneath the robe.

"Probably the usual shit," Carver said. "Literally."

She had explained on the tap tap that Fidelus kept busy doing whatever no one else would. And when it came to Haiti, that would probably be worse than the two Americans could imagine. Or, at least, one of the Americans. They had already seen him picking up any scrap of wood or metal that might be used for anything. There was no broom or mop or shovel anywhere, so Hayes imagined he'd use one of the cast-off shards to clean anything he needed to.

As the lion, tigress, and horse followed the jaguar slowly

up the long stairwell to a dimmer and cavernous second-floor landing, Hayes was tempted to ask whether Fidelus's associate had wondered who the trio accompanying the old man tonight was, but since the associate hadn't even bothered to appear, the point was moot.

"Is he sure Pasquette is here tonight?" he asked instead.

"As sure as he can be," Carver answered. "It's not like his friends have unlimited data plans with the best telecom companies."

"Yet, in this country, his associates might be even better than that," Toussaint whispered to them. "And more dependable, since they respond to the evidence of their own eyes and not tweets."

As they neared the second-floor landing, Hayes did a quick scan. The staircase continued to the left, facing a lone, large, heavy, oval-topped door that used to be white. Now it was streaked with black, brown, and red veins that could have been cuts. The only other thing on the second-floor landing was a grimy, cracked window looking out on one side of the unfinished six-story building across the plaza.

Fidelus stopped at the bottom of the stairs leading to the third floor and gave a curt nod at the door.

"All right," Hayes said quietly to Carver. "Stay with Jesula." Carver seemed about to complain, but Hayes quickly continued. "Protect Toussaint at all costs. I'm going to do a thorough search of the area before I enter, but keep in mind we have no time to waste."

Carver could have argued the points, but decided it best not to. Nodding, she motioned for Toussaint to accompany her, then started following Fidelus up the stairs toward an even darker floor.

Even before they got two steps, Hayes had taken off his lion mask and thrown open the robe. Although it might've been slightly preferable to remain incognito, it was more preferable to have a full line of peripheral vision. In addition, he needed his arms and legs completely free.

Given the emptiness of the area, his thorough search was short and sour. All Hayes had was his FN, low-vis ballistic vest, pair of Alpha gloves, and the element of surprise. He was about to find out if that was enough—if Fidelus's information was correct—and hoped that Carver and Toussaint were safe enough one floor above him.

"Dallys?"

At the sound of the voice, Carver's eyes bulged and her jaw dropped. She spun toward the noise, seeing a silhouette framed in a third-floor window looking out onto a higher, unfinished floor of the construction across the street. But when the shadow moved a step closer, just enough of the dim light from the floor below filled in the contours of his face.

"Chico?" Carver gasped.

Hayes gripped the second-floor door latch and pressed the steel toe of his boot against the bottom. With a strong, steady push on both, the partition shifted. That was enough for him to see that the room was mostly dark, except for a dim blinking light near a long, arched picture window that took up most of the far wall.

Hayes slipped in, his weapon at the ready, and slid the door closed behind him. Since it had no warning lights, the way any American construction site would, the unfinished Haitian building across the way filled the window like a skeleton's smile. Hayes, listening intently, took another step forward. But all he heard was a tiny, rhythmic beep emanating from where he saw the blinking light.

Hayes took another step, and another, until he could see that the light was coming from the other side of a screen on top of a dark desk. Hayes kept moving, peering intently in every corner until he was in a position to see the front of the screen.

On it was a map of Haiti. There was a yellow line from Pétion-Ville to this southeast section of Port-au-Prince.

The line stretched from where he had come from to where he was now. In an instant he realized why.

It was the Russian radio that he had delayed their escape to retrieve. They were tracking him with the Russian radio.

"That guy in Pedernales is ready," Chico Long told Carver, his hand out and his face pleading. "It's like I told you. He'll get us across the border. We can rent a plane."

Carver had her SIG out, up, and pointed between Long's eyes. "Where did you go?" she demanded. Toussaint and Fidelus were behind and equidistant from her on either side, tensely watching and waiting.

"Down to the bar!" he insisted. "I was sitting there, then the whole place came down. I was lucky to get out in one piece!"

It made sense. Carver's mind reeled, and her gun started to lower. "Where have you been?"

"Are you kidding?" he exclaimed. "I was looking everywhere for you. Where have *you* been?" He stepped toward her, waving the questions away. "Never mind, never mind, we got to get out of here!"

"Mesye Hayes, please."

The voice came from behind him.

Well, said his inner voice. *At least you're not already dead, so that's something.*

Hayes breathed deeply as a dim overhead light came on, bathing the large half-moon-shaped room in sickly yellow. Standing behind the entry door, holding a SIG M17 aimed directly at his head, was a man he had never seen. But by his attitude and expression, Hayes thought better of trying a fast draw. Especially when another voice came from the opposite side of the room.

"That is my new second-in-command, Inspector Louis Bernard. Formerly of the PNH, but now seconded to the ANI," said Felix Pasquette as he sauntered toward the desk, letting the silver-plated hilt of his machete reflect the flashing light of the Russian radio tracker. By the look on Bernard's face, Hayes guessed this was the first the inspector had heard of his new promotion. "Mesye Hayes," Pasquette repeated, "please." Only he used the machete tip to motion at Hayes's FN, then at the floor.

Hayes was sure he could take out one or the other, but sadly wasn't sure he could get them both before they either exploded his head or chopped it off. His son's face swam before his eyes as his gun started to shake.

"Slowly," he heard Bernard warn. "Slow-ly . . ."

"Or just drop it," said Pasquette. "If you want to keep your hand."

Haye's fingers opened and the gun fell. Even before it hit the floor, Pasquette came at him, letting out a gleeful cry of triumph, the machete swinging.

"Do you have the flash drive?"

That stopped Carver in her tracks at the top of the third-floor stairs. She waved Toussaint back, giving Fidelus a meaningful glance in the process. Suddenly the "coincidence" of Long's just happening to find her here started stinking worse than Jesula's shantytown.

"Who paid you?" she asked him point-blank, her SIG back up and aimed between his eyes.

"Nobody!" Long said vehemently, his hands out and pleading. "Honestly!"

Carver snorted, the truth appearing in her mind's eye. "I don't believe you, Chico," she spat out. "You took their promise, didn't you? How much? Five thousand? Ten?"

She backed away, motioning for Toussaint and Fidelus to get behind her. The former did. The latter stayed where he was—beside her, his eyes dark, his brow furrowed.

Long managed to keep his composure for a full two seconds before his expression collapsed and he confessed miserably. "Fifty."

Carver's jaw dropped. "Fifty?" she exclaimed. "*Estipid!* You'll never get that money. The middleman will pocket it. You know as well as I do that is Haiti's MO . . ."

The storm's first lightning bolt hit the moment the realization hit Carver. If Chico had been waiting for her up here, who was waiting for Hayes downstairs?

As the sharp crack of the lightning bolt distracted the ANI director, Hayes jumped and rolled, feeling the machete blade go past his shoulder. He came up equidistant between Pasquette and Bernard, his hands open, out, loose, and waiting. He didn't bother checking on the second-in-command. He would only come into play if Hayes got close to defeating the boss.

So that only left him a few options. Hayes started planning for them while hoping that Bernard didn't take it upon himself to execute the American despite his superior's obvious preference to hack him apart personally.

"Ah, yes, you are as good as *Carpenter* says you are, aren't you, Mesye Hayes?" Pasquette gloated, gracefully wielding his flashing machete like a symphony conductor.

At the sound of those three syllables, every question Hayes had as to why things shook down the way they did were answered.

Told you Shaw was lying, said the voice inside. *All the assassination rumors were true.*

Hayes would have loved to pass on a few choice words to himself, but he needed his full concentration as the machete-wielding lunatic got closer and closer, grinning like the maniac he was.

"Oh, you great all-powerful Americans, so much better than us stupid, incompetent Haitians, aren't you?" Pasquette started backing Hayes toward the corner, making it clear that there would be no jumping and rolling this time. "So what shall I send your friend Carpenter first? A finger?"

The blade flashed out, the tip actually tapping the fingernail of Hayes's left pinky despite everything Hayes did to avoid it.

"A hand?"

Pasquette kept coming.

Hayes anticipated that, so just managed to roll his wrist away from the darting, snaking blade. He figured a slice at his neck would be next and prepared to either direct the blade into Bernard behind him, or use an aikido move to windmill the machete back into Pasquette's torso before using him as a shield against the inspector's bullets.

"Or your head!"

The knife sliced, Hayes dodged, and felt the breeze as the blade just missed the back of his neck. Meanwhile his left hand was moving up to lock Pasquette's elbow before directing the blade into Bernard's chest.

That's when the door behind Bernard slammed open and Carver came in shooting.

PORT-AU-PRINCE, HAITI

Her intentions were good, but she made the same mistake he had by reacting to what was in front of her rather than checking all around her. Her shot was perfect, and if Pasquette were not a machete master it would have opened his face like a split lobster. Instead, it collided with his swung blade, bullet shards burning his cheeks and temples, while the rest of the round went whistling into the ceiling.

Carver immediately adjusted her aim as Hayes launched himself toward Bernard, who was also adjusting his aim to the back of the young woman's head. Hayes couldn't stop him, but the tips of his fingers connected with the inspector's gun arm just in time to throw off his balance.

As Carver pulled her trigger for a kill shot, Bernard's bullet slammed into the edge of her ballistic vest near her arm. One millimeter more to the right, and it would've shattered her shoulder. As it was, it threw her second shot from the thickest part of Pasquette's torso into the wall a foot away from him.

Bernard, like the survivor he was, instantly reacted to Hayes's charge. He let Hayes's push spin him all the way around, and he kept turning until he was one step out of the room and had yanked the open door between him and Hayes. For an instant, Hayes considered slamming the door into him, but there were already two more pressing distractions to take into account.

First, the aftermath of Bernard's shot. It may not have ruined Carver's arm, but it numbed—even deadened—it very effectively, and she watched, with growing dismay, as her fingers, against her will, slackened, and her SIG started to drop out of her grip. And second, Hayes watched Pasquette surge toward her, his machete coming down at her skull for a cleaving kill.

Hayes would normally have weighed his priorities, making a split-second decision as to which was the best choice for his survival and the completion of his mission. But all that went out the window when suddenly, in a mental lightning bolt, Dallys Carver suddenly became, in his mind's eye, Annabelle.

As his inner voice roared, Hayes launched himself like an eight-foot-two javelin, directly at the Haitian Intelligence Service director. If he had taken even a second to grab his gun or any other weapon, Carver's head would have already looked like a wishbone after Thanksgiving dinner.

Instead, Hayes slammed into Pasquette the best way he

possibly could have in the circumstances. His tough, thick neck was wedged into the Haitian's upraised machete underarm, so centrifugal force wouldn't allow the blade to come down on his neck or back.

Hayes's arms were locked around the man, his right fist clenched in Pasquette's hair, his left knuckles deep in the man's back, pressing as hard as he could on his left kidney. His jump was so strong that he brought Pasquette completely off the floor.

Carver watched in horror as the two men went irreversibly back, framed in the big window. Her gun hit the floor and skittered away. Hayes and Pasquette slammed into the glass—which cracked, then shattered—and they fell out of the window.

As Hayes and Pasquette fell toward the plaza ground in a shower of both glass and water, the storm reached its zenith. A few die-hard Carnival revelers realized that some of the droplets falling on them could cut skin and slice costumes. The rest were surprised when two men fell onto them.

Luckily for Hayes, several of these people cushioned his fall. Unluckily for him, others did the same for Pasquette. Both men scrambled to their feet at the same time, facing each other in the stinging rain and slashing wind.

Oh, great, said the voice.

Another lightning bolt illuminated the plaza, showing everyone the dangerous standoff. If the glinting silver machete didn't inform them of the situation, the two adversaries' expressions did. Hayes could soon hear the ANI chief's name being whispered in recognition all around him, drifting through the air like locusts.

As if in unspoken understanding, the Carnival crowd began to move away from, as well as encircle, them. Hayes hoped that Carver would shoot Pasquette before the fight could start again, but it was obvious there was no way to get a clear shot under these conditions.

On the second floor, Inspector Bernard ran past Jesula Fidelus as the garbage man moved quickly to the office door. Inside he saw Carver rubbing her shoulder, standing to the left of her fallen SIG, and the man she called Chico standing on the other side, staring bullets at her.

Fidelus's appearance in the doorway distracted Carver for a second, so that was the moment Long took to dive for the gun. Jesula was about to rush forward to help her when Long grabbed it, just before Carver fell on him. Fidelus kept getting closer, but stopped when the SIG started spitting bullets.

Toussaint dove under the desk while Fidelus ducked back outside the door. As Carver got her right hand around Long's gun wrist, her other fingers went for his eyes, while Jesula raced up the third-floor steps to his trash can.

Long screeched as her fingernails threatened to pierce his pupils—the pain and rage powering his flailing kicks and tearing hands. One foot caught Carver in the stomach. The other slammed onto her affected shoulder. Groaning in pain, she spasmed back, her eye fingers releasing, but her wrist fingers remaining tight. The two jerked apart, sending the gun spinning under the desk.

The two ex-partners scrambled to their feet and started to jump toward the desk. They both froze when Toussaint stood, the gun held in his shaking hands. Even so, the trembling barrel was pointed at Chico Long.

Carver smiled and stepped toward the banker with her arm out, but then, to everyone's surprise, Toussaint jerked the barrel toward Carver as well.

"No," he said, his voice shaking. "No, everyone, please, stay back!"

All three jerked in place when they heard the gunshot.

It didn't come from the SIG. It came from outside. The Carnival crowd had recognized Pasquette, and, realizing that they were masked, knew he would not recognize them to exact any retribution no matter what they did. Slowly but surely they began to move in toward him, apparently, as far as Hayes could tell, to risk machete strikes to show him what they thought of him. The American started to move with them, maneuvering to the front of the crowd to use his superior fighting skills to save them any unnecessary pain.

But that was when Bernard showed up at the entrance of the municipal building and got their attention with a shot skyward.

Everyone except Pasquette froze. Pasquette straightened and smirked.

"Everyone except the ugly white man, back away!" Bernard shouted in Haitian Creole, his gun lowering to crowd level, his voice carrying above the wind and rain.

Hayes didn't understand the words the inspector used, but he understood the result. The circle around them widened until only Pasquette and he were in the plaza.

"Director," Bernard said in English, motioning at Hayes with the gun. "Carry on."

Pasquette stood on no ceremony. He charged toward Hayes with glee, his machete raised high. To everyone's surprise, except maybe Carver's, Hayes ran right back at him. Both soldiers knew that extending an inevitable fight will only exhaust the one who retreats. Pasquette had his hatred and ego. Hayes had his training.

Pasquette swung, Hayes stopped, shifted, and moved his body so the blade missed. Then, as Pasquette's slicing continued, Hayes gave him a short, sharp punch in the ear.

He wished he could have made it a killing strike, snapping the temporal process from the zygomatic process bone, which would allow blood to drown the brain, but the rain—now falling almost horizontally in the wind—had thrown off his timing.

Pasquette reeled, stumbling, but also spinning the machete up, down, and around to fend off any attempt to follow up on the punch. He stood tall, one hand on the side of his head, the other pointing the machete directly at Hayes.

"Lucky shot," he sneered as the rain danced on the horizontal blade—playing for the silent crowd of masked, costumed onlookers. "Care to try for another one?"

Hayes moved toward him, his fingers wagging Pasquette forward. "Bring it on," he said. "Let's do it."

Hayes soon regretted his taunt. In his new charge, Pasquette was a changed man. He was now no longer a cat playing with a mouse. He was a panther stalking his prey. The machete now seemed to multiply and intensify into circles of strikes, forcing Hayes to contort, dive, roll, and ultimately take cover behind any column or wall he could find.

But there were precious few of those, and Pasquette continually drove him out from behind them until the best he could do was keep his distance. Through it all the rain poured down on them, but while it made Hayes feel heavier and more tired, it seemed to revitalize Pasquette.

"You are in my country now," he taunted, shadowing Hayes's every move. "That is why I wanted the privilege of ending you."

Hayes began to scan the area for any escape. The audience of Carnival revelers were still everywhere, despite the rain and wind. He might have been able to reach them, but he knew Pasquette wouldn't think twice about hacking any of them to get to him. In fact, he'd probably enjoy it.

"To trap you was so simple," Pasquette taunted. "My Russian guests were so certain you would be easy prey, but after you took them down, I promised to show them how it's done."

Hayes's eyes flicked all over the area. The surviving Russians could have been anywhere, but he could not pick them out from the Carnival crowd.

"Oh, no, don't worry about them," Pasquette called to him expansively. "They cannot have you until I'm finished with you. And then we can all feed your carcass to the panthers!"

That was when Fidelus, still wearing his jaguar Carnival mask, appeared in the broken window on the second floor, above and behind Hayes, and threw a long piece of rended, jagged metal onto the ground six feet in front of him. The garbage man had gotten it from his trash can where it was nestled under all the other junk.

Both antagonists knew the import of the long, sharp piece of steel. Pasquette screeched in rage and charged, swinging, as Hayes jumped forward just in time to grab the metal and parry the blow. The sparks, and the sound of the two weapons smashing together, elicited the first gasping noise the crowd made. Then, in the soaking rain and howling wind, the two men slashed at each other—one with finesse, the other with strength.

Hayes had used blades all his life, but had not been as thoroughly trained in sword fighting at Pasquette obviously was. The ANI director drove onward, slashing, forcing Hayes to retreat and weave. There was a bent, jagged piece on one side of the metal that Hayes hoped to use as some sort of blade catcher that would allow him to try snapping the machete out of Pasquette's hand, but it was too shallow. Every time he managed to catch Pasquette's machete blade in it, Pasquette snapped it out before Hayes could twist his wrists.

The soldier thought he could use sheer power to defeat the man, but Pasquette knew how to channel and redirect the force of Hayes's blows. Even so, that sheer muscle kept Pasquette from doing anything but forcing Hayes backward. He obviously wanted to deflect Hayes's weapon long enough to get in a slice or stab, but Hayes wouldn't let Pasquette's parries move his arms far enough to let the Haitian get in a killing blow.

But Hayes knew it was only a matter of time. He just wasn't skilled enough with the sword to do anything but defend. He thought about treating it like a knife fight, but a teacher in his memories only laughed at him.

The longer weapon wins, his inner voice reminded him. If he started acting like this was a knife fight, Pasquette would turn him into sashimi within a minute. Given how heavy his arms were getting, it wouldn't take much longer to accomplish that result no matter what he did.

Why don't they throw me a gun?

Fidelus, Carver, and Long were all talking to Toussaint up on the second floor—who kept the gun pointing at them with enough certainty that no one had yet attempted to jump him. Long was ready to take advantage of it if the others did, which was why the others didn't.

Fidelus was to Toussaint's right, Carver to his left, and Long in front of him, while the banker stayed behind the desk as if it were the other side of a moat. They all wanted him to give them the gun, but it was obvious he was in shock, and the fear that had been building ever since Carver turned him into a whistleblower, not to mention all the attacks he had survived since then, had finally become overwhelming.

"I just want it to stop," he kept repeating softly in Haitian Creole, tears dripping out of his eyes as the others soothed, pleaded, and lied, depending on their motivations. It was the most macabre, ironic, Haitian standoff any of them had ever experienced.

If Hayes had known, he would have empathized. But all he knew at the moment was that the long bar of twisted iron in his hand was getting heavier every second, the rain that poured over him was stinging his eyes, and the wind deafened him every few seconds.

The only thing he could think of doing that wouldn't sacrifice any innocent, or even guilty, bystanders, was to let Pasquette make him retreat into the unfinished construction on the other side of the plaza, and somehow use it to his advantage.

So Hayes kept backing toward it, while Pasquette kept hacking, slicing, and stabbing at him, seemingly becoming faster and more powerful with every strike of the machete blade. So fast and powerful, in fact, that Hayes didn't dare even look where he was backing up, or else the machete would find its target.

The only thing that was prolonging his life at that point was Pasquette's arrogant ego. He wanted to prove to himself and everyone watching how much better he was than the Russians, the man who had hired the Russians without checking with him first, and the pathetic, hulking American he was making a fool of.

That was fine with the pathetic, hulking American. He knew from the shadows above him, and the fact that the rain was no longer stinging him, that he was under the lip of the construction's first floor. He also knew because, once he had retreated inside, the unfinished floor, walls, and ceiling created howling wind tunnels that buffeted and battered him almost as much as Pasquette's machete did.

Hayes took a last step back. He felt his heel hit something, and then, as hard as he tried not to, he felt his balance shift. To his growing anger, he felt himself falling. His free hand went back, feeling the concrete step before his ass did. But then he fully landed on an unfinished stairwell, his elbow banging on a slab of cement.

It had the same effect on his arm and hand that Bernard's bullet on Carver's ballistic vest had had on hers. To his rage, he heard the piece of metal Fidelus had thrown him clatter behind him.

Then he saw Pasquette's triumphant, practically demonic,

face appear above and in front of him, the machete blade dancing like a buzz saw. It was obvious that the ANI director wanted him to die guessing whether his head would be chopped off or his skull cleaved.

As the sharp, shining, silver blade started to make its final descent, Hayes's vision was filled with Pasquette's derisive, hate-filled face. Then he heard the man's last, hissed words.

"This is for Emerie!"

29

Who the hell is Emerie?

Hayes would have to wait to find out, because that's when another gun went off. Both he and Pasquette stiffened in response. Then Pasquette's face slowly changed. The hate shifted to confusion, then realization, and finally, to resigned acceptance.

It was a shift of expressions Hayes had seen before, especially on the faces of people who had fought all their lives for the wrong reasons. It was as if, somehow, at the end, they knew they deserved such a fate.

Felix Pasquette closed his eyes and dropped between Hayes's legs, his face smashing into a concrete step. As he fell out of Hayes's view, he revealed his new second-in-command,

Louis Bernard, at the open entrance to the new construction's first floor, his SIG 17 pointed right where Pasquette's back, spine, and heart had been.

Now all the Carnival revelers parted as he walked, staring at the ex–Police Nationale d'Haiti officer differently than they had before. Even the masked revelers' postures were different—more reverential, less resentful.

Hayes reached to pick up the fallen machete between his thumb and forefinger, but Bernard stopped him with a flick of his gun barrel.

"I am going to need that for evidence," he said quietly as he kneeled by his fallen superior. His next words were for the corpse more than for Hayes. "Inspector Dorval was my friend. My good friend. Did you know his name was Daniel? I doubt it. It means 'God is my judge.'" His eyes returned to Hayes's face. "And now Felix Pasquette will meet his . . ."

Bernard never finished his sentence because that's when another shot rang out. A sharper, louder, more powerful shot. A shot Hayes recognized the sound of. It was the unmistakable scree of the Russian SVDK rifle, specifically created to go through body armor like a cannonball through cardboard. That weapon's 7N33 cartridge could go through virtually anything for miles. And, by the sound of it, it was right above them.

But neither he nor Bernard were splattered all over the unfinished stairway, so it had to have another target. As Bernard straightened and the crowd started running in all directions, Hayes immediately vaulted off the stairs and looked up across the plaza at the broken window of the municipal building's second story.

As Bernard joined him, Hayes was about to shout, but then realized it was way too late for that. Carver would know as well as he what they were dealing with. Now it was just a matter of deciding what was best to do about it. Before he could, he felt Bernard's hand on his arm. He looked down at the man who had executed Pasquette.

"Was that a gunshot?" Bernard demanded.

"Sniper," Hayes whispered back, then started to run.

Inside Pasquette's lair, Carver stared at Chico Long's corpse, or what was left of it. It was a spectacular work of high-caliber splatter art. The 254-gram projectile's 2,526 feet per second steel core had entered the defense agency's human intelligence junior officer between his first thoracic and seventh cervical vertebra, tearing his head off at the base of his first rib, while splintering his shoulder girdle, snapping his clavicle, and shattering his shoulder blades as if they were made of glass.

Long had just cried out in triumph, holding up the flash drive disguised as a key that someone had promised him fifty thousand dollars to retrieve after betraying his partner and country. He had only gotten his hands on it after Hugo Toussaint had been distracted by Inspector Bernard's shot that, unbeknownst to any of them, had saved Adam Hayes's life.

That's when Long had taken advantage of the distraction, lurched forward, grabbed the barrel of the gun Toussaint held, and viciously jerked it aside to point it at Carver, who was also reacting to her ex-partner's treachery.

As Long had hoped, the attack made Toussaint's muscles contract, and the gun had gone off. Carver saw it coming, too, so had already dropped and twisted as fast as she could, despite her forward momentum. She had felt the bullet whip past her jaw.

As she had hit the floor, Long had had a masterstroke. Rather than take on Fidelus directly, he'd wrenched Toussaint's arms up to jam the gun under the banker's chin, and latched on to the poor man's gun hand in a viselike grip.

"Don't, don't!" he had warned the others as he clawed Toussaint's finger tight around the trigger, while also frenetically shoving his other hand into every one of Toussaint's pockets. "I'll make him kill himself if you get any closer!"

Carver did not doubt him for a second. As Fidelus had shifted to try getting around Long's Toussaint shield, Long had moved in response, always keeping the powerful little garbage man at bay. Knowing better than to provoke her ex-partner, Carver had stayed down, but watched intently for any opening.

So both the young woman and the old man had watched Long's expression shift from disappointment to disappointment as his jabbing fingers had found nothing that felt anything like a flash drive anywhere on Toussaint's body.

But when he had yanked Toussaint's pathetic paper-clip key ring out of the man's pants pocket, he saw the plain, tarnished, tin, slightly-larger-than-usual "key" with the telltale user diagram protocol "fangs" at the tip—which had been a dead giveaway that it was a disguised flash drive.

"Ah!" he had exulted, holding the key upward. But he had

taken a second to celebrate and congratulate himself rather than keep an eye on the others, which had given them the split second to act. They had both leapt onto Long and Toussaint—Fidelus grabbing Long's gun hand, tearing it away from Toussaint's chin, and Carver grabbing his flash-drive-clutching hand.

Long had made one last enraged roar of frustration and desperation, then his neck, not just his throat, had burst open and his upper body had erupted as if a volcano was where his heart should have been.

All three survivors had been thrown back by the concussion, each splattered by Long's blood, guts, and bone. Carver was thrown to the floor near the place where Pasquette had originally hidden. Toussaint was thrown back under the desk, screeching in terror, surprise, and post-stress trauma. Fidelus, on the other hand, had simply hunkered down, then slid backward as if the storm winds were pushing him, before quickly slipping out the lair's door.

Throwing back her blood-splashed head, Carver sucked in her breath and screamed *"Sniper!"* louder than she had ever screamed anything. Then she twisted over onto her face, clawed, crawled, and kicked her way into Pasquette's hiding place, which was either a small closet or a large cabinet.

The cry sent Bernard scurrying so quickly it even took Hayes by surprise. One second he was there beside Hayes, the next he was gone. Hayes would've loved to have the luxury of looking for the man, especially if the inspector had wanted to target any of the survivors, but with that crack of the Russian SVDK, he had more pressing concerns.

As hurriedly as possible, and as carefully as he could,

Hayes scanned the second floor for any sign of where the sniper could be nesting.

Has to be the Russians, Hayes thought as he cautiously proceeded. *They always have a sniper as part of any incursion team.*

Given the speed with which they had to have been assigned to this godforsaken mission, it was most likely a trio. Maybe even one just coming off another assignment. Hayes had already killed one of them back at the safe house, and one of Poe's bozos could have taken out another, but somehow he doubted it.

So most likely there were two left. If the sniper was up there, where was the one who was most likely the point man? And why didn't he, or they, entrap Hayes rather than let Pasquette give in to his ego?

Hayes nodded to himself as he kept edging forward. Had to be a rush job, just like his was. Maybe some commander had something on these guys, or they were just good soldiers given the same song and dance Hayes had been given.

Oh yeah, easy-peasy, in and out, back in a day or two!

Maybe the point man was injured. Hayes doubted that, too. What was much more likely was that he was so sick and tired of all the bullshit he had to swallow that he let the local secret police megalomaniac fall on his ass, while hovering around the edges of this clusterfuck to pick up the pieces.

So maybe, just maybe, Hayes was caught in between two Russians. Hell of a place to be with nothing but a jagged piece of metal.

But Hayes, like them, had little choice. He was certain that the second he stuck his head, or neck, or any part of his body, out onto the street, the next 7N33 sniper cartridge would shatter it. So he carefully studied his environs . . . ignoring the corpse who still lay, facedown, at the bottom of the stairs.

The unfinished building was the architectural equivalent of skin and bones, and cancerous skin and bones at that—the skin being the floor and ceilings, with the bones being the girders that formed a basic box structure. All of them were either rotting, sagging, rusted, leaning, or all the above.

The lone concrete stairs on the first two floors could be considered the spine, and, like the human body, there was only one, going up the center. Despite being chipped, cracked, poorly cemented, and shabbily secured, it would hold a person's weight—at least for now. But, given its condition, there was no telling when it might collapse, bringing much of the floor and ceilings of its immediate area with it.

If Hayes were the sniper, he'd be on the third floor—given some cover by the last completed ceiling, but also above the window where the targets were across the street. Having gotten as much intel as possible given the situation, Hayes considered his limited options.

Try some insane swashbuckling shit to get up to the third floor and surprise the sniper without tripping over the point man, or try a run back into the municipal building and fire back alongside Carver?

Hayes shook his head curtly against the second choice. An FN and SIG against an SVDK? It was a little like setting two slingshots against a cannon. It didn't matter how good he and Carver were. Their guns couldn't turn body armor into Swiss cheese. Their guns didn't come equipped with variable zoom optics that could pinpoint a nose hair at six hundred meters.

No matter how Hayes pictured it, he, Carver, and Toussaint always wound up splattered all over the office walls, the 7N33 rounds going through them like rocket-powered drill bits.

Letting his instincts lead him, Hayes found himself moving as silently as possible back to the stairwell, where he got a surprise. Now, in addition to Pasquette's corpse, he was joined by Jesula Fidelus, who was silently and patiently waiting for him under the lip of the building, still wearing his jaguar mask.

Of course he was. If the sniper had seen the Haitian, he might have decapitated him. But a leftover Carnival celebrant might have been beneath the Russian gunman's notice.

Besides, it was still raining hard, and Hayes could just imagine Fidelus using the sheets of rain like his own personal curtain. Little wonder it was he, and not Carver, who risked making the transit. She wouldn't have gotten one step without being perforated. But then Fidelus raised, and opened, his hands, giving Hayes a piece of Carver's mind.

In the garbage man's palm was a governmental comm set—a relatively old secret service earpiece, the kind a Haitian secret police company would get as a hand-me-down. There was a small receiver station with a tiny microphone built in, and a compact mobile unit for the pocket. Without a word or questioning look, Hayes took both from Fidelus's hand and immediately stuck the earbud into his right aural cavity.

"Let me know when you got this," he heard Carver say quietly. "Let me know when you got this. Let me know when you got this. Let me know when you . . ."

"Got this," Hayes whispered, giving Fidelus a thumbs-up.

Fidelus nodded as Carver immediately continued. "Good. Don't want the shooter to hear you so I'll do the talking. Chico is dead. I think the sniper was aiming for Toussaint but Chico got in the way. This spy ear is just one thing I found in the closet where Pasquette was hiding. Another was a small drone."

Hayes wanted to say "good job." He wanted to inquire into how Toussaint was holding up. There were a lot of things he wanted to say or ask, but any word could be one too many when an SVDK could shoot right through three floors, straight down all the way through an American, and keep going deep into the Haitian ground.

"That's my drone. Can you . . ." Hayes whispered, but Carver cut him off.

"Yeah," she interrupted, well aware of his need for silence. "If you can use the drone, I can. Pretty foolproof. I've already done a full scan of the area. If I can spot the shooter without him taking the drone down, I'll let you know, but I'm pretty sure you think what I do—that he's under the lip of the third floor, waiting to pinpoint you, me, and Hugo so he can shoot through whatever wall is necessary."

Hayes wanted to say "great" again, but instead said, "Gun?"

"Hasn't Jesula given you that yet?" Carver replied, a little surprised as well as annoyed.

Hayes looked at the jaguar mask and made a fist with his forefinger out and his thumb pressing down two times. Fidelus immediately pulled Hayes's FN 509 Tactical semiauto pistol out from under his shirt, complete with its twenty-four-round magazine installed. Hayes raised his eyebrows as he nodded with appreciation. Rather than let him load the magazine himself, creating a noise that would get any gunman's attention, Fidelus had risked his own safety to make sure the weapon was ready to go.

"Did he give you anything else?" Carver said inside his ear. Then she cursed under her breath for asking Hayes something that required a reply. "Point at his pants pocket."

Hayes did so, and Fidelus pulled out the small emergency pack Hayes left behind when he crashed into the hotel lobby. Hayes nodded and gave him another thumbs-up, then, using what he just learned, made a series of short, pointed motions that he hoped would clearly translate to *anything else?*

The jaguar shook his head solemnly. *No.*

But by then Carver's drone reports were coming in. "There seems to be only one option with any sort of surprise element. It's a building kitty-corner on the northwest side of the construction you're in. It's one story taller. If you can get to the roof, you could make a jump."

Hopefully before the Russkie can take you down like a duck, said his inner voice.

Once again, Hayes considered risking his safety to ask a pertinent question, but once again, Carver beat him to it.

"Yeah," she said, and not without concern. "You may be wondering why Jesula is hanging around. Well, we decided that to make sure you make the jump without being too compromised, you needed a diversion."

Hayes looked sharply at the jaguar mask, which Fidelus took as a signal to pull it off. Hayes was sorely tempted to croak *no,* but one look at the man's strong, sad, eyes, and he knew they were right. Besides, having just known this man for an hour or two, Hayes gave him better odds than he gave himself.

Hayes nodded at Fidelus, who returned his previous thumbs-up.

"Jesula will wait at the exit just under where we think the shooter is," Carver explained. "He'll wait until you're ready to go, then will run at your signal in a way to get the sniper's attention."

Hayes nodded at Fidelus again, then started silently stalking toward the northwest corner of the construction site. As he went he checked the contents of his pack in case Pasquette had plundered anything. Inside was a flash-bang device, a smoke bomb, and his Ontario survival knife. By the time he reached the end of the construction floor, Fidelus was already in place and awaiting his cue.

No time like the present, Hayes's inner voice gently prodded.

Hold your horses, Hayes told himself. *Running blind will get us all killed.* He took a second to check the kitty-corner building.

It was right across a trash-strewn alleyway, and looked as bad as the building Hayes was presently in. But rather than unfinished, the place across the way looked abandoned. In any other city it would appear to have been in the process of being torn down, but here in Haiti, it was just another neglected earthquake remnant. The barometer of how bad came when Hayes could spot no squatters inside. A building would have to be dangerous indeed to chase away the impoverished masses here.

Taking a last look around, and grateful that there seemed

to be no Carnival stragglers remaining, Hayes stuck his survival pack under his vest. Nothing like a Russian sniper to
spoil the one party Haitians seemed to have left in their daily
misery. Not wanting his inner voice to ask him whether he
was waiting for an engraved invitation, Hayes turned and
gave Fidelus a big thumbs-up.

PORT-AU-PRINCE, HAITI

Even before he lowered his arm, the garbage man had taken off. And not directly at the municipal building entrance, either. No, he raced in a diagonal line, right across where any sniper couldn't help but see him.

But Hayes couldn't wait to see if the man made it. As he heard the first sizzling SVDK shot, he sprinted across the street and into the abandoned building. He was pleased there was no trouble getting in. There were gaping holes all along its walls; he just jumped through the nearest one. Like most of the buildings in this area, if it wasn't abandoned, it sure seemed like it was. It stank of bodily waste, and everything looked rotted. Hayes didn't have time to dwell on any of it.

He cleared the sodden threshold and moved to the rotting

stairs, but instead of heading up, Hayes paused at the doorway and retrieved the flash-bang from his pouch. Dropping to a knee, he drove the metal stake he'd mounted to the flash-bang body into the frame a foot above the floor, and then stretched the length of framing wire attached to the pin across the open stairwell. He pulled the tripwire taut, tacked it in place, and then moved back to the flash-bang, gently easing the safety wire from the spoon.

It was all just in case the infamous point man had been stalking him and decided to make an appearance from behind.

Better safe than sorry, his inner voice agreed.

With the makeshift anti-intrusion device guarding his backtrail, Hayes carefully followed the steps up to the roof, staying as close to the step edges as he could. The center of the steps looked ready to snap at the slightest weight. He was glad that the final set of stairs led to the roof. He didn't want to climb the exterior of the building.

As he looked out of the open door of the roof portico, the rain and wind slapped at him, but at least it wasn't as bad as before. And since Carver hadn't clued him otherwise, he assumed Fidelus had made it back in one piece.

Hayes envied him as he looked out on the crumbling, sagging, unfinished construction across the alley from him. Incredibly, its most distinctive feature was a two-story-tall circular staircase that erupted from the northeast corner of what was intended to be the floor of the fourth story, but now served as the entire structure's roof.

Some Haitian architect had, or was hired by a client who had, delusions of grandeur. Perhaps it was going to be a centerpiece for a two-story suite of offices. But then reality, the

2010 earthquake, the cholera epidemic, multiple hurricanes, and even a presidential assassination, spoiled those plans.

Besides the staircase, which jutted out into the sky, rain, and wind like a big metal middle finger, Hayes was tentatively optimistic about his chances of getting to the sniper before the sniper got him. Finding the building clear and the roof not actively falling apart, he was hopeful about the structure's serviceability. That vanished the moment he looked over the lip of the roof's front corner.

If this had been a Treadstone mission, the checkerboard of miscolored asphalt patches and dangling ridges, as well as the shaking steel spiral staircase that looked like a jutting sculpture of a DNA double helix, would have immediately sent him to an alternate position the mission planners would have preselected for him. But this was a Treadstone mission in name only, and the mission planners were either reassigned, fired, or corrupt traitors. Now, all he had was one lone sniper target on a used spy ear.

As if reading his mind again, Carver reported in. "I see you." He hoped she was doing it from someplace where the sniper couldn't crosshair her. Hayes kept studying the jump site as she continued. "I also see the shadow of the SVDK barrel. Unless it's a red herring, the shooter *is* on the third floor, about twenty feet east from the corner you're standing at. From my vantage point, you're going to have to make a jump between fifteen and twenty feet—closer to fifteen if I'm any judge of Haitian zoning laws."

There are Haitian zoning laws? Hayes wasn't sure if it was his voice or his subconscious that said it, but, ultimately, it made no difference. One way or the other, he'd have to make the jump with his pack, vest, and gun weight included. At least he was doing it from a height, which was good for any needed extra distance. Maybe he'd luck out even further and the diminishing storm wind would be at his back.

Wouldn't do to overshoot it, the voice reminded him.

Before stepping back and making a run, Hayes tested the area around the threshold with the toe of his boot, gradually increasing the weight on his front foot until he was sure that it would hold. Then he stepped back—the faded asphalt spread across the roof still tacky from the heat, rain, and wind.

He was almost across the space when the first rounds came snapping up from the neighboring construction. The first shot was high, but close enough for Hayes to hear the whiz of the bullet past his head.

"I'm spotted," he grunted. Made no sense to stay silent now.

Knowing the man wouldn't miss again, Hayes ran even faster forward, desperate to get to the ledge. He prepared himself to make the monumental leap, so he could land, roll, and come up running with his FN ready to perforate any target, but then he stepped into the center of a patch he hadn't tested.

He felt the thin section of wood flex beneath his weight, and then he was stumbling. The patch immediately broke with a spray of rotten splinters, forcing Hayes to throw himself forward, jagged bits of wood slicing across his ankles. He could hear Carver gasp inside his ear as he flailed in midair, halfway between the buildings.

He felt his body twisting, the rain and wind pushing his

head down and his feet up. He looked down to see the edge of the unfinished construction going by, which meant at least he wouldn't fall five flights to his death in the alley below. But then he slammed into the edge of the spiral staircase that poked upward out of the unfinished construction's roof.

"Shit!" Carver hissed in his ear.

The plate carrier in the vest saved him from a broken rib, but the force of the impact blasted the air from his lungs.

He ignored it, immediately shaking off the blow, because he had to concentrate on not bouncing off the staircase and slamming down onto the roof like a rag doll. His arms and hands scrambled, clawing at any surface they could find, while his legs bicycled in thin air as he searched for something solid to fall on. Then gravity took over, the weight of his gear dragging him down like an anchor.

"Not forward, not forward!" Carver called. "Back, side, or straight down!"

Thankfully, his momentum was conducive to sliding backward, so Hayes reached out and grabbed hold of one of the staircase slats. He tried to drop himself onto the top platform, but the metal tore free with a rusty shriek.

"Damn!" he heard Carver yell.

"Yeah," he snapped, jamming his left elbow down hard between the slats and using the friction of his skin to slow his tumble. Gritting his teeth, he reached down, searching for the handle of his Ontario survival knife. He missed on the first try, but didn't stop despite the way his limbs were threatening to send him off the staircase. Wrenching the knife out and stabbing down a second time, he got both hands around the handle and jammed the blade at anything that would take it as he slid to the edge of the banister.

He heard Carver gasping in his ear. She obviously couldn't help guide him, so, with less than a foot between him and a backbreaking drop, Hayes knew he was only going to get one shot at this. He brought the knife up over his head and, using the bared section of the staircase as a guide, stabbed down hard.

He punched the blade down through the rotten top layer of a skeletal beam at the top of the structure, and buried it deep into the solid core. The sudden stop snapped his arm straight. Then, as if taunting him, the rest of his body slowly toppled over, sending him off the edge of the platform. Hayes was left hanging off the top of the spiral staircase, dangling by one arm, his hand sliding off the knife handle.

"Shit, shit, shit, shit," said Carver's voice in his ear. He couldn't disagree.

Hayes could feel the bone grating on tendon, the lightning bolt of pain that ran up his arm and into his shoulder whitening his vision. Sensing serious damage to the joint, his brain screamed at him to let go, but Hayes ignored it and reached up with his left hand. Using both hands, he managed to pull himself up far enough to kick a leg over the lip, and then he was back lying on the top platform of the spiral staircase— right side up this time.

Hayes heard Carver's sigh of relief, but then 7N33s started coming up through the roof. The sniper either had a mirror set up or some hole in the tattered ceiling to look through. Three rounds came in succession, each screaming off a metal stair, banister, or slat, each as strong as a jousting lance. Hunks of metal went spinning like scythes.

Hayes didn't care. None of them had hit him so the FN seemed to jump directly into his hand, and using its low-profile optics and three-dot green Tritium night sight, Hayes made a nine millimeter target pattern directly where the 7N33s had appeared—four shots making a tight top, bottom, left side, and right side, with a fifth shot making the bull's-eye.

After all, the SVDK was not the kind of rifle you take away from your shoulder. If the sniper was actively aiming at him rather than just taking potshots, his return fire should have ripped off part of the Russian's trigger hand, parted his hair or skull, ripped off a cheek or ear, and, finally, punctured his forehead.

"The silhouette moved!" Carver cried. "I think you got him. I'm bringing the drone in."

Smart girl. With a more important primary target to take care of, Hayes doubted the sniper would split his attention trying to bring down a drone. Hayes crouched, hoping to make a less obvious target, and kept his FN ready. Five rounds down, nineteen to go.

"Damn this rain," Carver said. "It's pixelating the whole image. Wait a minute, he's on the move," Carver corroborated. "But he's hobbling. I think I see blood. He's gone down."

"Hard?" Hayes asked.

"No," Carver replied. "Kneeling. He's digging around in his duffel for something."

That can't be good. "What's his position?"

"Thirty, thirty-five feet from you. Same line of fire."

That meant he hadn't gone right, east, left, or west. Hayes adjusted his aim and was pulling the trigger when Carver spoke again.

"He's got an AK-74! Shoot, shoot, shoot, shoot!"

Hayes didn't have to be told a fifth time. The AK-74 was an assault rifle made for Russian special op units and airborne troops who worked in urban areas. It's the Russians' close-up killer, while the SVDK was its long-range assassin. The former wasn't accurate, but it could still kill him thirty, forty-five, or sixty times over depending upon which magazine the sniper was using.

Hayes's FN made a perforated line in the ceiling, spacing his shots a foot and a half apart, tracing the man's movements from where Carver said he had been to where Carver said he was now.

"He's hit but not stopping," Carver reported. "Take cover!"

Easy for her to say, since Hayes could only slide down the circular banister or jump off. Before he could do either, 5.45x39-millimeter rounds started erupting from the ceiling, making a straight line toward the spiral staircase. If he used the banister he'd slide right into them. If he jumped he'd fall right through them.

Instead, Hayes expertly judged where the man was shooting from and returned fire in kind. As the sniper's rounds came at him, Hayes's shots followed the same trajectory in the opposite direction. But he knew he was outgunned. The sniper had thirty rounds, but Hayes was down to about sixteen.

A moment later the odds changed again because Carver started firing up from the municipal building's shattered second-story window. Now they were three blind mice in a crossfire, and none of them had a clear view of their target. But that didn't stop any of them.

"Got ya, you bastard!" he heard Carver exclaim as the AK-74 rounds stalled at the base of the spiral staircase, digging up the structure's foundation, ricochets squealing off in all directions.

It was good timing, because Hayes's FN had just ejected its last shell. As he dug through his pockets and kit for a reload, he asked Carver, "Where?"

"Fuck," she replied. "Chest, near his neck, but he must have a vest, too. Shit, he's going back to the SD! Get down! Get down now!"

Hayes instantly tensed to make a leap as far away as possible, trying to decide which direction would be the safest, when the staircase made the decision for him. With a moaning, screeching, tearing bellow, it started toppling forward, its base ripping out of the weakened roof like a broken spine.

Hayes froze, knowing that if he jumped in any forward or side direction, the corkscrewing staircase would probably rip the floor out from under him, taking him down with it. But he was too close to the building's edge to jump back. If it gave way like it had before when he'd jumped across, he'd be back in the alley five floors below.

"Jesus, Adam, no!" Carver cried as she watched him grab the top banister and swing onto it when the staircase reached a forty-five-degree angle to the roof. "Jump, jump, jump!"

That's exactly what he did. As the staircase reached its top falling speed, Hayes jumped to the top edge like a diver on a board, and dove forward as far as he could.

Just as the sniper sent a 7N33 into the center of the falling staircase, Hayes remembered his college gym classes, tucked, rolled, landed in a crouch, somersaulted again, and came up running. For a split second he thought about trying to make the leap across the street, through the broken picture window and into Pasquette's lair, but that would've been impossible. He wouldn't have been able to get enough momentum.

At that moment, the staircase smashed into the roof behind him like a sledgehammer on a skylight, collapsing the ceiling in a progressive, almost falling-domino pattern. Hayes ran as fast as he could, hoping the destruction would stop before he reached the other end. Because of the city's darkness, and lack of regular electric light, he had no idea if there was any other building he could safely jump to from there.

He heard cracking and smashing just behind him as he reached the southeast edge, seeing the black, mostly lightless city yawning in front of him. Even the rain and wind seemed to diminish in respect to the destruction they had caused. As the lip of the building grew closer and closer, he lowered his head and charged forward even faster.

At that moment a lightning bolt smashed down in the plaza, creating a kinetic spotlight that made the hairs on the back of Hayes's neck stand at attention. In that not-quite-blinding light, he saw Fidelus out of the corner of his eye, running out of the municipal building entrance.

Then he had to ignore and forget everything, as he was about to run out of floor. That's when the collapsing construction caught up with him. Even before his foot reached the building ledge, what served as the ground cracked open beneath his feet, and he fell.

A utopsy NDC3012-67T. Decedent, Carol Mary Murphy. Identified by fingerprints and dental comparison."

Carol's dead, previously eviscerated, but now sewn up, body lay naked on the examining table in the middle of a small private clinic room, illuminated by an overhead medical lamp. The medical examiner remained mostly in shadow, but even in bright light, he would be mostly unrecognizable because of the face mask, magnifying protective spectacles, lab coat, and gloves.

"Rigor, absent. Livor, purple. Distribution, posterior. Age, fifty-nine."

Wouldn't have guessed, CIA Director Lisa Bratton thought. *Don't know if I would've gone higher or lower, but I wouldn't*

THE TREADSTONE TRANSGRESSION

have guessed. She was deep in the shadows, off to the side, a seemingly lone observer of her personal pathologist's findings.

"Race, Caucasian. Sex, female. Length, sixty-five inches. Weight, a hundred and thirty pounds. Eyes, hazel. Hair, gray. Body heat, refrigerated. Clothing, beige dress blouse, bloodstained . . ."

"You can skip ahead," Bratton's flat voice interrupted.

The autopsist looked up with slight irritation. "I need all this for the record," he maintained.

"No, you don't," Bratton replied calmly. "Cut to the chase."

"But you asked for a full workup," he complained.

"For which I am grateful," she replied. "But you need not go into all of it for my benefit right now."

"But . . ."

"I would appreciate details relevant to her death only, please," she interrupted. "Thank you." Although her tone was superficially civil, there was no doubting the finality behind it.

Momentarily flustered, the man scrolled through his notes. "External examination: well-nourished white female with multiple contusions on her throat and lacerations of face and scalp with fractures of the calvarium, facial bones, and cranial vault. X-rays demonstrate comminuted fractures of the skull. There are superficial penetrating injuries on the anterior aspects of the neck, with hemorrhage in the soft tissues adjacent to her laryngeal cartilages . . ."

"Cause of death?" Bratton interrupted again.

The examiner was no longer flustered. He looked over Carol's corpse into the shadows where the calm, curt, interrupting voice was coming from. "A blow to the zygomatic arch of the skull by a blunt object."

Bratton paused, then asked quietly, "Manner of death?"

"Homicide," he answered.

Bratton nodded, seemingly expressionless. "Got everything you need?"

The examiner looked down at the chart he had painstakingly compiled on his tablet. "Let me see . . . pathological diagnoses, individual examinations of pleura, peritoneum, pericardium, organs, glands, lymph nodes, vertebrae, bones, and genitalia, toxicology, photography, X-ray, microscopic examination . . ." He looked up, satisfied. "Yes, I believe so."

"Excellent," Bratton concluded. "Now erase it."

The pathologist blinked. "All of it?"

"All of it," Bratton ordered. "Now and forever. As far as you, and hopefully the rest of the world, is or are concerned, Carol Mary Murphy never existed."

The pathologist swallowed, then did what he was told. This was not the first time she asked him to do all this, then eliminate it. Although it never made him happy, it came with the job.

Lisa Bratton waited until the conscientious, patriotic man left, then stepped closer to the examining table upon which the last of who was once Carol Murphy lay. She, or at least her body, had been found by the night cleaning crew. The entire incident immediately went into "code coffee," named for the secret shop on the premises that very few were allowed to use.

The CIA chief's eyes lowered until she stared at the poor murdered woman's throat, where she had personally found, lifted, and preserved the fingerprints of one Michael Colossal Asshole Carpenter.

"He didn't even bother to wear gloves, did he?" Levi Shaw asked, moving out of the shadows on the other side of the examining table, opposite Bratton.

They both stood in the CIA's private, secure, secret morgue, where victims went to disappear, and be erased from the public record.

"No, he did not," Bratton said without looking up. "Apparently didn't even try to wipe anything off. Just took his laptop and sauntered away whistling 'Dixie.'"

Shaw returned his gaze to Murphy as well, but his eyes concentrated on the crushing wound at the side of her head.

"Ulster sap, my old friend," he muttered. "Smallest of the commercial blackjacks, but obviously effective—especially in the hands of a sadist. The best thing for closet sadists is, that since it is only seven inches long, it won't make a protrusion in any suit pocket." His gaze returned to Bratton's unperturbed face. "You never should have warned him."

Bratton's face seemed calm, but Shaw believed he saw a tiny twitch at her brow, the corner of her mouth, or both. But her voice, when it came, had the evenness of a laser beam.

"I'm sorry about how it worked out, but he wouldn't have done what he has subsequently done if I hadn't warned him," she said with measured patience.

Shaw pursed his lips, looking down at the innocent bystander, whose death was more an act of cruelty than a necessity. "All this and you still don't have that flash drive."

Her dark, sharp eyes snapped up to his. "Ah, you don't approve of my methods. Sure, I could have taken him into custody right from the start. That would have made for some impressive headlines, and believe me, Carpenter has enough important friends and connections to make sure he wouldn't go quietly. But I would imagine that even you wouldn't want anyone outside this room to know just how compromised the companies they depend on for their safety and well-being are."

Shaw breathed deeply as both high-ranking governmental watchdogs stared at the body on the table between them.

"The whole idea of public service," Shaw finally murmured, seemingly to himself, "is to be better than the enemy."

Bratton let out a short, incredulous laugh. "*You're* lecturing *me* now? I didn't make Carol a tool, Carpenter did. But since he did, I did not, and will not, hesitate to use that tool to end him." She leaned back and motioned to the dead body lying between them. "Or is losing to a murderous traitor preferable in the name of truth, justice, and the American way?"

Shaw nodded in understanding, his lips pursed. He didn't blame her. Now, with the reality of the once second-in-command of the CIA off the reservation with malice aforethought, there was no way for either of them, or anyone, to know who he had turned or who he already had in his pocket, ready to do his bidding against fellow agents. The concept of trust within the Central Intelligence Agency was now well and truly off the table.

"We all have our tools," he murmured.

That comment elicited raised eyebrows from her. She leaned forward, her head making a shadow across Murphy's corpse as she looked up at the director of the Department of Defense's elite ops unit.

"Would you like to continue this lecture in front of *your*

tool's wife and child?" she asked him with exaggerated in-credulity. "Would you like to bring them up to date on what their husband and father is doing, or even where, exactly, he is?"

Her words hung in the air like Ulster saps. The truth of them shook his reserve.

"I wish I knew," he admitted.

32

T he first thing Adam Hayes saw when he opened his eyes
again was blackness. But it was a gauzy blackness.
Burial shroud? his inner voice wondered.

Hayes jerked up, the gauziness revealed to be a tattered
blanket. As it fell away, Hayes could see he was in a rickety
cart being pushed by Fidelus, with the robed tigress on one
side and the robed horse on the other. He looked down at
himself. He was back to being the robed lion, although he
could feel his fighting clothes, complete with tactical vest,
beneath it. Underneath him, he could feel he was sitting
on other things that were piled under another gauzy black
blanket.

All around them, however, was darkness.

"How am I still alive?" he asked quietly.

"Ssh," the tigress said. "Keep your voice down. There's a lot you need to know, but we shouldn't disturb anyone who might be around here."

Hayes was not going to ignore her now, not after what they had been through. So he stayed quiet, but used all his other senses to get a head start on their current situation. To both his pleasure and concern, the rain had stopped and the wind was moderate. How long had he been out? He looked up. On the basis of the stars, it was around midnight. It also appeared that the starlight was about the only illumination there was.

He peered into the darkness around them. Behind him was the jaguar pushing the shallow, two-wheeled cart he was sitting in. Hayes would not be at all surprised if he had built it himself from throwaways. Fidelus was rapidly changing from a garbage man to a scrap king.

Beyond the scrap king, it looked like the crumbling, shadowy, metropolitan edge of Port-au-Prince was receding, as if at low tide. In front of him there loomed what appeared to be an endless bumpy blanket. They seemed to be alone in the inky, smelly night. But according to Carver's warning, the operative word was "seemed."

He heard Toussaint murmur from beneath his horse mask. "As ever," he said, "the storm-swept Carnival is, not surprisingly, being followed by a deep sleep."

"How do you feel?" Carver asked quietly.

"Not dead," Hayes replied.

Carver nodded. "You were lucky, if I can use that word, that you rode the falling floor for at least a story. Even so, you fell at least twenty feet, and landed just inches from the crashing rubble."

"So why am I in one piece?"

The tigress remained silent, as if she couldn't believe it herself.

The horse spoke. "Jesu caught you."

"You're kidding," Hayes replied.

"Believe it or not," Carver said, sounding as if she had a hard time believing it herself.

Then the jaguar spoke. When he finished, the horse translated.

"He says that he was not going to stand idle when he could do something," Toussaint explained. "So he did something."

"It *was* something," Carver said. "He caught you like a lifeguard. Stopped your fall in an arm-swinging catch so he didn't have to take the full brunt of your weight, then slid you over and across the ground to diminish the force of the landing. And then he carried you all the way back to Pasquette's office before the construction even finished collapsing."

"Pasquette's office?" Hayes echoed incredulously, rising.

Both Carver and Fidelus shushed him and put their hands on his shoulders.

"We need cover for some things," Toussaint said quietly, pointing down under Hayes.

He remembered the lumps beneath the black gauzy cloth, and had a sneaking suspicion he knew what at least some of them were. And, if his suspicions were correct, they were not things to be caught with on a dark Haitian night.

"Then come on," Hayes told the horse in hushed tones. "You cover whatever this is. I need to walk."

"Fine," Carver said softly as the men switched places. "We got to keep moving, and you need a debriefing, stat."

Once they finished the transfer of Toussaint into the cart, they continued talking quietly, their words disappearing into the night.

"Where are we going?" Hayes asked, checking his limbs' mobility as he took a position to the left of the cart.

"Someplace safer," Fidelus said slowly in broken English from behind them, "than where we were."

That was hard to believe. If he didn't know better, Hayes could entertain the thought that they were actually all dead, and making their way into the afterlife . . . although he hoped the afterlife wouldn't smell this bad.

Once he rejected that possibility, as far as Hayes could tell, they were walking through a twilight zone of dirt paths flanked by torn walls of sheet metal, rotted planks, mounds of rended cloth, plastic shards, and unidentifiable junk piles, all made sodden by the torrents of storm rain that had battered every inch of the city.

He concentrated on staying on his feet and asked Carver his most pressing question. "Sniper?"

By the way the tigress's head moved, he could imagine the grimace beneath her mask. "I saw the spiral staircase fall on him like a corkscrew guillotine," she answered. "Then the rest of the roof fell on what was left of him."

Hayes made a sucking sound at the corner of his mouth. "His commanding officer must be pissed."

"How do you know his commanding officer is still alive?" Toussaint asked.

"That's what good commanding officers do," Hayes told

him. "They lead, give orders, watch, and wait until they are needed to seal the deal. And once assigned, they never stop until the mission is accomplished."

Hayes couldn't help but look around, seeing if he could spot any green armor or angry Russian eyes staring back. He couldn't.

But that doesn't mean they're not there.

"That's a problem," Carver informed him. "But hopefully Bernard is not as much of one right now."

"Not as much? What does that mean?"

"He's now the head of the ANI," Carver informed them. "After we got you back into Pasquette's office, he appeared in the doorway with his hands up, then explained himself."

"That must have been something," Hayes sighed.

"It was. According to him, he felt trapped until he realized he could take over the ANI just as Pasquette was about to kill you."

"He feels for his country," Toussaint interjected from the cart. "I believe him when he said he had always tried to be a good man. That is why he became a police officer in the first place. But here, in Haiti, the corruption is like . . ." He looked around, unable to quantify it. "I feel the same way. It's a constant battle between hope and hopelessness."

Hayes waved the philosophy away like a pesky gnat. Even so, he agreed. "Yeah, if Pasquette killed me, Bernard was trapped for good. But if he could blame Pasquette's death on me . . ."

"Or on a building that fell on him," Carver added, "then nobody could prove he wasn't the heir apparent."

Hayes shrugged. "Well, then I have to accept that he was

a good man in a bad place. Or else we'd all be dead by his hand. After all, he couldn't just lock us up, since somebody who might want his job might pretend to believe our stories."

"And he did not want to kill us," Toussaint reminded them.

"He certainly had plenty of opportunities to do it," Carver concurred, "and if you want solid evidence of his good intentions, he let us take what we wanted from the supplies Pasquette had confiscated from the hotel and the safe house."

Hayes's eyes went back to the bottom of the cart, feeling the urge to inventory it immediately, but with another glance at the ominous darkness around them, he knew that wouldn't do.

"He even gave me what he knew about the Russians," Carver continued.

That got Hayes's attention. "Which was?"

"You were right. Three-person team. The man we hit with the car at the safe house was named Pavel Simonov. The sniper was Ivan Baben. Ring any bells?"

"Thankfully no," Hayes replied.

"Why 'thankfully'?" Toussaint wondered. For his peace of mind, he shouldn't have asked.

"Because if I had heard of them," Hayes told him, "there would be a very good, or should I say, very bad reason why." He looked back at Carver. "What's the commander's name?"

"Maxim Popov."

Shit.

The other two saw it on his face.

Carver saved Toussaint the trouble. Besides, the banker was swallowing very hard and blinking a bit.

"How bad?" she asked.

"His nickname is 'the Ghost,'" Hayes said flatly. "I'll let you guess why."

"Great," Carver said drily. "More good news? We're not out of the ANI woods yet, either." That got Hayes's full attention back, so she continued. "Bernard had good intentions, but this is still Haiti. He said Pasquette had loyalists who'd want the head of whoever killed him. The way Bernard described it was that all he could truly offer us was a 'head start.'"

Oh, I get it, said the inner voice. *"Head" start.*

"He strongly suggested that we get out of the country as soon as possible," Toussaint said sadly.

"Did he have any suggestions as to how?" Hayes asked with quiet exasperation. "Doesn't ANI have a private plane or something?"

"Not that *moun blan* can use," Toussaint said. White people.

"Especially *moun blan* that are being blamed for killing the previous ANI director," Carver sighed. "We're lucky that Carnival and the storm happened or the city would be crawling with ANI and even PNH screaming for our blood."

The night is still young.

Hayes ignored the voice and looked at the seemingly never-ending blackness around them while calculating how much time he had left. At this point he was even willing to try the airport at Pedernales. He would take whatever airplane he could find and kill anybody who tried to stop him. But first he would have to figure out where Pedernales was and how to get there. He doubted his schedule had time for walking all the way.

Still moving forward, he turned his head to look at Fidelus.

"So where is this safer place?" Hayes asked. "And how soon can we get there?"

Fidelus's English must have been getting better. In reply, he stopped the cart and smiled. When he had the lion, the tigress, and the horse looking at him, he nodded his head at two particularly large mounds of slimy trash that were flanking the dirt path like guardian garbage gates.

I swear, Hayes thought, *if we turn the corner and it's fucking Oz, I'm going to start shooting.*

But then Fidelus said something, and as they reached a wall of sheet metal, bent boards, and old, stained, billowing blankets, Toussaint translated.

"Welcome to my home. Be quiet. The wolves come out at night."

His guests took him at his word. Hayes and Carver had heard of the Port-au-Prince slum wolves secondhand, but Toussaint had seen them, and lived to tell the tale. Since the mid-eighties, the many self-created neighborhoods in these poverty-stricken and disease-ridden shantytowns had given rise to armed gangs that, like vampires, stayed out of sight during the day but went hunting at night. Word was they mostly fed on each other, but there were always exceptions.

Toussaint saw it get so bad that the authorities refused to police, or even enter, these slums. He had also heard about the residents who had, since then, tried to stem the violence, and he prayed he was following one such man now.

Fidelus took the lead, slowly and silently pulling a narrow section of the curtain aside. Stretching out in front of them was a rain-dampened shantytown that seemed to share a designer with Fidelus's cart.

Hayes looked over to see Fidelus smiling, seemingly proudly, at the section they stood in front of. Returning his attention to the bigger picture, he could see that the area that was reminiscent of the cart only stretched to a crude circle of cloth-covered, blanket-wrapped enclosures. Looming beyond it were even cruder fabrications consisting of rotted wooden slats, broken tree limbs, rusted sheet metal, loose cinder blocks, stacked boulders, plastic pails, hanging clothes, worn mattresses, and burlap sacks. Every ten yards or so there were also hollow concrete squares.

And that was just the dwellings. Everywhere else had piles of the same trash they had been seeing on their walk from the edge of the central city. Surrounding it all, for seemingly kilometers, were extensions of the fence Fidelus had led them through.

"Cité Lalin," Toussaint breathed. Moon City. It was what they called the smaller, more squalid, and hopefully more civilized, sister of Cité Soleil. Fidelus sighed some words, and Toussaint translated them: "They call it that because they want it to be the opposite of Cité Soleil."

But a slum by any other name, Hayes thought, *is still a slum.*

They continued to follow the squat, solid scrap king along the edge of the fence until he reached a worn, stained, torn, stitched-together child's bedding set that featured cartoon sheep and pandas on a background of red hearts and green polka dots.

Fidelus turned back to them, put his forefinger against his lips, pulled back the blanket curtain, then slipped inside.

It, like the hovel where Hayes first met Fidelus outside Pétion-Ville, was dark, dank, long, narrow, cramped, and low-ceilinged. But the big difference was that, lining the towel and blanketed ground around the entire circumference of the area, were sleeping Haitian children.

All three of Fidelus's guests looked from them to one another, then back to them, until Fidelus waved his hand in front of their faces to get their attention back to him. Then he waved them forward, to continue to follow him.

They complied, and, as he headed toward the opposite end of the elliptically shaped space, they couldn't help examining the sleeping children. There were both boys and girls, aged between five and ten. Hayes guessed that they were orphans or something similar. He imagined that Jesu would take them in after they were weaned and before they could be forced to work in legal or illegal ways. Or maybe he just gave them someplace to sleep.

The one thing Hayes was sure of, however, is that a child's sleeping face was the same everywhere. And he didn't pass a single one without seeing his son.

He raised his chin, nearly hitting his head, intent on asking how Fidelus could help them get out of this forsaken country, when the scrap king pulled aside another dark curtain to reveal another elliptical space. He motioned his guests in, his face beaming with pride.

What was inside the enclosure made Hayes's eyes widen.

It was a vehicle. An unconventional, glorified dune buggy with the engine, drivetrain, and exhaust system all visible on a steel skeletal structure within a strangely familiar frame. On the basis of the tires, struts, and shocks, it was obviously designed for off-road, as well as on-road, use.

There were no windows and no seats, just a welded metal bench that went from one side of the frame to the other. There was a platform with boxlike sides in the rear for storage, and a connecting rectangle that secured gas tanks as well as extra fuel cans. On any American road, it would be considered a compact, but here it filled the dirty slum workshop from stem to stern.

"Jesu has been working in automobile garages for fifty years before the earthquake," Toussaint quietly passed on to Hayes. "Suzukis, Chevrolets, Mazdas, Toyotas, Daihatsus, Fords . . ."

With the mention of that last brand, the ironic coincidence of it all came to Hayes. It wasn't just a strangely familiar frame, it was actually a modified F-150 frame.

"I got it," Hayes hushed back, still staring at the thing. Either Hayes or his inner voice immediately dubbed it the *F-150 Zombie*.

Hayes made his way slowly around the vehicle, marveling at Fidelus's mechanical ingenuity and automotive understanding. As he passed the others, he saw Fidelus whispering into Toussaint's ear. Two steps later, out of the corner of his eye, Hayes saw Toussaint motion to Fidelus to approach Hayes.

"You take, yes?" he heard, and, when he glanced in the direction of the voice, Fidelus was beside him with an urgent, hopeful look, motioning at the F-150 Zombie as if trying to move it off a used car lot.

Hayes was too conflicted to answer immediately, so Fidelus moved forward quickly, only turning back when he was in front of the machine. By then Carver and Toussaint were on either side of Hayes, and they all looked on as Fidelus pinched the edge of the cloth wall in front of the vehicle, then pulled it back slightly to reveal that this hovel garage emptied out onto the other side of the Cité Lalin fence.

"He's been working on it ever since the earthquake," Toussaint told them as Fidelus let the curtain drop and started back toward them. "He said for some months afterward it was the only thing that kept him sane." Toussaint looked up at Hayes. "He swears it runs beautifully. That's the word he used. 'Beautifully.'"

"I don't doubt it," Hayes said quietly, imagining Fidelus going from closed garage to closed garage, scavenging whatever he needed or wanted day after day. "Ask him why *he* won't use it to get out of here."

While Toussaint asked, Carver whispered into Hayes's other ear. "Now there's not enough room for the children, and, really, where would he take it, and how long would he have it once any wolf saw it?"

When Fidelus stepped forward, his motioning toward the other area where the children slept, and shrug when he looked back at the garage door said much the same thing. Then he looked back at Hayes while holding up a key.

Hayes looked down at him with a mix of gratitude and concern. Finally he smiled thinly and took the key. Now he had two keys to safeguard.

"All right, get ready," he told the others. "We leave as soon as we're packed."

Everything was going fine until they got to the bottom of the cart.

Carver busied herself planning the route to the Dominican Republic's border. Spread all around her were scraps of paper that Fidelus had repurposed from many office wastebaskets he had emptied over the years. On their backs he had scrawled information he had gleaned during the past decade from the many people who knew the safest routes to the border. Toussaint had been kind enough to translate them for her.

"Minimum roads, maximum trails," she promised. "Minimum cities, maximum countryside."

"Do you have trusted contacts there, too?" Hayes asked.

"Does a Haitian bear shit anywhere it wants?" she immediately answered.

Toussaint had watched worriedly as Hayes had moved their spy ears, drone, his FN, and Carver's SIG off the top of the cart's pile, but he was positively shocked when beneath those Hayes found an old American AR-15, a lightweight semiautomatic assault rifle, and an aged Israeli Galil ACE battle rifle.

"I think those were two of the actual weapons the rebels used to assassinate our president," Toussaint marveled.

What they were doing in Pasquette's closet, and why Bernard wanted to palm them off on them was not something Hayes had time to figure out. Nor did he have time to figure out why there was a full Haitian police tactical uniform, including helmet, ballistic vest, and boots at the bottom. He was just grateful they had something to protect Toussaint with.

"All well and good," Hayes exhaled. "What, they couldn't give us a box of grenades?"

Fidelus shook his head gravely at that comment, and Toussaint stepped up to explain why.

"You wouldn't want to make any loud noise here," he said.

"That bring wolves," Fidelus added solemnly. "And where one . . ."

". . . soon come many," Toussaint concluded.

Carver came over as the Haitians went back to their planning. "From what I discovered," she told Hayes, "these slums are mostly filled with children, but the men seem to be in two camps. Ones who do the best they can and others who are armed and looking for any way to take out their anger on anything that moves." She collected her SIG from the cart and pointed into the darkest corner at the bottom. "You missed a spot."

Hayes shifted his gaze, and finally saw a small, stained, overnight toiletry bag next to a soiled clump of cloth wedged in the corner. He reached down to grab them. As the other two busied themselves with their final preparations while Fidelus kept watch over the children, Hayes was surprised to find everything from the safe house's medicine cabinet in the toiletry bag, including the Treadstone meds.

He grimaced slightly and put it aside, not wanting to remember the worst of his training, or be tempted again, then redirected his attention to the most incongruous item from the cart. It was something small, a little more than hand-sized, and hard, wrapped in oil-stained cloth. He peeled back the cloth so the thing rested faceup in his hand, like a brick of poison belched up by a wilted Venus flytrap.

It was the radio he had torn off the first Russian assassin they had killed back at the safe house. It was the radio Pasquette had used to track them to the municipal plaza kill zone. It was the radio someone was, no doubt, still using to track them here. How could he have forgotten about it?

Hayes looked up at the others busy prepping their departure from Cité Lalin.

They were screwed. The Ghost was coming.

33

CITÉ LALIN, HAITI

From the night vision binoculars, Maxim Popov watched the man covered head to toe in a combination of special op and secret police tactical gear slink in the shadows on the inner outskirts of Cité Lalin.

Trying to find a decent vantage point to look down upon the cheap security of the crammed, crowded, fetid place took more time than he had wanted.

But what did I expect? he thought. *I'm still saddled with these Haitian hacks.*

Simonov and Baben had complained bitterly about who they had called the tactically inferior bastards they were forced to work with, and they had been right. Now Simonov and Baben were dead—one by a car and a bullet, the other by several bullets, a spiral staircase, and an entire building—while these *mu'daks*, assholes, were still alive.

Well, the Ghost would give them first crack at the targets who had proven as dangerous as Lieutenant Colonel Yutkin had suggested they were, while Popov watched from a safe distance. Not because he wanted to see if the approach the late and not lamented Felix Pasquette demanded bore deadly fruit the second time, but because it was better for him to learn the Americans' abilities through the Haitians' deaths rather than his own.

I never should have let the arrogant idiot convince me, he thought, remembering the power-mad Pasquette insisting that he had everything well in hand, and that Popov should follow the ANI's lead. It was no excuse, but Popov had to admit that he was, by then, truly sick of the man, the plan, and, in fact, the whole stinking country.

But Ivan had paid for Popov's impatience with his life, and Maxim would never forgive himself for that. Maybe even worse for his career, when he had returned from the airport, Baben and Pasquette were dead. Or, at least, he was told by these assigned *mu'daks* that they were dead because—despite the masses of Police Nationale officers "securing" the crime scene—no one was going to take the time to dig them out to see if they really were dead, or even actually under the rain-soaked and windswept rubble.

To top it off, in the chaos that followed, and the calm after the storm and Carnival, no one, including Popov, seemed to be able to find Pasquette's second-in-command, or even any-one with enough authority to redirect the assignment. And

Popov would be damned if he was going to fly, or even call, back and ask Lieutenant Colonel Yutkin.

So, as he often had, and preferred, to do, he took command. And thankfully, right there on the floor was Pasquette's laptop tracker device, still beeping away as if nothing had happened. So, in the waning wind and lessening rain, they had broken into, and stolen, a parked Suzuki Grand Vitara, then slowly and carefully followed the path where the tracker led them until the beeping dot stopped moving.

Only then, he couldn't get any of the Haitian bastards to actually enter the shantytown.

Am I going to have to do this myself? he wondered. *No, he answered, I'll be damned if I have to do this myself. These mu'daks got my team killed, so they're going to take their place, or I will kill them myself.*

Put to them that way, the ANI ops figured out a way to lessen their chances of being killed by the slum residents before they eradicated their assigned targets.

So now Maxim Popov stood on the roof of the Grand Vitara, which was parked on the biggest mound of dirt and debris he could find, overlooking the shabbily walled slum, watching the progress of the beeping dot as well as his Haitian stalkers. Those stalkers would only creep into Cité Lalin if they could remove any identifying intelligence service clothing or paraphernalia. Now they were just Haitian men in plain T-shirts, pants, and shoes with short, dark machetes in one hand and Taurus PT-809 nine-millimeter automatics in the other.

The Taurus was not standard issue for the Haitian authorities. But if any slum wolf saw an M1911 Colt in their hands, they might as well have been wearing a "please kill me" sign on their backs. The Taurus was one of the handguns of choice for the myriad Haitian terrorists, gangs, and criminals who had been lumped together under the general title of "rebels."

Idiots, Popov thought. *Fire a Taurus, a Colt, or anything else in there, and the very thing you fear will come down on you in abundance.* Popov was even tempted to fire off his MP-443 Grach just to see the bastards swallowed up by their angry countrymen. But first things first: He wanted to witness the primary target go down before he personally tracked and exterminated the secondary targets.

So he stood and watched through the night vision glasses as two of the Haitian bastards took advantage of the sleeping post-Carnival slum dwellers to track their tactical-geared quarry. If they failed, Popov didn't care. There were more where they came from.

He watched as the closest ANI op came to within six feet of the slowly moving man in the tactical getup. But just as he seemed about to thrust the machete, the target appeared to stumble, then fall behind a pile of trash.

Popov twitched with surprise. He craned his neck forward and tried to focus, just in time to see the ANI op stumble as well, then also disappear from sight as the second Haitian bastard lurched forward, apparently to help the first bastard up.

Popov lowered the binocs and straightened, trying to see where the target and the pursuers were. But a moment later he saw only the target come trudging out from behind the trash pile and continue along his cautious, unsteady path near the edge of the small Cité Lalin square.

What just happened? he wondered, snapping the goggles back over his eyes.

Adam Hayes could've told him. Once he had found the radio that had been so carefully covered and stuck at the bottom of the cart, he had approached Hugo Toussaint with a dangerous and difficult plan.

To his surprise, the understandably frightened but consistently brave and uncomplaining whistleblower had agreed to do his best. He explained he still felt guilty about his behavior back in Pasquette's office, and fully believed Hayes's contention that their escape would fail if their pursuers weren't stopped. So he let himself become a decoy, disguised as what they hoped their pursuers would think was Hayes.

Hayes also had night vision goggles. Fidelus had "emancipated" them from one of the thousands of cleaning jobs he had done over the years, because he wanted them available for any night driving trips that might become necessary.

Hayes had those on his forehead, and had already undressed down to his black synthetic military undergear T-shirt and bike pants. Fidelus had shaken his head at Hayes's tanned but still obviously Caucasian skin. He held up a forefinger in the generally accepted sign meaning "wait a minute," and slipped out of the hovel carrying a dark plastic bucket.

Hayes and Carver didn't want to think about what the

bucket was most often used for, but when Fidelus returned, in what turned out to be under a minute, it was filled with dark mud, which, to the Americans' surprise, did not stink of excrement.

"Jesu knows the nonpolluted puddles nearby," Toussaint had explained as Fidelus himself quickly but carefully helped smear Hayes's exposed skin with the sludge.

So, as the stalkers grew close to Hugo in the tactical gear, the camouflaged Hayes got close to them, but not before locating each of the three other ANI avengers, so he could, figuratively and literally, keep them in the dark.

Digging and crawling around through and up into the trash pile, he let Hugo pass, but as soon as the first ANI agent appeared, it looked to the bastard as if a dark arm shot out of the trash itself, crushingly grabbed his throat, and yanked his head into the pile. Between Hayes's choking fingers and the surprised op having rubbish filling his open mouth, the attack effectively gagged him. The silencing was complete when Hayes shoved his knife under the man's sternum and right up into his heart.

By then the second ANI op had grabbed his associate's shoulders, thinking he had tripped, and sought to assist him. He said nothing, of course, certain that even the softest whisper would be heard by the wolves. But as the first op's head drooped, the second op saw something dark and sharp, but for only a moment. The dark and sharp thing shot under his chin and then the second bastard felt as if his throat was being replaced with a blender.

Hayes knew that this would've been more effective from behind, but he had no choice. He stabbed his knife through the second man's carotid artery, then immediately yanked the blade down to slice the man's vocal cords. As the man tried to jerk back, Hayes grabbed his hair, yanked his head over the first man's shoulder, then cut both the man's trachea and jugular vein with a deep, strong slice.

That kept the second op from yelling, but it wouldn't keep him from gasping and coughing. So, as the first man, now dead, dropped, Hayes plunged his knife through the second man's ribs and into his heart as well. Holding the second op's head deep in the trash, Hayes waited until he stopped twitching, then let him fall as well.

"Third ANI spotted," he heard Carver's hushed voice in his ear. "Next left, moving diagonally toward tach."

No one had wanted Carver involved in this operation, Fidelus least of all. He knew what happened to women ambushed by wolves after dark. But all of them knew that the operation would be twice as dangerous, if not more so, without her. So she, too, was down to her moisture-wicking base layers of a black synthetic short-sleeve T-shirt and bike shorts, with her exposed, even paler, skin doubly muddied. She had even taken the cloth the radio had been wrapped in, covered that in mud, and tied it over her telltale blond hair. Just to be on the safe side, they also muddied as much of the spy ears as they could without breaking them.

She now lay on top of Fidelus's hovel, having crawled up there through a meticulously crafted escape flume the man had created over the years just in case he needed to evacuate quickly without running directly into whoever or whatever was forcing him to evacuate. From that vantage point, just under the top of the fence Fidelus had built around his dwelling, she could see much of the surrounding four square blocks.

She peered into the darkness, watching the disguised Toussaint make his slow, careful way toward the far corner of the adjoining area as Hayes pulled the twitching, bleeding corpses into the trash pile. He crouched, craning his neck to keep watch on the moving tactical gear as, behind him, the dull brown garbage started being streaked with growing tendrils of dripping red.

Popov was annoyed. How could these bastards be so incompetent? From the way the target was walking, he might even be drunk. And where had the first two attackers gone? If the target had killed them, why hadn't he seen or heard it? It's not like the storm was still raging. Now he wished these cheap night vision goggles were equipped with heat-signature apparatus. But then he realized where he was. Alone, in Haiti.

Once that had sunk in, Popov wanted to kill something, very quickly and very badly. At this point, he admitted he really didn't care who. Yutkin had always quoted Trotsky to him.

"The commander will always find it necessary to place the soldier between the possibility that death lies ahead, and the certainty that it lies behind."

Popov was fully intent on proving that true. He hopped off the stolen car's roof. It wouldn't do to come driving up to the shantytown beeping the horn and flashing the headlights. He made sure his Grach was secured, then checked that his combat tactical Storm knife was in its usual place on his belt. That nasty-looking 170x35x4-millimeter, spear-shaped, single-edge, anti-glare-treated steel blade, with its meaty, thirty-centimeter handle, complete with wire-bending notch, had held him in good stead for decades.

"Do not fret, my pet," he whispered as he started making his way down toward the shantytown. "Tonight you will feed on the blood of our enemies."

CITÉ LALIN, HAITI

Dallys Carver did not see the Ghost. But she did see a squad of six Police Nationale D'Haiti officers, complete with their dark blue short-sleeved uniforms, caps, and holstered .45 automatics coming through the Cité Lalin entrance.

What are they, insane? she thought. *Drunk?* Even from this distance she could see their disgruntled expressions. *Did they follow the ANI agents looking for a fight? Don't they know what will happen the moment the residents lay eyes on them?*

It was not her place to figure out their motivations—it was only to give Hayes ample warning. Hopefully he'd just take Toussaint out of the line of fire and let the Haitians finish each other off.

"Six officers to your east, coming in from the main entry," she whispered. She watched and waited, but nothing changed. A third ANI op was making his way toward the disguised Toussaint, his machete at the ready. She scanned the area for any sign of the other ANI agents, but couldn't find them. Meanwhile, the PNH officers were getting closer. In just a few moments they would appear directly in front of Toussaint.

"Six officers are about to turn the far corner," she said, trying to keep her voice down. "Do you read?"

Still no response, but she finally saw Hayes's form rise up behind the third ANI op. His looming shape blotted a portion of the ANI op's body from her view. Did Hayes know about the local cops, and was hoping that he could time the execution so the approaching PNH officers wouldn't see it? Did he already know where the other ANI ops were positioned?

Stay still, Dallys, she told herself. *Don't move. Anything else you do now will only make it worse.*

But then the officers were right around the corner, pulling their guns out of their holsters.

"Guns drawn," she hissed. "Appearance imminent. Do you read?"

Still no acknowledgment or reply. Not even a crackle. Not even a nod.

Cursing herself, Carver found she was already sliding off the top of Jesu's hovel and starting to run toward the corner. She got there just as Hayes was about to hand-gag and kidney-spear the third ANI op who was right behind an oblivious Toussaint.

But Toussaint was only oblivious to the ANI op behind him. He could now clearly see two of the six PNH officers who had just come around the corner, their .45 automatics coming out of their holsters. At the same moment, Carver could see the fourth ANI op behind a cinder-block wall to her left, aiming his Taurus at Hayes's darkened form behind his fellow operative.

She opened her mouth to shout a warning, but everyone else beat her to it. Hayes jumped forward, the fourth ANI agent fired at where Hayes had just been, and all six NPH officers crowded around the corner, their guns drawn.

Hayes leapt forward, tackling Toussaint. They both went down to the ground as the half-dozen officers started firing at the three remaining ANI ops, who started firing back.

They might as well have blown a wolf whistle. The nine Haitian law enforcement officials should have known, but they couldn't hear themselves think over the sound of their gunfire. Carver spun completely around, already seeing the flutter of ragged window covers as the criminals prepared to retaliate and the innocent bystanders hid.

She didn't know which were the gang neighborhoods within this shantytown, but she hoped and guessed they wouldn't be too near to where Fidelus lived. That meant they had at least a few seconds to spare. She started toward where Hayes and Toussaint lay, but Adam stabbed an open hand toward her, clearly communicating *Stop!*

Carver realized that one of her worst fears for the evening's plan had come to pass. The spy ears had died, either from old age, the mud bath, or both. That had to be true, since there was no reason for Hayes to stay silent now that the gunfight had erupted. In fact, she saw his lips moving near Toussaint's ear, but didn't hear what he was saying.

Carver crouched by some cement and watched in amazement as Hayes and Toussaint stood at the same time, the disguised banker facing the street and the American behind him. As the Haitian officials kept shooting at each other, the figure in the tactical gear, and his shadow, kept moving, slowly but surely, closer to where Carver crouched.

It's working, Carver thought. *They might actually make it out of the line of fire.*

But then the wolves appeared on the horizon, seemingly from everywhere.

Carver's unmistakably foreign-colored eyes widened as dark T-shirted figures wearing shorts—some in sandals, some barefoot—started appearing from every street, from many doorways, and even in what served as glassless windows within the corrugated metal, wood-slatted, concrete-poured, and cinder-blocked dwellings. And they didn't come empty-handed.

Carver saw knives, machetes, hatchets, and axes. There were even two sledgehammers—one two-handed, the other a short, one-handed, version. But there were also more Taurus automatics and a double-pistol-grip Remington pump shotgun with six buckshot shells on its exposed sidesaddle.

Immediately, the ANI and PNH officials stopped shooting at each other and started shooting at the wolves. The wolves had no problem or hesitation shooting back.

Hell had broken loose.

In the chaos, Hayes grabbed Carver by the arm and shoved her toward Toussaint.

"Get back to Jesu!" he shouted over the gunfire, but before he could do anything else, the third ANI op, whom he had nearly killed, screeched, broke out from his hiding place, and charged at him—seemingly thinking that, if he was going to die, he was going to take his attacker with him.

Hayes pushed Toussaint back against Carver, then charged at the ANI op. Carver grabbed Toussaint's elbow and started running toward Fidelus's hovel. Carver spared only a moment to see that Hayes took advantage of the fact that the third ANI op was still protecting himself by firing back at the wolves. Hayes grabbed the op's other arm in an aikido hold, using the man's motion to throw him back toward his hiding place.

By then Carver had turned and propelled Toussaint forward, cowering behind him so any errant bullet would hit his vest, arm, and leg shields instead of her. From her crouched position, Carver could just make out the edge of Fidelus's hovel to the left of Toussaint's thigh, but then she crashed into his back when he suddenly and completely stopped.

What the hell? Why did he stop?

Carver fell on her ass, and from that vantage point she could look through Toussaint's legs. There, standing in the middle of the dirt street, was the Ghost. There was no mistaking him, from his green-armored tactical gear to his cruel smile. He was pointing his MP-443 dead center in the middle of Toussaint's chest.

Yes, Toussaint had on a tactical vest, but would that be enough against the all-but-point-blank nine-millimeter Parabellum? Horrified, Carver did the only thing she really could to help: She sprang from the ground and leapt onto Toussaint's back just as Popov fired.

The tactical gear was heavy, but Carver's strength and

energy was enough to bring them both down fast and hard. She felt the bullet graze her shoulder and burn a line across her back. She had stayed Toussaint's execution, but knew the Grach had seventeen more 9x19 millimeters.

The face she looked up into as she crouched atop Toussaint's prone form was a sadistically amused one. It was the face of an executioner who truly enjoyed his work. And never more so than when his assignment had fallen right in front of him on a trash-strewn platter. But his greatest happiness was also his flaw. He took one second too long to finish the job.

Four wolves appeared, two behind him, and one more each on either side. The one behind shot him in the back with a seventy-year-old Winchester Model 12 shotgun.

Carver heard the boom. Hell, anybody in the surrounding few kilometers probably heard the boom. Then she stared as the Ghost was propelled off the ground, flew over her and Toussaint, and slammed to the street face-first, mere inches in front of them.

But before she could scramble up and try retrieving Popov's Grach, the wolves descended on her—one grabbing her left arm, one her right, and the third seizing a fistful of her hair, ripping her disguising rag off. Yanking her to her feet, they started dragging her away.

The wolf with the Winchester smirked smugly and started sauntering after the three who were dragging Carver along, but the wolf with the shotgun had made three mistakes. One, he had used a buckshot shell, so the many tiny balls within had spread out, making for less effective penetration power on the green-armored back. Two, the wolf hadn't shortened the thirty-two-inch barrel, which would have transformed it into a far more deadly sawed-off variety.

And three, he didn't realize that the Ghost was wearing, unlike Toussaint, the latest in ballistic protection. Toussaint knew all this, either intrinsically or in actuality, when he saw, with growing horror, Popov rise from the dirt, aim at the wolf's receding form, and shoot him in the back of the head.

The wolf's skull exploded through his face, and he dropped to the ground like a brick. His three fellow wolves had to make an instantaneous choice: retaliate or stick with their captive. They stuck with their captive, dragging the screeching Carver into a concrete blockhouse.

Popov merely grinned, thinking, *One eventually down, one more right behind me, one more to go.* He turned, his Grach out and pointing where Toussaint had fallen, then blinked. The man in the tactical gear was gone. Popov took a step to start finding out where, so he could finish the execution, when more bullets started smacking into his back and ripping up the dirt all around him.

Bellowing with both frustration and expectation, Popov spun and started marching to the adjoining square, firing with pinpoint accuracy and pleasure at the gunmen who were now targeting him. As he reached the corner, his experienced eyes took it all in. ANI ops and PNH officers were alternately trying to kill each other when they weren't trying to keep from being killed by the wolves.

The Ghost let out a derisive chuckle. Either one or the

other, or both, thought one or the other was responsible for either Pasquette's death or the plaza destruction, and their Carnival-fueled drunkenness led to the worst decision of their lives. Popov was about to leave them to kill each other, as well as to find his targets, when one of his targets made himself known.

Popov moved swiftly out of the line of the Haitians' fire so he could watch the big, mud-covered man in military undergear move swiftly from one wolf to another along the shantytown's eastern wall, taking each down quickly and effectively. By this time, more cheap handguns had appeared, but the muddy man didn't seem to care what weapon his opponent had.

The first wolf stabbed a knife at the man's middle. The man grabbed his knife fist, not his wrist. That's how Popov knew he was a professional. If you grabbed his wrist, the knife man could still move the blade in many directions, including into your flesh. But if you clamp his fingers shut, the knife can only move in one direction, especially if the clamper controls that direction.

Which is what the mudman did. He moved it wide then slammed his other hand into both the wolf's throat and jaw as if piston-powered. The wolf's reaction excited Popov. The wolf's feet snapped up and off the ground as if being yanked by wires. He nearly did a tight, fast, backward somersault and crashed onto the ground with a neck-breaking slam.

But by then the mudman had moved on to the next wolf, who was bringing his snub-nose revolver up. The mudman grabbed the gun's cylinder. The gun couldn't fire if the cylinder couldn't move, unless the gun was already cocked, which this one wasn't. At the same time, the mudman slammed the heel of his other hand up into the man's nose, spearing his nasal bone into his brain. The wolf dropped like a rock.

Popov had been briefed on his targets, and there was no doubt in his mind that the mudman was Hayes.

Popov actually giggled, then decided whether he was going to shoot his attacker or the wolves. When another Taurus round slapped into his vest, Popov decided to err on the side of the attacker. But no matter how many wolves, ANI ops, or PNH officers he executed, he promised himself to save three bullets to complete his assignment.

CITÉ LALIN, HAITI

C arver heard it all, even within the big cement square the three wolves had dragged her into. She continually wrenched her body around, forcing them to hold on to her lest they lose control of her. They were strong and wiry but also clearly malnourished and possibly sick with cholera, malaria, respiratory infections, or any of the other diseases this country was prone to.

They kept trying to throw her down, while constantly babbling about her hair, eyes, and body, but she kept twisting, turning, and anchoring her legs. Their frustration that they couldn't just get her on the ground was building, so the one with his hands in her hair only kept that up for a few more seconds before he let go, said something she guessed was "hold her" and started to pull down his pants.

Carver immediately stomped on the left foot of the wolf holding her right arm, tromped on the leg of the man holding her left arm right where his shin met his thigh, then slammed her head back into the nose of the man behind her.

She heard the cracking of several of the foot's twenty-six bones to her right, sensed the knee caving in on her left, and felt the splatter of nose blood on the back of her head as the hands holding her fell away. She did not stop to consider the damage. Unless the hair-grabbing wolf fainted at the sight of his blood, she had just made him angry.

Not giving him a chance to react further, she swung around and, in the same motion, kicked him between the legs. As he doubled over, she slammed the heel of her right hand into his jaw, even harder than she had split Poe's lips, which drove the hair-grabbing wolf's jaw up into his zygomatic bone, cutting off blood to his brain.

She didn't have time to see whether the kick had sent him into shock or the palm strike had rendered him unconscious, because both wolves to her side were still awake. They were also in excruciating pain, but they were probably used to that, so she couldn't depend on that affording her any time to escape.

Seeing that the wolf with the collapsed knee was down, she spun on the wolf with the broken foot, slapped her open palm on the side of his head, and slammed it into the concrete wall. As she turned to the collapsed-knee wolf, she was gratified to see the spiderweb-cracked dent the broken-foot wolf's skull had made in the concrete, but that could've been from the cheapness of the concrete, not from her power.

As she spun on her last attacker, he went to grab her, but his ruined leg wouldn't support his weight. He went down again, as if bowing to her, just as she slapped her palms on both his ears, as if she were trying to pop his head like a balloon.

Instead, her strike had the effect she was looking for—rupturing his tympanum. Whether it deafened him temporarily or permanently he'd have to find out if he lived. Whether he just collapsed from the severe pain or lost consciousness from the shock, she wasn't going to wait around to see.

Carver charged through the concrete square's opening, just in time to run into a half-dozen more wolves who were looking to join the fun.

Too many, she immediately thought. With the first three she could control their attacks and take them on one at a time. Now, no matter who she started on, even if she managed to hurt two, eight more arms could grab, and four more bodies could tackle. Sure enough, they were all over her, no matter how she kicked, scratched, and punched.

She went down hard just inside the concrete opening, and their hands were already clawing at her flesh and tearing her clothes in a frenzy. She gave one agonizing screech and swore that she would never stop fighting. Even so, she felt two hands at her left wrist, two more at her right ankle, then more at her other wrist and ankle. She was down, spread-eagled in the dirt, with more hands at her shirt and shorts, when bullets started smashing into the cement all around them.

The wolves all over her started scrambling as if they had fallen into a hornet's nest. As she saw three of them take bullets in their head, neck, and chest, she snapped into a self-protective ball, watching between her knees as a figure in tactical gear and helmet walked by with a smoking AR-15 in one fist and a Galil ACE in the other. Carver was up immediately and running to him.

"I'll kiss you later," she told the still-disguised Toussaint, who had obviously hidden back in Jesu's hovel until he could no longer stand by and let his protectors fight alone.

Carver easily grabbed the AR-15 and the Galil ACE out of his hands and swung around to make sure they were safe from snipers—whether they be wolf or ghost. Thankfully the concrete enclosure blocked the sight of them from the fighters in the next square, so she had time to check the remaining rounds: four in the AR, five in the ACE.

"Now get back to Jesu," she instructed, "and stay there unless he says otherwise."

Then she hopped onto the back of one of her slumped, dead attackers, and vaulted onto the top of the concrete blockhouse.

Hayes must have heard her screech, because she saw he was fighting back toward her along the west side of the square, a snub-nose revolver in one hand and his knife in the other, as three wolves were coming at him with a brick, a machete, and a sledgehammer. She knew he wouldn't waste bullets if he didn't have to, so he was preparing to take on the three with just his knife.

"Hayes!" she shouted, "Down!"

Recognizing her voice, he immediately dropped, so she

quickly shot his attackers with three of the AR's remaining .223 Remington rounds—all in the chest because she hadn't had time to check the aim of the hand-me-down semiautomatic to see if head shots would've hit their targets. No matter how used and dirty the AR was, the human torso was wide enough that a straight shot from a trained shooter wouldn't miss completely. The same was not true of the head.

By then Hayes had his back against the wall of the concrete enclosure, so Carver just swung the Galil ACE down in front of his face.

"Five rounds left," she informed him.

His knife and the snub nose clattered on either side of her as he stepped forward in a perfect sharpshooter position, then pulled the trigger, taking down the wolf with the Remington shotgun.

The majority of the PNH officers and ANI ops had been killed minutes ago, and Carver watched in growing amazement as a muddy man in military undergear had target practice on four of the remaining wolves who were armed with guns.

Even Popov was impressed. It didn't matter where the wolves were in the square, and it didn't matter where or how they were hiding. Hayes put them in perfect timing order, and dropped one after another, clearly readjusting his aim as each shot told the shooter the deficiencies of the weapon.

The wolf who was farthest away had to go first, lest he escape to return later with more guns. He was at the back corner of the square, aiming at the one remaining ANI op, when Hayes's 7.62x51-millimeter round went through the cheap Taurus and into his face.

A second later Hayes took out the wolf at the mouth of the entry road before he could escape through the garbage gate. The wolf's head snapped back and he fell like a scarecrow onto his own snub nose. A second after that, Hayes sent a 7.62 into the forehead of a wolf who was diving over a trash mound to try killing the surviving, cowering PNH officer.

That left a wolf, who, after Hayes had taken out the entry road wolf, had started running toward Hayes from the other side of the square, repeatedly firing his shaking Taurus as Hayes shot the other gun-toting wolves. The first Taurus shot was five feet to the right of Hayes. The second was three feet to his left. The third was one foot in front of him. The fourth was four inches to the right of his head.

By that time Hayes had finished off the other three, so he dropped the fourth armed wolf just before he got off his sixth, possibly last, and probably killing, shot. The wolf slammed down face-first just ten feet away from Hayes.

For a split second the square was still and silent. Then Carver screeched "Ghost!" and fired her AR-15's remaining round at Popov, who appeared from behind a tattered sheet in the northwest corner of the square, holding a Haitian woman in front of him as a shield. He had his Grach pointed at Hayes from over the woman's quaking shoulder, next to her crying face.

There was no standoff. There was no gloating. There was no hesitation. Hayes immediately fired the Galil, not knowing how poorly it had been calibrated the last time it was cleaned.

Obviously the answer was "not well enough," because, although Hayes was aiming for Popov's eye, which was glaring at him from beside the woman's ear, the ACE bullet hit the Grach instead—ripping it out of the Ghost's hand, and sending both he and his hostage spinning to the ground.

The cry the woman made was unlike anything the Russian and Americans had heard before. It sounded like the agonized rage of an entire tormented country.

Popov spun to find his gun. Damaged or not, it might still be useful, but just as he spotted it in a puddle eight feet away, another shadowy figure slowly leaned down to pick it up. It was an old Haitian man who had come out of the hovel next to where Popov had found the woman. The old man studied the rended weapon for a moment, then pointed it at Popov's face. Popov simply stared back, showing no fear. The old man pulled the trigger, but nothing happened. Not even a click. The guns were done.

The reaction from within the slum was staggering. The surviving wolves surged forward, seemingly to tear the foreigners limb from limb. But then, from the other dwellings, came more men, and even some women, carrying sticks and pans and boards—anything they could use as a weapon.

Popov scrambled to his feet and started toward the old man who still held his ruined Grach, but before he could get to him, Hayes appeared out of nowhere and swung the ACE at his head like a baseball bat. Popov ducked, dodged, and weaved, then leapt forward—the Storm knife appearing in his hand from the scabbard on his thigh.

Hayes parried with the Galil, driven back by Popov's strength. As the two men circled each other, more and more older men and women began to appear, emerging from their homes to finally confront the wolves who Hayes had all but defanged.

As the two forces raging within the slum collided in a flurry of punches, kicks, and flailing all around them, Carver looked from Hayes's expressionless face to Popov's grinning death mask, made her decision, and ran toward Jesu's hovel.

"So, *pindo*," Popov sneered at Hayes as he stepped closer, using the Russian curse word for *American*. "I guess it is up to me to kill you, after all." He glanced back at Carver's receding back, pointing the knife blade at her. "And her." He looked at the growing group of Haitians that were now all around them. "So where is the Haitian I must kill as well?" He pointed his knife at a nearby man. "Is it you?" The man skittered away.

Popov then kept walking after Carver, everyone staying away from him. Hayes walked faster until he was between Popov and Jesu's hovel, making the Russian finally stop. It was as if the two were alone in the shantytown. He was sure the two opposing Haitian forces would bellow and posture and show their teeth, then finally go back to where they started. That would not happen with the Russian and American man.

Popov gave Hayes a wide, knowing, evil smile. "She won't get back in time to save you, you know," he said with assurance. "And whatever weapon she finds, I'll still make her take me to the Haitian and then kill them both." He pointed the

Storm directly at Hayes's face. "What do you say, Mister Adam Hayes?" he asked. "Want to give them a show before you . . ."

He attacked before he finished the sentence, as Hayes knew he would. The Russian was under a time constraint now. Despite what he said, Carver would come back with her SIG or Hayes's FN, or both, and would shoot him dead unless he killed Hayes first and ambushed her.

He also knew he was going to attack because Hayes had seen him prepare. He was a trained Russian soldier, so most likely he would use their Systema Spetsnaz knife-fighting system, which was taught to Russian Special Forces personnel. That combat system used a foundation of four pillars—body position, breathing, movement, and relaxation. Despite the situation, Popov had slowly drained himself of tension, and there was no mistaking that to Hayes.

Nor was the explosive attack that followed, which Hayes parried with the Galil, banging the Storm five inches to the left with the barrel, while swinging the buttstock up in a scything strike to bang Popov in the elbow and wrist with the rifle's hand grip and magazine.

Popov's reaction was fast. He snapped back, and quickly covered up his surprise with cocky assurance. Hayes merely stepped back and remained motionless. Against any other opponent he might have tried to press his advantage, but knowing that Popov was trained to have any reaction be as explosive as the attack, Hayes wasn't going to fall into that trap.

After all, it was a man in Kevlar body armor with a Storm knife versus a man in microfiber undergear with an empty rifle. Just about the only weapon that Hayes had right now was his knowledge. Popov may have been trained by the Russian military, but Hayes had been trained by Treadstone.

And if there was one thing Treadstone had taught him—consciously, subconsciously, and even maybe by osmosis—was how to fuck with an opponent's strongest, as well as weakest, weapon—their mind.

Popov immediately started to move again, like a boxer sizing up his opponent. Hayes, however, remained still, holding the Galil in front of him, like a downward-facing samurai sword, from his chin to his crotch. He watched Popov without expression, because the whole idea of Spetsnaz was to be confident and fearless. In attitude and posture, Popov wanted to remain superior to his enemy. He wanted to feast on fear and doubt. Hayes was not going to feed him, either.

Spetsnaz also stressed adaptation. Popov would not be taken in by the same move twice. But he was also trained to kill his enemy in the shortest amount of time possible, and Hayes was ruining that.

"Better kill me quick," Hayes commented, keeping his eyes veiled and his expression blank. "The girl *will* be back. In fact, I think I see her now."

He most certainly did not. In fact, he got the distinct impression that Carver was having a tough time making it through the melee of wolves and residents without getting stabbed or grabbed. The impression remained distant because it was important for him not to lose focus. The goal here was to see how Popov reacted, not to show Popov how Hayes reacted.

Hayes achieved his goal. Although he kept his eyes on Popov's feet because Spetsnaz was also dependent on footwork, he could see in his peripheral vision that Popov had reacted to his comment. His eyes had not stayed locked on Hayes. They had shifted. He was checking all the wolves and Haitians, as well as keeping an eye out for the woman. Hayes's comment had shaken him, because he secretly agreed with it. Time was on the American's side now. It wasn't on the Russian's unless he took it back.

Popov had been taught to be flexible and adapt to any circumstance. There was plenty of circumstance all around them, but none in front of him. To Popov's mind, Hayes was just waiting—waiting for Popov to move, waiting for a wolf or slum resident to attack, waiting for Carver to return. But Hayes knew better. He wasn't just waiting. The American was reflecting and redirecting Popov's weakness back onto him. Because the Russian's greatest weakness was his arrogance. And arrogant people were, at their core, stupid.

Sweat was beginning to form on Popov's brow. *I was trained to execute the enemy in the shortest time possible,* he remembered. *I was trained that once I got to striking distance, I must eradicate the enemy immediately.*

But this entire experience, from the moment he had stepped off the Antonov AN-12 in Port-au-Prince until now, had systematically stripped him of everything he had thought he had become. He had failed his comrades, he had failed his superior, he had failed his country, he had failed himself.

Hayes saw the explosion coming. He prepared himself by remembering his training. "Rule number one in a knife fight: Don't get in a knife fight," the teacher had said. "Rule number two: Didn't you listen to rule number one? Don't get in a knife fight. Rule number three: If you're stupid enough to ignore rules number one and two, understand you're going to get cut. Your job is to minimize the damage."

Hayes turned his arm so the outside, the meat, faced Popov, not the inside where the veins and arteries were close to the surface.

That was all the Russian needed. All his frustration and anger exploded. The Storm knife launched forward, prepared to shift into another killing direction no matter what Hayes did to parry the attack. Any direction it was blocked, the knife would rise, fall, shift, curve, turn, and strike. And once it started striking, it would not stop. Neck, inner thigh, elbow, shoulder, it did not matter. It would cut deep and sever any artery it could find.

Popov's mouth twisted, a triumphant cry beginning to rise in the back of his throat as his eyes locked on to the gleaming blade. But then the cry was choked off as something clamped on to his neck and waist.

Carver *had* returned. She had no gun or knife. In the few endless seconds since Hayes had blocked Popov from following her any farther, she had, in turn, been blocked from getting back to Jesu's hovel by wrestling Haitians. Knowing the impossibility of Hayes's position—an empty rifle versus a knife, an armored man versus a nearly naked one—she took the only possible course she felt she could: get behind the Russian.

So, using the shantytown combatants as cover, she slipped to the far fence and made her way back. Some of the Haitian women saw what she was doing and went alongside her, blocking her from Popov's view. Finally, when she was in position, she ran toward Popov's back.

Hayes saw her do it. That was why he moved his arm when he did. Had Popov not been lunging forward, the Russian would have jammed the knife into her side, neck, or head. It may have given Hayes a second to spare, but given the Russian's training, maybe even that wouldn't have been enough to keep the knife from also plunging into him. That would've resulted in two dead Americans and a doomed Haitian whistleblower.

But that Russian training had not been lessened by the surprise. In fact, it only revitalized it. Hayes used the Galil like a sword, smashing its stock against Popov's knife hand. But instead of disarming him, Hayes watched in shock as Popov lessened the impact by moving his arm with the blow. At the same time, Popov reached up with his free hand to grab Carver's hair.

That's when she bit him as deeply as she could on his neck.

Popov howled, wrenching her off him before throwing her over his shoulder to crash into the mud at Hayes's feet. That forced Hayes to try getting around her. If he tripped over her, they would both be helpless against the enraged, now bleeding, man. At the same time, Carver let the momentum of the throw roll her to her feet, and she immediately sprang back toward the Russian as he charged toward them.

Popov could see, feel, and even taste the inevitable. The Storm would slice across one and then plunge into the other. He didn't care who got cut first, because the Storm would move on, ripping out of the second victim to plunge back into the first. And he didn't care where his enemies were cut or stabbed, because once it started, nothing could stop it. It was impossible for them to hurt him with their bare hands as badly or as quickly as the Storm would tear them apart.

They were coming at him as he swung the Storm. He imagined and savored the feel of rended flesh traveling through his arm.

But then a dark cloud passed between them. The Storm plunged into it. Maxim Popov stared, astonished, into the sad, wet eyes of Hugo Toussaint.

He no longer wore the tactical gear. He was back in his shirt and pants. He had run in from the side when he saw that the Russian was about to kill one or both of his protectors. He had wanted to just hold Popov off. He should have known better, and probably did. Hayes was certain of that when Popov tried to yank the knife out of the man's stomach, but Toussaint purposely turned his torso, driving the knife in deeper and tighter.

Neither Hayes nor Carver wasted that moment. Having already gotten a taste for his blood, Carver sunk her teeth into the wrist of Popov's knife hand. Hayes grabbed the pinky of Popov's knife hand and broke it backward at the same time he plunged the thumb of his other hand as deep into Popov's right eye as it would go.

As the Russian jerked unavoidably back, screeching unrecognizably, Carver kicked him between the legs while Hayes plunged his other thumb into the nerve cluster between Popov's knife wrist and hand. The Russian's grip snapped open like a pop top, allowing Toussaint to fall back into the mud.

Carver immediately went to the fallen banker, and not just to comfort him. She had intel to protect and she didn't want anyone, wolf or otherwise, to accidentally take it as they were trying to strip the man of his clothes, shoes, or even the knife still stuck in him.

Hayes had no problem with that. In fact, he agreed, and was glad she was there to do it because he had a Russian to dismantle. Popov stumbled back, trying to straighten up and reignite his attack, but the damage he had already taken made him shamble like a hunchback.

Seeing that one of his eyes was already ruined, Hayes stabbed the knuckle of his forefinger into Popov's other eye as if trying to pulverize a grape. Then, the Russian sufficiently blinded, Hayes crushed Popov's nose with the palm of his other hand.

The Russian's head snapped back, his arms swinging upward, his feet sliding in reverse. As they did, they kicked up splashes of mud and waste, which gave Hayes a fittingly savage, deserved inspiration.

Grabbing Popov's wrists from the air, Hayes wrenched them around until he was behind Popov, holding his arms as if they were handles of a Russian plow. Then he kicked the back of Popov's knees so the man fell onto his shins. With his mangled eyes, Popov couldn't see the deep puddle of dark, viscous liquid just beneath him, but he could certainly smell it.

Still wrenching the man's arms up and back, Hayes drove Popov's head down, plunging his face deep into the sludge pool with enough force to mash his lips across his face.

Keeping his grip on Popov's arms tight, Hayes slammed his knee onto the back of the Russian's head and held him down until he stopped writhing.

Finally, when all movement left the Russian's body, Hayes

let go of the man's arms, which flopped down as if they were empty of muscles. Hayes stayed kneeling as he looked up and around. The fighting had stopped. The wolves were on one side of the area, closer to their neighborhoods, while the older men were on the other side, now joined by more women, and even a child or two.

The one thing both groups had in common was that they were all staring at the American and his vanquished foe.

Adam Hayes stood up, scanning both groups. It was deep into the morning hours, and everyone looked tired. As he watched, the surviving wolves started backing up.

He wasn't surprised. The wolves had learned who the new alpha was, and that the rest of the herd was now willing to protect themselves. So the wolves, as wolves do, would slink back to their dens, lick their wounds, and rearm until life here drove them crazy again.

Hayes turned toward Carver, who was kneeling with Toussaint's head resting on her thighs. The man's breaths were coming short and shallow. As Hayes watched, Carver bowed down and kissed the fallen man on the forehead.

Fidelus was standing behind them in the entry of his hovel with all his children gathered behind him. They looked sleepy. He looked immeasurably sad.

Hayes breathed deeply, then looked down at the man he had drowned in a puddle of mud, blood, and shit.

"Now you really *are* a ghost," he said, then turned to retrieve his knife and get the hell out of Dodge.

36

SEDONA, ARIZONA

eputy Director of CIA Operations Mike Carpenter was reminded of the staring contest he had with a tarantula when he first came out here. The hairy thing as big as his fist was just standing there in the middle of the driveway, seemingly waiting for someone to come along and mess with him.

"Standing" was a fairly accurate description of what it was doing, too. It wasn't just resting there on all eight spiky, porcupine-needled legs. Its four front legs were up, like a rearing horse, basically giving the impression that it was saying, "You looking at me?" Carpenter must have studied it for a full minute before he walked away. For all he knew, the tarantula was still standing out there.

That staring contest now made Carpenter feel the same way as he stared at Sofia Belov on his laptop screen. She might as well have the nickname Tarantula since Black Widow was pretty overused by now. Even so, she, like the driveway arachnid, was all bluff and no bite since the word came in about what had transpired in Haiti.

That's what this new darknet webchat was predicated on. Carpenter had hoped to get in a nice hike among the red rocks, grab a pork tamale at Tamaliza, and get back here to Casa Astin for a nice long swim in the pool—secure in the knowledge that Belov's handpicked operatives would make quick work of Adam Hayes, and leave them all safe in their beds, visions of twenty-nine million dollars dancing in their heads.

But it was not to be, so Carpenter sat in his shorts and a Kokopelli T-shirt in the pool's changing room mini-cabin with the glorious night views of mesas out a small window, and not nearly as glorious views of three deeply corrupt international power players on his laptop screen.

"You had one job!" Paulo Morales laughed. It was so rare that the Russian black marketer bungled anything that the Brazilian arms dealer happily took the opportunity to tease her.

"I had three jobs," she reminded them. "And only three hastily recruited operatives on a tight deadline. Could you do any better?"

"That is what we are here to find out," Colonel Quan Park of Chinese counterintelligence said sourly. "Mr. Carpenter, what is the status of your moles? Has your investment in them paid off?"

"Colonel," Carpenter replied with great respect. "You know the deference with which I hold your skill at establishing sleeper agents, so I'm sure you're well aware that one can never know a mole's status until they are called upon to awaken."

"Considering that you have your future at stake, Senhor Carpenter," Morales reminded him, "wouldn't it be wise to awaken all your moles on the off chance that any of them are in striking distance?"

Carpenter snorted. "My future is already staked, Senhor Morales. As you well know, I am officially on the run."

"Not officially," Park interjected. "Not yet."

"No," Carpenter said, fighting the urge to add *of course not*. "Given the magnitude of my . . . shall we say, transgression, it would be far more damaging to the reputation of those I left behind at the agency if the news of my . . . naughty behavior got out. But you all know that, don't you?"

"Yes," said Morales with a smirk. "But I just wanted to hear how you would describe it. And I was not disappointed. At least 'transgression' is also a 't' word, along with 'trea—'"

"Enough," Carpenter snapped, feeling like a teacher dealing with unruly students in detention. "Each of you stand to lose more than I do if the evidence Hayes is guarding gets out. To the tune of at least eight million dollars each at last count, I believe?"

Morales slapped the table as he lowered his head and laughed. "That's only a few million more than you would lose," he said.

"And that is only in a monetary sense," Park added. The

colonel sniffed. "That is only a *diu jin tong li*—drop in the bucket—for us."

"Bucket?" Belov scoffed. "Barrel, swimming pool, lake . . ."

"Ocean!" Morales exclaimed. "And you are conveniently ignoring that, even if this evidence does come out, it's not like our reputations will take a hit. As it is, our reputations are not what anyone might call *limpissimos*. Squeaky clean. In fact, it will probably enhance our standing in our communities."

"And Colonel Park can again blame the decadent westerners for daring to impugn his imperial patriotism to the communist cause," Belov said sardonically, but accurately. "This evidence gets out, we get more likes on the internet. You get a hangman's noose."

Carpenter found himself chewing on the inside of his cheek. The students, it seemed, were now the teacher. "What," he said vacantly, "do you want me to do?"

"Enough, enough," Park chided. "Our friends here have a wicked sense of fun," the colonel told Carpenter, shaking his head at the others on the screen. "But it is not ill-timed to remind you that you have a bigger—" Park paused and glanced at Morales. "What's that term?"

"'Dog in the race,'" Morales said immediately, since he ran both dog races and dogfights, among other things. "Reminds me of another term," he continued, looking directly at Carpenter. "'Lie down with dogs, get up with fleas.'"

"Bowwow," Belov said drily.

"Enough," Park repeated to the woman in Russia and the man in Brazil. "Comrade Carpenter, as I said, they are just having their idea of fun with you."

"Yes, yes," Morales chimed in, waving it all away as if it

were a minor practical joke. "Of course Colonel Park and I will retrieve the rose the fair maiden Sofia so daintily dropped. Please be so kind as to inform us as to the whereabouts of our quarry. Just to give us a running start, of course."

"Of course," Carpenter said tightly. "All intel suggests that he will be in the Dominican Republic in a matter of hours."

"Where in the Dominican Republic?" Park inquired blithely. "I'm told it's a fairly large island state."

Belov chuckled. "Oh, Quan. You know that it would fit in the Sichuan Province with room to spare. China is two hundred times bigger than the Dominican Republic. Who's having fun with our little Carpenter ant now?"

Carpenter wondered if they could hear the sound of his teeth grinding. They were well aware that he did not have the full access to the network he used to control. But until an hour or so ago, he didn't think he would need it. He thought, he *hoped*, that he could just take the money he had stolen and run.

"I will get you more specifics as soon as I receive them," he said. "But the quarry cannot complete his mission until he gets back to America, so I think we should concentrate on the airports, at least for the time being."

"What do you mean 'we'?" Belov said quietly, as if it were a casual remark.

"I will get you the intel!" Carpenter snapped, "If you will send the operatives I cannot. And may I remind you that none of this would be necessary if your initial operatives had not bungled their part of the job."

"Oh, the ant has teeth," Belov said with mock fear.

Chill the fuck out, Carpenter told himself. *She's just trying to cover up for her failure. Don't chomp at her bait.*

"I am certain you will," Park said flatly. "Now, Senhor Morales, do you know the percentage of Latin residents versus those of Chinese descent in the Dominican Republic?"

"What does that have to do with anything?" Belov wondered.

"The question is well taken, *meu docinho*," Morales said. *My sweet.* "Given that the next portion of the operation might take place during the day and in public, it wouldn't be prudent to have a team that will stand out." He shifted his attention back to Colonel Park. "I believe Asian people make up less than one percent of the population."

"Well then, that settles it," Park said. "Do you have a team prepared and nearby, Senhor Morales?"

Morales gave a small, knowing smile. "Yes, I believe I have more than enough quality operatives in the area."

"Very good," Park said. "Will that be satisfactory, Comrade Carpenter?"

"Of course," Carpenter said with relief, apparently not knowing, or not acknowledging, that the Chinese now used "comrade" for people they secretly wanted to insult. "Thank you."

"*Tudo bem!*" Morales said pleasantly, with a wave of his hand. *No problem.* "By this time tomorrow we can pretend this conversation never happened."

"With any luck," Carpenter said with a forced smile.

Morales leaned in until his face filled his part of the screen. "My people don't require luck, *puta.*"

Before Carpenter could respond to Morales's use of

the Portuguese word for *bitch*, the Brazilian connection winked out.

Belov grinned and gave a little wave before her connection ended as well.

Carpenter was left with just Colonel Park on his screen.

"Thank you, Colonel," he said slowly. "I pray another call will not be necessary."

"I don't care whether or not another call is necessary," Park immediately replied, which took Carpenter aback. "At this point the money and scandal are of secondary concern for me. They have been since your previous call. My primary concern is your unfortunate, unproductive, and ineffective dependence on us to solve a problem that I think we have made clear is now at least ninety-nine percent yours."

Carpenter blinked. "Yes, please believe me, Colonel, I do . . ."

Park went on as if Carpenter hadn't spoken. "We are willing to clean up your mess out of appreciation for your cooperation in our endeavors, but I truly think you should prove your future worthiness, and be prepared to do what is necessary to fix the problem at the source. Do you not agree?"

At the source. The words echoed in Carpenter's mind for a lingering moment. Then Carpenter's head went up like a dog smelling a bone.

Park's face grew concerned. He recognized Carpenter's expression, and disconnected without another word.

Carpenter had not smelled a bone, despite having lain down with dogs. He had heard something instead. Several things, in fact. First, the sounds of approaching vehicles, then the higher, more distant sound of rotors.

The laptop's plug was torn from the outlet by the time his host had burst into the pool house's changing cabin. He had a look of concern on his face.

"I heard," Carpenter told him, already running for the pool's filtering unit. "Thanks," was his final word to his host as Carpenter disappeared behind it.

His host turned back to the main house, his face now masked in grave resolve. "If this works," he said, "thanks will not be necessary."

37

SEDONA, ARIZONA

L isa Bratton," Carpenter's host said as he looked out on his expansive front lawn, which stretched for many acres until it reached a remote Sedona route five miles away.

From his front porch roost, he looked down upon two armored SUVs flanking a woman in a long coat and a wide-brimmed hat who had just stepped out of a helicopter that had neatly landed in the middle of his circular driveway.

She was surrounded by ten men in dark clothes, each of whom had spy ears that were far more modern, advanced, and dependable than Astin's. And they all wore sunglasses.

"Jeremy Astin," replied the woman. "Long time no see."

"Won't you come in?" her previous tormenter at the CIA training farm politely inquired.

The woman did not reply. Instead she marched up the long, wide, marble staircase toward the front door. Six of her entourage came with her.

Astin, wearing shorts and a Hawaiian shirt, led them through the spacious foyer, under a massive chandelier, and into a nearly cavernous, sumptuously appointed living room.

"Nice place," she commented.

It was an understatement. The mansion, nestled at the top of a hill with Red Rock views overlooking the Coconino National Forest, was awash in picture windows, fireplaces, Venetian plaster, Ming marble, Bisazza tiles, Italian travertine, and was about $8,900,044 more than an instructor at the Central Intelligence Agency training farm could afford.

"Glad you think so," Astin said. "It was paid for with a lot of blood, sweat, and tears." Then he smirked and said, "Yours." Not waiting for the woman's reaction, he approached her, his arms wide. "May I give you a guided . . ."

But before he could say "tour," another voice was heard. This one emanated from a radio inside the woman's coat.

"Out! Everybody out!" it commanded. "Now!"

Two of the men in the black outfits blocked Astin's way, their guns drawn, while the others hustled the woman to the front door.

Astin gawped, his eyes wide and his jaw bobbing.

"Faster!" the voice demanded, so one man swept the woman up into his arms and carried her like a baby out the front door and onto the porch.

"Faster, faster!" the voice repeated with even more urgency, so the man carrying the woman literally threw her to another man coming up the steps from the driveway.

This other man caught the woman and threw her over his shoulder in the same motion, then turned and leapt just as the whole porch shook. The last remaining man by the vehicles ran up the steps to catch and cushion the woman as she fell onto him.

A moment later the explosions started.

"The devices had been built and placed to detonate inward to immolate and eradicate the house using bursts of pressure vessels with flammable and detonable gases, deflagration and detonation of particulates, intentionally detonable gasses in semi-confined spaces, modified military weapons, and a variety of commercial blasting devices."

"Thank you, Doctor," the real Lisa Bratton said, then turned from the forensic pathologist to check the condition of the woman in the long coat, who sat propped up against a gate post almost a mile from the house. She still had on all the body cam that sent what she saw to Bratton, and broadcast what Bratton said to everyone around her.

Although she was badly shaken, with minor cuts, scrapes, bruises, and burns, she would live. Unless the farm instructor had a trapdoor and a fire-, shockwave-, debris-, and shrapnel-proof containment unit under the house, Bratton doubted Astin would.

But the CIA director was putting nothing past these pricks. The search team had already found the underground tunnel through which Mike Carpenter had made his escape, starting from a trick door in what appeared to be a pool filtering device. They had also found the tire tracks at the end of the tunnel a half mile into the desert behind where the house used to be. What was left of the house was a smoking pile of extremely expensive rubble.

Bratton turned her back on it, then stared out into the beautiful desert and the surrounding scenic glories as she lifted a sat phone from her pocket and thumbed a button.

"Let me guess," Levi Shaw answered without a hello, hardly waiting for the encryption to take hold. "You were right."

"The trail was too obvious for me not to be," she replied. "For a rat skilled at hiding, he was practically screaming, 'look at me.'"

"How'd you find him in the first place?"

"For hours, nothing, then suddenly some self-proclaimed hotshot in IT finds a cyber trail? I arrested the hotshot and took the bait."

Shaw paused a moment, which made Bratton listen all the more.

"Maybe the guy in IT was just really good at his job."

"That was my first thought, but when we looked into his background there were just too many connections to Carpenter for it to be a coincidence that this particular guy was the one to pick up the trail."

"In that case, maybe you should have let the hotshot remain free," Shaw finally suggested, "then watched him."

"I considered that," Bratton replied, "then decided against it. What if the person I assigned to the surveillance was also turned? Better we let everyone involved know that their benefactor is no longer in a position to give them what he promised."

"Speaking of their benefactor," Shaw sighed. "Let me guess again. Carpenter had his escape route ready."

"Of course. And, naturally, he gave us the slip."

"Then the problem remains the same," Shaw said sourly. "The more people we use to help, the better the chance that Carpenter has turned at least one of them."

"And Carpenter is willing to sacrifice any one of them. From what I could see on the body cam, Astin was shocked by what was happening."

Shaw let out a short sniff. "He's a real winner. How's your double?"

Bratton glanced back to see the woman was getting a small tank of oxygen. "Singed but unbroken. At least she's learned to listen when I interrupt."

"What clued you in?"

"The tour offer. If their goal was to kill me, and Astin wasn't a human bomb, the only reason to get me deeper into the house was to ensure I didn't get out alive. If I had actually been in the living room or foyer, there was a chance that the detonations would hurl my body out the front door or any of the picture windows."

"When did he buy the house?" Shaw wondered. "That should've been a red flag."

"He didn't," Bratton answered. "Neither did Astin. They were glorified squatters. Carpenter knew the owner's schedule, and that the place was empty six months of the year. Astin thought he was just delaying me. He didn't know that Carpenter was going to sacrifice him."

Bratton could practically sense Shaw shaking his head on

the other end of the line. "All to kill you?" he asked incredulously.

"He knew that if there was a chance of catching him, I would want to be in on it personally," she confirmed.

"He appears to be subscribing to a scorched-earth policy."

"He's clearing the deck," Bratton surmised. "Settling all scores."

The first thought that popped into Shaw's head was *what for?* But a moment after that he recalled others in his past who behaved the same way.

"He may be planning a grand exit," Shaw mused.

"Seems like it. But where to and with what? I hope he's not expecting to collect his CIA pension."

"What's your next move?" Shaw asked.

"I'll leave that to him," Bratton answered. "The traitor is in the wind. He's sure we won't institute an all-points bulletin, to avoid panic if the public found out about this. But I'm going to stop jumping every time he yanks my chain. I have to figure out a way to get ahead of him."

Shaw became quiet, remembering the late-night alert about the new head of the Haitian intelligence service announcing the discovery of a Russian spy ring, which was captured and killed in Port-au-Prince.

Bratton paused for a few seconds before realizing they no longer had time to waste. "Where are you?" she asked.

"Undisclosed location," he muttered, obviously still thinking. "I'm remaining isolated until I decide who I can trust." Bratton could practically hear the DoD director grimace. "I've already made a substantial misjudgment on that front."

"The tool?" Bratton asked incredulously.

"No, not the tool," Shaw replied. "The tool remains as constant as a Swiss Army knife. But it was someone I didn't suspect or expect. If Carpenter could get to him, he could get to anyone."

"But not any longer," Bratton reminded him. "He no longer has the leverage."

"Not enough people know that yet," Shaw reminded her. "And even if they all did, his willingness to kill anyone for any reason continues to put us at a disadvantage."

"That very well may be true," she said sadly. "What's *your* next move?"

"I'm not sure yet," Shaw replied. "But I agree with you— it's time to stop thinking against him and time to start thinking *like* him. We just need the tool to get ahead of him."

PEDERNALES, DOMINICAN REPUBLIC

Jesula Fidelus was as good as his word. The F-150 Zombie *did* ride beautifully. But it was a few hours before Dallys Carver could appreciate it. Hugo Toussaint had died in her arms, holding up the flash drive disguised as a key in his shaking, bloody fingers. He had waited to speak his last words until Hayes had gotten to them.

"Protect her," Toussaint had said. "Then take them down. Take all four of them down."

Carver's wet blue-green eyes had burned up at Hayes. *All four.* Toussaint had only mentioned three. Pasquette was kind and stupid enough to have already revealed the fourth.

"I will," Hayes had told him. He'd never know if Toussaint had heard him before he died.

But Cité Lalin was accustomed to death, so, after that, all there was to do was disappear into Jesu's hovel and never appear to the wolves or the residents again. If anyone nearby had recognized the purr of a Fidelus-tuned engine coming to life, they gave no hint of it.

When they finally left, Jesu's farewell was unceremonious, to say the least. Carver considered giving the man a hug but thought better of it. Without a word, she and Hayes had gotten into the vehicle, Fidelus had opened the "garage door" sheet, then held up a hand in farewell as they drove quietly out of his life. Or perhaps the hand was to signify good-bye and good riddance. If it was, neither Carver nor Hayes would blame him—but somehow they both thought the extraordinary man was above that.

In any case, the man's scrawled, secondhand directions also held up. The roads deteriorated from their already low quality the closer Hayes and Carver got to the Port-au-Prince border, but that was what the Zombie had been designed for.

Hayes knew they were out of the city the moment the roads turned into abased trails. But only then did he see the country's natural beauty. The green-carpeted, forest-dappled landscape was a welcome change from the overcrowded shantytown.

Thankfully it was still so late that roads and trails alike were empty of vehicles and people. Even so, Hayes had to avoid an armadillo, donkey, and lizard or two along the way.

The fact that Haiti was the poorest nation in the Western Hemisphere was certainly driven home as even the glorious vistas of mother nature were diminished by the pervasive signs of poverty in every non-natural thing that littered the landscape—up to and including the air around them. But the farther they got into the adjoining Ouest region, the more breathable it became.

They drove in their undergear, the drying mud threatening to meld with their skin, for two hours until they spotted a tributary of Lake Azuei, the largest lake in the country. They were able to park in some tall grass and walk only twenty yards before the trickle opened onto a natural pool, which was being fed by a waterfall that crawled down an incline.

Keeping their undergear on, both waded into the water up to their waists and happily stuck their heads under the waterfall, which led to the first thing Carver had said in more than a hundred and twenty minutes.

"Don't swallow," she advised. "You never know what might be in it."

Hayes was just about to drink, but he quickly spit it out of his mouth. It was good advice, but it reminded him that he hadn't had a drop of water since the safe house. Feeling both hunger and dehydration, he started to move back to shore, but stopped as Carver raised her head into the waterfall and began to cleanse her reddish-blond hair.

Hayes wished he could allow her this one indulgence, but they still had miles ahead of them.

"Come on," he grunted. "Let's get going. The sooner you're safe the happier I'll be."

There would have been a time when she maintained she could take care of herself, but not after last night. They both moved quickly back to the vehicle where they retrieved the shirts, pants, and boots that Jesula, Toussaint, or even some of the children had folded and piled neatly on the Zombie's bench.

They were approaching the northern end of Lake Azuei, which stretched along the Dominican border for sixty-six miles, but Carver insisted they move on rather than trying to cross over at that point.

"No trusted contact who owes you a favor here?" Hayes asked.

Refreshed, but still smarting mentally and physically, Carver simply gave him a curt nod, and directed him farther southeast. By the time they had been driving for five hours, the appearance of a long yellow-orange line of sunlight on the horizon seemed to shake Carver out of her well-deserved funk.

"There's a daily binational market near Rio El Mulito on the border," she told him, "ten miles north of Pedernales."

"Won't we stand out?"

"Like sunflowers?" she said, grinning for the first time in a while. "No. The Dominican Republic has far more American tourists than Haiti, and this is one of the go-to spots."

"Won't we need visas?"

"No again," she said. "For three reasons. First, a western tourist can stay in the DR for thirty days without one. Second, Haitians are free to cross the border to buy food that's too expensive back home or sell extra clothing and medicine donations."

She paused, so Hayes took up the slack. "And three?"

"And three," she said, glancing at him out the corner of her eyes, "I have a trusted contact there."

"Let me guess. Someone who owes you a favor?" he asked.

"Not exactly," she answered, shielding her eyes against the sunrise's glare. "Look for a big cement blockhouse with all kinds of conveyances outside."

"Conveyances?"

"Everything from oxcarts to tap taps," she explained.

"Is there a parking lot?"

"I wish. More like wheeled chaos."

"Okay," said Hayes. "Give me a ten-minute warning. I think we better find a place to hide this vehicle nearby."

Carver looked like she wanted to discuss the pros and cons of such a thing, but quickly accepted it as a decent idea.

Finding a hiding place was relatively easy since virtually everything from north Pedernales to west Santo Domingo, a hundred miles to the east, was river-threaded countryside. Hayes carefully drove over crumbling concrete paths linked by rocky, bumpy trails until he pulled into a foliage-enclosed area just big enough to squeeze the vehicle into.

"Will they search us at this market?" Hayes asked as he pushed his FN into his waistband under his shirt.

"I doubt it," Carver answered, doing the same with her SIG. "Let's find out."

The walk along the Mulito River as the sun rose was the first oasis of peace Hayes had experienced since falling asleep on the plane out of New Mexico. Although he never stopped watching for a glint of a rifle scope, telescopic sight, or green armor, the sound of the rushing water, insects, and birds lulled him into an unwanted feeling of hope.

This trusted contact better be gold, he thought.

His inner voice didn't fail him.

More likely fool's gold, bobo, it said. *Don't let your guard down.*

The waterway narrowed and coursed around a large, wooded patch of light brown earth dotted with gazebos made of narrow tree trunks topped with roofs made of leaves. They led to an unpaved driveway widening to a warehouse-sized cement blockhouse surrounded by hundreds of people looking to buy and sell.

Carver and Hayes stood in the buyers' line, and quickly discovered that the holdup was not because of guards checking IDs or searching the entrants, but because so many people wanted to get in, even at this early hour.

Once inside, Hayes was impressed by the sheer volume of goods—from running shoes and clothes to luggage and kitchen appliances—stacked everywhere, all of it separated only by small doorless, roofless, numbered cement booths.

"We're looking for E-001," Carver told him.

They found it in the southeast corner, where a tall, strong, handsome Black woman with close-cropped hair, ankle boots, a vented khaki short-sleeve shirt, and matching cargo pants leaned against the booth's concrete wall, surveying the crowd with her arms folded.

"What are you selling?" Carver asked her.

"The usual crap," she answered with an American accent before she stood up, nodded at Hayes, picked up a burlap bag, and said, "Let's go."

He didn't ask questions. It was obvious that Carver and the woman knew each other, and, on the basis of their ease, had known each other for quite some time. He followed them to the exit door where a fairly disinterested security guard held up his hand, then listlessly pointed at Carver and Hayes.

Hayes's hand shifted to his side for quick access to his FN, but the woman simply pulled out a billfold and flipped it open. At first Hayes thought it might be a bribe, but just before it was in the security guard's face, he got a glimpse of it. It was unmistakably a US embassy ID. The security guard reacted to it as if it was a get out of jail free card.

The woman stepped aside, and motioned for Carver and Hayes to go out the exit door first. She followed, pleasantly telling the guard *gracias*.

Once outside, she retook the lead and brought Carver and Hayes through the wheeled chaos to a dark red Toyota sports utility vehicle.

She unlocked the doors with a push of her key button, and Carver got in the passenger-side front without even offering it to Hayes. When he hesitated at the rear seat door, Carver looked at him with a knowing smile.

"What?" she said. "Do you think I wasn't going to call shotgun after what we've been through?"

Hayes shook his head and got in the back without complaint, taking advantage of the position to scan the entire area.

The woman tossed the burlap bag into the back next to him, started the car, and pulled away from the lunacy.

"What did you get?" Carver asked, glancing at the bag in the backseat.

"Some things that might come in handy," the woman answered, then concentrated on threading through the riverside maze of trails and crumbling concrete bridges, before she turned onto Avenida Duarte, heading south.

"Adam," Carver said, "this is my friend Jessica." She smiled over at the driver. "A trusted contact."

The driver glanced in the rearview mirror to lock eyes with him. "Captain Jessica Knell to you, sir," she said without irony. "Dallys and I met at the Defense Intelligence Agency Operating Training Course at Camp Peary."

"That's where the CIA does its training, too," Carver added.

"Thanks for telling me," Hayes said drily.

Knell snorted. "If that was sarcasm," she said, "I'm surprised you have any sense of humor at all after what Dallys told me."

"How much did she tell you?" he asked.

"Not enough and too much," Knell said honestly. "Let me start by saying I signed out a medium-security vehicle for this trip. It has a rudimentary bullet-resistant coating. It won't stop an SVDK but it should work on a Taurus round."

"Well, that's something, at least," Hayes said without humor.

"I didn't want to alert any possible turncoat at the embassy garage," she informed him.

Hayes was impressed. "I appreciate that."

"I wanted you to know that I'm taking this seriously," she replied. "And I know from experience what that means."

Carver breathed deeply. "Ever since Jess and I met," she said, "it's been us against them. You can guess what training was like. A white chick is bad enough, but a Black woman? There's still too big a percentage that can't have that. That *won't* have that."

"I can imagine," Hayes said, unavoidably having memory

shards of the Treadstone training slice across his brain. Compared to that, their DIA course was like Junior's first day of t-ball.

"Enough reminiscing," Knell interrupted. "Fill me in on what's been happening so I can adjust my plans as needed."

Between the two of them, they told Knell everything they knew. Everything but the trio of names they didn't know on the flash drive key. By the time they finished, Knell's expression was as hard as Hayes's—and she was scanning everywhere for everything from green armor to drones.

"Shee-it," Knell breathed as the car crossed the Pedernales border, and recognizable civilization began to appear around them. "I wish I could trust the embassy personnel enough to bring you in and read the flash drive, but I can't. In any case, except for the severity of the corruption quotient, I don't think I've compromised your security yet. Fortunately, I haven't mentioned either of your names to anyone."

"I told you not to," Carver reminded her.

"Yeah, but I would have decided that on my own anyway, DC," she answered. "Thankfully any trusted contact I have wasn't in the office the day you contacted me." She looked back at Hayes via the rearview mirror again. "But I did put into motion a plane out of here back to the States. But now I've got to vet everyone involved, from the crew to any other passengers."

"Don't rush on our account," Carver said.

"*Do* rush on our account," Hayes disagreed. For the first time in hours, he grabbed on to the thin lifeline that he might be able to make it back to Jack's birthday in time.

"I understand," Knell said, although she didn't. Hayes

hadn't told anyone about his family emergency deadline. "I will do the best I can."

"Which is very good, I can tell you," Carver assured Hayes.

"And hopefully we'll get you out on a flight tonight or tomorrow."

"And in the meantime?" Hayes asked.

"In the meantime, you get to enjoy the comfort and security of what passes as a safe house in my neck of the woods."

What passed as a safe house in her neck of the woods was ecotourism.

"For treehuggers," she said as she pulled the SUV into a forest-lined driveway, "it's about conservation and supporting the locals. For me, it's secrecy. No one at the embassy knows about this place." The driveway opened out into a small, well-designed beachside community by the Caribbean Sea. "For you, it's privacy and security." She stopped at the edge of the sandy parking lot. "Welcome to the Eco del Mar."

Carver could have visited Knell before so she might have had a head start on adjusting to this surprising safe house, but Hayes got slowly out of the backseat as Knell retrieved the burlap bag. He stared at the glorified campsite spread out before them from the lip of the parking lot.

The "rooms" ranged from Caribbean cabins on platforms through upscale huts to tents right by the beach. They were all extremely clean, nicely thought-out, cleverly designed, and well constructed. Knell nodded at the largest structure at the apex of the site.

"That's yours," she said. "I chose it because no one can approach without you seeing them. And you don't have to approach anyone else if you don't want to."

Hayes was about to express some concern, but whether it was his hunger, thirst, or exhaustion talking, he quickly appreciated that Captain Knell was crazy like a fox. It was not only beautiful and refreshing here, but remarkably secure.

Knell saw Hayes's expression and smiled. "Always do favors for hotel owners," she murmured, then cocked her head at Carver. "I taught *her* that."

Captain Knell then brought them up the steps of the circular, up-raised platform their teak cabin rested on, and unlocked the door. She left them inside the loftlike space, under the vaulted ceiling, and between the two queen-sized platform beds that faced a bathroom, which inspection revealed had a rainfall showerhead.

Hayes was glad that the windows were only uncovered at the top, just below the wood-beamed ceiling, so even a sniper couldn't get a bead on them. The rest of the glass was thickly covered by eight-foot-tall pleated curtains.

"I'll get you out as soon as possible," Knell said, "so rest, eat, drink, and, whatever else you do, wash." Knell tossed the burlap bag to Carver and the room key to Hayes, then headed for the door. "Because believe me," she said, "from the way you two smell right now, you need it."

Inside the burlap bag was bottled water, takeout containers of sancocho—the local stew with seven types of meat, vegetables, and tubers—and even a change of clothes.

Hayes showered first, since Carver decided he stank the worst. It was a different man who emerged, a fluffy white towel around his waist. At first Carver's face clouded as she saw the full road map of scars across his torso, but then her expression cleared when she saw his assured, even serene, face.

"My turn," she said, taking the pile of clothes Knell had bought for her at the binational market. "Hope yours fit. Jess only had my guess of your size to go on."

"I'm sure they'll be fine," Hayes replied. Not surprisingly, Knell had bought the most utilitarian, practical, and functional fashion she could. They looked much like hers—vented long-sleeved shirts with big pockets and cargo pants; dark blue for him and olive for Carver. Thankfully she even thought of boxers, briefs, and undergear. They weren't military grade, but at least they were decent knockoffs.

As he heard the rain shower head go on inside the bathroom, Hayes looked around at the inventory they had spread out during and after wolfing down the stew and guzzling the water—in his case one long pull that emptied fifty-eight ounces. Over on the writing desk next to the bathroom door, across and between the beds, he saw their guns, his knife, and, lying beneath them, the two keys—one Fidelus's, the other Toussaint's.

Hayes looked down at the fresh, clean clothes on the seemingly soft bed, and tried to decide whether to change or simply fall face-first and not wake up until it was time to go. At that moment, he heard Carver start to sing in the shower. It was as if a guardian angel had lifted a two-ton weight off his shoulders.

That's just the exhaustion talking, said the voice. Hayes couldn't disagree, but maybe it would shut up when he fell asleep.

Hayes was lowering his head when Carver's sat phone buzzed.

His eyes snapped open, all exhaustion leaving him. His head whipped toward it.

Had to be Knell.

Too soon. She just left.

She probably forgot to tell us something.

So answer it and find out. What, you're going to wait until Dallys gets out of the shower?

Hayes was off the bed and at the phone. He checked its ID screen. *Anonymous.* Makes sense if it was an embassy line. He pressed the accept button and put the phone to his ear.

"D-daddy . . ."

The second he heard his son's tiny voice on the other end, the exhilaration that came with having survived drained from his body and, in that moment, Hayes knew his post-Treadstone life was over.

"Jack, what's wrong?"

"The bad men are here . . . they—"

Before the boy could finish, a familiar voice came on the line. "You know who this is, and you know what I want."

"You fucking monster," Hayes spat.

"You've got twelve hours," Mike Carpenter said, and then the line went dead.

39

The man who emerged from the Eco del Mar was devoid of serenity or even assurance. What had replaced them was far worse.

Adam Hayes marched double-time to the parking lot. A group of teenagers were unlucky enough to be lounging around a Yamaha V Star 250 motorcycle near the steps to the beach.

Forgetting about checking every vehicle to see which would be the most easily stolen, Hayes made a beeline to the teens, then, without pausing, straight-armed the one on the cycle seat with such power that the kid vaulted up five feet and spun backward over the low parking lot fence.

As the bike owner thudded to the beach below, Hayes jumped onto the cracked, worn seat and roared away so quickly that the other teens didn't even start yelling until the bike was disappearing into the tree-lined drive.

Hayes knew this ride. Fifteen cubic inch, air-cooled, two-valve with a five-speed multi-plate wet clutch, dual exhaust, and front disc brake. It was older, somewhere between a 2012 and 2015 model, but it would do. Even if it had not been recently tuned up, and Hayes doubted that it had been, it should get at least seventy-five miles a gallon, and reach a top speed of around eighty miles an hour. As he tore out onto Avenida Duarte, heading north, he saw how close he could get to it.

On the avenue, old cars were outnumbered by old bikes, and both had the same casual attitude toward driving that he had seen elsewhere in the Caribbean. If there was a helmet law in effect, Hayes saw no evidence of it. But within minutes, the traffic, pedestrians, and buildings on either side were just a blur to him.

First stop, the place where the F-150 Zombie was hidden. He wasn't happy to see the toiletry bag was still under the bench where he left it. He had hoped someone would come along and relieve him of the temptation caused by the addictive Treadstone pills inside. Why was there never a thief around when you needed one?

He hesitated but then snatched the bag up and shoved it into a pocket of the cargo pants.

He paused for a second, weighing the options of the two vehicles, but he quickly settled on the bike. Once someone saw the Zombie they'd never forget it. But trying to spot a stolen Yamaha motorcycle in the Dominican Republic would be like trying to pick out one specific person with brown eyes.

Hayes grabbed one of the fuel cans, snapped open the Yamaha's gas tank, and poured until it spilled over. Then he climbed on the bike and sped out of there.

Back on the open road, it was every vehicle for itself, but Hayes was no longer just another driver. Although the other bikes seemed to defer to the larger vehicles, the Yamaha's rule was if you can't help, get out of the way. As he weaved, dodged, and passed, no matter how narrow or small the space seemed to be, he thought furiously.

He swore he could remember something that Carver said Chico Long told her. That he knew a guy in Pedernales who could get them to an airport nearby. Airports were near the water. Hayes headed south, the way he had come, and tried to hack his way out of his rage jungle to see daylight.

He mentally checked his inventory. Gun, knife, pills, and keys, that was it. He had no phone—sat, cell, or otherwise. No way he was going to take Carver's sat phone, not after what the Russian one he took did to him.

Normally he'd try to figure out how they found him, let alone call him, but this was no longer normal times. If the Russians and the CIA deputy director of operations were two of the four entities on the flash drive, at least one of the other two was likely to be China. The fourth was a coin toss.

Frustration mingling with his fury, Hayes yanked the V Star onto main road forty-four. The back streets, which virtually all the streets were, would not be helpful in finding an airport, but if anything would, it would be the signage on one of the country's main paved roads. Although normally the trip would be start and stop as a regular driver navigated the slowdowns, Hayes did not slow down, speeding past the other motorbikes and weaving in and out between the cars and trucks.

Seventeen minutes down Route 44 and he saw the first bent, rusted, pockmarked sign with the universal airport symbol. Ten minutes later he saw a beige tower that was shaped like a window-ridden torch of the Statue of Liberty. He sped up again.

Like most airport exits, the one off Route 44 was crowded, but that made no difference to him. He rode in, around, and among other vehicles as if threading a maze. Moments later he broke through to the main entrance road of the airport, lined with tropical palm and caoba trees.

The fenced-in runways were to his right, and the parking lots to his left. The lone terminal was straight ahead. There was no gate on the parking lot entry so all he did was slow down, aim for an open space, cut the engine, put his feet down, and let the Yamaha slide out from under him. As it thumped against the curb and fell over, Hayes kept walking.

The place looked like any medium-sized airport in America—glass walls, windows and sliding doors, floor tiles in geometric patterns, plastic and steel seating along the windows, and a variety of overpriced shops selling mediocre food and trinkets. Hayes gave that a cursory look and moved toward the arrivals and departures screens. They were displayed on a wall over the airline counters—the domestic flights to the left, which were plentiful, and the international flights on the right, which were sparse.

In fact, the only international flights were to New York, Boston, Madrid, and three Florida cities: Fort Lauderdale, Miami, and Orlando. Any of those would work for him. He wasn't surprised when the flights to Orlando outnumbered the others three to one. He looked for the flight that departed the soonest. There was one at twelve-thirty that arrived at three-ten.

Hayes moved quickly to get as many details on the aircraft as he could. He didn't have a passport or ID, but he had hidden on planes before. Given the size of the airport, he hoped that smaller cities in the Dominican Republic still let loved ones accompany passengers to the gates. It did. Checking the trash can to the side of the gate's ancient printer, he saw the plane's call letters. In just a few minutes he saw the plane itself, taxiing to the gate.

The setup was perfect for his purposes. The passengers would move out onto the tarmac while a rolling staircase was brought over for them. He would have a variety of opportunities to find a way on board. He started to move to a blind spot by the doors, then glanced around to make sure no one was looking.

Dark hair and a flash of reddish-blond caught the corner of his eyes. Hayes immediately pressed himself deeper into the blind spot. It was Carver and Knell. How the hell had they tracked him here? They had to have some sort of tracker on him. They couldn't have just found him by accident. What, did Carver call her friend right after she found him gone, and she came speeding back?

Didn't matter. Since they were here, they'd search. He saw them already talking to an airport employee, who pointed in the direction of the Orlando flight gate. As the white and Black women started in his direction, Hayes sidled away until he could turn a corner and look for any employee entrance or exit. He found it midway down the hall, between lavatories and the back of a food stall.

Incredibly, it wasn't locked and he found himself in a maintenance hallway that was used by the baggage handlers and ground crew. To his left the curving hall moved deeper into the bowels of the terminal. To his right, it opened out onto the runways.

The winding hallway was designed so the employees could have a clear view of the field. Before anyone could spot or question him, Hayes moved away from the terminal and toward the light. As he went, the curve of the hallway revealed more of the tarmac, as well as an overhead walkway that connected the terminal to the observation tower.

When Hayes looked down from it, he saw two men in zip-up jackets coming toward him. They were smiling and had their hands at their sides. Hayes slowed. Although they had chestnut-colored skin, their features looked as Dominican as his did. Hayes stopped and looked behind him. A third man in the same outfit was moving slowly toward him from that direction as well, but this man was considerably larger than his compatriots. He kept his hands loose and by his side.

Hayes leaned against the wall. He looked right, toward the two smiling men, and smiled back—a big, wide, almost feral smile. Then he charged.

As he expected, the men reacted like assassins, not airline employees. They immediately split up, their hands going inside their jackets, but, by then, Hayes was on them, grabbing one by the hair and yanking him into the other man, while sweeping the first man's ankles with his right leg.

The first man collided with the second, who stumbled aside, giving Hayes time to shift back to his original target. He let go of the man's hair for just a second, then regripped it even tighter from the back. Immediately, he yanked the first man up and around—just in time for the giant, who had been behind Hayes, to pull out a Glock G43X, the most sought-after handgun on the market, complete with a Banish 45 suppressor, which cost twice as much as the gun.

As he tried to get a clear shot, Hayes kicked the man he was holding up between the legs from behind, which jerked the man completely off the ground, his hands spasming to his side. The hand that had been inside his jacket came out, clutching his own Banished Glock, which Hayes ripped out of his hand as the second man tried to get his silenced Glock clear of the encroaching bodies of his partner as well as Hayes, who snapped a shot at the third man.

The giant seemed reluctant to fire back with his partner still in Hayes's grip, but self-preservation left him no choice.

As even the man who was firing feared, Hayes merely ducked behind the man he was holding and shoved him higher still. The bullet thudded into the first man's chest as Hayes looked from behind him into the second man's eyes. The second man tried to move his gun to aim at Hayes rather than his partner, but he was too slow. Hayes shot the second man between the eyes, then immediately pushed the first man forward.

"*Largá-lo,*" hissed the gigantic assassin. "*Ele está morto.*"

That wasn't Spanish, Hayes thought. Sounds like Portuguese, the main language of Brazil. But he recognized the word *morto*, which made him smile grimly.

He knew the first man wasn't dead, or even really shot. He had felt the sensation of the nine-millimeter round thudding into the man's ballistic vest beneath the zip-up jacket. He even felt the extra weight of it when he was jerking the man around. That was why the third man shot his associate so quickly and readily. He hoped Hayes wouldn't know or realize that the man was wearing a bulletproof vest and let his guard down.

He doesn't know you very well, does he?

No, he does not, Hayes thought as he pushed the first man out in front of him, even closer to the giant, who kept shifting his position, trying to get a clear shot at someone other than his fellow killer. He couldn't retreat, because as soon as he did, Hayes would drop him with the silenced Glock he still possessed.

The only other thing the third man could have done was feint as if about to run, hoping that Hayes would expose enough of himself from behind his shield so the third man could nail him. But that all depended on Hayes not making a kill shot, and even the third man—*especially* the third man, being a professional killer—knew that was unlikely. The Glock G43X was sought after for a reason. And one of the prime reasons was its accuracy.

So the third man tried to take advantage of that accuracy by continuing to try shooting Hayes around or past his partner, who Hayes kept pushing forward and jerking around by his hair. The reason the first man didn't fight back was that he was still trying to recover from Hayes's genital-crushing kick. Hayes knew how to kick a man in the balls. Hard enough to take the fight out of him, but not hard enough to make him deadweight.

So as the first man kept spasming in agony, the third man's second bullet hit him on the right side. The third bullet hit his left shoulder.

Idiot, Hayes thought. *Good luck hitting my hand in his hair. You may have the best silencer money can buy, but you don't have a laser targeting sniper scope.*

If Hayes had been here for any other reason, he might have started feeling bad for the man he had by the short scalp hairs, but he wasn't, and didn't, so he kicked the man between the legs from behind again. As the man unwillingly leapt back into the air, Hayes finally shot the third man in the face.

The Glock G43X was as accurate as they said, but it only held six rounds, and time was a-wasting. The third man went down onto his back, and as Hayes lowered the first man, his hair ripped completely out from under Hayes's fingers, and his body flopped down at Hayes's feet. Hayes nailed him there with another shot from the Glock.

It had been less than a minute, and even if someone had been listening, all they would have heard was a couple of quiet coughs. The Banish 45 is the lightest, most versatile, and effective silencer going. That's why it costs a thousand bucks.

Hayes dropped the fistful of the man's hair and his Glock onto the second, already dead, man. He retrieved the second man's silenced weapon because it was still fully loaded. It could come in handy, along with Hayes's non-silenced FN.

Hayes looked quickly around while shoving the Banished Glock inside his shirt, but the area was still empty of workers or innocent bystanders. He moved swiftly and quietly to the end of the semicircular space and saw that the flight to Orlando, which was parked at the gate nearest to his right, was loading both passengers and luggage.

Wow, he thought. *I just might be able to do this.*

Right, his inner voice answered. *Especially after all the good luck you've had so far.*

As usual, the voice was correct. As Hayes neared the last remaining open luggage compartment, he saw the baggage handlers talking among themselves, leaving a path to the hold. Just before he decided to make a silent, smooth, slouching run toward it, he took one last look up to make sure he wasn't being watched.

Hayes froze, then pulled back into the shadows at the edge of the open-ended curving hallway. He slowly and carefully stuck as little of his upper face around the corner as he could. Once again he saw a second-story observation picture window, where all the friends and family of the passengers were smiling and waving.

But that hadn't made him stop from trying to slip into the cargo hold. Not even Carver and Knell, who were also watching the field from that vantage point, were the ones who canceled that plan. It was the three more chestnut-skinned men in zip-up jackets ten feet down the line of family and friends who had frozen him.

The Russians had sent three. The Latin Americans had

apparently doubled down and sent six. And just one glance, as well as the cutting-edge equipment they were supplied with, convinced Hayes that their instructions were to do anything necessary to kill him—even if that included taking an entire plane, and all its passengers, down with him.

40

PEDERNALES, DOMINICAN REPUBLIC, 11:45 A.M.
GRANT COUNTY, NEW MEXICO, 9:45 A.M.
(11 HOURS, 15 MINUTES REMAINING)

ayes looked upfield. There was nothing but the end of the
runway and the Caribbean Sea beyond. Hayes looked
the other way, and immediately started sidling down the
terminal wall in that direction. Beyond a patch of crab-grassed
lawn and a chain-link fence topped with three strands of
barbed wire was the private plane lot and hangars.

Just from a quick glance he saw at least a dozen small
planes parked in the long, narrow lot, and beyond them two
hangars for fueling and prep. Staying close to the terminal
wall would hopefully keep him out of sight from observers,
even if they craned their heads downward and to the side.

He increased his speed slightly when he neared the fence. He had started developing his fence-jumping ability as a kid. Some of the most interesting things he found throughout his life were on the other side of barbed-wire-topped fences. And at least this one didn't have barbed-wire rolls attached at the top. These were the three-strand types, which were strung out by intermittent flat metal wands attached to the top of the fence posts, which basically just added a foot in height.

Hayes grabbed the chain links in both hands, just under the barbed wire, pulled himself up, then swung his right leg up until he could plant his boot bottom flat on a metal wand. Then, with his hands, arms, and anchored right leg, he propelled himself up until he was essentially standing on the wand, over both the fence and barbed-wire topper. From there he hopped over, just enough to clear the barbs. He landed as lightly as he could on the other side, just eight inches from the fence.

He took a quick glance back to see if anyone had spotted him, but being so close to the terminal wall shielded him from any onlookers. There was a small drop to the private plane lot, and then Hayes moved quickly toward the hangars along the far left side. He passed a Beechcraft Musketeer, a Grumman AA, a Piper Cherokee, and a Cirrus SR20 as he neared the fuel hangar. What he didn't pass was any owner or airport employee. He imagined the lot might get more crowded on the weekend, but no hardworking Dominican was going to spend their time at the airport midweek.

As he sidled into the fuel hangar his eyebrows raised. Tucked on the far side was a Cirrus Vision jet, but right in front of him was a single-engine, fixed-wing Cessna 172S, the most successful single-engine aircraft in history. Hayes didn't pause. He grabbed the gas pump nozzle hanging on the fuel dispenser that was bolted just inside the hangar opening, climbed up to the top of the wing, opened the twist-off cap to the fuel tanks in the wings, and checked the level of gas. They were already three-quarters full. He topped them off. Jumping down to return the gas nozzle to the dispenser, he glanced inside the small cockpit.

Good timing. By the rolling carry-on and golf clubs across the rear two seats of the four-seater, it looked as if someone was planning a lunchtime jaunt. With any luck the owner's flight plan had already been approved. Hayes stood on no ceremony—he pulled himself up into the pilot's seat and checked the ignition. The key was in it.

Another one for your collection.

Hayes smiled tightly at the upgraded avionics panel. Most often the Cessna had a traditional flight instrument dashboard with circular dials displaying altitude, airspeed, attitude, heading, and navigation. But this one had digital and electronic screens along with a multifunction communication and navigation display that included traffic, weather, and a cutting-edge autopilot.

Hayes quickly switched on the circuit breakers, put the master switch on, gripped the throttle, and turned the key. The dependable engine thrummed on as Hayes checked the fuel flow and mixture. He adjusted the throttle, retreated the flaps, and made sure the transponder was on.

"*Oye!*" he heard from outside. "*¿Qué estás haciendo?*"

The owner had arrived, wearing an all-golf ensemble. Hayes didn't know Russian, Haitian Creole, or Portuguese, but he knew some Spanish.

"Hey yourself," Hayes answered tightly, starting the Cessna rolling out of the hangar, directly at the amazed, angry golfer who was waving his arms. "Can't you see what I'm doing?"

He knew the golfer couldn't hear him over the noise of the engine, and saw that the man didn't care. He kept waving his arms until it was abundantly clear that couldn't stop the plane-jacker, then he skittered off to the side. But even Hayes increasing the taxiing speed didn't deter him. He ran around to the passenger side, jumped up on the wing strut, and started yanking on the door latch, shouting, *"¡Parada, parada! ¡Ayudar!" Stop, stop! Help!*

Hayes gave him half of what he asked for. He kicked open the passenger door, which knocked him back, but he held on. Then he threw his rolling luggage bag at him. It caught him square in the chest, sending him down to the tarmac. The owner rolled to the side of the grass and watched as the Cessna picked up speed toward the private plane runway—his golf clubs falling out of the door one by one, finally followed by the gold bag. The jolt of it landing sent six golf balls bouncing after the plane.

Back at the Orlando flight, most of the well-wishers still had their focus on the travelers. All still waved at where they thought their friends or family were sitting, while some pointed at windows where they thought they saw their friends' or family members' faces. None of these people paid any mind to the noise and activity down on the southeast part of the runway.

But three people on the left side of the crowd, and two

people on the right side, did. Carver slapped Knell's shoulder with the back of her hand, and, when she got the DR Embassy's HI officer's attention, pointed at the Cessna heading for the private plane runway, as well as the golfer floundering at the top of a grassy ditch among his clubs and bouncing balls. As the two hustled in that direction, Knell was distracted by three chestnut-skinned men in zip-up jackets racing down to the still-open gate outside the Orlando plane.

Knell grabbed Carver's sleeve to stop her, then nodded at the three men, one of whom was waving rectangles of paper at the gate stewards while the other two headed toward the baggage handlers.

"They had tickets for the flight," Knell breathed. She looked sharply around for the exits, then started running, waving for Carver to follow.

Meanwhile, one of the Brazilians was arguing with the gate steward while another was yelling at the baggage handlers— both in Portuguese. The airport personnel looked perplexed until they realized it was a diversion for the third man to find his checked bag in the luggage cart. He yanked the satchel from the other bags and yelled at his two partners while waving it. The airport employees started to yell at the Brazilians to prove the bag was theirs, but by then the trio in the zip-up jackets were already running down the field.

The closest baggage handler grabbed the back of one of the jackets, but that Brazilian just spun around, smashing the airport employee in the head with the bag. The baggage handler slammed down to the tarmac as the trio kept running toward the private plane runway. Two kept running while the third did a hard left toward a standard motorized airport cart, which, ironically, was called a passenger utility golf cart at airports around the world.

All he had to do was press the engine button and, within seconds, he was cruising alongside his two associates, who jumped on. Then the driver tromped on the accelerator and the cart jumped forward, reaching its top speed of twenty-five miles an hour in just three seconds.

By then, airport personnel had gotten to the fallen golfer as well as the baggage handler while Hayes had gotten the Cessna to the wrong end of the private plane runway.

Normally international flights took off to the southwest, over the water, while the private planes took off northeast over the Dominican Republic. But Hayes wasn't planning a domestic trip, and the Orlando flight would not take off for at least a half hour, so he ignored the increasing intense chatter coming from the cockpit headset that he left on the copilot seat and concentrated on takeoff.

That concentration was disturbed by the appearance of an airport passenger cart stopping at what was supposed to be the start of his runway. Hayes was not about to wait, for the golfer, the golf cart, or anything. He lined the Cessna up with the runway, checking that the directional gyro matched the runway heading. He checked that his fuel mix was at its most potent, then advanced the throttle all the way to full.

As the plane started to pick up speed down the runway, the Brazilian with the bag opened it up and pulled out a nasty little weapon that looked like a T-shirt cannon attached to a sawed-off shotgun. As Hayes tried to concentrate on the oil pressure and temperature gauges, he glimpsed the Brazilian pulling a stock section of the device to his shoulder before squeezing his eye to a suction cup attached to a scope atop the device's large round barrel just as the Cessna's airspeed indicator lit up.

Shit, he thought, *is that one of the grenade launchers the Army Contracting Command's weapons product manager announced the search for?*

Hayes remembered the notice well. The new weapon, variations of which were being developed all over the world for consideration, had to be an "ambidextrous precision engagement weapon that destroys personnel targets in defilade and in the open with increased lethality and precision, with rounds specially designed to counter light armored targets and hovering, unmanned aerial system targets at a minimum distance of 500 meters, with an armor penetration of between 1.0 to 2.0 inches."

With sweat appearing on his brow, Hayes pulled back on the throttle as the knots of indicated airspeed gauge reached fifty-five. He tore his gaze from the gauges to glance to his right just as a second Brazilian shoved what looked like a fat roll-on deodorant stick into the side of the weapon.

The Cessna could take off in as little as seven hundred and twenty feet, but not if any part of it was blown off by a rocket grenade. The speeding plane's wheels just started coming off the ground as Hayes lowered the plane's nose, hoping that the Brazilians would overshoot, but he could see they were right on target.

The Brazilian aiming the weapon started squeezing the

trigger, perfectly targeting the grenade launcher so the explosive would catch the cabin just as it was passing. Hayes saw his wife and son's faces seemingly reflected in the Cessna's windshield, and he prepared for the worst.

Then one nine-millimeter Parabellum round went into the back of the head of the man aiming the grenade launcher, perfectly separating his brain from his skull pan before tearing open both, as well as his face.

The grenade, which would have hit the Cessna right in the cockpit a second earlier, flew just above the plane's wings and exploded at the edge of the grass near the seaside seconds later.

By that time it was irrelevant, because right after the Glock bullet destroyed the head of the man aiming the grenade launcher, a V-Crown jacket hollow-point projectile hit the satchel, setting off an altitude-sensitive explosive device inside it. The subsequent explosion enveloped the three Brazilians and caused thousands of dollars in damage to the private plane runway.

It also made the eyes water and hair ruffle of Dallys Carver and Jessica Knell of the Defense Intelligence Agency as the heat and wind of the explosions reached them fifty yards down the runway.

"Just because you've got the arms," Knell quietly said as an epitaph for the homicidal trio, "doesn't mean you know how to use them."

Carver, holding her SIG by her side, and Captain Knell, holding her Glock—two of the most accurate long-range pistols in the world—watched the Cessna climb into the sky over the sparkling water of the Caribbean Sea while airport personnel struggled to react to the situation. All they knew for sure was that someone's amusement park vacation would be ruined for the moment.

"Do you think he betrayed you?" Knell asked as the Cessna climbed higher into the Dominican sky.

"There was an untraceable anonymous call on my sat phone just before he left," Carver answered. "Whoever it was and whatever they said, it was enough to get him running."

"Do you think he thinks *you* betrayed *him*?"

Carver shook her head. "If he did, I think we might have had a violent little discussion before he left." She returned her attention to the Cessna. "Whenever he is able to think clearly, I'm pretty sure he'll know we did the same thing he would have done if I had run. I mean, where else would I have gone except to Jesu's vehicle and the nearest airport?" She glanced up at her trusted contact. "And the Brazilians probably had killers at every Dominican international airport waiting for him."

Knell snorted sardonically. "All two of them?"

They took a last look at the plane heading northwest toward Cuba, the Bahamas, and Florida—wherever his fuel ran out—then turned to offer assistance to the authorities.

"Well, at least him keeping the flash drive will take some of the heat off you," Knell surmised. "Whoever wants it will all be after *him* now."

41

Elias Jones thought he was hallucinating when he first heard the voice on his citizens band radio coming from the den.

"Captain," Hayes said. "Sweet Charity."

Jones tripped over the Persian rug, stumbled across the coarse floorboards, and bumped into the worn easy chairs to get to the small CB radio rig on the top shelf of his rolltop desk against the window.

He grabbed the hand mike, clicked the send button, and barked, "How the hell are you even doing this?"

The CB had a very narrow frequency—only forty channels

near twenty-seven megahertz in the high frequency shortwave band, and, unless the person speaking was in a thirty-year-old tractor-trailer rig, what Jones was hearing was nigh near impossible. Which is why Jones thought he was dreaming.

But the ache he felt in the toe he had just stubbed on the carpet was real enough.

"Captain," Hayes repeated, "Sweet—"

"I heard you," Jones grunted. "What's your twenty?"

Jones might have thought he was hallucinating when he heard Hayes's voice, thought he was dreaming when he heard him invoke their secret SOS code phrase after all these years, but when he heard where the man was and what he was about to do, Jones knew it had to be all too real, because it was too crazy not to be.

That's why he was now out twelve nautical miles south of the Key West International Airport on his twenty-eight-by-eight-foot fiberglass R-25 Ranger Tug cruiser watching a Cessna 172S float down in a long descending line from four hundred feet, its engine off.

It had to go that low and that far out to sea because, although Key West was the southernmost city in the contiguous United States and was known as the eccentric epicenter of America, the area around it was so carefully patrolled that if Hayes got closer he'd bring every police and military authority in the surrounding fifty miles onto his head. As it was, Jones still kept a sharp eye out for anyone or anything that might go boo until the Cessna appeared under the clouds.

Jones stopped watching the plane when he saw Hayes drop out in a low, modified BASE jump, his parachute opening immediately, but only fully deploying just before he hit the water. It was enough. Hayes was conscious when Jones quickly pulled the tug up close. Hayes even grabbed the side without help and vaulted on board as Jones hustled back to the cabin and the controls.

To Hayes's eyes, Jones hadn't changed since the last time he saw him, or really from the first time Hayes saw him. Jones seemed to be the type of man who was born crusty. He also seemed to be the kind of man who stayed with something he liked, and in this case, it was a captain's cap, cargo shorts, army boots, and a linen button-up short-sleeve shirt.

Hayes didn't even look back to where the Cessna had crashed into the sea. He just pulled out a wrapped package from his wet clothes. As Jones opened up the Yamaha F250 engine to its top speed, Hayes stripped off his shirt, pants, and boots, laid them out to dry, then unwrapped his FN, the Banished Glock, his knife, and the pill bag on the cabin's table.

"You got a clean kit?" he asked the captain.

Jones didn't reply. He just stared at Hayes's body map of wounds for a split second, then reached down to a cabinet below the wheel and slapped a small rectangular box into Hayes's hand.

Hayes should have known better. He should've asked "*Where's* your clean kit?" As he began to disassemble his guns, he asked, "Any issues?"

"Flight plan submitted and approved," Jones said, turning his attention back to the sea. "Aircraft refueled."

"On schedule?"

Only then did Jones allow himself a crooked grin. "I've got seniority."

Dallys Carver wasn't the only person with trusted contacts.

Jones had taken Hayes under his figurative and literal wing when he first started training. Hayes had flown with more than his fair share of pilots, and most of them were like Jones—former fighter jocks who'd been there, done that, and had the T-shirt. They were pros, men who ordered another beer and called mayday in the same tone of voice. But even among them, Jones had a strange and special place—he was a man who was respected, feared, loved, and hated all at the same time.

They had felt an instant kinship, and between sharing many a beer, not to mention many other spirits, as well as surviving several life-threatening scrapes, they had formed a bond unlike any Hayes had in his life, up to and including his family. Neither would call it a friendship. There was no place for friendship in the game they played.

But after the last, and hairiest, emergency they had survived together, they had, in the drunken aftermath, established an emergency code phrase that, when uttered by either of them, would bring the other running if at all possible.

It was just Hayes's good luck that Jones had retired to Key West five years ago at the age of seventy. It was especially lucky since Hayes had to fly the Cessna at the lowest possible altitude, the propeller biting thick air, to get here at all. With only fifty-six gallons of fuel to go seven hundred and eighty-five miles, the Cessna was coughing on fumes by the time it arrived.

But it had made it, and, even now, Hayes thanked the golfer he had stolen it from for having the most advanced avionics possible in the cockpit, including GPS, autopilot, and a comms system that had extraordinary versatility. After all, Hayes had attempted every other way he could to electronically reach Jones before trying the last-ditch citizens band frequencies.

"Don't you have a smartphone?" Hayes wondered, moving on to the Glock after cleaning and reassembling his FN.

"Of course I have a cell phone," Jones growled. "But not one you could reach."

Hayes nodded slightly. That figured. Jones continued piloting the boat as Hayes kept preparing the weapons. There was nothing more to discuss. In addition to the code phrase, the Cessna-ditching plan, and the need for the fastest flight home, he only added five words. "They have my family hostage." Jones hadn't even asked who "they" were.

Both men were ready when they reached shore less than a half hour later. They went from the dock to Jones's 2012 Ford F-150 in the parking lot. Two and a half miles later along Route A1A, they were pulling into the private plane lot at Key West International Airport.

The airport employees were ready. The gate man waved Jones through. The captain drove past the maintenance garages and pulled right up to a C145 Skytruck. Jones had flown virtually every military vehicle during his decades-long career, but it was this used, Polish-made, twin-propeller, light cargo and troop transport that he chose to take with him into retirement.

Hayes looked it over as Jones tossed his truck keys to a hangar worker, who caught them and jumped into the F-150 as if he had done so hundreds of times before. The Skytruck was forty feet long and had a wingspan of more than seventy feet. Hayes recognized the landing gear, knowing it was specially made for short takeoffs and landings, even on unpaved runways.

Jones noticed Hayes's examination as he hurried to the door. "It used to do combat airdrop, search-and-rescue, humanitarian assistance, casualty evacuation, and disaster relief," he said, waving Hayes on. "Today it's doing all five, and probably more."

As soon as Hayes boarded, the steps were tossed up behind him, and the door sealed. Hayes only had time to take in the twenty feet of open cargo space filled with rifle cabinets, toolboxes, storage units, foot lockers, ammo cans, and netting. It looked like an Army Surplus store's back room. Then the starting engines shook the entire area.

Hayes moved quickly forward and stuck his head inside the cockpit in time to see the brightly lit digital and traditional control panels. Jones had obviously been using the aircraft as his combination workshop and workshop project. He already had his headphones on and was deep into takeoff prep. Hayes wanted to make sure all the stuff in the back wouldn't make them too heavy for a quick flight, but kept his mouth shut. He had faith that Jones knew exactly what he was doing.

Hayes watched as the captain taxied to the end of the runway and turned into the wind.

The Skytruck shot down the runway like a sprinter from the blocks, the sudden acceleration pushing Hayes toward the tail of the plane. He grabbed the netting, holding on tight as the plane leapt into the sky.

Thirty seconds after leaving the ground the world turned

gray, the cloud cover so thick that Hayes couldn't see the engines or the wing. The sudden loss of visibility was nothing new to him, but always worrisome. It was the first pocket of turbulence they hit at three hundred feet, however, that caused his guts to tighten up.

Jones looked up at Hayes as he reentered the cockpit, a mirthless smile of recognition on his face. He motioned for Hayes to sit in the copilot's seat and pointed at the headphones that were hung on the seat arm. Hayes sat, slipped on the headphones, and heard what Jones was saying.

"Takeoff in world record time. Now a three-hour, forty-five-minute flight if we're lucky." Jones checked his gauges. "ETA nineteen-fifteen"—seven-fifteen p.m. non-military time—"almost two hours ahead of deadline."

"And if we're not lucky," Jones continued, seemingly using one of Carver's magic mind-reading tricks, "I'll try to make some luck. Meanwhile, you might want to check some of the stuff I have back there. You might find something useful."

Hayes had almost four hours to fill, so he did what was suggested. What he discovered in the containment units caused his guts to untighten. Neither Jones nor Hayes knew what they would find at his home. Was Carpenter alone? Would he have other men with him? Where would he be holding Hayes's family? The overwhelming odds were that they'd be used as a body shield for their captors, so Jones had brought along some nonlethal weapons—a few flash-bang and teargas grenades as well as handheld electroshock weapons, including a stun gun, a shock prod, and even a Taser.

But it was the small collection of both hard and soft body armor that monopolized Hayes's attention. There was a ballistic T-shirt, long-sleeve, vest, hoodie, and even a tan, ventilated, seven-pound ultra-high-molecular-weight polyethylene full armor system that purported to protect the neck, collarbone, shoulders, stomach, groin, and even thigh from anything up to a forty-four Magnum.

Hayes tried it on over his shirt and pants and appreciated how well balanced it was. No way of knowing how effective it was, however. As he thought about it, he found himself staring at the Israeli-made hoodie. It felt soft and was pliant, but weighed almost as much as the armor system. The one thing he liked most was that it included two concealed pistol holders.

Hayes frowned. As inviting as the gear was, this was no time to do a field test. Better he trust the one thing he knew for sure: himself.

Hayes took off the hoodie and armor and laid it by the grenades and stun weapons. His hands moved up to rest on his FN, the Glock, and then the knife, before he returned to the cockpit.

Jones's eyebrows raised when he saw just the shirt and pants, then duly noted Hayes's dark, distracted expression. They were well into cruising altitude by this time, so the headphones were not completely necessary.

"Nothing?" the captain growled.

"Want to go in light and fast," Hayes said absently, the memory of his failed I-can-still-hack-it run back at the Lazy A taunting his ego.

Jones shrugged and let it lie for a few seconds. He stared out into the gathering dusk then spoke, seemingly to himself. The words were quiet, but Hayes heard them.

"You know, I spent my entire life trying to prove how tough I was." He exhaled deeply. "If I haven't proven it by now, I never will."

As soon as the old man shut his mouth, Hayes saw his wife and son's faces in his mind's eye. They stayed there, their expressions going from love to fear, and then terror until Jones interrupted.

"Can you sleep?"

"I doubt it," Hayes answered truthfully.

"Try," Jones said. "Any is better than none considering what you're going into. If you can, I'll wake you in plenty of time. If you can't, well, that answers that."

"Can't argue with that," Hayes said, standing up.

"Good," Jones said. "And let me tell you something from experience—"

Hayes stopped in his tracks. With all his experience, when Elias Jones was willing to share some hard-earned wisdom with you, you'd be stupid not to listen.

"I've learned that no matter what you do, you can't get stronger as you get older." The old man took his eyes off the sky to lock them onto Hayes with a wicked, knowing, grin. "But you sure as shit can get smarter."

Hayes stopped and looked down at one of his few trusted contacts—maybe even the only one.

Jones's eyes went back to the sky as storm clouds began to form ahead. "And remember. You're not here to prove anything. You're here to save them."

42

BLACK MOUNTAINS, NEW MEXICO, 7:00 P.M.
(2 HOURS REMAINING)

The C-145 Skytruck was fifteen miles from the drop zone when the storm hit, the howling wind and jet-black thunderheads pouncing on the transport like a pack of ravenous wolves. In the cockpit, Captain Elias Jones fought to keep the aircraft level, all too aware of his lone passenger standing at the cockpit door.

"Can we make it?" Adam Hayes asked from inside the hoodie and full armor system, his blue eyes cold as death beneath the camo face paint he'd smeared on.

As an instructor with the 58th Special Operations Wing, Jones's job was to teach Air Force Special Operations pilots how to push their machines to their absolute limits—to remain calm no matter how bad the weather. But even with the conditions outside the Skytruck worsening by the second, getting to the drop was the *least* of his troubles.

"Making it to the DZ isn't the probl—" Jones began, but before he had a chance to finish, a violent crosswind sent the Skytruck skittering across the sky, the impact shoving Hayes off-balance.

"Might want to strap in," Jones advised.

"Good idea," Hayes replied.

He was moving back to the nylon bench when his body began to tingle, and he noticed the hairs on his arms were standing on end. It was a strange but familiar sensation, one that reminded Hayes of the time he'd shown his son how to rub a balloon over his hair and use the static to stick it to the wall.

But with more important things on his mind, he brushed it off and dropped into the bench, hands reaching out for the seat belt when there was a brilliant flash of white from the starboard wing followed by a resounding *bang*.

Hayes blinked away the stars and looked out the window, the jet of flame sprouting from the engine combined with the chlorine choke of ozone and raw fuel telling him everything he needed to know.

Lightning.

He was trying to shout a warning to the pilot when the Skytruck nosed over and yawed hard to the right. The violent maneuver sent Hayes pinballing across the cargo hold, his helmet slamming into the forward bulkhead hard enough to crack the plastic.

It was a stunning blow, the impact dropping him flat on

the deck in front of the cockpit door. He shook off the stars and looked up to find the instrument panel lit up like a Christmas tree, the relentless *"altitude . . . altitude . . ."* of the ground avoidance radar echoing loud through the speaker.

"Ops, this is Ghostrider 1, calling an emergency . . ."

In the left seat, Jones shoved the throttles to their stops and hauled back on the yoke. "I've got to abort!" he yelled.

With just one engine, scrubbing the op was the only call, but Hayes didn't care about safety. All he cared about was getting to the ground and killing the men who had his family. With the Skytruck pulling up and away from the drop zone, he was running out of time.

"Do what you have to," Hayes yelled, standing up, "while I open the doors!"

Any other pilot would have yelled *Are you crazy?* at him, but this was Elias Jones. He kept doing what he had to.

Hayes turned and, stumbling back to the bench, retrieved the black duffel he had prepared from the deck, managing to snap one of the carabiners into the ring before the clamshell doors cracked open and the storm came screaming into the cargo hold.

It was twenty degrees outside the aircraft, and the bitter blast of wind shoved him back, the weight of the guns and gear already strapped to his body threatening to bend him double. He braced himself against the cold and fumbled with the last carabiner, fighting the sway of the aircraft beneath his feet and his rapidly decreasing dexterity.

C'mon.

Finally, he got it snapped and then, with a final check of

his gear, turned to the open doors, his mind instantly recoiling at the yawning abyss waiting for him outside the aircraft.

Like most men in his line of work, Hayes had long ago come to terms with his own mortality. For him, violence and death were hazards of the trade, obstacles you could avoid, but never outrun. Yet standing at the edge of the ramp, Hayes's biggest fear was not that he'd die—but that he'd be forced to live *without* his family.

Clock's ticking, the voice said. *Let's go.*

With that, Hayes took a deep breath, rotated the night vision goggles over his eyes, and then threw himself from the aircraft. For an instant he was weightless, body trapped in a smooth pocket of air behind the retreating Skytruck. Then the prop blast found him, the rush of hot exhaust from the overworked Pratt & Whitney PT6 backhanding him across the sky. He was tumbling through the black, the PVS-23s all but useless in the endless gray wash of the clouds.

Hayes arched his back hard enough to make it pop and, while the subtle change in posture managed to flip him onto his face, he was still spinning. With his vision already darkening at the edges, he knew it would not be long before he passed out.

He fought to bring his arms in tight against his chest. Doing that while falling at one hundred and twenty-five miles an hour was like trying to swim through wet concrete. Hayes stuck with it, the only measure of time being the spreading burn of lactic acid through his muscles and the altimeter on his wrist unwinding like a broken stopwatch.

7,000 . . . 6,000 . . . 5,000 . . .

Straighten out, the voice in his head snapped, *or they'll be cleaning you up with a mop.*

By the time he hit two thousand feet and burst through the clouds, Hayes had given up trying to control the spin. He was exhausted, his clothes were soaked with sweat despite the frigid air, and his vision had shrunk to the diameter of a soda straw.

Pull now or die.

Blinking through the frozen tears, he reached over, his numb fingers fumbling for the D-ring.

Where the hell is it?

Unable to feel anything, he forced his fingers into a claw and, relying on muscle memory, raked them across his chest until he felt tension. Then, summoning the last of his strength, pulled as hard as he could.

The canopy fired out of the pack tray and fluttered in the wind like a dying jellyfish. Finally it caught air, inflating with the crack of a rifle shot. The sudden deceleration snapped his head back, the pair of PVS-23s slamming into the bridge of his nose with a sickening crunch.

Blood spattered across Hayes's face and his vision swam, but at least the blood was warm. With a craggy outcropping rushing up to meet him, the pain was instantly forgotten as he grabbed the steering toggles and pulled hard to the left.

In the high wind the normally deft parachute turned reluctantly, and Hayes lifted his knees to his chest, preparing for the bone-crunching impact he knew would follow. But at the last possible instant the wind shifted directions and he swung clear of the obstacle.

Wiping the blood from his face, Hayes took a shuddering

breath and felt his heart rate return to normal. He checked the GPS strapped to his wrist, saw that he was still seven miles short of his intended drop zone and made the necessary corrections.

He settled in for the ride, suddenly tired as the adrenaline that had been pumping through his body for the previous ten minutes began to ebb.

Hayes was a half mile from the drop zone when the thunderheads that had ambushed the Skytruck over the Black Mountains came scudding west. The accompanying rain slapped against his exposed skin hard as buckshot. Any other time Hayes would have been pissed, cursed the rain and his bad luck, but this time it was exactly what he needed.

His original plan was to land to the south of the mesa and use the low ground to shield him from anyone watching the valley from the ranch house, but caught beneath the rain curtain there was no need.

He stuck the landing, collapsing his chute and shrugging out of the parachute harness, before shoving both into one of the large holes that dotted the summit. Once he was satisfied, Hayes moved to the western edge of the mesa and lay flat behind the rifle. He took a quick glance all round, and seeing no plume of crashed plane smoke anywhere, hoped that Jones and the Skytruck had gotten out of their latest scrape.

Get down to business.

Through the Nikon P-223 scope mounted to the new AR-15 he had taken from Jones's surplus plane, the ranch and surrounding terrain looked empty and void of life, but Hayes knew better. Thanks to the captain, he had arrived early and that, plus the rain, was keeping the men inside. But Hayes knew it wouldn't last.

Better get moving, he thought.

He finally pulled out one of the pills he had avoided for so long from his chest pocket.

You've got nothing to prove, he heard Jones say. *You're here to save them.*

He dry-swallowed the pill, shouldered the duffel, and followed the game trail down to the arroyo. As he went, he remembered the "proving he could still hack it" run he had attempted just hours before Shaw showed up and his life turned to shit. Back then, he had strapped on a weighted vest, which had felt like anvils. Now, suddenly, the gear he wore and carried felt like nothing.

He worked his way west, bypassing the drop zone and heading directly for the house. There was nothing subtle about his plan. That time was long gone. With that thought at the forefront of his mind, Hayes probed the perimeter, marking the sentries arrayed around his property. He was searching for a hole in the security bubble, praying his mud- and rain-soaked clothes were shielding him from the men's optics.

Hayes crept through the arroyo, the night dark and still around him—the only sign of life the distant howl of a coyote off in the mountains. That sound froze him in his tracks. His senses strained in the darkness, the mud-splattered Israeli hoodie blending perfectly with the charcoal gray shadows that hung low over the ground.

When he was sure it was clear, Hayes inched forward, his

blue eyes cold as dry ice beneath the black and green grease-paint smeared across his face.

He made it to the edge of the arroyo and was about to step out to cross the twenty meters to the back side of the barn when a familiar itch at the back of his skull stopped him. It had been too easy to get this close.

Or maybe they're afraid of a little rain?

Then he saw it, a blackness in the shadow, as if someone had cut a man-sized hole out of the night.

My first victim, he thought.

Dropping to his belly, Hayes slithered through the mud, his progress toward the shadow measured in inches rather than feet. The pill had kicked in, warming him from the inside out, and by the time he was halfway to the barn he no longer noticed the pain that had bear-hugged his body.

Finally, he made it to the edge of the barn and silently got to his feet. He moved to the corner, the weathered wood still warm from the guard's body.

He reached behind him, fingers closing around the hilt of the knife strapped to the small of his back, and started a slow count in his head. In the silence his mind balanced the things that could go wrong.

The only thing that can go wrong is you.

He nodded, pushed the doubts away, and closed his eyes—senses straining over the steady thump-thump of his heart. Then he heard something else: the gentle crush of gravel and the whisper of fabric coming from his left.

The blade came free with a silent hiss of steel on leather, and Hayes held it low against his body, the matte black spray paint on the cold steel rendering it invisible.

All sense of time fell away as he watched the man. He was less than a foot away, so close that Hayes could smell the musk of his cologne when he stopped, his head swiveling back to the ranch house.

Still Hayes waited. Killing a man with a knife was tricky, especially in cold blood, and Hayes knew from experience that even the slightest error would cost him. Some men went for the throat, others for the heart, but Hayes didn't have time to stick around, wait for the man to bleed out, so he chose his target accordingly.

Hayes reached out, left hand snaking around the man's head and covering his mouth, and right hand driving the blade into the base of the man's skull.

The man was dead before he ever knew Hayes was there.

One down, he thought, easing the man's body to the ground. He was about to stand and continue when his sixth sense stopped him.

Hayes gripped the man's shoulder and turned him over. His first victim was Chinese.

43

*W*ell, of course. First Russian, then Brazilian. Now Chinese. Suddenly the three secret people on the flash drive went from being three out of eight billion to three out of roughly one-point-eight billion. The bad news is that Chinese assassins were on his farm. The good news is that Carpenter apparently needed them to supplement his family-attacking assholes.

Hayes stood up, resting against the barn. He slowly shut his eyes and used his remaining senses. He felt a small lump of grief in his throat but quickly swallowed it, letting it be dissolved by the growing rage that was crawling up his neck— all because he smelled a dead dog.

Týr.

Well, of course they killed Týr. They would have had to kill the black Malinois or, based on the way Hayes had trained him to protect his family, he certainly would have torn their throats out.

All his aches and doubts left him like vapor. All his training and experience locked in.

Rest in peace, boy, Hayes thought, the rage spreading through him like cold steel. *Master's home.*

They had apparently dumped Týr in the barn. They certainly wouldn't have left him near the house. That would have disturbed Carpenter's delicate sensibilities.

Hayes wanted to get to the shop where he had his weapons, but there was no hope of getting there without being seen from the house.

Instead, Hayes slid along the barn wall as quickly as possible, making sure his boots made no sound and his hoodie didn't rub against the coarse wooden planking. It would only be seconds before the other sentries noticed their first man didn't return.

Hayes got to the narrow wooden tree house–style steps he had personally nailed to a supporting beam so he could climb up into the hayloft from outside. And because he had done it himself, he knew one step wouldn't suddenly break, leaving him hanging.

Hayes reached the loft with an M84 stun grenade in one hand and the Brazilian silenced Glock in the other. He glanced down onto the barn floor and there they were. Five more Chinese in work clothes, standing around a hay bale, checking their Smith & Wesson M&P Shield automatics.

They had to be local sleeper agents, Hayes realized. Given the relatively short amount of time since he left the Dominican Republic, whoever Carpenter's Chinese collaborator was couldn't have flown these men to New Mexico from Asia. And they were obviously just awoken sleepers at that, since their nine-millimeter, nine-round weapons were most likely CIA hand-me-downs Carpenter had collected or stolen.

Well, let's see if I'm right about this, Hayes thought, stowing the Glock, then pulling the pin from the slim M84 in his fist.

And get ready, his inner voice added. *That bang will let everybody know daddy's back.*

He tossed it in a high, slow arc right over the hay bale the men stood around, then turned, dropped, screwed his eyes shut, and covered his ears as tightly as possible.

Thankfully Jones was too experienced to let a dud remain in his collection. The magnesium-based charge went off perfectly, igniting the seven-million-candela magnesium charge right at eye level in the middle of the five men. One second they could see. The next second they were blind, the light receptors in their eyes near bursting.

That was the flash of the weapon's name. Then the ammonium nitrate went off at a hundred and seventy decibels. The jet engines Hayes had been near were only a hundred and forty. That was the bang in the name.

Even from the hay loft the weapon had hurt his ears and eyes, but that was nothing compared to what it did to the Chinese mercenaries. Hayes got to his feet, ran to the ladder, and started firing the Glock. He was using it for its accuracy. He sure didn't need its silencer anymore.

They had invaded his house for less than a day. He had

been living here for months, so he didn't pause when he got to the ladder. It was laid from the loft lip to the barn floor at a forty-five-degree angle so he could walk, even run, down it in a standing position, which he did now. His only problem was nailing them as they writhed, kicked, and stumbled in all directions.

Hayes worked outward. First he took out the one firing the hand-me-down Smith & Wesson blindly, next the one stumbling sightlessly toward the barn door, third the one by the side window slat, fourth the one spasming between the hay bale and the back wall, and then the final man was right in front of him. Hayes fired but missed, because the man had tripped over the last ladder rung. So Hayes shot him with the Glock's last round, in the head, as he fell.

Hayes did not pause. He tossed the empty Glock while bringing around the AR-15. Before he could deploy it, guns started going off, and rounds started slicing into the barn.

Hayes threw himself down while slamming open the right barn door with his shoulder. He hit the ground, his legs and waist inside, his head and torso outside. He immediately saw four men he didn't recognize fanning out of his front door, firing at the barn with HK416s.

They obviously had no concern for the Chinese, and somehow thought their target would be standing up. *More leftovers firing obsolete weapons from the CIA armory,* Hayes thought, as the four stooges adjusted their aim.

Hayes ducked through the cloud of dirt and earth kicked up by the bullets and thought it was about time he showed them that he wasn't caught out in the open with them. They were caught out in the open with *him.*

His first 5.56x45-millimeter bullet hit the closest man in the center of the chest, the impact knocking him off his feet. Hayes shifted his aim to the next target without taking his eye from the scope, and fired. He moved across the line of men from left to right, killing three in the first salvo before rolling toward the house.

"Can anyone kill this motherfucker?" Mike Carpenter seethed, slapping his palm on the kitchen table.

"Not these guys," Gunner Poe said, sitting next to him.

"Well, what did you expect?" Annabelle blurted from the seat next to him, "when you take Adam Hayes's family hostage?"

"Shut up, bitch," Poe snarled, backhanding her across the face. He hit her so hard that she flew out of the chair and smashed into a tray of washed dishes at the sink. At the sight, Carpenter's eyes shone and his lips twisted into a satisfied smile. The tray spilled off the counter, scattering crockery and cutlery across the floor.

"Adam Hayes, Adam Hayes!" Poe sneered. "All I hear from big boss Shaw is *Adam Hayes*. So I don't need to hear it from you!"

He hunched down, his hand up to slap her again, when a gray-haired man named Titus Knox leaned over from the fourth kitchen table chair and gripped Poe's arm.

"This is not helping, Gunner," he said quietly.

At that moment, more gunfire came from outside, and they all looked in that direction before Annabelle looked up with a glare of defiance.

"So what *will* help?" Poe seethed. "Trying to kill him has gotten us shit-all."

"It's also made us lose some of the last associates who haven't already deserted us," Knox reminded them.

"So," Poe snapped, pointing at Annabelle, "why don't we hand her head to the cocksucker?"

"No, no, that would be too extreme," Knox said, seemingly benign, as he pulled up a Remington 870 that was leaning on the back of his chair. "Why don't we just bring her out, make her scream, and, as he reacts, I fill his ass full of lead?"

That suggestion brought a big smile to Poe's face, but before he and Knox put it into action, Carpenter slammed his fist on the table.

"Did you forget what this is about?" he hissed. "Adam Hayes has something I want. So shut up and follow me." Carpenter rose, grabbed the crook of Annabelle's arm, dragged her up to her feet, and started pushing her toward the living room as she waved her fists. "Let's give him something he wants and get this all done."

Got to keep moving, Adam Hayes thought.

He burst from cover and started darting to the porch. He almost made it to the front steps when someone opened up with a shotgun.

Boom, boom, boom! rang out the Smith & Wesson M&P Shield.

Diving out of the line of fire, he hit the ground and threw himself behind the aluminum water trough. While the thin-skinned trough was good for concealment, he knew it wouldn't do much to stop bullets. He was low crawling to the far end when a load of buckshot came blasting through the trough, water spraying from the dinner plate–sized hole over his head.

Well, shit, he thought, the water spraying across his back. The ground turned to mud around him as he jumped forward.

He made it to the edge and peeked out to engage the shooter, but the man was gone, the only sign of him the wisp of gun smoke from the porch. Hayes waited, scanning the area for any sign of movement. He watched everywhere—except for behind him. The shotgun man had run around the barn, then came through it to get behind Hayes.

While still inside the barn, the man must have ejected the used, hot casing, and racked up a new cartridge, and the hay must have muffled the sound. Obviously Hayes hadn't heard it because the man got to within ten feet behind him. He raised the Browning BPS, and was pulling the trigger when the hot casing he had ejected in the barn set off the box of fireworks Hayes had gotten for his son's birthday.

The man with the shotgun jerked down, hunching, looking wild-eyed behind him while Hayes flipped onto his back, raised the pistol and was squeezing the slack from the trigger when the man's face turned back toward him. Hayes fired the moment he saw flesh and watched his target's head disappear in a cloud of blood and gore.

The man was down, but the fireworks, not to mention the resounding echo of the gunshot, had given away his new position. Hayes was scrambling to his feet when a burst of fire came ripping in from the east. The bullets snapped over his head and he fired without bothering to aim, dumping the magazine to suppress the threat. But before the slide locked to the rear, he felt the clawhammer strike of a bullet on his left arm.

Hayes spun like a corkscrew in the air and slammed down to the right of the porch, silently blessing Captain Jones for the armor, and the fireworks for drowning out any noise he made. He automatically counted four boot steps coming toward him across the porch as he rolled toward the latticed skirting he had built himself. Two men, one with a forty-five Colt Commander, the other with another HK416 hand-me-down, pushed their guns over the railings first and ripped up the ground with their bullets.

When they hazarded a glance, they saw the ground was torn up but empty. They didn't stick their heads out far enough to see the lattice was broken. That's when Hayes fired his FN through the porch floor from beneath them. The first nine-millimeter round went into the HK416 man's chin and out the top of his head. The second went right between the Colt man's legs, through his genitals and up into his intestines.

The porch floor exploded as the shotgun made a basketball-sized hole in it, but Hayes had already rolled out the front of the lattice. As the moaning, collapsing shotgun man's face appeared over the front banister, Hayes put him out of his misery with one hand and raised the tear gas grenade with the other.

He was halfway through the throw when someone bellowed, "Enough!"

44

A dam Hayes lowered the tear gas grenade when he saw his wife on the porch, standing in front of Mike Carpenter, Gunner Poe, and a gray-haired man who looked vaguely familiar. He didn't raise his FN, but he didn't drop it, either.

Each of the men behind Annabelle on the porch had a different gun. Carpenter had a Glock 19 at her head, Poe had a SIG Sauer P320 pointed between her shoulder blades, and the gray-haired man beside her had a Remington 870 pump shotgun, whose barrel floated between her and her husband—obviously able to go in either direction in a blink of the eye.

"Do you think you could nail us before—" Poe started, before Carpenter cut him off with a raised hand.

"Wait," he admonished, making a vague movement toward the gray-haired man. "Wait until Mr. Hayes gets it."

Hayes blinked, and the image of a bright red Porsche Carrera GT flashed in his mind. "Oh, my God," he breathed.

Carpenter smiled as if he had just become chief of the CIA. "See?" he said. "See how long and how well I've been planning this? As soon as I knew you were going to be assigned for the Haiti extraction, I sent Mr. Knox here to start laying the groundwork just in case we couldn't stop you."

"I'm sorry, Adam," Annabelle said with true regret. "He came to apologize for making you run off the road. I let him inside . . ."

Well, that explained why all the security measures he had installed weren't working. And he also didn't have to ask how Carpenter knew about the assignment. Gunner had been instrumental in that, no doubt.

"Must've pissed you off, Poe," Hayes said, "that you could do shit to stop me, no matter how hard you tried, huh?"

That made Poe's eyes flash and his shoulders jerk forward, but Carpenter foiled Hayes's hope to instigate a wrong move. Carpenter pointedly smiled back at Poe, his free hand up, his gun hand still pointing the Glock at Annabelle.

"No need to ask Mr. Hayes about our little New Mexican standoff here, Gunner." Carpenter smiled down upon the subject of their attention. "You wouldn't shoot any of us at the moment, would you, Mr. Hayes? After all, we're civilized men here, players of the great game, so why don't we make our little exchange and go our separate ways?"

They knew that was bullshit, but they also knew that Carpenter not only had the queen of hearts, but also an ace up his sleeve.

"Where's Jack?" Hayes asked, his voice dripping blood.

Carpenter lowered his head as the moon rose higher behind it. "Well, you have the key to that answer, Mr. Hayes. Just give it to me and you'll get it."

Adam Hayes breathed deeply. He looked into his wife's eyes, and her expression told him everything he needed to know. She might have nodded imperceptibly. She might not have. The men behind her certainly didn't register it. All their eyes were on the dull silver key Hayes held up, moonlight glinting off it.

Nothing happened for just a moment, then what Carpenter said was music to Hayes's ears.

"Toss it to me."

Hayes did as asked, but too wide and too high. The key flew through the air, went over the porch railing, and hit the house wall near the porch roof. Before it could drop and clatter on the floorboards, Carpenter had instinctively swung his arm around to try catching it. Worse, his eyes followed it. Worse still, his Glock's barrel cleared Annabelle's head.

Poe, thinking himself smart, didn't look at the tossed key. Instead he kept focused on Hayes, his lips twisting into a smirk as he shoved his SIG at his nemesis. Knox remained calm, still holding his shotgun loosely, and only reacted when the small, sharp bird's beak paring knife Annabelle had palmed after Poe slapped her to the floor sliced the femoral artery of his inner thigh.

She did it so quickly and strongly, with no change in her

expression, that even Poe didn't pick up on it until Knox started going down and the shotgun went off. That sudden, unexpected explosion threw off Poe's aim so the SIG bullet he wanted to put in Hayes's face went into the night instead. Then Knox started screaming, knowing that, if the blood wasn't stanched, he'd bleed out in five minutes.

That threw off Poe's second shot at Hayes, who was already running toward the part of the porch where Carpenter was. The man scooped up the key and raised his Glock to shoot Hayes between the eyes as soon as he jumped, but then more bullets began slamming into the house.

The first went directly by Carpenter's head, and, as Poe reached out clutching fingers toward Annabelle, the second slammed into his reaching shoulder, sending him back through the open front door.

"Kill the fucking kid!" Carpenter bellowed as he scrambled up and practically slithered off the porch to disappear into the darkness on the left side of the house.

Adam and Annabelle took only a second to lock eyes, then he went after Carpenter and she grabbed the shotgun as Poe scrambled up and charged toward Jack's room. Annabelle yanked, but Knox held on in a death frenzy. With hardly a pause she slammed her foot into his wound and wrenched the shotgun out of his writhing fingers.

She saw Poe at the top of the stairs and blasted the Remington at him. It tore a watermelon-sized hunk out of the stairwell, and dotted his other shoulder with buckshot, but he kept going. Annabelle never questioned, never despaired. She got to the top of the stairs just as Poe got to Jack's door. She pumped the next round in and fired, blasting the door off its hinges and sending Poe down in a heap.

But he kept going, and so did she.

By the time she reached the wrecked door of her son's room, Poe was on his knees, dropping his gun so he could tear open the closet door with the arm of his less wounded shoulder. Inside Jack lay wrapped in a blanket that was duct-taped around him, his mouth and eyes also taped.

As Poe grabbed for his gun, Annabelle swung the shotgun like a baseball bat. The butt and comb of the weapon went into the side of Poe's head like a Maori war club. She was not going to risk running out of rounds or hitting her son with any of the buckshot. She couldn't help splattering Jack's face with a bit of Gunner Poe's blood, but she could live with that.

The other side of Gunner Poe's head went into the left side of the closet frame, and then he slowly dropped back onto the carpet, where a pool of blood began pillowing his crushed skull.

Annabelle wrenched the dead, or nearly dead, man away from her son, grabbed his SIG in one hand while grabbing a pillow from her son's bed, then used the pillow as a silencer while shooting Poe in the chest and the other side of his head. With monsters like these, it paid to be sure.

"Never," she whispered, "get between a mother and her son."

Lights danced across the farmland as Hayes raced after Carpenter. He obviously thought that he might lose Hayes in the darkness, but the headlights and spotlights of approaching vehicles soon swept across his back as he charged toward an outbuilding. He never turned, even as he reached it and went inside. A moment later, a power engine roared, lights came out through the shed's slats, and a four-hundred-and-eighty-five-horsepower Dodge Challenger V8 on black sidewall performance tires came blasting out and tore across the field straight at Adam Hayes.

Hayes stood his ground, leveled his FN between the eyes of the shadowy shape of the driver's head, and emptied all the remaining shots in its twenty-four-round magazine.

The car kept coming straight at him, but Hayes didn't move as the vehicles behind him got closer. Then, a hundred feet away, the Dodge's hood began to shake. At seventy-five feet, the car began to slide. At fifty feet, it started to drift. At twenty feet it swerved, the driver having fallen to one side, turning the steering wheel with him.

The Challenger shot by Hayes. As it passed he looked into the window and saw a slumped form. He turned as the car passed the house, then the barn, and then into the open ground as four vehicles and a helicopter converged toward it.

Before they could catch it, the Challenger's performance tires hit a bump and a hole, sending the car skidding and screeching sideways, where the inevitable happened. It snapped upward, spun in midair, and rolled four times. As the four vehicles surrounded it and the copter hovered overhead, Hayes ran as fast as he could toward them.

As people began to emerge from the cars, Hayes waved his arms. "Take cover!" he shouted. "Take cover!"

A moment later the Challenger exploded in a roaring fireball, which burned until there was virtually nothing left.

Hayes looked at Levi Shaw, who had exited one of the cars. The older man motioned, seemingly emotionlessly, for Hayes to join him for a debriefing.

Hayes stared at him for a second, then looked away toward the porch of his home, until he saw his wife, Annabelle, standing by the front door, holding their son in her arms, Jack's head resting on her shoulder. She nodded once, her face certain. She wasn't smiling, but she wasn't frowning or crying, either.

Hayes stood in the front yard of his once happy home, equidistant from his family and the man who represented his responsibility to his country. Both were waiting to see who he went to first.

Instead, Hayes checked the time.

His deadline had just ended. It was nine p.m. on the dot.

Mike Carpenter strolled along Bay Street, savoring the warmth of the salt air across his skin. He stopped in front of the Rolex boutique and checked his reflection in the glass, the scars from his facelift hidden by the side brim of the Panama Jack hat.

Might as well do some shopping, he thought.

He stepped inside, the woman behind the counter flashing him an eager smile. Two months earlier, Carpenter didn't have the money to buy a pair of socks, but that was then and this was now.

He ran his hands over his clothes, the feel of the fabric against his fingers bringing a smile across his face. His thoughts drifted back to New Mexico and the smile broadened.

Carpenter had never felt so alive as he did standing on that porch, his gun centered on Hayes's forehead. He'd been concerned that the Treadstone man would figure it out, but when he switched places with his double at the back of the house, and Hayes kept running after the wrong man he knew that Hayes never had a clue. Meanwhile Carpenter was already moving toward the dark F-150 he had secreted in a nearby ravine.

What a fucking idiot, he thought.

Getting out of New Mexico had been the hardest part. He'd never seen snow like that and, even with the truck's four-wheel drive, it had taken three hours to make it out of the mountains.

The original plan was to head north to Canada, but Carpenter hadn't been relishing the thought of the twenty-three-hour drive. He'd toyed with the idea of flying, but quickly abandoned the idea. It might have been faster, but he knew the agency would be watching the airports. That, plus the fact that there was no way in hell he'd be able to sneak through the security checkpoint.

The only acceptable option was to head south. He'd driven through the night, stopped once for fuel in Las Cruces, and again in Tucson, where he dumped the truck and used fake papers to rent a car. By the time he hit Interstate 19, Carpenter was exhausted, his head pounding from the amphetamine crash and guts churning from the cups of truck stop coffee.

But with Hayes still alive, sleep had to wait until he was across the border—and even then, it would be dangerous.

He had crossed into Nogales before dawn, and the rest, as they say, was history. The loss of the money was a huge blow, but that hadn't been his first rodeo. He had other sources that he could access.

So, now, he settled on a Submariner and was stepping outside wearing his new purchase when his new phone chirped to life.

Recognizing the caller's ID, he answered happily. "Hello?"

"Mr. Reed? This is Jonathon Summers from the Central Bank of the Bahamas."

"Yes?"

"I am calling to tell you that your deposit has cleared and is now available to be transferred to an account of your choice."

Finally.

"Is that something I can do over the phone?"

"I am afraid not. The law requires a signature and proof of identity."

"I wish someone had mentioned that earlier," Carpenter sighed. "I've left my passport back at the hotel."

"I apologize for the oversight," the man said.

"It's all right. I am heading back there now."

"Very well," the man said, "and thank you for trusting the Central Bank of the Bahamas."

Carpenter ended the call and moved to the line of taxis parked across the street.

"Where to?" the driver asked.

"Colonial Hilton," he said, climbing into the back.

From his current position to the hotel was less than a mile, but due to the prevalence of one-way streets in downtown Nassau, it took fifteen minutes.

By the time the taxi dropped him off at the door, Carpenter was sweating, the incisions from the cosmetic surgery he'd gotten itching like screwworms. He paid the driver and flashed a halfhearted nod to the white-suited doorman before entering.

The lobby of the British Colonial Hotel was stunning in the way Carpenter liked best—spotless, controlled, subservient, and devoid of any undesirables. Carpenter strode to the bank of elevators, stepped inside, inserted his key card into the reader, and pressed the button for the Governor's Suite. The doors swished closed, and the car began its ascent, the lights dancing off the Rolex like a disco ball.

The elevator settled on the top floor and Carpenter stepped out, his Ferragamo deck shoes silent over the marble floor. He stopped in front of his door, paused to make sure the matchstick he'd stuck between the door and the frame was still there, and then swiped his card across the reader.

Carpenter stepped inside, dropped the key and his wallet on the table, then threw the security latch before heading to the shower. He was just passing the bed when he glanced at the mirror and caught the reflection of a figure seated in the far corner, his face hidden by a ray of sunlight through the blinds.

Shit.

Carpenter dove onto the bed, snatching the Beretta from beneath the pillow and thumbing the safety free, then rolled off the other side of the bed. The second his feet touched the marble floor, Carpenter dropped into a crouch while his index finger curled around the trigger as the pistol came on target.

Carpenter didn't know who was sitting in the chair, and

to be honest, he didn't care. He'd already made up his mind how this was going to go down, and the moment the sights were lined up, he pulled the trigger.

Click.

Adam Hayes smiled mirthlessly. "Really?" he said. "A man is waiting in your room and you think your gun is loaded?" Hayes's tight smile thinned as he leaned forward, the Walther P22 with the Banish 30 Gold suppressor in his hand coming into view. "Now, *my* gun . . ." he started, then fired a first round into Carpenter's right knee, ". . . is loaded."

Carpenter's right leg collapsed, his surprised face twisting in pain. He opened his mouth to screech, but then Hayes shot a second round into his left knee. Carpenter went down onto his face.

He never knew whether he hit his head on the marble floor or fainted from shock, but when he next opened his eyes he was seated in a chair facing Hayes in a matching seat three feet away, holding the Walther and a pillowcase.

"That was just to make sure you don't go anywhere," Hayes informed him.

Carpenter took just a second to realize that this Adam Hayes was not the Adam Hayes he knew before. Carpenter had not gotten into the highest ranks of the CIA without knowing the difference between a tool and a tool master.

Carpenter immediately started babbling. "Listen," he begged, "my man at the bank just called. I've still got millions in my account. You can have it. You can have it all."

"I thought I already had it all," Hayes replied quietly.

"Until you came along. You think money will save my son from a lifetime of dealing with the trauma you caused him? You think money will keep my wife from deciding whether she can stay with a man who will always be vulnerable to assholes like you? Do you think I would take money from a man who killed my fucking dog?"

Carpenter just blinked at Hayes as if the words were in a foreign language.

Hayes breathed deeply then spoke to Carpenter as if he were mentally handicapped. "Remember what I told you on the sat phone?"

Carpenter blinked. The pain in his knees radiated through him, making it hard to think. "Uh, that you were going to kill me?"

Hayes frowned and shook his head. "No," he answered. "I would never say that, because it's an empty threat. You're already dead inside." Hayes raised the gun and the pillowcase. "I called you a fucking monster." As he finished the last word he shot Carpenter in the left elbow.

Just before Carpenter began to howl, Hayes shoved the wadded pillowcase deep into the man's mouth. As he cried and choked, Hayes showed him the gun. "Twenty-two caliber," he explained. "Best chance to lodge lead in your bones and muscles and not come out the other side. Wouldn't want to add damages to your hotel bill."

As Hayes sat back in his chair, he studied Carpenter's face. He had to hand it to the monster. He could see the ex-CIA man was trying to think of ways out of this, but it wasn't going to happen.

"You might be wondering how I found you. Well, I went

to visit your Brazilian friend. He was quite happy to help me out. Face it, you just don't have a lot of friends, probably because you spend your time betraying and blowing up the few people who trusted you, including that dope who agreed to double for you."

Carpenter's face got very red, and all the veins in his head got very prominent, as he tried to shriek in pain and rage.

"Amazing," Hayes mused. "You are incredibly evil, but you think that all the good people you look down on would never betray you. Not *you*."

Hayes then shot him in the right elbow. As Carpenter writhed in the chair, Hayes continued.

"Levi Shaw apologized to me. Yeah, hard to believe, right? He figured out you were going to go after my family, but too late. By the time he neared you and your gang, you'd already invaded my home. So he decided, probably wisely, to wait for me, figuring that anything he'd do would result in the death of my wife and son. That was why the sniper shots at the end there were not as accurate as they could be. To make sure there were none of your people on the assault team, he had to quickly recruit trainees. Ironic, huh?"

Carpenter's head began to droop, but by his expression and body language, Hayes figured that he wanted to say something. And since he had made sure Carpenter couldn't run or fight, he leaned forward and pulled the pillowcase from the man's drooling maw.

Carpenter tried to laugh. "You never were the sharpest knife in the drawer," he gasped. "You think, in that tiny brain of yours, that anything you say will make up for how I ruined your life?"

Hayes smiled thinly and shoved the balled pillowcase back in Carpenter's moaning mouth.

"Ah, right on time," he sighed, then pulled out a Kershaw Faultline pocketknife with one hand while holding up Carpenter's right hand, palm down, with the other. "Now that there's little hope, they said you'd try to get me to kill you. But don't worry. Both Bratton and Shaw will have their long overdue interrogation time."

As he finished the statement, Hayes stabbed the blade through the top of Carpenter's right hand, between his middle and fourth fingers. As the ex-CIA man reacted as if being electrocuted, Hayes held the crook of Carpenter's right thumb to make sure he wouldn't cause himself more harm. Not much chance of that with both his elbows shattered, but you never knew with monsters.

As he pulled out a second Kershaw Faultline, he continued. "No, Mike," he said sadly. "You didn't ruin my life. Other operations, organizations, and I did that job better than you ever could."

Hayes lifted the knife and Carpenter's left hand as he looked directly into the monster's wet, shaking eyes. "But you better pray you didn't ruin my loved ones' lives."

He stabbed the second knife through the top of Carpenter's left hand, straight through to its hilt. Then he stood up and walked over to the door. "Bratton's got some guys waiting outside for you. As a favor, she gave me these five minutes alone with you. Now I'm headed home. I've got a lot of work to do."